JACQUOT AND THE WATERMAN

Also by Martin O'Brien

All The Girls

JACQUOT
AND THE
WATERMAN

Martin O'Brien

Thomas Dunne Books
St. Martin's Minotaur
New York

THOMAS DUNNE BOOKS.
An imprint of St. Martin's Press.

www.minotaurbooks.com

Library of Congress Cataloging-in-Publication Data

O'Brien, Martin.
    Jacquot and the waterman / Martin O'Brien.
        p. cm.
    ISBN 0-312-34998-X
    EAN 978-0-312-34998-1
    1. Police—France—Marseille—Fiction. 2. Women—Crimes against—
Fiction. 3. Marseille (France)—Fiction. 4. Serial murders—Fiction.
I. Title.

PR6115.B755J33 2006
823'.92—dc22   2005051995

First published in Great Britain by Headline Book Publishing

First Edition: January 2006

10 9 8 7 6 5 4 3 2 1

For my three girls
Fiona, Katie and Polly
with love

Part One

1

Lac Calade, Salon-le-Vitry, Thursday

They had called there four summers now, at the end of their holiday, on the northern shore of Lac Calade, in the wooded hills above Salon-le-Vitry. It was always the family's last stop, their final lunch before the airport at Marignane and the evening flight home. And in all the time they'd been there, on this narrow strip of sand, they'd never had to share it. Maybe a scatter of sails far off from the slipway at Salon-le-Vitry, but nothing closer. The track they followed, more than a mile of clumpy weed and rutted stone that seemed to go nowhere and promise nothing more than a broken exhaust, put most people off.

There were five of them. The grown-ups and three children. As usual they'd arrived mid-morning, driving down from their holiday home near Courthézon. And just as they always did on this last day of their holidays, they'd taken their lunch early so the children could play. On a grassy bank above the shoreline, in a pool of shade beneath the single olive tree that grew there, they set about the bread, pâté, sausage and cheese they'd bought at the charcuterie in Salon-le-Vitry, the rug from their car soon littered with breadcrumbs, smeared waxed-paper wrappings, discarded bottles of Orangina and an empty plastic vrac of local rosé wine.

Now the man dozed in his low picnic deckchair, ankles crossed, feet in sandals and socks, shirt unbuttoned, hands clasped across his stomach. *Behind him, in the olive's shade, his wife read her book, smoking idly as she turned the last few pages, the three children ranged along the shore and in the woods. Around them, crickets beat out a static summer hum, lizards skittered from stone to stone and the midday sun laid a shimmering column across the water.*

'Daddy! Daddy!' The voice came from the point of land that separated their cove from its tinier, stonier neighbour. His twelve-year-old daughter, Mandy.

'Dad, I can't see Julie.' The words were distant and scared.

The man's eyes sprang open and he struggled to his feet. He felt suddenly hot and unsteady, staggering a little to gain his balance and his senses as he came awake.

Under the olive tree, the woman put down her book and tipped off her sunglasses. 'What is it? What's wrong?'

'It's Julie . . . Something . . .'

The man shaded his eyes and looked to the spit of land where Mandy stood.

She was pointing to an air-bed drifting thirty metres off shore.

Their nine-year-old son, Ned, came out of the trees and joined her.

'Jesus!' said the man under his breath, and his blood ran cold.

His wife spun round, looking back to the woods.

'Julie,' she shouted, short and sharp. And then, throwing away the cigarette, putting down the book, standing: 'Juuuuu-leeeee.' Long and hopeful, but somehow not convinced.

'She was playing with the air-bed,' said the man. 'Last time I looked. Right there. On the beach. I told her not to . . .'

He spotted the child's armbands, like little red apples, on the sandy skirt of beach. A suffocating chill spread through him.

He knew where she was.

Heart hammering, he ran to the shore, pulling off sandals and socks, hopping from one foot to the other, damning the delay. A moment later, tearing off his shirt, he was splashing through the shallows, a bed of hard, slippery pebbles shifting underfoot, bruising the balls of his feet, propelling him forward. In an instant he was out of his depth, arms flailing, head coming up to take a breath and a bead on the air-bed.

'Daddy! Daddy!' he could hear the kids shrieking. But all he could think was – how long? How long had she been off the air-bed? How long had she been under?

Thrashing through the water, heart pounding, he reached the air-bed, grabbed it, chest heaving, and looked down, holding the air-bed up to provide shade from the sun, a better view into the depths.

Nothing. He could see nothing.

He took a breath and flipped down, pulling himself into chill, coppery depths. He opened his eyes but could see only a dusty brown glow cut with slanting shafts of sunlight and, further down, the tops of some swaying grass.

But nothing else. No Julie.

He burst to the surface, filled his lungs again and dived a second time, hauling himself deeper into the gloom, feeling the water sluice through his fingers with every stroke, slide past his arms and shoulders. What had she been wearing? What colour?

But still nothing. Nothing . . .

A second time he broke surface, gasping for breath, head hammering, the air-bed floating away in the commotion. Legs bicycling, he spun himself in the water, frantically, full circle, catching his breath, wishing he was fitter, getting his bearings, the lake shore wheeling past. Filling his lungs he pushed down again, legs flailing in the air till they found purchase in the water and propelled him deeper.

And then . . .

Oh God, no . . .

As he kicked out, a dozen feet down, somewhere in the murk to his right, he felt his foot push against something, something weighty, something suspended in the water, and he turned to see a dim white shape roll away, out of sight, out of reach.

But his breath was gone, chest cramping. He had to go up. As he burst into the sunlight he took only the time to blow out the air from his lungs, drag in another breath and plunge back down, so fast that the water raced up his nostrils and into his mouth. He blew it out and felt the remains of his lunch rise up and follow, filling the water with a reddish cloud of crumbs and his throat with a burning acid tang. But there was still enough air, just.

Oh God . . . oh please God, don't let it be . . . he prayed, lungeing his way down.

But there she was. Suddenly. From nowhere. Right there beside him. A lolling head, drifting coils of hair . . .

. . . Oh God. Julie . . .

And he wrapped his arms around her, kicked out his legs and dragged her up with him.

But even before he reached the surface he knew that there was something wrong, something not as it should be. There was no swimsuit on the body. Had she taken it off? And the flesh against his chest, in his arms, shifted like a puppy's coat, loose on the frame. Swollen. Slippery. Somehow larger and heavier than six-year-old Julie the closer he came to the surface.

Then, suddenly, he was back in sunlight, water cascading from him, facing out across the lake, then turning to shore, hauling her with him . . .

And standing there, thirty metres away, he could see . . .

Four of them. On the beach.

Not three. Four. His wife, Ned and Mandy . . . and Julie, their youngest, all of them waving at him. None of them able to see what he held in his arms.

'She was in the woods,' he heard his wife shout across the water. 'She's okay, she's here . . . She was back in the woods.'

Which was when the man knew for certain that the body in his arms, the body he'd pulled from the depths of Lac Calade, was not his daughter's.

2

Daniel Jacquot cupped his hands and splashed water on his face, gripped the sides of the basin and looked in the mirror. Long strands of black hair stuck to his cheeks and water dripped from his chin.

I need a rubber band, he thought to himself, absently, as if there was nothing else worth thinking about that first Monday morning in May.

A rubber band. A rubber band. He'd seen one somewhere, he was sure of it. The one he'd used the day before. But where had he put it? He glanced around the bathroom, a small, angled space set beneath the eaves where he'd learnt to keep his head low, its single window giving onto pantiled roofs, its pastel walls bright with a distant, shifting sea-glitter from the Vieux Port.

Nothing. He couldn't see one anywhere.

Jacquot dried his face on yesterday's T-shirt and tossed it into the wicker basket beneath the sink. Rubber band, rubber band. Sometimes, in emergencies, he used string. But it never worked as well as a rubber band. That was what he needed, and he went back into the bedroom to find one.

Sunlight splashed through the room, the sound of Monday-morning traffic rising up like a hot murmur from rue Caisserie. And then, in an instant, his search for a rubber band was forgotten. There was something wrong, something out of place. He tried to register what was different, how the room had changed. And then he realised. He hadn't noticed the night before. She'd taken the curtains, the length of muslin she'd dyed a cobalt blue and trailed over the pelmet to fall in folds onto the bare wood floor. The curtains. She'd taken the curtains.

Jacquot dressed in the clothes he'd worn the day before, save for the T-shirt that he'd used to dry himself. Pulling the hair from his collar he looked around for something to tie it. Nothing here he could use. And nothing in the bathroom. In the kitchen he slid open drawers, trawled his fingers through the contents, shifted the containers on the shelves to see if there was anything suitable, but found nothing.

Then, beside the kitchen door, wedged under his service Beretta and holster, he saw the mail – a stack of circulars, bills, a postcard from Boni's friend Chaume furloughed in Tahiti – which he'd brought up to the apartment the night before. All of it bound in a thick rubber band. He snapped it off, gripped his hair and wound it round into a ponytail. Then he buckled the gun to his belt, pulled on a jacket and closed the apartment door behind him.

Taking the stairs two at a time, fingers brushing the wood banisters, shoes scuffing the worn stone, Jacquot swung down two flights to the ground floor, crossed the tiled hallway to the Widow Foraque's door and knocked on the coloured panels of glass.

It opened before his hand had dropped to his side.

'Thank you,' he said, handing Madame Foraque the saucepan she'd left outside his door the night before and the plate that had covered it.

The old concierge took them both, tipped the plate, looked into the saucepan and nodded.

'Rabbit,' she said, sweeping her mascaraed eyes up at him from beneath her black beret, the way she did when she talked to you. 'The man at the *tabac*. His son's got a smallholding over Aubagne someplace.'

'It was good,' Jacquot told her. And it had been. Thick and meaty. But cold by the time he'd got back. While he'd walked around the emptied apartment, taking it all in, the stew had warmed on the stove.

He'd only been away a single night. Not thirty-six hours. But Boni was gone. Nothing left of her. The clothes in the wardrobe behind the bedroom door and in the chest of drawers beneath the windows, her shoes, her toiletries, her tapes and CDs, pictures, books, the silly little things she'd bought for their second-floor apartment above the old cobbler's shop. She'd taken everything. Anything she could lay claim to, and some things that she couldn't. The place was empty, as if she'd never been there. Jacquot wondered how long it had taken her, how long she'd been planning it. She must have found herself somewhere without him knowing. All she would have needed was a couple of trunks in which to pack it all and the apartment to herself.

'She left in the afternoon,' Madame Foraque began, telling Jacquot what she knew, whether he wanted to hear it or not. She'd have told him the night before if he hadn't got back so late. She gestured to the stairs with the empty saucepan. 'First I see of it there's men coming up and down, carrying bags and whatnots. Boxes and the like. They told me she was moving out. Couldn't have taken them more than an hour. Loaded everything in a van and drove away . . .'

'Did you see her?' asked Jacquot quietly.

Madame Foraque shook her head. 'Stayed upstairs the whole time. Just the key, left out here on the table while I took my nap.'

'Well, thanks for the rabbit,' he said. 'It was kind of you to think of it.'

'She leave you anything? Was anything left?'

'Not much.' Jacquot tried a smile. 'This and that,' he said, then turned to go.

Madame Foraque watched him cross the hall – the hair, she thought to herself; when was he going to do something about his hair? Far too long. And those boots! The pointed toes. He'd regret it one day.

'She was no good, Jacquot,' she called out as he pulled the door open. 'No good. You're better off without her, believe me.'

'That's what you always tell me, *Grand'maman*. Maybe this time you're right.'

And with that, Chief Inspector Daniel Jacquot stepped out into the glare of a Marseilles morning and was gone.

3

Boni. Boni Milhaud.

The tight, sky-blue jacket and the pencil skirt with that winking pleat behind the knees. The silver wings on her lapel and that crisp little airline cap of hers clipped to a brunette bob.

Jacquot remembered every detail. Flight 427, Charles de Gaulle to Djibouti, via Marignane, Marseilles. Air France. A Sunday night. Last flight out. Two years come July. The plane was packed, but she'd caught his eye as she went through the safety drill, pulling the tapes on the life jacket. Those eyes just latching onto his as if to say I hope you're paying attention.

He'd been surprised to see her walking the crew channel at Marignane where he got off, even more surprised to find her still waiting at the cab rank when she'd had such a head start. He spotted her from the concourse where he'd stopped to buy cigarettes. While he waited at the counter, a half-dozen cabs had come by and she'd shaken her head at each. He wondered if she was waiting for someone. So he went out to the rank. And she *was* waiting for someone. Him. They took the next cab that came along. She didn't go all the way on a Sunday night, she told him. To Djibouti. Not Sundays.

Which had made him smile.

At his suggestion, the cab dropped them at Chez Peire in Le Panier. They'd only got a table that late because it was him. Jacquot. Halfway through their meal, Boni had looked at him over her wine glass and told him how tired she was, and how she just hated taking off her own stockings. And that was that. So much for not going all the way on a Sunday night.

That first night, after Chez Peire, she'd taken him to the Hotel Mercure overlooking the Quai des Belges. And every time after that, whenever she passed through, stopping overnight, she'd call him from Charles de Gaulle, and that's where they'd end up. Hotel Mercure, fifth floor. Where the Air France crews put up. Where Jacquot quietly fell in love – and she, he believed, fell in love with him.

One of the things that Boni liked was that people knew him, recognised him. Jacquot noticed it early on, whenever someone looked at him in that particular way, placed him, remembered. How she'd tighten her arm around his, making it clear that he was hers, sharing the glow when people stopped to shake his hand, buy him a drink. Even after all that time. The celebrity. That's what appealed to her. His past. What he had done on the playing field all those years before. In his blue shirt with its gold *coq* insignia. The winning try. Against the English. All this time and people still remembered. The ponytail. The double takes. The smiles of recognition. Nothing to do with the police, the job he had, though Boni liked that too – its glamour, its roughness, the way Jacquot knew his city.

Then, three months after that last flight out from Paris, Boni relocated to Marseilles and moved into his place, the apartment on Moulins, top floor, under the disapproving glare of Madame Foraque. Of course they were never going to hit it off, the two women. The smell of the Widow's soups, bubbling thickly on her range, the reek of her cheroots, the rolled-down socks she wore, the too-heavy mascara globbing her eyelashes and the pink pools of rouge on her cheeks. The way she peered round the glass-panelled door of the *conciergerie* whenever she heard a footfall in the hallway, always greeting him with a 'Jacquot, *ça va?* Some soup?', but never saying more than a 'Mademoiselle' to Boni, a brief little toss of her head. No, those two were never going to get on.

At first, in Marseilles, Boni worked as ground staff at the Air France office on Canebière in the centre of town. But it wasn't long before she was back on flights. Twenty-seven years old. Chief purser now. Transatlantic routes from Marseilles to New York, Boston, Los Angeles. Back and forth. Six days round trip, door to door, four days off. Which was not the way that Jacquot liked it. The week crept by and the four days zipped past. But Boni never seemed to mind, bustling up the stairs loaded with bags from Fifth Avenue and Rodeo Drive, this and that, four hundred filterless Gitanes for him, a bottle of good cognac. And her smile and that warm scented hug and, in the early days, the searching hands, shedding her uniform, drawing him through the bags and the wrappings to the bedroom or the sofa, or the small balcony when it was warm enough. That was what it was all about for Boni. The leaving and the returning. The heat and the passion of it.

Then, one afternoon while she was away, Jacquot was calling at the Novotel to check some credit-card fraud that the management had reported when he saw her leave the bar with a man, watched her cross the reception area and get into the lift with him. If Jacquot had worked in an office, he'd never have seen her. But he did see her, caught her red-handed, while she was supposed to be serving lunch in first class thirty-five thousand feet somewhere above the Atlantic. That was what really hurt Jacquot. The deception, as much as the infidelity. But he'd said nothing. She was younger than him, nearly twenty years. So what? A little on the side. Who didn't? He could maybe imagine doing the same himself. In the time they'd been together, he'd come close, he'd be the first to admit. But coming close was as far as he'd got. Whereas Boni . . .

For a while he persuaded himself that he didn't mind. It wasn't important. And she still loved him, regardless, the thing he was sure of. But then, sometime later, they'd argued about some silly, stupid trifle – the way she always left a coffee ring on the bathroom windowsill and how she never wiped it away, leaving the job to him, the lack of consideration – and before he could take it back he'd said it, said what he should have kept quiet about. Seeing her at the Novotel, adding something spiteful about the last flight from Paris, not going all the way to Djibouti, just for good measure. At which she'd given him a stunned, then pitiful look and slammed out of the apartment.

Six days later she was back, tearful, tanned and sorrowful. And he'd forgiven her, and they'd made it up, under the stars, out on the balcony.

Then, not six months later, she was pregnant, throwing up into the basin he'd just washed his face in. The sheer wonderful joy of it for him. Fatherhood. He'd walked to the office, the morning she told him, with a spring in his step and a whistle on his lips. But a week into the third month, Boni lost it. A smeared stain on the bedsheet and a gentle smile creasing her bloodless face, her head settling back on the pillow, no tears brimming in her eyes. And he'd known, kneeling beside the bed, known as certainly as he could, that she was relieved, known too that the child she'd lost had not been his.

Now, thought Jacquot as he made his way along the lanes of Le Panier, now it looked like Boni had gone for good.

4

Yves Guimpier, Chief of the Marseilles *Police Judiciaire*, turned from the window when Jacquot knocked and entered.

Guimpier was tall, gaunt and round-shouldered, a short-sleeved singlet visible beneath his cream striped shirt, the loose knot of his tie not quite hiding the collar button. His hair was a comb-tined mix of grey and white, slicked straight back off a high forehead, his eyes blue and slanted, lips thin as splinters, cheeks long and hollow. *Le Chef.* The Man. He might look like he'd been squeezed out of a tube but Jacquot knew that Guimpier could handle himself. Thirty years with the force and only the last four behind a desk.

Guimpier nodded to a chair and Jacquot sat down. Guimpier stayed standing, slid his shaking hands into his pockets and looked back down into the street where a jackhammer grunted. The shaking hands were the reason he found himself behind a desk.

'You hear?' began Guimpier, keeping his back to Jacquot.

'Hear what?'

'Rully. Broke his leg. All we need.'

Jacquot closed his eyes. Opened them. 'When?'

'Saturday.'

'How?'

'How do you think?'

'Where is he?'

'Conception. You should call in, see him.'

Jacquot nodded.

'Any luck with the body?' continued Guimpier.

The body. The reason Jacquot had been out of town. There'd been no need to go but it beat staying in the apartment. Boni had returned home Friday evening, still in her uniform, and they'd started straight in. The way it had been the last few weeks. The sniping, the scratching. Little things. Then a weighted silence. Moving around the apartment like shadows, no word spoken.

The drive north had soothed him, the chalky bluffs, the clear, snaking highway, a high blue sky and the lulling salsa rhythms of Stan Getz and Joao Gilberto. And then in Aix the company of his old friend Desjartes, from way back. He'd arrived in time for lunch, a little place off Cours Mirabeau, just the two of them talking over old times, then seen the body and noted the tattoo – eleven letters in red and blue and green, elegantly scrolled and stitched into the skin high up on the inside of the thigh. The tattoo and the welts, a web of them criss-crossed over her buttocks and the tops of her legs, the original red stripes leached by the water into a cross-hatching of black lines. The third body they'd retrieved in as many months.

'Like they said,' Jacquot shrugged. 'Nothing. Except the tattoo. We're checking prints and missing persons. Something'll turn up if she was from round here, or has form.'

Guimpier turned from the window, pulled out his chair and sat down.

'How long was she in the water?' he asked, stretching out and clasping his hands round the back of his head.

'According to Desjartes's boys, a week, ten days.'

'Drowned there or dumped?'

'They're pretty sure she was drowned there. Fresh water in the lungs – no trace of salt, chlorine or fluoride.'

Guimpier took a deep breath, let his eyes drift to the ceiling, then dropped them back on Jacquot. 'Access to the lake?'

'Not easy. There's the slipway at Salon-le-Vitry, but this time of year there's too many people around. A restaurant, the sail school, camp-site. He'd never have managed it. And there's no current to account for the drift. Three kilometres, at least, to the beach where she was found.'

'Any other possible drop-offs?'

'The rest of the shoreline is too thickly wooded. Maybe a ten-metre bank most of the way round and difficult to reach. Too much trouble to carry or walk her through. The beach is different. I went out yesterday, took a look with Desjartes. There's a track leads down from the road. It's rough going, but not that rough.'

'So he knows the area?'

Jacquot shrugged. 'Not necessarily. He could have checked it out beforehand. It's pretty deserted round there.'

Guimpier nodded, took it in. 'Whose land?'

'A farmer called Prud'homme.'

'Anything on him?'

'Not a thing. Too old, anyway. Late seventies. Maybe eighties.'

'Family? Workers?'

'According to Desjartes, all accounted for.'

'Anything on the track? The beach? Tyre marks? Footprints?'

'Nothing. No rain up there the last month.'

'Who found her?'

'An English guy. Stopped there with his family.'

Guimpier looked interested. 'Could there be any involvement?'

Jacquot shook his head. 'When the body went into the lake, they were staying at a *gîte* outside Orange; place called Courthézon. Desjartes checked their story and it all held.'

'She drugged?' asked Guimpier, moving on.

'They're still waiting for the tests to confirm it, but Desjartes reckons if she was, she was maybe coming round. Realised what was happening and tried to fight back.'

'And how does he figure that?'

'There were traces of a rubbery black material under two of her fingernails. Actually a sponge. Neoprene. Looks like our man wore a wetsuit.'

'Water gets cold up there at night,' said Guimpier thoughtfully. 'Sex?'

'Hard to say. Again, we'll have to wait for the report. But she'd been beaten.'

Guimpier gave him a questioning look.

'Caned,' explained Jacquot. 'What with the tattoo, Desjartes reckons it might be work-related.'

'On the game?'

'It looks that way.'

'The other victims? They weren't hookers.'

'Not so far as we've been able to establish.'

'Any clothes? Jewellery? Anything lying about?' This last was said hopefully. They needed something.

Jacquot shook his head.

'Not a thing. No watch, no rings. Nothing to trace.'

'So what do you think?'

Jacquot measured his words. 'It certainly looks the same. Young woman. Naked. Drowned. The lesions on the hairline where he pulls the head back. The bruise between the shoulder blades, like the others, consistent with holding the victim under. We'll know for sure when we get the autopsy report.'

Guimpier nodded. 'So, Daniel. What next?'

'See what Records come up with. That'll be a start. And chase up the tattoo.'

'Don't tell me, a heart?'

'Three words. *Le Vieux Port.* Like some kind of signpost.'

Guimpier gave a grunt. 'Which makes you think she's from around here?'

'Seems a fair bet to me.'

Guimpier tipped forward, reached across the desk and flicked through a file.

'With Rully down, I'm putting you with Gastal. Bring him up to speed.'

'Gastal? The one from Toulon?' Jacquot had seen him around. Like a fat little puffer fish, the kind Chez Peire had hanging from the ceiling. A year or so younger, maybe, same rank, but Jacquot's senior in the force by a couple of years. 'Isn't he Narcotics?'

'End of the month. For now he's roving . . .' Guimpier pushed the file aside and tapped his fingers on the desk, something to cover the shakes. 'He's been doing a bit of time on Vice. But you'll need help and he's all I've got right now.' Guimpier shot Jacquot a look. 'Just don't let him get to you. What I hear, he's not the easiest customer.'

Jacquot nodded and got to his feet. 'I'll be a pussy cat.'

'And go see Rully,' said Guimpier, pushing back from his desk and digging his hands into his pockets. 'Give him my best but tell him not to expect flowers. He's too old to be playing football.'

'Rugby. And he's only thirty-three.'

'Exactly. And look where it's got him. Leg in plaster and halfway through an investigation.'

'Let's hope we're a little further than that.'

17

5

They were, Jilly thought, like some joyous, extravagant escort guiding them home. Perched in the prow of *Anemone*, her bare, tanned legs dangling free, hands gripping the salt-crusted rails, cobalt water splashing and hissing along the hull, Jilly Holford watched the three dolphins rise and fall beneath her, marvelling at their speed and grace. One minute their long, arched bodies swerved and shimmered beneath the surface, the next they broke above it, dorsal fins slicing through the water, sleek humped backs glistening in the morning sun. Sometimes they came so close it seemed she could stretch out a pointing toe and touch them before they peeled away out of reach.

Tim, at the wheel, had seen them first and had called down the companionway for Ralph and Jilly to come topside to see them. His brother, still sulking, had remained below with his charts, plotting their final course for Marseilles, but Jilly had climbed up, clambered forward to the bows and had sat herself down to watch, the brisk westerly that filled *Anemone*'s sails snatching at her T-shirt and filling the pockets of her shorts. They weren't the first dolphins they'd seen on this long, difficult voyage, but Jilly felt something stirring and comforting in their presence. They seemed to say, you're nearly home and we're so pleased to see you. Let us show you the way.

It had been a great trip to begin with, just the two of them, Ralph and her, sailing north from Grenada, up through the islands to Antigua. She'd been waiting tables in a quayside restaurant in St George's when they'd met. He'd just wandered in one evening, tattered shorts and T-shirt, tousled hair and a big, slow smile, taken a table by the bar and ordered beer and a snapper fillet. When the kitchens closed he was still there and, at his invitation, she joined him for a drink. He asked where she was from, what she was doing in Grenada, said he was sorry when she told him about her parents, wiped away by a drunk driver, and nodded when she tried to explain how she'd needed time out, time to travel, time to wash away the grief. In six months she'd be starting university, she told him, a new life. Till then . . .

When the restaurant closed, he'd waited for her to grab her bag and they moved to another bar along the quay, ordered tots of rum. With that slow smile hovering on his lips, his knee touching hers, he'd told her how much he liked her cap of auburn hair, her freckled nose, and asked about the topaz necklace she wore that matched her sky-blue eyes.

Warmed by his attention, the touch of his leg against hers, Jilly'd asked what he was doing, where he'd come from, where he was going?

Looking for crew, Ralph told her, staying long enough in Grenada to resupply his yacht *Anemone*, then heading up the islands, and out across the Atlantic. Did she sail? Did she know boats? Maybe she'd like to join him?

Two hours later, naked, locked together on the *Anemone*'s deck, with the stars blinking down at them and the lights of St George's shimmering across the water, Jilly had said yes. The following day she'd quit her job and three days later they'd set sail, island-hopping their way to Antigua where Ralph was picking up his younger brother.

'You'll like Tim,' Ralph told her. Six months bumming his way round South America and now headed home, an extra pair of hands for the voyage.

Which was the problem. Jilly did like Tim. Very much. A younger, fresher version of Ralph who suddenly didn't look quite so good beside his younger brother, getting all skipperish once Tim was aboard, something he'd never done before, something Jilly didn't much like.

They were two days out of the Azores, heading for Marseilles, when Ralph discovered what was going on, saw the way Tim gave her a nod to go below, before following a few minutes later. When Ralph confronted them as they came back topside, and as Tim tried to deny it, Jilly had interrupted the exchange to say yes, right out, it was true. That's all there was to it, and if Ralph didn't like it he could turn back for San Miguel and drop her off, get someone else along the quay to take her place. But Ralph wasn't having any of it and, setting his lips in a thin, silent line, had sailed on.

And then the storm broke.

Ralph would have known it was coming. Jilly and Tim didn't. Not until they noticed the heightening swell rising up behind their transom, the cool breeze off its crest ruffling their hair and licking their bare ankles. The first smacking pellets of rain, from a line of black clouds banking up above their wake and gaining on them fast, confirmed it.

The blow carried them north-east, had them clinging on tight, sails down, all-hands-to, and lifelined. By the time the storm overtook them and raced on ahead, they were only a day from Gibraltar.

Jilly had asked to get off there, but Ralph sailed on regardless – Gibraltar made no sense, he said; Marseilles was the place to be – and when Tim, for obvious reasons, agreed with his brother's decision she'd barred him from her cabin and put both brothers out of mind. They were good guys in their different ways, she liked them both and didn't want to hurt their feelings, but . . .

Now, just a day's sail from Marseilles, Jilly watched the dolphins play and plunge only inches from her toes. They were leading her home, she decided, and she felt the future beckoning, up ahead, across the blue water.

Then, the very next moment, the wind veered, the sails luffed and *Anemone* swung to starboard. The bow crushed through a wave and a spray of cold sea water dashed up between her thighs, spattered across her face and snatched the breath from her body. With a rush of delighted laughter, Jilly let go of the rail, pushed back her cropped, salty hair, and raised her face to the sun.

6

Raissac favoured cars that didn't draw attention. Brown, grey. Anything dark blue or green. And always unwashed. A skirt of mud, dusty windscreens. Citroëns, Peugeots, a couple of old Renaults, the beaten-up Toyota off-road that looked like a Nissan. Just the kind of cars you'd use to get round town without being noticed, visit a site, call in on a contractor or supplier without giving the game away. And all of them registered as company vehicles, Raissac et Frères, kept in half a dozen lock-ups around Marseilles. Of course there was the Bentley, tucked away in his garage, but Raissac only used that for long journeys. To Lyons or Paris. Or along the coast road into Italy. Anywhere else, it was the anonymous family saloons that Raissac preferred.

And he always sat in the front. Beside his driver, Coupchoux. Never in the back seat.

That Monday morning Coupchoux arrived with a seven-year-old Renault, scarred along the flank, its aerial a wire coat-hanger, the bodywork around its windows speckled with rust. As Raissac came down the steps from the house, unwrapping a toffee bar, he saw the driver's door swing open and Coupchoux start to get out, shoulders straining against a black T-shirt, arms and neck layered with muscle.

Raissac waved the toffee, caught the man's eye and Coupchoux settled back in his seat. Too much weight-training, thought Raissac, strolling round to the passenger side, too much attention to the body beautiful. Compensation, he guessed, for the man's weak chin, the dull black eyes brooding under a bulge of brow, and those ridiculous baby teeth of his set in wet pink gums. The parts of his body that Coupchoux couldn't do anything about. At least, Raissac reflected, the muscle had its uses. Not to mention his other considerable talents.

'Where to, Monsieur?' asked Coupchoux as they pulled out of the gates and turned inland, uphill, away from Cassis. A wooden crucifix, strung by its rosary beads to the rear-view mirror, swung across the windscreen like a pendulum.

'Marseilles,' said Raissac. 'And get rid of the trinket.'

'Of course, Monsieur,' replied Coupchoux, not needing to be told what trinket Raissac had in mind. He unwound the rosary from the mirror and slipped it into his breast pocket, pressing the beads against his heart. 'Anywhere particular?'

Raissac finished his toffee, crumpled the wrapping and tossed it onto the floor. 'The Sofitel,' he replied, trying to get comfortable. There was just one problem with the cars he used. Space. He was over six feet tall and it was difficult knowing what to do with his legs. After a few minutes squirming in his seat, Raissac found a suitable position, then leant forward to the dash and realigned the air vents in his direction. Not that it made much difference. The air-conditioning was crap too.

The call came as Coupchoux turned left onto the D559, the old secondary route into Marseilles. Raissac slid the phone from an inside pocket and flicked it open.

He said nothing, just listened. And then:

'When did she leave Accra?'

He nodded. 'How long till she gets here?'

Another silence.

'And the other young lady? Sylviane?'

Raissac smiled. 'Good,' he said. 'That's right. Sofitel bar round twelve-thirty.'

There were no adieus. Raissac snapped the mobile shut and slid it back into his pocket. For a moment or two he looked ahead, then noticed the trees flashing past them.

'You're going too fast,' he said.

Obediently Coupchoux eased his foot off the gas and Raissac felt their speed drop. No point getting pulled over, he thought, and settled down as best he could for the trip into town.

So far it was all good news. According to Carnot, the ship was on its way – four, maybe five days out – and the people they needed were in place. All of it down to Carnot, his man in Marseilles. Carnot and one of those tidy little breaks that come along when you least expect them, a slant of sunshine from a cloudy sky, usually some juicy weakness that laid their victims wide open, made Raissac's life so much easier. Over and over again, hundreds of them, just asking to get hit. Sometimes it was the sex thing, or greed, or debt, or love, or hate. Emotions let loose. Life spinning out of control, isolating them from the herd. Leaving them vulnerable.

Whatever the reason, it always boiled down to stupidity; pure and simple. And weakness. Raissac had a nose for weakness. More effective than the barrel of a gun pressed to the side of the head. Like the building inspector who liked a flutter on the horses with other people's money. Or the union boys with their big bellies and their Corsican weekends who made sure his work-gangs were solid. Or the Customs boys in Toulon who got to take their family holidays in Martinique, and the new one here in Marseilles that Carnot had set up, a married man playing with boys. Even the cops. You could even get to them. And once you had one of them . . . well, then you were well ahead of the game. Like that cop in Toulon, or the other one in La Ciotat. All it took was a little time, a little patience, a little perseverance. Like his old Maman used to say, misquoting Richelieu: 'human frailty is only a matter of time.'

And now de Cotigny – of all people. The man himself. Raissac couldn't believe his good fortune. And all thanks to Carnot. A single chance encounter, and an interesting set of coincidences. First there was the American woman, de Cotigny's wife, coming on to their girl at the gym and Vicki, knowing money when she saw it, going along with it. The wife first, and then with the husband. And Raissac wouldn't have known a thing about it if Carnot hadn't gone round to Vicki's one evening and seen the two of them on the stairs, coming down from her apartment. According to Carnot, he'd heard their footfalls on the landing above and had had time to stop at a door on the floor below and fiddle at the lock with his keys, as though he lived there, until they'd passed. The husband and wife. Carnot had recognised the man immediately – de Cotigny, Hubert de Cotigny. Head of Marseilles town planning. A very important gentleman. And paying a call on Vicki, the only apartment they could have been visiting.

Knowing Carnot, Raissac suspected it wouldn't have taken him long to find out what was going on: that it was the third time they'd met up – twice before with the woman, and that evening with the husband too – and most important, that it was an ongoing thing.

Silly bitch, thought Raissac, as they pulled up through the bends of Monts de la Ginestre, the Renault groaning with effort, its automatic transmission playing between first and second as though it couldn't make up its mind what kind of revs the corners and gradient needed. Silly, silly little bitch. Hoping to make a little on the side, was she? Trying to go independent. If it hadn't been for Carnot calling by, she'd never have said a word. And after they'd set her up like that. Some stupid twenty-something trying it on for size. Trying to get the better of them after all they'd done for her.

In Raissac's game, you always had to look out for that. Girls thinking they could go independent, and get away with it. Which, Raissac acknowledged, was yet another fatal flaw. Underestimating the opposition. Who the hell did she think they were? Choirboys? But she'd soon discovered how far out of their league she was.

As the Renault rounded the last bend on the Ginestre Col and started the long, winding descent into Vaufreges and the city beyond, Raissac put Vicki out of his mind and settled his thoughts on more pleasing matters. New friends to tap, a new route to use, and the money as good as in the bag. All in all, he decided, everything was shaping up pretty much as planned, and by the time Coupchoux drew up at the Sofitel, Raissac was feeling very contented.

Equally contented was Toni, the Sofitel doorman, in his braided hat and burgundy topcoat. Conference delegates on business expenses – it didn't get any better. Only an hour into his shift and already a thousand francs up. The notes were easy to carry, but any more coin and the seams in his pockets would split. The thought of his money rolling across the forecourt made him wince. Pretty soon he'd have to unload at the *Caisse* desk inside, or have one of the porters take a bag of it down to his locker. Neither prospect appealed. Rudi at the *Caisse* would be sure to touch him for a cut, and not being able to count it out there was no telling how much the porter would lift en route to the staff changing room.

Toni was considering his options when a dusty old Renault swung up the drive and rattled to a stop not twenty feet away. One look at the scraped paintwork, the coat-hanger aerial and mismatched hubcaps was all it took. A franc if he was lucky, and he had enough of those already. Without another thought Toni turned his attention to the 'Welcome Delegates' board, busying himself with minute adjustments to the lettering until he heard a car door slam and steps approach.

Dusting off his gloved hands he stood back to check his handiwork, then turned to greet the new arrival. How he kept his cool, he'd never know. Strolling towards him across the forecourt, buttoning up a slickly double-breasted suit and loosening a silk scarf, was the nastiest piece of work Toni had ever set eyes on. And ugly. Jesus, what a face. Jesus . . . The kind of man you didn't want to cross if you could possibly help it. The kind of man you opened a car door for, or God help you. That long thin face, those sleepy eyes, that tight, icy smile. Sent a chill right through you.

'*Bonjour, Monsieur, bonjour,*' Toni managed, but the man was past him, trotting up the steps.

Out on the forecourt, the Renault driver caught Toni's eye, shook his head and smiled.

7

'It was the other side's prop. He just came out of nowhere. Not so fast, you know. But heavy, and looking for trouble.'

Rully, hair awry, bare-chested, his groin artfully crumpled with a sheet, peered mournfully down the bed.

Jacquot looked with him. The left leg was plastered in a bright white cast that reached to the top of his thigh, the peeping toes a bruised red, the joints blackened with bristly black hairs. An inch above the ankle, the cast was cradled in a sling, the sling attached to a steel cord stretching up through a system of pulleys and secured to a large silver weight.

'Last match of the season, you know? *Amicale*. Just a testimonial,' sighed Rully.

'Prop, you said. Left ear gone? Nose flat?'

Rully nodded. 'That's the one.'

'Mastin, from Brives. Has to be. Used to play for Perpignan.' Jacquot knew the man. A tough little bugger. Any excuse. And he didn't care if the referee saw him. It was what those Brives fans wanted. And Mastin gave it to them. 'Nasty piece of work,' continued Jacquot, sliding a finger into the neck of his T-shirt. Not mid-morning yet and the temperature was already climbing into the twenties.

The two men fell silent. Jacquot leant back in his chair and looked around. Third floor in La Conception. A private room at the back. Jacquot had been here a few times – other colleagues. Knife wounds, bullets, baseball bats – anything sharp, heavy or blunt. Now it was Rully.

'I was turning to pass and he hit me like a train,' his partner began again. 'I went down over the leg. Heard it break.' Rully nodded at the lower half of the cast. 'Then the knee twisting. Funny,' he continued, looking at Jacquot. 'Didn't feel a thing.'

'You don't,' replied Jacquot. 'I know.'

And he did. Not a bone for him, but the long stretch and surrendering snap of an Achilles tendon, the foot trailing, a wave of nausea. But no pain. Not then.

Outside in the corridor a trolley rattled past.

'I'm sorry, Dan,' said Rully quietly. 'I know it's not a good time.'

'Hey, it happens,' replied Jacquot, waving it away. 'But I'm sorrier for you. How long?'

'Week here like this. Then maybe I get out. Who knows? They don't tell you much.' Rully shrugged, then changed the subject. 'You get any leads up in Salon?'

Jacquot brought his partner up to speed, the same information he'd given Guimpier an hour earlier. 'The victim was in the lake a week, maybe longer. Naked. Mid-twenties. Nothing bar a tattoo to identify her. No jewellery and no clothing. The local boys went over the shoreline as much as they could but didn't find a thing. They can't say for certain where she went in, but this little beach the far side of the lake looks the most likely.'

'So what do you think?'

'It's got to be the same guy. A copy of the autopsy report is on its way but Desjartes called me on the way here with a few details. Pronoprazone, just like the others, but administered above the shoulder blade this time, which means he was probably coming up from behind. And definite penetration. She was badly bruised internally, with significant laceration.'

'But no semen?'

Jacquot shook his head. 'And no evidence that he used a rubber. No trace of lubricant or spermicide. They're water-based, remember?'

Rully nodded. 'Have the papers got it yet?'

'Sailboat accident. Just a local story so far. No one's linked it with the other deaths. Not yet anyway.'

'Well, let's hope it stays that way.'

27

There was a tap at the door and a nurse breezed in. She was young and fresh-faced, a junior's striped cotton shift showing tanned arms and bare legs.

'And how are we today?' she asked, plimsolls squeaking on the lino floor as she moved around the bed, checking the weight and pulleys before asking Rully if she could get him anything.

Rully smiled and told her no, unless she knew a way to get him out of there.

'You want to leave us already?' she exclaimed, giving them both a hurt look, tucking back a stray wisp of dark hair that had slipped from her cap. 'Maybe we need to make you a little more comfortable,' she continued and, sliding an arm around Rully's shoulders, she drew him forward and held him against her while she plumped up his pillows, glancing across at Jacquot as she did so. Her fingernails were painted, Jacquot noted, which surprised him. Pink – easy to miss but there all the same.

'There you go,' she said, easing Rully back down, fingers brushing across his bare shoulder. 'What would you do without me?' And with that, and a smile, she straightened her cotton shift and left the room.

Jacquot and Rully looked at each other, thinking the same thing.

'It's that dress does it for me,' said Rully with a wink. 'The older nurses wear slacks.' He picked at the folds of sheet between his legs. 'Better have a book here for next time,' he said.

'Nothing so weighty,' replied Jacquot. 'A newspaper should do it.'

The two men smiled at each other, not really sure where to go next. Rully started it: 'You see Guimpier?'

Jacquot said he had, told him about the flowers, that he shouldn't expect a visit any time soon.

'So who's taking over from me?'

'Gastal.'

Rully frowned, trying to place the name.

'You'll have seen him around,' said Jacquot, getting to his feet, pulling on his jacket. 'Came in from Toulon a couple of months back. Worked with Sallinger and the Vice boys to start with. Transferring to Lamonzie in Narcotics at the end of the month.'

'Fat guy?'

'Fat guy.'

Rully thought for a moment.

'Doesn't he do some trick with *escargots*?'

8

It was Sylviane's friend Carnot who'd arranged everything. He'd phoned her that morning and given her the time and place. The bar at the Sofitel. Twelve-thirty. She'd know him when she saw him, Carnot had said. And best behaviour, he reminded her. Monsieur Raissac was very particular about people's manners.

Sylviane had been waiting for the call. Carnot had briefed her a month into their arrangement, the way things could go, the opportunities. So long as she behaved herself, showed willing. Did as she was told. It was just a matter of time, he'd said. As soon as there was an opening, she was in. And now, it seemed, the opening was there. Her big chance. At last. The step-up she'd been waiting for.

Locking the door of her apartment, Sylviane took the lift down. It was small and cramped but big enough to rest a shoulder on the carpeted wall and slip a finger into the side of her shoe, ease it off her toes and heel. New shoes. Laboutin. And right now they were playing the very devil. She should have gone for the Manolos, she thought as the lift doors opened. They might have been a bit scuffed and worn but they were a whole lot more comfortable than these.

That morning Sylviane had dressed for the occasion. Cool and sophisticated. Just the kind of outfit you'd wear at a place like the Sofitel. The new shoes, of course (damn them); black silk stockings; a grey pinstripe Chloé suit; blonde hair secured at the back of her head the way Deneuve sometimes did it; and red lipstick, the colour Monsieur Raissac favoured, according to Carnot. For all the world she could have been a business executive representing some important corporation. Exactly the look she wanted.

Out in the street Sylviane let the first cab, an ageing Opel, go by, then spotted a Mercedes, flagged it down and slid into the back seat. She told the driver where she was going and used the time to check her make-up, her teeth, take a few deep breaths, and dry the sweat off her hands with a tissue. At precisely ten past twelve the Sofitel doorman was ushering her into Reception.

Sylviane was nervous. She needed to make a good impression and could feel a fluttering in her stomach. She might know the way to play it, had done it enough times after all, but this was different. This was serious. If she got this one right, she knew it wouldn't be just the one Chloé in her wardrobe, the single pair of Laboutins and the old Blahniks. This could be the big time. Big money. No more bars or private clubs, no more conferences or anonymous hotel rooms. A select clientele, arranged through Carnot. For which she'd get the new apartment he'd told her about. Off the Cours Lieutaud some-place, good and central. And a lot more money. Even with Carnot's cut, it was more than she'd ever earned in her whole life. A few more years and she'd be on her way.

At the reception desk the hotel staff were pleasingly attentive when she asked if they could direct her to the bar, called her 'Madame' and pointed across the foyer where a flight of stairs descended in a series of railed terraces to a long picture window overlooking the Vieux Port.

'I'll know him when I see him. I'll know him when I see him,' Sylviane repeated as she crossed the creamy marble expanse of the foyer, Laboutins tapping, and stepped down into the main bar on the first level. But she couldn't see him, couldn't see anyone who looked like they could be this Monsieur Raissac. So Sylviane found herself a small table, ordered a vodka tonic from the steward and made herself comfortable.

As time passed the bar grew busier, men mostly, a dozen or more business types in sharp suits and polished shoes, briefcases laid on the floor or on stools, mobiles on the bar, ordering their drinks from a white-jacketed barman who smiled and nodded and wielded the various bottles with the sure hands of a fairground juggler. Sipping her drink, helping herself from the bowl of smoked almonds on her table, Sylviane took it all in. She knew these kinds of men – all of them middle-aged, successful, away from their wives, their homes. There wasn't a single one there she couldn't have seduced away from their bored, nondescript lives. Not one. She'd worked crowds like this so many times, it was second nature. The likely ones. The generous ones. The tricky ones. But in a place like this, she knew, discretion was the watchword – or she'd be out of the door faster than a bullet from a—

'*Excusez-moi, Mademoiselle . . .?*'

The voice was low and warm and inviting, but when Sylviane looked up it was all she could do not to gasp. His face. His face. Carnot had been right – 'You'll know him when you see him.'

'You are Sylviane?'

She nodded, unable quite to find her voice.

The man stepped forward, reached for her hand and bent over it, dry lips brushing the skin. '*Enchanté.*'

9

C hief Inspector Gastal, a napkin tucked into his collar, was sitting alone in a booth in Fabien's, over the road from the Vieux Port, the sun's reflection off the water playing Hockney patterns across its ceiling. Picking up the last *escargot* from his plate, Gastal held it between ringed middle finger and thumb and, with the nail of his index finger, scratched a hole in the top of its shell. Satisfied with his handiwork, he clamped the shell's opening to his mouth and sucked loudly, the coiled black body and warm juices bubbling out like the last drops of a child's drink sucked through a straw.

Jacquot, making his way to Gastal's table, watched the performance and wondered at it. He was glad he had already eaten.

Gastal put down the empty shell, pulled the napkin from his collar and wiped away the trail of melted butter that glistened over his dimpled chin. When he spotted Jacquot approaching, he tossed down the napkin and held out his hand.

'Gastal,' he said with a shiny grin. 'Alain to you. Take a seat, why don't you?' he offered, hauling his backside along the banquette to make room. 'The *paquet*'s good if you're hungry. Or I'd offer you one of these,' he said, indicating the pile of empty shells, 'but, as you can see, that was the last.' Having made enough room, Gastal reached back for his glass and the newspaper he'd been reading, leaving the dish of empty snail shells and dirty napkin where they were. 'Go on, take a seat,' he repeated, pointing beside him where the warm shape of his buttocks, gently inflating, was still impressed in the seat's red plastic cover.

'One of Sallinger's boys on the third floor told me you'd be here,' said Jacquot. 'I was on my way back so . . .'

'It's Danny, isn't it?' said Gastal, reaching for a clean napkin and working it into his collar.

A waiter appeared, cleared away Gastal's plate. 'M'sieur?' he asked, turning to Jacquot.

Jacquot shook his head. He wouldn't be staying.

'Come on, sit yourself, have a drink.'

'If it's okay with you . . .'

Gastal shrugged. 'Sure, sure. Suit yourself,' he said, not appearing to be bothered one way or the other. He picked up the last bread roll, broke off a piece and smeared it across the top of the butter dish. 'How's your partner? I heard he's down.'

'He'll live.'

Gastal's cheek swelled with the bread. 'Rugby, wasn't it? Bastards. Football, you break a leg and you can retire. Didn't you play one time?'

Jacquot nodded, watching Gastal's jaws work the wad of bread, a buttered crumb caught in the corner of his mouth.

The waiter reappeared with a rack of lamb and a dish of *pommes lyonnaise* the colour of old ivory.

'So,' said Gastal, lifting the hunk of meat and sawing a cutlet off the end of the rack. 'See you back at the office, then, if I can't tempt you.' He picked up the cutlet, turned his wrist and looked at his watch. 'Say three? Thereabouts?'

'Three's fine,' replied Jacquot, and turned for the door.

'Why don't we meet on the third, eh?' Gastal called out. 'My office.'

Jacquot looked back, raised a hand to say 'understood'.

At his table, Gastal took his first bite of the cutlet, stripping away the meat. His cheek ballooned again and he waved back with the clean, curving bone.

10

R aissac wasn't expecting visitors. It was late afternoon and he was lying in bed watching Sylviane dress. The shutters were closed but the windows were open. He could hear traffic below, the screech of seagulls on a nearby rooftop and somewhere out across La Joliette the distant, mournful hoot of a merchantman. The sun was beginning a slow descent towards the city's pantiled roofs, the shutter blinds throwing bars of gold across the girl's body.

They'd had lunch at his favourite restaurant, Le Chaudron Provençal on nearby rue Lafonde, just the two of them, its formal, faintly intimidating atmosphere the perfect test.

And Carnot's latest girl had passed with flying colours.

The way she peeled and delicately dunked the quails' eggs, for herself and for him, dipping their sides in the celery salt, rinsing her fingers afterwards with an almost hypnotising delicacy, the lime-scented water trickling from her fingertips.

So impressive a performance that Raissac had left the choice of courses to her and she'd ordered for the two of them, with an easy confidence, barely glancing at the menu as though she knew it off by heart, only occasionally referring to it when she suggested he might like . . . what? Oysters? The *moules farcis*? Langoustines?

And then performing as adeptly with the wine list, choosing a half-bottle of a white Châteauneuf-du-Pape to accompany the grilled oysters, and a meaty red Gigondas for the *daube*. She even made a point of saying which Gigondas she preferred, the one from Domaine de la Vauquaquillière, the name tripping perfectly and prettily off her tongue, the sommelier bowing acknowledgement as though agreeing absolutely with her choice.

Nor did it stop there. When the food arrived Sylviane had eaten carefully and daintily, the knife and fork held just so, elbows tucked into her sides, back straight, sipping her wine and water but never leaving a trace of lipstick on either glass or napkin. And all the time she held his gaze, never once letting her eyes drift to the scarring on his face and the angry pool of claret splashed across his cheek and neck.

Later, when he began to ask his questions, getting down to business after the bright and insignificant chatter over drinks at the Sofitel and on the cab ride to the restaurant, she'd answered politely and concisely, holding nothing back. Everything that Carnot had told him – about her background, how she'd got into the business – she repeated it all with never a blush nor a stammer. She knew the score and she was looking to move up, she told him. They could rely on her. She wouldn't let them down.

Raissac nodded. Of course, of course. Sizing her up.

She was young and pretty with a flinty edge he rather liked. And if she didn't match up, or tried getting smart like the last one, there were plenty more where she came from. By the end of their meal he'd decided she'd do very nicely indeed. A perfect choice.

There'd been only one more piece of business to attend to.

Back at his apartment.

'You want another, help yourself, and then skedaddle,' said Raissac wearily, reaching down beneath the sheet to coddle his balls.

The girl had been stepping into her panties and pulling them on, but left them where they were, mid-thigh, and moved over to the chest of drawers where he'd left the kit. She looked faintly ridiculous, shuffling around the bed like that, panties at half-mast, but when she leant over to cut the line he'd offered, Raissac changed his mind. Not ridiculous at all. And she knew it, stretching her hindquarters out at him as she snorted up the cocaine, wriggling her hips like a dog wagging its tail.

A good arse for spanking, he decided, and no mistake.

With a sigh, Raissac changed his mind a second time. 'Stay like that,' he told her, 'just stay like that and—'

He was halfway across the bed, reaching out a hand, when the buzzer sounded.

11

At three, as agreed, Jacquot went up to the third floor of police headquarters on rue de l'Evêché. At the top of the stairs he bumped into Corbin, one of Sallinger's Vice boys. He was dragging a plastic sack crammed with video-cassettes across the landing.

'Gastal? Any ideas?' asked Jacquot.

'The fat one?' Corbin reached forward and pushed the button for the lift.

Jacquot smiled. 'That's him.'

'Down the end, last on the left,' said Corbin with a sour look. 'And you're welcome to him . . .'

When he reached Gastal's office, Jacquot tapped on the door jamb and looked in. The man had his feet on his desk and a box of dates in his lap. Licking his fingers, Gastal tossed the dates onto his desk and struggled out of his chair.

'We'll talk and drive,' said Gastal, bustling past Jacquot and heading down the corridor to the lift. 'Your car. I got something I need to check. Over near the Opéra. Shouldn't take long. You mind?'

Five minutes later, with Gastal buzzing down the window and sliding his elbow out, they turned past the striped flanks of the Cathédrale de la Major and set off down rue de l'Evêché. There was a hold-up a hundred metres ahead on the corner of rue du Panier, so Jacquot took the scenic route, working the wheel and gears through a maze of sun-starved alleyways with only a few inches to spare either side of the wing mirrors. Above them the tenement balconies were strung with washing. Peering up, Jacquot remembered his own clothes hung out to dry. Even now he could still hear the squeak of the pulley as his mother strung them out across the street like a set of flags on the mast of a ship – the short trousers, the shirts, socks and, most embarrassing, his underpants. Back then, he was certain everyone would know the underpants were his.

'You know your way around,' observed Gastal as they rejoined du Panier a half-dozen blocks past the hold-up.

'Years of practice,' replied Jacquot.

'More of the old stuff here than Toulon, and that's for sure,' said Gastal. 'So, what you got on the boil anyway?'

'Three homicides. All women. Spread around. The first two in Marseilles, a third up near Salon-le-Vitry. Rully and I reckon they're related.'

'Related?'

'Water. All three drugged, sexually assaulted, then drowned.'

'And you're thinking the same guy?' said Gastal, releasing his tiepin to use as a toothpick.

'That's how it looks,' replied Jacquot, drawing up at a set of traffic lights on rue de la République.

'So what you're saying, it's serial?'

Jacquot nodded. 'That's how it seems.'

Gastal withdrew the pin from his teeth, inspected the morsel from lunch, or maybe a shred of date, that was speared on its tip and licked it up.

'Yeah, well . . . That's why I'm moving,' he said, looking down to clip the tiepin back into place, his jowls folding over his collar. 'You don't make money chasing skirt squeezers – serial or otherwise.'

Which brought Jacquot up short. Was this a line from his new partner, feeling him out? And what exactly did he mean by 'make money'? Was he talking cash or career?

Jacquot decided not to pursue it, pulling out onto République when the lights changed and turning right. At the Quai des Belges, at the head of Marseilles's Vieux Port, he manoeuvred into the flow of traffic around the old harbour and played the lanes.

'Opéra's up ahead,' said Jacquot.

'Take the next left and pull in wherever you can,' Gastal replied, pointing vaguely ahead. 'I just need to see if someone's in. Lamonzie has his eye on someone. Something going down; and I want to be up to speed when the time comes to join his team.'

Jacquot did as he was asked, reversing into a tricky space between a van and motorcycle, wondering what Gastal was up to and when they could get on with the homicides they were meant to be investigating. In his pocket Jacquot had a picture of the tattoo – *Le Vieux Port* – found on the body at Lac Calade. There was a tattoo parlour close to the office, another near Longchamp, even one behind the Mercure Hotel that he wanted to visit, show the photo around. Maybe someone would recognise the pattern, the style. Maybe tattoo artists kept records, recognised each other's work. Maybe there'd be a lead they could follow. Right then the tattoo was all that Jacquot had to go on, unless they came up with a print match from Records or a Missing Persons report. Three women – drugged, sexually abused and then drowned – and here he was playing driver for Gastal who seemed to have his own agenda, out to score points before moving to Narcotics and Lamonzie. At Jacquot's expense.

'You know the name Raissac?' asked Gastal, winding up the window and adjusting the air-conditioning.

Jacquot shook his head. 'Raissac? Should I?'

'Not necessarily. Alexandre Majoub Raissac. One of our North African cousins. Ugly bastard. See that apartment block there? By the underground-parking sign?'

Jacquot nodded.

'Well, that's where he lives when he's in town.'

'And?'

'So I want you to ring his doorbell and see if he's in.'

'And if he is?'

'Tell him you're looking for someone. Wrong bell. Whatever.'

Jacquot knew that he could easily override these instructions. They were the same rank, after all, even if Gastal did have a couple of years on him, and they did have three homicides to investigate, a killer to track down. Gastal might be transferring to Narcotics some time soon, but right now he was working with Homicide, whether he liked it or not. For a moment Jacquot was tempted to say something but he remembered what Guimpier had said about not making waves. It wasn't worth the effort. He'd play the pussy like he'd promised. Another five minutes and they could be on their way. Switching off the engine, Jacquot pulled himself from the car and crossed the street.

There were five buttons on the entryphone. Raissac's was the top one. Jacquot pressed and waited. When there was no answer, he tried again, holding the button down a little longer.

'Yes, yes, what the hell . . . ?' came a voice over the intercom.

'Madame . . . Berri?' asked Jacquot.

'Madame who?'

'Berri,' Jacquot repeated, surprised he should pick that name, the name of his grandfather's dog, all those years ago in Aix.

'And what does the name on my bell say?' the voice demanded.

'Monsieur Raissac.'

'Doesn't sound much like Berri, does it, you fuck—' and the connection was broken.

Jacquot looked up at the front of the building. Four windows a floor, the top four shuttered.

Back in the car he told Gastal the man was in.

'So let's wait,' said Gastal, settling himself into his seat.

'Wait?'

'You anything better to do?'

'As a matter of fact . . .'

'Or just trying to get off early?' said Gastal with a wink.

Biting his tongue, Jacquot explained about the tattoo. He wanted to check it out. There was a *tatouage* parlour only a few blocks away.

'So do it tomorrow, why not? First off. Right now I just gotta do this one thing.'

Nearly an hour later, leaning his elbows on the roof of the car, smoking a cigarette – Gastal had made such a fuss about it that he'd gotten out – Jacquot saw a young woman come out of the apartment block, go to the kerb and hail a cab. He watched her slide into the back seat and the cab move off, making an illegal turn twenty metres ahead and coming back towards them. As they passed, Jacquot saw the girl snap open a mobile phone and dial a number. She was pretty, nicely tanned, but had a hard look to her. He recognised the type.

Seconds later, he glanced back to the apartment block in time to see a black Mercedes with tinted windows slide up out of the underground car park, pause at the kerb, then swing into a gap in the traffic heading away from them. Only the Merc didn't turn back as the cab had done.

'Your man drive a black Merc?' asked Jacquot, leaning down to the window.

Gastal looked perplexed. 'Get in. We'll follow and see.'

By the time they edged out into the traffic, the Merc was some distance ahead. A set of lights went against them on Quai de Rive Neuve and their quarry drew even further away, up past Fort St-Nicolas headed for Catalans. As the lights changed, Jacquot put his foot down and when they turned into Avenue Pasteur they were only two cars back.

'Looks like he's making for the Corniche road,' said Gastal. 'You get a look at the number plate?'

'Not so far.'

'Well, let's stay on him, just in case.'

At the end of Pasteur, the Merc turned left and away from the Corniche road. Before either of them could get a fix on the number, the Merc pulled in to the kerb, the driver's door opened and an elderly woman got out from behind the wheel.

'Fuck,' said Gastal as they drove past. 'Fuck. Fuck. Fuck.'

12

After Sylviane had gone Raissac took a bath, ankles resting either side of the taps, head cushioned on a towel. A brandy glass floated among the suds.

A good day, he decided. The ship was on its way, distribution was in place and the new girl Carnot had found was top of the range. Much classier than the last one. Things were looking . . . good. He glanced at his watch. Another hour and Coupchoux would be back, ready to drive him home.

Finishing his brandy, Raissac hauled himself from the bath, reached for a towel and rubbed himself dry. Pulling on a gown, but leaving it untied, he wandered over to the mirror and ran a hand over his cheeks and jaw as though considering a shave. The skin beneath his fingers was deeply pitted with smallpox scars, pink and shiny below the left ear where an adversary's blowtorch had once scorched the skin, his right cheek purpled with a birthmark that had never lost its lividity. He thought of the doorman at the Sofitel and smiled. The man had near wet himself, seeing this face. And you couldn't really blame him.

Turning his head from side to side, Raissac inspected the damage. It really was quite dramatic, especially around the lips and eyes. Back when he was young, he had thought that it made him look hard and dangerous and he'd worked it to his advantage. Now he just accepted it, amused by the effect he had on people – their surprise, their embarrassment, their discomfort.

Raissac pulled back his lips, inspected his gums and teeth, then opened his mouth wide, like a snake dislocating its jaws. Raising his chin, stretching his neck, he felt the burn-mark tighten but watched with satisfaction as the cratering of scars across his cheeks creased into a kind of smoothness. Only the birth-stain remained, oddly distorted but no less colourful. Quite a sight, he thought to himself. Quite a sight.

Back in the bedroom Raissac slipped off his bathrobe and began to dress. He was buttoning his shirt when he heard his mobile. It was Basquet, over at Valadeau, returning his call from the day before.

'Paul, thanks for getting back to me . . . Yes, yes. I thought we could meet up . . . Tomorrow? The *calanques*? Of course. No trouble. Say ten . . .? Give or take . . .?' Raissac listened a moment more, nodded, then broke the connection. As he tossed the phone onto the bed, he felt a smile play over his lips.

Greed, thought Raissac as he continued with his dressing, that was Basquet's problem. His problem, and his weakness. Wanting it all, and never thinking to watch his back; putting it all at risk for the promise of more. A dog with a bone, looking for a bigger bone. And Raissac had determined to play that dog for all he was worth.

Just twice a year. The two trips – that was what Basquet was expecting. That was what Raissac had told him. Just two cargoes out of the twenty or thirty that Basquet Maritime moved each year. A little space in the hold. That's how Raissac sold it. Just that. Two cargoes; and Customs in their pocket, he'd added for good measure, even though, back then, arrangements had still to be finalised. Two hundred kilos a time. Pure cocaine. Four hundred kilos a year. At three hundred francs a gram and leave cutting and distribution to someone else, the mathematics were mesmerising. Take out production and delivery costs, and they were looking at what, a hundred million? A hundred and twenty million the first year? Not that Basquet had wanted to hear any details. Forty million clear, no questions asked, had been enough bone for this little doggie, invested on his behalf in a cover corporation in Rabat, accessed through Raissac's property and building divisions. As for the rest – say sixty, seventy million – well, that would suit Raissac very nicely – *merci beaucoup*.

And Basquet had believed him. The doggie had rolled on his back with his little legs in the air and believed that Raissac would keep his word – keep it to the two trips, keep it to the four hundred kilos. Bumptious little shit, thought Raissac, tightening the knot of his tie and reaching for his jacket. Basquet liked to think he was sharp, but the man didn't have a clue. It astonished Raissac that his new friend had got so far.

It was the builder Fouhety, over in Batarelle, who'd put Raissac onto Basquet. A debt repaid. Apparently the boss of Valadeau et Cie had overextended himself. He'd just launched into a massive redevelopment scheme, said Fouhety, and money was tight. He was vulnerable. So Raissac called in another favour from one of his Union contacts and suddenly life had become very precarious indeed for Monsieur Paul Basquet. Which was when Raissac arranged a suitably discreet introduction through Fouhety.

And not once, not for a single second, had it ever occurred to Basquet that Raissac might have been behind the hold-up in the first place.

Remarkable.

Leaning across the bed he picked up the phone and dialled Carnot.

'De Cotigny. Is it fixed?'

He listened a moment.

'Good. Make the fucker sweat.'

13

S ardé was done in. It had been a long, hot, tough goddamned day
at Piscine Picquart, but at least he was finishing on a high note.

It had started first thing, before they even opened, when usually
Sardé could put his feet up and enjoy a coffee and croissant before his
boss, Picquart, made an appearance. But for some reason Picquart
was there before him, striding around the forecourt, opening this,
checking that, like some platoon sergeant inspecting a barracks.

First the old bastard had him move the flower tubs and shake out
the AstroTurf in front of the showroom; then sweep the forecourt,
making him squeeze behind the blue pool moulds that rested against
the side wall to finish the job off properly; and then, when Sardé
should have been stopping for lunch, Picquart had him dismantle and
fix two faulty filtration units that had come back to the workshop in
the last few days. It was an easy enough job, but in the early afternoon
the heat in the workshop was cruel. In twenty minutes the sweat was
rolling off him as he manoeuvred the units around the workbench.
And dirty work too. Oil on his fingers, working its way into his
cuticles, the very devil to get out. As if Picquart had known it would
annoy him.

Then, last of all, right when he was thinking he could call it a day –
the yard swept, the filtration units sorted, the van cleaned inside and
out, stock-checked and re-equipped – out comes the creep to the
workshop, fanning his face with the collar of his shirt, and tells him
there's a chlorine job needs doing. Pronto. Out in Roucas Blanc.

Which made Sardé's heart beat a little faster. He took the order form from Picquart and read the address.

The de Cotigny place. Ta-daa!

Thirty minutes later he was parking the Citroën van outside the back of the lady's house and calling up on the intercom from the lower gate.

The maid answered and buzzed him through. Three terraces later, each one densely laden with hibiscus and flowering jasmine, lawns cropped to a uniform toothbrush texture, Sardé set down his kit beside the pool and, taking his time, started the prep for the chlorine tests. But the setting sun was against him, burnishing every window with a sheet of gold. No matter where he went around the pool, taking his samples, no matter what the angle, standing or squatting, the sun had got there first. No chance to see through a single one of them.

Not like the first time, a few weeks back. Sardé had been right here, checking the flow gauges and drain flues, when he saw her in the library, running her fingers along the shelves like she was checking for dust or looking for a book. Only the lady was naked. Not a stitch. He couldn't take his eyes off her, and when she turned he was certain she must have seen him, couldn't have missed him where he was standing, shirt off in the sun, boner in his shorts. But she'd carried on like he wasn't there, just checking those shelves until she seemed to grow bored and left the room.

And it wasn't just the once, either. A week later he'd called by unannounced, on the maid's day off (easy enough to find out from the file in Picquart's office), wandered around the side of the house and there she was, Madame Suzie de Cotigny, in all her glory, spread out on a lounger by the pool. When she opened her eyes and saw him standing there, not twenty feet away, the coils of the suction cleaner slung across his shoulder, she'd just got to her feet and walked back to the house, naked as the day she was born, not a word, dragging a towel behind her.

Just like that. Like he wasn't even there.

Or maybe, precisely because he was there.

And the arse on her. The tits. Those legs. Holy Jesus, but she was brazen, parading herself round like that. As far as Sardé was concerned it was there on a plate, his for the taking, just a question of opportunity, timing. Just like the rest of them. When it came down to it, there was only one thing these rich, bored, spoiled women wanted and that was a little bit of action. A little work-out with the paid help. A little bit of rough and tumble while hubbie was off at work earning the bucks.

And he, Sardé, was the man.

Right now though, it looked like the lady of the house was a no-show, just the maid calling out to ask if he wanted a beer.

Which he did.

And a lot more besides.

14

B oni Milhaud loved underwear. Jacquot often wondered how she
ever managed on her salary.

In the two years they'd been together, Jacquot could swear to it,
every time they passed Secrets Dessous on rue Saint Saëns, or Pain
de Sucre on rue Grignan, or Nocibé on rue St-Ferréol, or Clairtiss on
rue Pisançon with its lacquered blue door and cabinet windows, Boni
would tug at his arm, draw him back, look with imploring, then
promising eyes, and lead him in. As easy as that.

Probably because Jacquot loved it too. All those flimsy, wispy
nothings which, later, she would bring to such animated, stunning,
unimagined life. For Boni, underwear wasn't clothing, it was costume.
Theatre. Extravagance. All colour, texture and form. The black and
the white; the pastels and creams; the scarlet, greens and blues.
Clean, crisp cotton; rough, abrasive lace; shiny, sliding silk and satin.
The panels and trims, straps and hooks, ruffles and cups; all those sly,
secret conjunctions and gentle overlappings. All of it, delicious
counterpoint to her smooth, tanned skin.

And shopping was Boni's way to sharpen his appetite, quicken his
pulse. Her passion for it, her mischievous tempting, making sure to
include him in any decision – smoothing the satin cup of a bra against
his cheek, taking his hand to run it across the ribboned bodice of a
wasp-waisted basque, a questioning look as her fingernail traced a
stiffened border of filigreed lace or a dangling length of ruched
garter.

For Boni, it was all a part of the performance. The first act. Intimacy in public. A conspiracy of sorts. With Jacquot to begin with and then, when the sales assistant approached, with her as well. Boni would draw in the newcomer as though she, too, had a part in the action, creating – with a smile, a touch, a shared confidence – a teasing, taunting complicity between the two of them that played to his role in all of this, both of them looking to him for confirmation, a nod, his own complicated smile of approval.

'Hey, dreamer. Wake up. We're off.'

Jacquot came to with a start. Beside him Gastal nodded ahead impatiently. The traffic was moving again, thanks to an old Citroën van merging from the right. It had run up against a corner bollard, crumpling its corrugated flanks, and was blocking the busy one-way street feeding into theirs. For the last five minutes he and Gastal had been waiting for the gridlock to ease, stalled on rue St-Ferréol, right outside Nocibé's show window. Now, with the van driver clambering out to inspect the damage, waving off the blare of horns from cars caught behind him, the road was clear. Jacquot put his foot down and Nocibé's shop window slid behind them.

Nocibé. Of all the places to be caught in traffic, thought Jacquot, making the lights and swinging out towards Le Panier.

For most of the day – briefing Guimpier, calling by on Rully at La Conception, meeting up with Gastal, chasing down this Raissac character, and then trailing the wrong car – Jacquot had managed to forget his lonely apartment, forget the woman he'd spent the last two years with, forget the fact that she was now – he was certain of it – gone for good. But five minutes stalled in front of Nocibé's front window and it had all come streaming back.

The only good thing, Jacquot decided, turning onto Quai du Port, was Gastal's ferocious mood, stoked up by getting it so ridiculously wrong with the Mercedes. By the time they reached Headquarters and Jacquot pulled in to let him out, Gastal had worked himself up into quite a state.

'Fucking door,' he swore, tugging at the handle until Jacquot leant across to release the lock. Without bothering to acknowledge Jacquot's help or his cheerful 'À demain', Gastal hauled himself from the car, brushed past the guards at the security barrier and disappeared inside the building.

Jacquot chuckled as he pulled away from the kerb and headed

home. Serve the fat bastard right, he thought. Playing the big deal like that. Watching *The French Connection* too many times. Who did he think he was? Popeye Doyle?

15

The Mozart was soft, sweet, lulling in the darkness. Steady and graceful. Flute, harpsichord and a weeping violin. The Third Concerto in G major. Just enchanting.

Hubert de Cotigny sat in his favourite armchair by the study window and watched his wife step onto the terrace. He'd switched off his desk lamp so the window held no reflections – just the watery blue light from the pool, a golden hammock moon through the trees . . . and his wife.

Suzie de Cotigny was barefoot, dressed in a long silk wrap that licked at her heels as she walked. And Suzie de Cotigny knew how to walk. A slow, measured progress, like the music, shoulders back, hands brushing her hips, tossing her hair like a catwalk model. He watched her glide to the side of the pool where she paused to untie the gown. Parting it, sliding it from her shoulders, she let it drop around her ankles. As usual she was naked, belly flat as a board, breasts taut and full. Raising her arms with a languorous grace, she drew back her hair into a coiling black snake and took time slipping on a band from around her wrist. A fabulous body, de Cotigny decided, long and svelte, not an ounce of fat, not the slightest tan mark, his eyes ranging down the length of her, from the dark puckered tips of her breasts to the curve and swell of her hips and the trimmed shadow between her legs. As he watched, she stepped to the edge of the pool, went up on tiptoes and her slim brown body knifed forward into the blue illuminated water, lost to view. He knew he wouldn't have to wait long. Soon enough she'd haul herself from the water and the performance would continue. The new world performing for the old, youth for age. One pleasure providing for another. And beyond it all, lacing the darkness, a sublime soundtrack.

They'd returned home later than usual, after drinks with the mayor at the Miró opening at the Musée Cantini on rue Grignan, and dinner at Aux Mets de Provence on the Vieux Port with his daughter, Michelle, and her husband, Thomas. Which de Cotigny counted as something of a triumph, the four of them sharing the same table, only the second or third time they'd managed it. Michelle was the very devil to pin down and had yet to be won over by her American stepmother.

'She's too young, Papa,' Michelle had told him tartly the afternoon he'd broken the news that he and Suzie were getting married. A small ceremony at the Préfecture the following week; he hoped his daughter would come. 'I mean, she's only a couple of years older than me, you know?'

'Six, to be precise,' de Cotigny had replied. 'And how old exactly is Thomas?' he'd continued. He didn't need to be told. Deputy editor of *Le Provençal*, vegetarian, environmentalist, all-round do-gooder and bore, Michelle's husband Thomas Thénard was only a few years younger than Hubert was. He'd given his daughter a look and she'd flushed with annoyance.

'It's not the same at all, and you know it,' she'd snapped, determined to have the last word as usual, marching from the room and slamming the door smartly behind her. But a week later she'd come to the wedding, and grudgingly toasted the bride and groom. And though she'd kept a certain distance since then, it seemed to de Cotigny that recently his daughter's resolve was weakening.

Down to Suzie, of course. Suzie was the one who made the calls, kept up a dialogue, refused to be snubbed. The invitations to lunch or dinner, the boat, the picnics, the villa, the little soirées she hosted. When she put her mind to it, Suzie de Cotigny could charm the scales off a rattlesnake.

Which was what Suzie was really good at, the talent Hubert de Cotigny valued above all others in his young wife. The way she played people, seduced them. Found them out. Sensed what they wanted, sensed how to please them. And, in so doing, pleased herself. The control she enjoyed.

Which was how it had been with the two of them, right from the start. The only woman he'd ever met who understood what he wanted and found no fault with it, made no judgement, happy to pander to his particular requirements and draw her own pleasures from them. The reason he'd pursued her. The reason he'd asked her to become his wife.

They were two of a kind, Hubert had told her, outsiders who liked the same things, albeit from different ... perspectives. And she'd agreed, to the marriage, and the ... perspectives. Just so long as he never, ever, laid a hand on her. That's what she'd said. She could easily and happily accommodate the watching, she told him, but she wouldn't tolerate the other. Those were her terms and, being the gentleman, Hubert had given his word – and kept it.

For which, he discovered, there were substantial rewards. All he had to do was say that he was going to the study, as he'd done this evening when they got home from dinner, and he knew she'd happily oblige with a last night-time swim. Or he'd specify his dressing room on the first floor, next to their bedroom, where he'd watch on his console as she prepared for bed or bath. What a show she laid on.

But nothing compared to those other times when she took the initiative. The young girls she found, the waifs and strays. For him, and for her. Bringing someone home he could watch her play with, someone he *could* lay a hand on.

How well Suzie knew him, reflected Hubert de Cotigny, feeling himself stir as she climbed from the pool and positioned the lounger just so, only a few feet from his study window, lying back and spreading her legs, her long, slim fingers reaching down.

So very different from his first wife, Florence. Just as pretty as Suzie but in no way as accommodating when it came to satisfying his peculiar requirements. She'd divorced him when Michelle went away to school, generous enough to cite irreconcilable differences but canny enough to make it worth her while. She'd pretty nearly cleaned him out.

Unlike Florence, there wasn't any question of Suzie being in it for the money. Wealthy herself, she didn't need a bean – about the only thing that comforted his redoubtable mother, Murielle de Cotigny, when Hubert announced their engagement – a fact his mother had been quick to grasp when she met Suzie's family at the wedding. Murielle de Cotigny might not understand the attraction between her son and his new wife, but she knew money when she saw it. And the Delahaye family had a great deal more of it than the de Cotignys.

Later, after Suzie left the terrace, de Cotigny stayed where he was in the darkened study. It was close to eleven and he was expecting a guest. He wondered if the man would try to make a point by being late, just to prove something.

De Cotigny sighed, levered himself from the chair and went to his desk. He switched on the reading lamp and selected a cigar from the humidor. He snipped the end, lit a taper and drew in the first of the smoke, rolling it round his mouth. Some things in life you can rely on, he thought to himself, savouring the taste of his cigar, closing his eyes for the last plaintive notes of the Mozart.

And some things you can't.

De Cotigny glanced at his watch. Already a little after eleven. Which irritated him. But not as much as the reason behind this late-night visit.

All in all it had been a most regrettable lapse of judgement. His, and Suzie's. Visiting that girl she'd found, being persuaded to play away from home. Skin white as alabaster she had, hair black as night. But she was common. Trash. Just a greedy little scrubber, with that dreadful tattoo.

He should have known better. Now he did. Because now it looked like someone was going to make him pay the price for their endeavours.

16

It was not a face that Jacquot had been expecting. Out of the past. Years back.

For a moment, sitting there in Molineux's glass-walled kitchen-office, Jacquot was certain he must be mistaken. It couldn't be. Not Doisneau. But in the puffy old face, twisting round from the sinks in the tiled, steamy washroom off the main kitchen, Jacquot recognised the same darting eyes from long ago, that hook of a nose, the high, triangular, clown-like eyebrows. Doisneau. No question. After all this time. Up to his elbows in a *plongeur*'s yellow rubber gloves. And trying to catch his attention.

Jacquot had never planned calling in at Molineux's. But then, he hadn't planned any of the things he'd done in the hours after dropping Gastal at Headquarters. It was just that going back to his empty apartment was not a prospect Jacquot relished. So he put it off, parked his car in rue Thiars and did the rounds – a cold Guinness at O'Sullivan's, another drink along the *quai* at Bar de la Marine, before ducking down rue Néot for a steak at La Carnerie and some attentive mothering from Gassi, the proprietor's wife. Fifty dressed as thirty, Gassi's smile was as wide as her hips and her skirt as short as her breath. Jacquot adored her; and she adored him right back.

La Carnerie, a basement bistro that served only meat in a city block that at pavement level served only fish, was as it should have been at a little after nine on a Monday evening – a few meals ending, others just beginning – but not so busy that Jacquot's favourite spot in a

54

screened corner was taken. The table might still be covered with dirty plates and breadcrumbs but the chairs were as empty as the bottle and glasses. He nodded to Léon in his chef's whites, taking a restorative *marc* at the bar, and settled himself down. In an instant, Gassi was at his side, shooing away the waitress and doing the job herself, clucking away as she cleaned the table and set it for one.

'Such a long time, Monsieur Daniel, we don't see you . . . you're looking pale, and thin, you need some more weight, and someone to go home to at night, *n'est-ce pas?*' She'd snapped open a napkin, used it to flick away the last remaining crumbs from the chequered cloth, then spread it in his lap. 'Don't tell me. The *pavé?* Just a little bit over the rare?'

Jacquot smiled, nodded. 'And a *demi.* Bandol,' he added, as she turned to go.

While he waited for his steak and his wine, Jacquot decided he had two choices. Think about Boni, or think about work. He opted for work and fell to musing about the case that had come to occupy most of his time, the murders he'd been investigating with Rully and the rest of his squad, going over the facts to see if there was something they'd missed, some connection they hadn't made. Like the journey home, he knew the route by heart.

Three bodies in the last three months. Three young women. The primary-school teacher Yvonne Ballarde drowned in her bath; the shop-assistant Joline Grez dumped in the fountain at Longchamp; and now the owner of the tattoo in his pocket, the body in the lake up at Salon-le-Vitry. Not to mention four naked bodies washed up along the coast between Carry-le-Rouet and Toulon since last summer. Bodies that could have been tagged as murder victims were it not for the absence of matching forensic evidence, any likely indication of foul play long compromised by the fishes and the rocks after weeks in the water. Three confirmed homicides, four 'maybes'. Seven possible murders in less than twelve months. Maybe others they hadn't found. Would never find.

But always the water – salt or fresh – the victims routinely drugged, abused and drowned. And still not a single suspect, no one worth bringing in for questioning. They'd been over Grez's and Ballarde's families and friends like a rash. Nothing. No links. No leads. No coincidences or inconsistencies. And nothing that touched Jacquot's instincts, nothing that gave him pause for thought. Painstaking, time-consuming investigation with no return.

But now, with this third confirmed victim, Jacquot sensed a way forward. This time, this girl up at Salon-le-Vitry, this one would set them on their way. Jacquot was sure of it. And the tattoo was the place to start.

Two hours later, the *pavé* demolished and three *demis* downed instead of one, Jacquot was standing beside his car and wondering whether he should drive home. He shook his head, pocketed the keys, and decided to walk. Which was how, ten minutes later, he'd found himself outside Molineux's. Set back from the Quai du Port, its picture window framed in a sagging, breeze-ruffled scarlet awning, Molineux's was a Vieux Port institution–fifty years, two generations, serving the finest bouillabaisse in this city of bouillabaisses. If Jacquot hadn't had Gassi's steak, he'd have sat himself down and ordered up the house special. Instead, he'd tipped a wink to the maître d' and headed for the basement where Molineux junior, seventy if he was a day, coaxed a soufflé *au citron* on him, piercing its sugar-dusted dome with a knife and pouring a shot of vodka into its steaming lemon heart.

It was there in Molineux's office – chewing on a final shred of lemon, his mouth slick with sweetness, Molineux called away to bid farewell to some favoured customer – that Jacquot spotted Doisneau, saw the nod indicating the back of the restaurant and five yellow-gloved fingers held up.

Five minutes later Jacquot received his customary hug from Molineux, thanked him for the soufflé and went out the back way, past a dumpster overflowing with the restaurant's rubbish, and into a dark cobbled yard pooled with shadow. He looked around. No movement, no sound. And then:

'Miaaaooow.'

Despite himself, Jacquot smiled, turned to the call.

And smiling, too, but with fewer teeth than Jacquot remembered, was the familiar lanky figure stepping from behind the dumpster.

'Long time,' said Doisneau, holding out his hand. 'You're looking good, Danny.'

Jacquot wished he could say the same for his old pal. The handshake was firm and affectionate, the skin still warm and damp from the sinks, but the features were battered and bruised.

'*Chats de Nuit.*'

'You remember,' said Doisneau.

'Of course,' replied Jacquot.

The *Chats de Nuit*. Their gang. Doisneau the leader. Not because he was the oldest but because he was the wiliest. A real schemer. Up for anything.

Doisneau released Jacquot's hand, steered him down the yard, nodding towards the street. 'I wondered, you know? Thought maybe you wouldn't get it. You moving on and all.'

'Some things you don't forget,' replied Jacquot. 'Even if you want to.' And then: 'You been at Molineux's long? I've never seen you there before.'

'Couple of months. You know how it is . . . Been away.'

Jacquot knew what that meant. A little time. A *peu de vacance* courtesy of the State out at Baumettes prison. Jacquot wondered how long Doisneau had 'been away'. And what for.

By now the two of them had reached the end of the yard. They passed under an arch and stepped out onto the pavement. A few late cars spun by, a bus for the airport at Marignane, its blue-lit interior empty save the driver.

'You got a minute? I know a place,' said Doisneau, guiding Jacquot to the right and setting a swift pace, limping a little. Three minutes later they were sitting in a booth in a late-night café-bar off avenue Tamasin.

'So. The cops,' said Doisneau, taking a sip of his *pression* and wiping away the resulting white moustache. 'I heard, you know?'

'It's a small town.'

'I heard about your mum, too. I'm sorry. I never got the chance to say anything. Otherwise . . .' Doisneau shrugged. Just the way he always did. He might have put on a few kilos but the old movements were still there.

'It was a long time ago. But thanks.'

'You went away,' said Doisneau.

'To Aix. Went to live with my grandfather.'

It was thirty years ago now. The moment Jacquot's life changed. The fork in the road and no signpost. He remembered how his mother looked that last morning, tired and drawn, but putting on a show for her boy. And the clothes she wore – the red, flowery print dress, the coral necklace his father had given her, her favourite red shoes clicking on the pavement as they walked together down the slope of Le Panier into town, the kiss on both cheeks when they parted at the school gates, the wave she gave him when he turned back to see if she was still there. And then, three days later, the shop windows at Galeries Samaritaine, boarded up when they drove him past, bound for the orphanage. An anarchist bomb, lobbed from a passing car, while his mother painted a shop-window backdrop, insulated from the blast by nothing more than a sheet of plate glass.

He'd read about the attack in the newspaper, searched for some mention of his mother. But there'd been nothing. Just one of the fifteen bodies recovered from the wreckage. For Jacquot, three months after his father had been lost at sea, those rough wood panels hammered into place over the shattered display windows meant that things would never be the same again.

And that included the *Chats de Nuit*. At the orphanage in Borel, curfew was ten. The *Chats* never met before eleven.

Jacquot wasn't the only one thinking of the past.

'And then that try!' continued Doisneau, looking up at the ceiling and smiling gleefully. 'That was the next we heard of you. Oh boy, when we saw you make that run . . . oouffff – from nowhere!' he said, skimming one hand off the other to indicate the speed of it. 'And you were always the slowest, remember?' Doisneau chuckled. 'How many times you nearly got nicked . . . But that day, against *Les Rosbifs*, you had wings, man, wings on your boots.'

Jacquot remembered it too.

A low steely sky and sheets of rain pelting down. Twickenham. Outside London. A sodden pitch, mud as thick and sticky as fridged honey. Seventy thousand crowd. A merciless game. No quarter given. Brutal.

Jesus, thought Jacquot, he'd die if he tried it now.

And right from the start all the luck going the English way. Every try, every kick going to the English, somehow clawed back by the French until, in the closing minutes, the English captain, stood deep for the purpose, dropped the ball to turf and toe and sent it spinning like a Catherine wheel between the posts.

Two points up. Minutes to go. It was surely over. French supporters groaned like an upset stomach, the band from Dax started packing its instruments and people began making for the exits.

Out on the pitch, as fast as they could, desperate now, the French had kicked from their twenty-two. Horrifyingly, one of the English pack caught it cleanly and ran like an old bull, dragging half the French scrum with him, barging on only to be mauled down a few metres from the French line.

Around the pitch, that moment, you could have heard a cat walk on concrete, it was so silent. As the French coach said afterwards, seventy thousand scrotums squeezed tight as walnuts.

So the referee calls a scrum five metres from the French line. And, unbelievably, gives the put-in to the English. Only a splinter of injury time left to play and *La France* two points down. In goes the ball, a solid grunting from the pack, and the English hooker gets it, heels it back to the Number Eight who tiptoes round it until the scrum-half sees his chance and reaches for it.

That was the moment it all went wrong. The tiptoeing fazed him, made his hands skitter. He didn't get the grip he needed and fumbled it on the turn, juggling the ball like it was hot.

A second, maybe two, that was all. But it was enough. Jacquot, debut flanker, brought on with twelve minutes to go, took his right shoulder off Souze's arse, slid free of Mageot and Pelerain in the second row and came out fast, like a runner from the blocks, from the blind side. He scooped the ball from the man's cradling arms, shouldered him aside and set the hell off.

What Doisneau meant by 'oouffff – from nowhere!'

But someone had seen him coming, the English wing – Courtney he was called. Except Courtney, like the rest of the English line, was wrong-footed. By the time he spun round, Jacquot, not the fastest runner in the world, was pumping arms and legs and eight metres clear.

The thing Jacquot always remembered was the view. The distant posts, the mud-churned field of play, the rain slanting through the floodlights. So far to go. So empty. The sideline inches from his left boot, the stands a blur of faces, scarves, hats, umbrellas, flags.

All he had to do was run.

And, somewhere behind him, an Englishman in hot pursuit. Just the two of them. And thirty thousand Frenchmen rising to their feet, raising their fists, letting their scrotums unwind and their voices loose from deep down in their bellies. Urging him on, realising what was happening here. *La France* has the ball. Only two men. A race for the line. Run, man. Run, run, run . . .

Jacquot never once looked back. Didn't dare. Just put his chin in the air and made those legs pump.

Just run.

For a moment, he wondered if the whistle had gone for some infringement. A knock-on? A forward pass? Some technicality he wouldn't know about. Maybe he should stop so he wouldn't make a fool of himself, going the length of the pitch when the whistle had blown. Or maybe it hadn't, and he'd make an even bigger fool of himself coming to a halt in the centre of the pitch for no good reason – handing the ball, and victory, to the English.

So he didn't stop. He kept running. And now he could hear Courtney coming up behind him, boots sucking the turf. Which was when he knew for certain there'd been no whistle. Not if Courtney was still after him.

Extravagantly he'd swung out into the centre of the pitch, wrong-footing his pursuer a second time, gaining a few more metres. Out in the open, you could really hear the crowd. French and English. Each baying for their man. But it was impossible to see them out there. Only the pitch he galloped over, the low grey sky and the wind gusting floodlit splatters of rain in his face.

Across the halfway line – Jesus, he'd never forget how that felt – and now the posts were coming up, coming up. Closer. It didn't look so far now. Possible. Suddenly possible. Home not so far away, and the ball in the crook of his elbow, pressed to his chest.

But somewhere behind him he heard a grunt, a final, desperate expulsion of air from the lungs as Courtney launched himself, five metres from the English line.

And Jacquot felt the man's fingertips clip the heel of his boot.

There was nothing he could do.

The next second his left foot hit the back of his right knee and he was tumbling forward, reaching out with his free hand, his right leg managing just a final, hobbled step.

But the Englishman had left it too late. Jacquot was close enough for that final, desperate hop to work and over the line he went, ploughing through the mud, the ball pressed against his ribs and a plug of English turf up his nose.

Five points. *La France* wins. On the touchline, the Dax band brought their instruments to their lips and started up a triumphant *Marseillaise*.

'You'll never buy a drink again, *ami*,' said Touche, the other flanker, as he hauled Jacquot to his feet and hugged him.

Sixteen seconds, that was all it took. Jacquot timed it on the replay. Later he found out that Courtney was a solicitor. A solicitor chasing a policeman the length of England's home ground. Jacquot loved that bit.

But it was all a long time ago now. Deep in the past. Another country. Now it was a café off Tamasin. Sharing a beer with an old comrade.

'You see the others?' asked Jacquot, trying to recall the *Chats*. The names, the faces. Blanchard with the blond hair, Gouffrat, Kovacs, and Dee-Dee something . . .

Doisneau shook his head. 'Décousse one time. Watching Olympique. He ran a hot dog stall there. Did the races too, at Borély. And Didier, Dee-Dee Ronat? Remember him?'

Jacquot nodded. Didier Ronat, of course. 'Three-finger' Dee-Dee, the other two lost in the sawmill where his dad worked. An expert pickpocket even without the full complement.

'Dead now, Didier. Cancer.' Doisneau sighed, looked to the ceiling, shook his head.

The two men were silent for a moment, remembering.

'You need something, don't you?' said Jacquot gently, making it easy for the man across the table, an old friend he hadn't seen for close on thirty years. For all the memories, the chance encounter, Jacquot was certain they weren't there just to talk about old times. He was right.

Doisneau hooked his hands round his glass and levelled his gaze on Jacquot. 'A break, that's all I'm looking for, Danny. A word in the right place. I got four more months' parole work and no choice but hanging on to that stinking job.' He held up his hands, whether to show the effect a dishwashing job had on the skin or simply as a gesture. Jacquot couldn't decide. 'Another four months? I can't do it. I'll go nuts.'

But if you don't, thought Jacquot, if you break parole conditions, you're back inside to work out the rest of the sentence. A week to find a job and six months holding it down. Working your way back into the community, they called it, starting you off. That was the deal. That's what they wanted. After that you were on your own. Sometimes it worked, most times it didn't.

'I gotta move on, see, before it's too late,' continued Doisneau. 'My son René's down in Spain. Got himself well sorted. Said he might be able to fit me in someplace. Better than this, you know?'

Jacquot took a sip of his beer, pinched his lips from side to side, wiping away the froth. His old friend was looking for a way out and reckoned that Jacquot, the cop, could wangle something for him.

'So what do you need?'

Doisneau smiled, shook his head. 'Not money, don't worry. Just get them to lighten up, is all. I'll do another month, Danny. I just want to know they won't come after me.'

Jacquot nodded. 'I'll try. No promises.'

Doisneau's face lit up. 'I knew you'd help. Jesus, you've got no idea . . .' And then he hunkered down over the table, cast around the bar and leant forward, speaking low. 'And now here's something for you. Up front, if you like. Just to show willing.'

'Okay,' said Jacquot. 'What have you got?'

'You ever hear of a man called Raissac?'

Only the second time that day.

'Raissac?'

'That's the name. Ugliest son of a bitch you ever set eyes on. Real bad pox when he was a kid, a birthmark slapped across half his face. And if that wasn't enough, he's got a burn from a blowtorch across the other half. A war wound, you might call it. Used to live in Toulon but moved out a few years ago. A real big operator back then. A real *parrain*. Girls. Drugs. You name it, he was into it. But things got tricky and he lives out Cassis way now. Villa someplace. Word is he's started up again. Going for the big time. And very soon.'

'Big-time what?'

Doisneau glanced around. 'Drugs. Coke, you know . . .? A lot.'

'And how soon?'

'Could be any time. This week. Next week. End of the month, latest.'

'Where?'

'The word is L'Estaque. Or the harbour at Saumaty. One of them for sure.'

'And?'

'He's got someone on the inside. Your lot.'

'Any names?'

Doisneau spread his hands, shook his head.

'So why are you telling me this?'

Doisneau finished his beer and got to his feet.

'It was Raissac got me done. Put me away. And you know the *Chats*, Danny. Always return a favour. See you around,' he said, and as Jacquot felt in his pocket for the bill Doisneau slid from the booth and slipped away into the night.

By the time Jacquot got back home on the Moulins hill, Madame Foraque's door was closed, no light coming through the panels of coloured glass.

Monday, he realised. The weekly card game over at her brother's. Which was a relief. He didn't fancy a repeat of her observations and opinions on the subject of Boni, even if she wasn't far off the truth.

Up in their apartment – his apartment now – Jacquot pulled the rubber band from his hair, stripped off his clothes and fell onto the bed. Their bed. In a few moments he was sleeping deeply, and alone.

17

Tuesday

Resting the backs of his thighs against the cream leather trim of the skipper's chair, Pamuk eased back on the Ferretti's throttles and the seventeen-metre cruiser buried her bow into the inky blue Mediterranean. As he steered her into the wind, a low chop slapped against the hull and the sound of her twin engines dropped to a chesty rumble. Pamuk knew this stretch of coastline like the back of his hand, but he cross-checked their position on the chart display and glanced at the echo sounder – it was shallow enough to anchor if they had to.

Leaning over the wheel, he reached for a pair of binoculars and scanned the horizon – a few distant sails taking advantage of the blow around Calseraigne and the Ile de Riou, the ladened bulk of a container ship heading west past Cap Croisette, and an incoming Tunis Line ferry shivering in the heat off the water. Then he turned and trained the glasses on the scrubby headlands of pine and glaring white limestone that rose up not two hundred metres off his starboard side. Satisfied, Pamuk put down the glasses, reached for the phone cradled on the dashboard and called down to the master cabin to let Monsieur Basquet know they'd arrived.

There were only the two of them aboard.

Pamuk had arrived at the *Vallée des Eaux* berth in the Vieux Port at six-thirty that morning, at about the same time that the fishermen's wives were setting out their stalls on the Quai des Belges. Geneviève, Monsieur Basquet's assistant, had called the evening before to schedule the trip. By the time Monsieur Basquet boarded at eight-forty-five the tanks were full, the air-conditioning set low and the engines warming at a purr over eight hundred revs.

Pamuk had brought with him a bag of fresh croissants and chocolate brioches from Joliane's, and some fruit and dates from the Capucins market. Down in the galley, the fruit had been juiced to Monsieur Basquet's specifications, the Blue Mountain coffee had been brewing since eight-forty, and the saloon TV was tuned to CNN. Pamuk had also stopped off at the *tabac* on the corner of Pythéas to buy a small tin of Lajaunie's *cachou* pastilles. They were Monsieur's favourite brand, but he was always forgetting where he'd put them, leaving them places. Pamuk made sure he carried a fresh supply just in case.

The *Vallée des Eaux* may have been a splinter over fifty feet but she handled like a dream. You could berth and tie her up single-handed if you had to, and set off the same way. Five minutes after Monsieur Basquet disappeared below deck they were cruising down the channel alongside the Rive Neuve quay and drawing looks before heading out to sea between the twin forts of St Jean and St Nicolas. Now, twenty minutes later, they drifted gently some six kilometres west of Cassis, the idling engines a soft rumble somewhere aft.

'You see anyone?' asked Basquet, coming up onto the bridge and looking around.

'Nothing, Skip,' replied Pamuk, playing the wheel, glancing across at his employer. Heftily built, in his late fifties, with a crop of grey hair bristling over a tanned skull, Basquet had a short, muscly neck, a fat, shiny face and small button ears. He'd come aboard wearing a silk two-piece suit that caught the light and a well-buffed pair of lace-up brogues, but had changed below deck into shorts, a polo shirt and leather espadrilles. A gold chain and cross hung from the roll of his neck and a diamond Rolex sparkled on his wrist. He wore mirrored sunglasses and carried a mug of coffee which slopped messily over the deck when the Ferretti swung through a larger than average chop.

Apart from the Rolex, Paul Basquet looked like any middle-aged tourist waiting for a table at a Prado beach club. But Pamuk knew better than to be fooled by appearances. The man beside him was certainly no tourist. Monsieur Basquet was one of the region's most prominent businessmen, a property developer who'd turned large stretches of the coastline into a country-club fairway of pantiled villas, swimming pools, golf clubs and tennis courts. And all of it in less than a decade.

Everyone knew the story. For two hundred and fifty years the Valadeau family that Basquet had married into had made their money from soap and essential oils. When his father-in-law died and Monsieur Basquet took over the running of the company, he'd used that security to underwrite a programme of diversification that had started with residential and commercial property development in the centre of town, before spreading out along the coast. It was said there wasn't a brick laid between Marseilles and St Raphael that didn't bear the Basquet stamp. And Pamuk believed it.

Tossing the remains of his coffee over the side, Basquet hoisted himself onto a seat and leant an elbow over the rail. 'Take her in,' he said. 'Let's have a look.'

Gunning the engines, Pamuk turned against the offshore breeze and powered in towards the coast, a craggy wall of limestone that ran from Montredon, a little east of Marseilles, to the outskirts of Cassis, its desolate, thirty-mile length cut with narrow, fjord-like *calanques*. It was the mouth of one of these, maybe fifty metres across, that now opened up ahead of the Ferretti's prow. Passing between the headlands that guarded its entrance, the chop flattened and Pamuk reduced speed, letting the cruiser chortle along between the bluffs, the sound of its engines growling off the stony sides of the inlet.

Beside him, Basquet looked to port and starboard, the sloping sides of the inlet rising a hundred metres above them. Slim, twisted pines and bursts of golden mimosa clung to its rocky skirts, their roots trailing out for a precarious grip on the stony soil. At a little past ten in the morning it was already hot, the sun climbing high above the canyon rim, warming the deck beneath their feet and the handrail that Basquet gripped.

One day soon, thought Basquet, this stretch of water will be the most sought-after address on the coast, nothing to compare with it between Marseilles and the Italian border. A dozen sumptuous villas cantilevered into the sides of the *calanque*, each with its own wrap-around terracing and private dock, the peculiar geography of this twisting inlet ensuring that no two villas were in sight of one another. Complete privacy. Basquet could see the properties now, superimposed onto the slopes and bluffs that rose around him: the mahogany decking under low pantiled roofs, Jacuzzis and glass walls, each estate connected by roped pathway to its private jetty and headland terrace.

Right now, of course, all this land, every *calanque* between Marseilles and Cassis, was protected, development forbidden. You couldn't spit without a permit. But all that was going to change if Basquet had his way. He took a deep breath, puffed out his chest and smelt the fresh salt tang of the sea in his nostrils.

And what the hell was the objection anyway? Why shouldn't he start development here? Over the years they'd done it all the way from Catalans Plage to Prado without anyone saying squat. Even built an autoroute right bang along the coast. Four lanes of concrete and tarmac. And if that wasn't bad enough, they'd gone and called it after a fucking American president! So what was the problem going a little further east, Basquet reasoned, as he did a hundred times a day? The way the city was growing, the way people swarmed down here from the north to spend their money on somewhere swanky to live, someone was going to do it someday. So why not him? Paul Basquet. And why not now? In a couple of days he'd have the money. And permission. And who was going to stop him then?

Of course the old man, his ever-cautious father-in-law, would be spitting nails. While he'd been in charge, it was soap, essential oils and absolutely nothing else. It had taken Basquet six months to persuade the old *pingre* to develop a line of scented candles, for fuck's sake. And when the stock sold out in less than a month, the old man refused to consider another run. It wasn't their core business, he'd argued; it diminished their position. What the company was founded on, the old man declared, was what it lived on, gently smacking the back of one hand against the open palm of the other in that irritating, patronising way of his.

Which, Basquet had been at pains to point out, hadn't been enough to keep the family business all that healthy. Profits were acceptable but unremarkable, the company share price never more than a few *sous* one way or the other, and yearly dividends increasingly disappointing. The business was ticking over, more or less, but nothing more. Which was why, when the old man passed on and Basquet finally took control, the company headed off in some unlikely directions. And it was those various directions – property development, leasing, insurance, remortgaging and, most recently, maritime trade – that had kept the family business on line, recording the kinds of profits the old man had never even dreamed of. So much for playing safe.

Rounding a stony bluff, the Ferretti reached its limits, the furthest point inland, cobalt depths rising to aquamarine shallows and the gentle slap of surf on a curve of white sand some sixty metres across.

Basquet leant forward, took off his sunglasses and shaded his eyes. He could see it all. There, where the rock and scrub began to slope upwards behind the beach, built out on a stilted deck, would be the clubhouse and restaurant; there the chandlery, workshops and supply mall; and there the double jetty large enough to accommodate a dozen cruisers.

Slipping his sunglasses back on, Basquet followed the scrubby path that wound up through the trees, the only land access to the *calanque*, leading to a stony goat track that cut through pine and olive to the D559. That was the route the driveway would follow, from the security post and pillared gates through nearly two kilometres of landscaped grounds, two hundred hectares of tended lawns, tennis courts, a driving range . . .

Right now, it seemed, the biggest problem Basquet faced was what to call the place, trying to get the right name. The Calanque Club? Or just Calanque?

Or, as his mistress Anais had suggested, Calanque One. That was smart. Basquet liked that – doing the same again, the next inlet along. Another Basquet development. More units, lower overheads, higher prices and profits.

Closing now on the beach and beginning to roll with the surf, Basquet had Pamuk power up and put the cruiser into a tight sweep, going back the way they had come past the three-million-dollar homes whose draft architectural plans Basquet kept in his office safe. By the end of the month he'd have what he needed.

As the Ferretti reached the final bend, Basquet glanced at his Rolex. Right on time.

Beside him, anticipating open water, Pamuk eased the helm to starboard and slid the throttles forward. But as they turned out of the *calanque*, Pamuk suddenly stiffened, brought the revs back a notch. A hundred metres ahead lay a black-hulled cigarette boat, the weight of its twin outboard engines lifting the bows above the chop, its name,

Pluto, painted in flames along its lacquered flanks. There were two men in the cockpit – one, in a black T-shirt, wiry but well built, standing at the wheel, the breeze whipping his fair hair; the second, just head and shoulders, sitting back, arms spread across the top of the cockpit lounger, the side of his face smeared with a startling raspberry stain.

'It's okay,' said Basquet, putting out a hand to calm Pamuk. 'Just draw alongside, there's a good boy.'

Five minutes later, the two boats were fendered and secured, bows pointing up into the wind, the *Vallée des Eaux* five metres longer and much higher in the water than the speedboat, but a good twenty knots slower. Pamuk, holding her steady, watched Monsieur Basquet appear at the bow and lean over the rail. In the cockpit beneath, the man in the lounger got shakily to his feet and the two of them began talking. The low revving of the engines and the whip of the breeze made it impossible to hear what was being said, but the meeting seemed amicable enough.

The rendezvous, Pamuk realised, had been planned. And about as discreet as you could get.

A few moments later the exchange was concluded with a wave, since hands couldn't be shaken, and Basquet returned to the bridge. Down in *Pluto*, Black T-shirt slipped the tethers and the two boats rocked apart.

Pamuk glanced at his boss and Basquet nodded towards Marseilles. Turning the bows and gently applying pressure to the throttles, Pamuk eased the Ferretti away from the speedboat and set a course for port.

Beside him Monsieur Basquet patted the pockets of his shorts, his shirt.

Pamuk recognised the movement. He took a hand off the helm and reached for the pastilles he'd stashed in a drawer on the console.

18

Thirty years earlier Jacquot would have made for La Joliette and the alleyways off Quai du Lazaret. That was where the tattoo boys hung out back then. Pumping red and blue inks into meaty, seafaring biceps, the recipients either comatose with drink and carried in by giggling shipmates, or holding back their own sleeves to more closely inspect the needle's whining progress across their skin.

But it was a different world down there now, along La Joliette, from when Jacquot was a boy, loitering along those streets with Doisneau and his pals. Now it was cranes and hard hats, the rattle of jackhammers, bulldozers and Metro extensions, and a recently completed and widely acclaimed office conversion, the old warehouses set against the Littoral flyover transformed into chic and elegant office space – six-floor atriums, glass-walled lifts, glades of giant fern and pools of golden carp among the teak decking and gravelled Japanese landscapes.

Nowadays the tattoo parlour nearest to La Joliette was tucked away in a courtyard behind République, and it was here that Jacquot was headed. Tuesday morning. First thing, just as Gastal had suggested. On foot. Feeling a little weak and ragged from Gassi's *demis* the night before but every sense alert.

This, Jacquot decided, shading his eyes as he stepped out from Le Panier's shadowy side streets onto the sun-warmed quay of the Vieux Port, was what it was all about, everything he loved about police work. Real police work. Down in the trenches. A photo in your pocket and a whole city to trawl, people to seek out, questions to ask, leads to follow.

Of course, Guimpier wouldn't have approved. As chief investigating officer it wasn't the kind of police work Jacquot should have bothered with, a job more usefully delegated to one of his team – that bloodhound Peluze, or the wily, devious new girl Isabelle Cassier, or Chevin with his disarming stutter, or Laganne, Serre, Muzon. Any of them on the homicide squad could have done the job. But Jacquot couldn't resist it. Out here in the morning sunshine, following a hunch, with only the flimsiest evidence to work on; knowing that somewhere in the city there was an answer to every question, a solution for every crime, a killer for every victim. You just had to look. Like the old times. Read the passage of play, keep your eyes and ears open, and take your opportunities where you found them.

It wasn't so different from the time he'd spent with Doisneau and the *Chats de Nuit*, young kids, out on the street, looking for mischief. Only this time Jacquot was on the right side of the law, with a badge in his pocket to prove it and twenty years' service under his belt. From a gendarme walking suburban beats to hunting down killers for Homicide, he'd played his part in countless dramas. But the thrill of the chase never palled. It was what Jacquot loved, and never tired of. Maybe something, maybe nothing, but always worth the ante.

And what a place to do it, he thought, breathing in a lungful of salty sea air along the Quai du Port, and the very next moment, as he turned the Samaritaine corner into République, catching a warm, rotting whiff of drains. Marseilles. The city he'd grown up in, left and come back to. A city by the sea. Wherever you went – in its darkest alleyways, its busiest markets, in its parks and suburbs, along its most fashionable thoroughfares – the ocean was always there. The watery play of its reflection when you least expected it, a slice of blue at the end of a boulevard, or a flash of distant sun-glitter between buildings. And always the clean, salty scent of it sluicing through the city streets.

And this morning he was a part of that city, as close as you could get, the pavement under his feet, the sun on his shoulders, a cool breeze licking at his neck. And on his own, the way he liked it. The way Rully had always fallen in with, understood; the reason they got on so well together. Following his nose, letting instinct rather than procedure set the pace, point the way.

Instinct. Jacquot knew it was his strongest card. Growing up in the back alleys of Le Panier, playing fast and loose with the *Chats*, instinct had been his key to survival. Knowing who to trust and knowing when to run. And instinct too, knowing, when the moment arrived, to follow an old man with white hair and his mother's gentle eyes who came to claim him from the Borel orphanage. A man he'd never met, didn't know. His mother's father.

It was the same instinct that served him from the moment he stepped onto the field of play, encouraged by that same old man; knowing somehow where the ball would go next, knowing which of his opponents was the real threat, knowing which of his own team-mates to shadow. Sensing the passage of play.

Instinct. And Jacquot could feel its gentle, goading presence now, as he sought out his first port of call, in a sloping, rubbish-strewn yard a few steps back from the traffic on République. There was no shop window, just a door with an unlit neon sign above it, *Tattoo-Toi*, and three stone steps leading down into a dim semi-basement parlour that smelt of damp plaster, old sweat and spilled antiseptic. In the middle of the room was a barber's chair surrounded by the paraphernalia of tattooing: needle gun, inks, a tray of plastic bottles, an unlikely-looking bag of pink cotton wool balls and, beneath the chair, a patch of bubbled lino stained with blots of ink – red, blue, black, green – and scarred with a worn furrow where, Jacquot supposed, the soles of customers' shoes rasped as the needle bit.

'*Allo*. Anyone around?' called Jacquot.

With a swish and slap, a curtain of beads at the back of the room parted and the proprietor appeared, his grubby sleeveless vest revealing bulging tattooed shoulders under a mat of black hair. Holding the beads to one side, he gave Jacquot a surly once-over before bringing up his other hand and biting into the brioche he was carrying.

At which point, saying nothing in return, Jacquot pulled the picture from his pocket and held it up.

Usually it would be a face, features to identify, but all they had was the tattoo – three words one above the other on a curled and shadowed scroll of parchment incised into the victim's upper thigh – the face too bloated and fish-snacked to be of any practical value.

The tattooist looked once, thrusting out his chin as though scrutinising a work of art, swallowed his mouthful of brioche, sucked at his teeth with his tongue and top lip, then shook his head.

It was the same story at the second tattoo parlour that Jacquot visited, behind the Mercure Hotel on Quai des Belges, and at a third address near the Gare St-Charles. But at the fourth, off rue Curiol, Jacquot came a little closer.

Grunt work, it got you there in the end.

Surrounded by sample images of coiled serpents, fire-breathing dragons, roaring lions, daggers plunged into bleeding hearts and intricately worked native designs, a bare-chested customer was slumped forward across a table, head resting in his arms. Beside him, perched on a stool and leaning over the canvas of his back, a rubber-gloved tattooist worked on the wing feathers of a bird or an angel. Like the other parlours Jacquot had visited, the room was filled with the sharp smell of antiseptic, a bottle of which the tattooist tipped out one-handed onto a swab to wipe away the beads of blood from his customer's shoulder blade.

'Not mine,' said the tattooist, studying the photo but not taking it, needle humming an inch above his customer's skin, cotton swab tossed into a metal bin at his feet. 'But you ask me, it looks like Vrech's work.'

'Vrech?' asked Jacquot, pocketing the photo.

The tattooist didn't respond immediately, as though Jacquot had left the shop and he was alone with his client. And then, without looking up from his work: 'Fausse Monnaie. Up on the Corniche, near the bus stop,' he said, giving Jacquot the lead he'd spent the best part of the morning searching for.

Ten minutes later, as a sleekly lined motor launch rumbled down the channel to its berth in the Vieux Port, Jacquot turned off the Quai de Rive Neuve and down rue Thiars where he'd left his car the night before. Fausse Monnaie was on the road to Prado and too far to walk. Already a flyer had been tucked under his windscreen wiper. A sale somewhere, best prices, the usual thing. He balled it and tossed it behind the passenger seat. Pulling out into the traffic he set off for Fausse Monnaie.

It didn't take long to find the place he was looking for. A few steps back from a covered bus stop, across a narrow municipal garden and sharing a semi-basement frontage with a *tabac*, an estate agent, a baker and a greengrocer, stood Studio Vrech. Leaving his car in the nearest side street, Jacquot walked back to the parlour. The closer he got, the more certain he was that he was about to get a break.

Vrech's tattoo parlour was bigger than the others he'd visited that morning – bigger, brighter and better cared for. Its reception desk was furnished with a vase of plastic flowers, its tiled floors slanted with morning sunlight and its waiting room tidily piled with magazines. Around its walls, framed certificates and a gallery's worth of photographed tattoos attested to Vrech's qualifications and artistry.

Behind the desk, in the parlour beyond, was the man himself. He was unmistakable. Dressed in white T-shirt and black cycling shorts, he was sitting with his back to the door, bare feet up on a mirrored vanity, reading a newspaper. From where Jacquot stood the capital letters spelling his name were clearly visible on the back of his skull, branded onto the skin beneath a helmet of blond stubble. As far as Jacquot could see, it was the only tattoo the man possessed.

'You don't look like you've come for a tattoo,' said the man called Vrech, glancing up at Jacquot in the mirror before turning back to his newspaper.

'You're right, I haven't,' replied Jacquot.

Vrech turned a page lazily, casting his eyes over the spread to see if there was anything that caught his fancy. Outside, beyond the studio window, the traffic beeped its way back to town or out to the beaches of Prado. A bus pulled into its stop with a wheeze of brakes and the doors shuddered open.

'So, Monsieur Gendarme, what can I do for you?'

Jacquot noted the emphasis and how swiftly the tattooist had identified him as a policeman.

'Someone told me they recognised your handiwork,' said Jacquot, pulling the photo from his pocket. He placed it on the counter.

Swivelling round in the tattooist's chair, Vrech put down the paper and came out to the desk. He took the photo, looked at it intently and started nodding.

'Very difficult work, that,' he said. 'The skin's so pliable there, so soft. Not like the arms or the back. You have to stretch it, you know? To get the smooth surface. And compensate, otherwise the outline blurs. It can be painful, too . . . well, not painful, you understand, as much as . . . ticklish. It is difficult to sit still, yes?'

Vrech's voice was rough and deep, the French heavily accented. Dutch, thought Jacquot. That hoiky way Lowlanders speak, as though every word is a shard of gravel caught in the throat.

'It's yours?'

'Did you hear me say that?'

'Let's say I detect a certain professional pride.'

Vrech looked at the photo once more, then snapped it down onto the counter rather than handing it back.

'And you'd be correct in your assumption, Monsieur Gendarme. Let's see . . . Maybe eighteen months ago, couple of visits. The colours, you understand, the closeness of the lettering, the . . . discomfort.' Vrech tipped his head back to stare at the ceiling, as though making a calculation. Then he turned to Jacquot, looked him straight in the eye. 'Maybe four, five hours' work total.'

'A name?'

Vrech gave it some thought. 'Nicki? Vicki? Something like that.'

'You have an address?'

Vrech shook his head. 'The boyfriend paid.'

'The boyfriend?'

'The boyfriend. Cash. Sat beside her the whole time.' Vrech nodded at the chair he'd been sitting in. 'Both visits. Which, you know, makes it difficult when I'm tattooing pretty much the highest place you can get to on a woman's leg. I mean centimetres from it. You can smell it, you know what I'm saying . . . ?' Vrech smiled. 'And there's the boyfriend watching. I tell you . . .'

'What about the boyfriend?'

'No address, sorry.' Vrech shook his head.

The negative and the headshake were dispiriting.

'But I know who he is,' continued Vrech.

'And that would be?' prompted Jacquot, as the tattooist went back to his seat and picked up his paper, as though he'd said all he planned saying.

'He's called Carnot.'

'First name?'

'Jean, Jean Carnot,' replied Vrech, making himself comfortable, straightening out his paper. 'You see him around, you know. Young guy. But hard. A real *gorille*. He used to hire out as a bouncer up Cours Julian way, then moved on. Private security. That sort of thing. And a fixer, too – you want something, he gets it. If the price is right. And he always has a couple of girls working for him. A kind of sideline. I guess she was one of them. Very pretty – very, very sexy, you know?'

'Anything else?'

Vrech gave the question some thought. 'I remember, while I was working, she was talking about some photos she'd had done. For the Internet, you know, the porn sites. It sounded like he'd set it all up. She sounded real pleased with them.'

Jacquot reached for the photo, slid it off the counter and into his pocket.

'And if I wanted to find this Carnot? Where would be a good place to start?'

19

C oupchoux paused in the entrance, his body split by sunlight and shadow, the skin on his face and neck still tight with salt spray from the morning's outing with Raissac in *Pluto*. Dipping his fingers into the holy water and leaving them there longer than he needed to, he gazed ahead, down the aisle to the altar, stone-panelled and plain, and the rose window behind it. Taking his fingers from the water, he brushed them against the edge of the font and dabbed them against his forehead and heart, the cool liquid trickling between his eyes before he wiped it away.

It felt good, that abundance, running off him, scouring a path through the salt. Powerful. Powerful, and God-given.

He put wet fingers to his lips, kissed the knuckles and turned to the left, making for one of the side chapels. When he reached it, the altar of Sainte Matilde, with its plainly draped altar cloth and damask-curtained confessional to one side, he genuflected, crossed himself a second time and slid into one of the four pews reserved for penitents. He was the only one there, though he could hear an earnest whispering from behind the confessional curtain and could see beneath it a pair of thick ankles and wrinkled hose bulging over stout brown shoes. Not long now, he thought to himself, pushing aside the mat and dropping his knees to the stone floor. Closing his eyes, he clasped his hands and lowered his head in prayer.

Of all the churches Coupchoux knew, this was his favourite, this narrow-naved, coolly stoned basilica a few blocks back from Cassis port. Such an inspiring, restful place, he always thought. Such a glorious, peaceful sanctuary, the bevelled columns rising upwards into a web of simple ribbed vaulting, the stone paving polished and shiny, the still, stale air suffused with the scent of snuffed candles, hot wax and incense. He could sit there for hours, and often did when Raissac had him do something really bad, something that reached down deep and squeezed at his soul.

The problem, Coupchoux knew, was that he was powerless to do anything about it. When Raissac wanted something, he felt only a bursting compulsion to comply, a pressing, irresistible desire to obey and to please. Except here, his knees burning on the cool stone slabs. Here was the strength to deny his master, here the will to resist temptation. Here was cool faith and fortitude, and always, as he stepped back into the sunshine, a burning determination to change his ways. Redemption. In Coupchoux's line of work, there was nothing like it. The trouble was that his resolve never seemed to last longer than a few days – just until Raissac called, told him what was needed, and it began once more.

With a swirl of musky damask and a rattle of wooden rings the confessional curtain was pulled aside and Coupchoux heard an old woman's shoes tap across the stone flags. Headscarved, bustling into the pew in front of him, she set to work on her rosary.

The moment had come. Getting to his feet, kneecaps aching, Coupchoux stepped from the pew and made for the confessional. Drawing the curtain closed behind him, the panelled space still redolent of the old lady's lavender, he settled himself in the dark. With a dry click the grille slid open. He took a breath, kissed his fingers and began: 'Forgive me, Father, for I have sinned . . .'

20

J ean Carnot had considerable form. Going back a long way.

Sitting at his desk, Jacquot scrolled through the details he'd accessed from Records, starting with Carnot's first arrest at the age of fifteen for car theft, through a litany of drug-related offences, various breaches of the peace, living off immoral earnings until, three years earlier, he'd been picked up for aggravated assault. The victim, Jacquot noted, was a woman. According to the file, Carnot had tied her to a chair, beaten her with a belt and knocked out two of her teeth with the heel of his shoe. In the last seventeen years, since his first arrest, Jean Carnot had spent four of those years behind bars. If the woman he'd assaulted had pressed charges, he'd still be inside. Since then, as far as Jacquot could confirm, Carnot had been clean.

But Jacquot knew that meant very little.

While he was at it, Jacquot pecked out Doisneau's name on the keyboard and waited for the screen to bring up the information he wanted. Seconds later, his old friend's face flashed onto the screen. In the photo, Doisneau looked tired and washed-out, his hair standing untidily on end. Probably a dawn pick-up, thought Jacquot. Hustled out of his bed and down to Headquarters with no time, save for dressing, to tidy himself up or gather his thoughts.

Jacquot scrolled through Doisneau's sheet. The usual – theft, obstruction, handling stolen goods, assault: a sad chronicle of a life. Like Carnot he'd been inside, his latest stay, as Jacquot had guessed, at Baumettes on the back road to Cassis. A six-year term, reduced to three and work parole.

Jacquot went to the notes on Doisneau's last arrest.

Following a tip-off – no source credited – officers had raided a garage lock-up in a Toulon suburb and found four kilos of hashish jammed under the front seat of a Renault van and a .45 automatic taped to the steering column. When they arrested Doisneau, the registered owner of the vehicle and the lock-up, he'd denied any knowledge of the drugs or the gun but it hadn't done much good. According to Records he'd been released into parole work only two months earlier.

Fitted up, Doisneau had told him the night before, and the police report seemed to support it. Someone plants the evidence and calls the cops. Raissac? One of his team? It made sense. Doisneau does something stupid and pays the price. And now, three years later, here he is looking to square the account and get out of the firing line down in Spain.

Jacquot tapped out instructions on the keyboard and Carnot returned to the screen.

The two men couldn't have been more different. Doisneau nearly twenty years older, unshaven, bleary-eyed, his face a map of discontent and abuse. And there was Carnot. Over six feet tall, judging by the laddered measure behind his head in the custody picture. Arab blood for certain – black curly hair; smooth, tanned skin over a clenched jaw and high cheekbones; a strong, jutting chin and a bored, mocking stare from eyes black as barbecue coals. The lips were full but impatiently drawn, pushing out thin, bracketing lines into his cheeks. The teeth, Jacquot suspected, would be white and even, gritted, too, under the insolent glare. He was also pretty sure that Carnot could throw out a hell of a smile when he wanted to.

Pushing back his chair, Jacquot swung up his legs and rested his boots on the desk. He crossed his ankles and felt the leather rasp gently. Snakeskin. His favourite pair. Twenty years old and soft as Boni's Air France gloves. Good support for his bad ankle too, even if they did raise a look from Guimpier and the Widow Foraque. Perfect walking shoes as well. Which was why he'd selected them that morning.

He was just about to call up Gastal one floor above, still out to lunch the last time he'd tried, when the door was flung open and

Lamonzie marched in, face clenched tight as a walnut, red as an early cherry. Lamonzie was head of Narcotics, senior in rank but a few years younger than Jacquot, and he wasn't happy.

'And just exactly what the fuck do you think you were doing?' he demanded, leaning over Jacquot's desk, his weight supported on splayed pool-player's fingertips.

On reflection 'Where?' was probably not the right thing to say, but Jacquot said it anyway. What the hell? He'd always thought Lamonzie a shifty, jumped-up little *rigoriste* who behaved like police head-quarters was his own personal playground. No one ever knew what Narcotics were up to, which meant that whenever some poor bastard trespassed on a stake-out that Lamonzie had set up and not told anyone about, down came Lamonzie, brandishing his wrinkled red face like an offensive weapon. Which was exactly what this little outburst was all about. Jacquot must have crossed the line without knowing it.

'Where? Where?' Lamonzie lowered his voice, looked around, then glared back at Jacquot with an even greater intensity. 'Rue des Allottes, that's where, Jacquot. Number 65. A certain Alexandre Raissac. Or is it your mother you were calling on?'

'That's right. Allottes.'

'And? And?'

'Just checking out a lead, you know.'

'Just – checking – out – a – lead . . .'

Jacquot's patience gave way. 'Look, Lamonzie, give it a rest. You're not the only one around here who's got a job to do. You keep everything buttoned up the way you do, sooner or later someone's bound to cross your patch.'

'And how exactly does Monsieur Raissac figure in these inquiries of yours?'

'Raissac? He doesn't.'

Lamonzie gave him a squinty look.

'Berri. Madame Berri was who I was after. She's a tattoo artist. One of the best, they say.'

'Well, next time you want a heart on your arm make an appoint-ment someplace else. You got that?'

Lamonzie pushed himself away from Jacquot's desk. 'I don't want to see you a hundred metres in any direction. Clear enough for you?' He gave Jacquot another hard little stare and marched out of the office, rattling the glass panel in the door as he pulled it shut behind him.

'*Bite*,' whispered Jacquot, leaning forward to wipe at his boots where he'd noticed a fleck of Lamonzie's saliva land. Brushing off the leather, he wondered why he hadn't just said that Gastal had had him do it. Finger Gastal. But like it or not, Gastal was on his team, and you didn't do that to one of your own.

Still, taking the blame rankled, and a couple of hours later, sharing a terrace table with Gastal outside the Club Maras, Jacquot decided to have it out with his new partner.

'Lamonzie dropped by,' he said.

'Oh yeah,' replied Gastal.

'And he's not a happy man.'

Gastal nodded, covering a smile as he cracked a stubborn pistachio between his teeth and added the splinters to the pile of shells in front of him.

'So next time,' continued Jacquot, 'have someone else do your dirty work.'

Gastal raised his neck out of his collar, as though squaring up for some verbal. But he let it go.

Which was a pity. They'd only been working together a couple of days but already Jacquot felt an unhealthy compulsion to bury his fist in Gastal's fat little face. A real *face-à-claque* if ever there was one.

They'd been sitting at Club Maras for more than an hour, Jacquot watching the street and Gastal facing the bar. It was one of the places that Vrech had said was a likely Carnot haunt, a new set-up on a side street back from the Cours Julian. There was a members-only club downstairs, the bar at street level, and a so-so fish restaurant on the terrace above them. It was a long shot, Carnot turning up at the first place they tried, but something told Jacquot that it might be worth a call. A beer-after-work kind of thing, even if your drinking partner was Gastal.

'Isn't that him?' said Gastal, nodding over Jacquot's shoulder.

Jacquot took a pull on his cigarette and reached around to the table behind him for an ashtray. As he did so he glanced up at the bar. Twenty feet away Jean Carnot was slapping one of the waiters on the arm, swaggering over to shake the barman's hand, nods here and there, glancing around the room, taking a stool, looking at his watch. Unmistakable.

'You wanna do it here?' asked Gastal.

Jacquot shook his head, repositioning his chair and stretching out his legs.

Carnot was now in full view at the bar. He looked like he was dressed for a night on the town: clean blue jeans, a cream silk shirt, and a bright green jumper draped over his shoulders. He was swinging a ring of keys in his hands, like a set of worry beads.

'Let's give it a few minutes,' said Jacquot. 'See if anything turns up.'

Nothing did. Carnot finished his beer, swigging elegantly from the bottle, kissed and hugged a couple of the waitresses who didn't look to be enjoying the encounter as much as he did, then made his farewells.

Jacquot had been right about the smile. Pure platinum.

They caught up with him two blocks along as he was getting into his car.

'Jean Carnot?' said Jacquot, bending down to the driver's window. Gastal leant against the rear door as though his weight might somehow stop the car from moving off.

Carnot must have heard those words a hundred times. He knew immediately who they were. He looked up at Jacquot from under thick black brows. 'And? What of it?'

'I believe you may be able to help us.'

'Oh yeah?' Carnot replied, sliding a key into the ignition and disengaging the gear.

Jacquot slipped the photo from his jacket pocket and passed it to Carnot.

Carnot took it, turned it, looked. Looked closer. Then handed it back.

'And?' It was a good act, given how he hadn't been expecting them, hadn't expected to see the photo.

'Wondered if you'd seen that tattoo before?'

Carnot pushed out his bottom lip, shook his head. 'Couldn't say,' he replied.

Of course Jacquot could have got down to it straight off, said how Vrech had given them his name, how Vrech had confirmed that Jean Carnot had been there when the tattoo was done, how he'd been the one who paid. But Jacquot didn't want to put the Dutchman in a spot, even if he was the most likely source for the information. So he came at it from a different angle.

'We found it on a body.'

Carnot didn't react. 'And?'

'And we think you might know who it is.'

'Like I said . . .'

'You got a moment?' broke in Jacquot. 'Maybe come by the hospital and take a look, make an ID? You know, on the off chance?'

Jacquot hoped Carnot didn't bluff it too far, what with the victim's body being a couple of hours north in a chill drawer in Salon-le-Vitry's morgue.

Carnot took the photo back, gave it another look.

'She dead?'

The girl's name was Vicki Monel, Carnot told them. Lived up near St-Charles someplace, in a block by the station. Maybe still there. Hadn't seen her in a year, maybe two, not since the tattoo, anyway.

They were sitting in Carnot's car, its interior filled with the citrus scent of Carnot's aftershave. Carnot was fiddling with the ignition key, flicking the engine off and on. Lighting up the dashboard dials, then killing them, as though he was impatient to be off. It was getting dark and street lights were coming on, quivering and warming into life.

A name, thought Jacquot. Vicki Monel. Another name. Another line of inquiry. Maybe there'd be something more from this one than they'd managed to get on the two previous victims. Something that went somewhere.

'Address? Phone number?'

Carnot shook his head. 'Never went there.'

'How'd you meet her?' asked Gastal from the back seat.

'I don't know. Party somewhere. Don't remember.'

'She a local girl?' asked Jacquot.

'Toulon? Hyères, maybe,' replied Carnot, as though he couldn't care one way or the other.

'Did she have a job?' Jacquot continued.

Carnot shrugged.

'Is she one of your girls, Jean?' Gastal again, leaning forward between the two front seats.

Sitting beside Carnot, Jacquot saw the jaw tighten. Was this the man who had drowned Vicki Monel, he wondered? And Grez? And Ballarde? Hard to say. Certainly up to it. Strong enough, and mean enough with it.

'Listen . . .' began Carnot, shifting in his seat.

'Come on, Jean,' said Gastal. 'This Vicki Monel's on the slab and you know her. She worked for you. One of your girls. Right?'

Carnot came as close to a nod as you could without actually nodding.

'So, she give you a hard time or what? Pocket a bit here and there, think you wouldn't notice?'

'Maybe tie her to a chair, Carnot,' added Jacquot. 'Knock a few teeth out.'

'I swear I don't know what . . . It's got to be a year, more, since I seen her. She was a friend, you know, but it didn't last. Drugs. She was always out of it.'

'Where you been the last few weeks?' asked Gastal.

'Here. There. Around.' Carnot gave them a cocky look.

Jacquot knew the way Carnot's brain was working. They haven't got a thing on me, he was thinking. If they suspected me they'd be doing all this at police headquarters. They just want information.

'Out of the city?' continued Gastal.

'Nope. Here the whole time.'

'You know anyone who might have done this?'

Carnot shook his head. Now he knew he was off the hook.

'Like I said, she was always drugging it. Could have put someone out. Pissed someone off.'

'So tell us about the photos,' said Jacquot.

They kept Carnot in the car for an hour, Jacquot beside him, Gastal behind, niggling away at him, probing for more information. But Carnot's story held. He hadn't seen Vicki Monel in more than a year. She was a druggie. Unreliable. The last he heard she was modelling – for an Internet porn site. He'd started her up, he told them, but she'd done a runner, cut him out of the deal. *Tant pis*, he shrugged; she was a loser.

So they took his address, noted his car registration, told him not to leave town and let him go.

Back at Headquarters, while Gastal chased down the Internet address that Carnot had given them, Jacquot checked Vicki Monel in Records, searching through known felons and missing persons. It didn't take long for him to draw a blank – no sign of her. Next he looked up her name in the city telephone directory. If she was listed, they'd get an address. And with an address, they'd find someone who knew her – a neighbour, friends, family. But she wasn't listed for Marseilles. Which meant an official ex-directory enquiry and all the hullabaloo that would entail. And if they didn't get any joy there, they'd have to go through the same procedure for Toulon, Hyères. Maybe even Salon-le-Vitry.

Jacquot was getting himself a coffee from the machine on the landing, thinking it could wait till morning, when he heard Gastal's 'Gotcha' in the Squad Room.

Hunched forward, his fat little fingers cupping the mouse, Gastal was glued to the computer's monitor, a slice of red tongue sliding over his lips.

'You find her?' asked Jacquot, leaning over his shoulder.

'Oh yes,' said Gastal, moving aside for Jacquot to see. 'The one in the middle.'

On screen three young women lay side by side on a bed, legs in the air, held apart at the knees, limbs criss-crossing. Given the angle it was impossible to see their faces.

'How do you know?' asked Jacquot.

Gastal tapped the screen, between the middle pair of legs. There, high up on the inside of one thigh, was a small black mark, more bruise than shadow.

'Can you make it any clearer?' asked Jacquot.

Gastal chuckled, dragged a cross-hair from the control strip, squared it over the mark, selected a high zoom and double-clicked. A second later, the screen went fuzzy, then shivered back into focus. Still a little blurred from the magnification, but clear enough for Jacquot to see the three words, even if they were upside down.

'You got a face to go with it?'

Gastal clicked out of the image, back to the three girls on the bed, and then clicked out of that. In an instant another image rolled down over the screen. The bed and wallpaper were identical to the previous set so Jacquot assumed that the three girls – a brunette and two blondes – were also the same. This time the brunette was sitting on the edge of the bed, legs apart, looking straight at the camera while her companions, kneeling beside her, stroked and licked her breasts.

Gastal repeated the procedure with the cross-hair, aiming it between the brunette's legs. The same tattoo materialized on screen. He clicked the mouse again and the original picture returned. He squared an outline around the brunette's head, clicked again and her face filled the screen – lips apart, eyes dreamy, fingers pushing through her hair.

Gastal pointed his fingers like a gun. 'Badaboum.'

21

A little more than an hour's drive north of Marseilles, Max Benedict turned off the Rocsabin road and lurched down a bumpy track, marking his trail with a plume of swirling, chalky dust. The sun was low in the sky and cast a warm, golden glow across the landscape, pooled with shadows in those hollows where the sun no longer reached. Through his open window Benedict could smell rosemary, pine and wild fennel, and up ahead, across the tipping bonnet, he caught sight of the house flickering beyond the trees – its pantiled roofs and honey-coloured stone walls, its blue-shuttered windows and the spray of golden mimosa that sheltered its big oak door.

Benedict had arrived in Paris that morning, flying north the previous day from Palm Beach to New York's La Guardia airport. Without contacting any of his friends in the city, he'd transferred directly to JFK and made the connection for Air France's last transatlantic service. An obliging stewardess had recognised him and, once they were airborne, invited him into First Class. In Paris, his head feeling tight and woolly from too much airline claret, he'd taxied to the Gare de Lyon and caught the train south to Aix. Three hours later, he'd picked up a rental jeep and driven the thirty kilometres north-west to Cavaillon, then up into the hills of the Luberon, following the signs for St Bédard-le-Chapitre, Chant-le-Neuf and Rocsabin. As the road became narrower, his hangover began to feel more manageable, his shoulders appeared to be loosening and his mood grew less frustrated. As he pulled through the last stand of pines, before dropping down into the gravelled courtyard of his home, Palm Beach suddenly seemed a very long way away.

Benedict had spent the last three months in that seaside haven for the rich and famous, attending the trial of one of that city's more illustrious names, a Senator's son accused of aggravated rape and assault. It had been a professional assignment, covering the proceedings for a magazine that specialised in, and was required reading among, those very same rich and famous, particularly when the pampered lives of one of their own went astray and the perpetrators believed themselves beyond the law. Which, in the Palm Beach rape trial, much to Benedict's dissatisfaction, had proved to be the case. After three 'Letters From The Courthouse', published in consecutive issues, the defendant had been acquitted of the charges against him despite a mass of evidence. It had been a sobering, frustrating three months and Max Benedict, veteran crime diarist and roving editor-at-large, reckoned he was due a break. And there was only one place in the world where he could do that.

Max Benedict had bought La Ferme Magny eighteen months earlier, a run-down Provençal *mas* whose occupants – the farmer Magny and his wife – had finally decided that life in town looked altogether more practical and comfortable than life in the country running three sloping hectares of vines. But the place was more of a mess than Benedict had anticipated, and back home in the States he joked to friends that all he had done was buy a view, and was now building a home from which to enjoy it. For more than a year he'd had a team of builders in there, tearing out floors and walls, repointing, replumbing, rewiring . . . re-everything. And then – even more work, more expense – installing a pool, set on a terrace between the house and the vines, facing west through a bordering line of cypresses, its blue depths now slanted with bars of golden sunlight.

It seemed an age since he'd been there and he felt a surge of affection for this ancient farm perched on the side of a valley with the Lubaron highlands rising away to the south, as well as a deep and abiding gratitude for his good fortune. Pulling up at the front door he switched off the engine and, over the ticking of the hot metal, listened to the sounds he'd been waiting for. The buzz of crickets, the hum of bees, a distant birdsong, and the creak of a breeze through the pines.

It was the first time that Benedict had been to the house without builders there, the place littered with their rubbish. Now it was finished – everyone gone – and he relished the solitude, the peace, and was surprised by the unexpected sense of ownership he felt. Without switching on any lights, beyond checking to see that the electricity had been connected, Benedict walked through the rooms, their rough stone walls painted white, the tiny windows opened up, and the rotting Magny floorboards replaced with stripped maple and cool marble – everything according to his specifications. And in the centre of every room stood the packing cases he'd sent over from the States, packing cases which over the next few weeks he'd work his way through, unwrapping his possessions, deciding where everything should go.

By summer's end La Ferme Magny would be home.

22

There was nothing like a plan. Preparation. The attention to detail. If you'd asked, the Waterman would have told you that it was half the fun. The satisfaction of knowing a name, friends and family, home and work, sharing the same bus, browsing through the same shops, deliberately brushing past the object of your affection in the street, sometimes even stopping them to ask directions – gradually drawing the prospective victim closer, closer.

Then, with all the information to hand, selecting the time and the place, confident that everything planned and provided for will be rewarded. Almost as a right. The uncontested prize for your thoroughness and your diligence. The watching, the waiting, the gathering momentum, sometimes spread over weeks at a time, that led, inevitably, to the act itself and that glorious, gratifying consummation.

But then, the Waterman sometimes reflected, preparation wasn't always everything. There were also those unplanned moments when life conspired to provide an unexpected opportunity. Something unforeseen. A moment's weakness, a second's hesitation: that fatal carelessness. A gathering of chance events to be seized upon and taken.

Thinking about it now, the Waterman was hard pressed to say which approach was the more enjoyable, the more satisfying. Preparation or opportunity. It was just like business, the Waterman decided. You either did your homework, or you just struck it lucky. Both, in their different ways, were equally rewarding.

This evening the Waterman had no special plan, no whispering need. In the last three months, there had been two such chance encounters and a third that had taken weeks of preparation before the final strike. Perhaps, tonight, this city by the sea would offer up something else, another opportunity. And either the Waterman would seize it, or let it slip by like a leaf carried along in a stream.

Scoop it up or leave it be.

Yet another pleasure to be savoured.

For there was, the Waterman knew, a certain satisfying contrariness in knowing that you could do something, yet not do it. If you had the discipline, if you could resist and carry it off. For there was little doubt in the Waterman's experience that denial of this magnitude only sharpened the appetite for the next encounter, increased that beguiling sense of edge, gave a certain thirsty need for the next headlong plunge.

And always, close by, wherever the Waterman prowled, the comforting sound of the ocean, or a sense of it pulling at the shore. Its distances and depths. Moods and movement. Its cool, cleansing influence.

Tonight, driving through the city, the Waterman enjoyed a moment's buoyant, brimming confidence. It was all so good here, so enlivening. And so easy. So easy that there was always the possibility you might make a mistake. Take your eye off the ball.

And there, the Waterman conceded, was yet another frisson to relish – the possibility of error, something going wrong. That single, unseen snag in the weave, only mitigated by the sheer, head-spinning exultation of the close call, the narrow escape. There had been a few of those, the Waterman would tell you. The breathless, heart-thumping rush of it.

And so, in a spirit of almost reckless abandon, tools of the trade stowed away in the glove compartment, the Waterman cruised the streets once more, hands idly playing the wheel, eyes darting left and right, searching out prey.

23

Jilly Holford had a date.

The cab slowed and she leant forward over the front seat, looking out for the name of the street. Somewhere off the road to Prado, he'd said.

Back from the sea. Away from the boat and away from the brothers, at last.

She'd left them moored in the Vieux Port, said it was a family thing, told them she was meeting her sister in Nîmes. Which was nowhere near the truth. She didn't even have a sister. It was just a story she'd spun to put them off the scent, to get away from them, to find herself some breathing space.

Because she knew that she wasn't going back that night, nor the next if she could manage it.

Grudgingly they'd let her go, passing up the knapsack – her 'stay-over bag' – with only her make-up inside, her toothbrush, some clean knickers and that dress she'd bought in Grenada the day before they set sail. The one with the full skirt, tight top and low front, the squared shoulders and the swirl of colours, the one she'd never worn outside the privacy of her cabin. As soon as she saw Marseilles looming above them as *Anemone* sailed into harbour, she'd known that dress was a Marseilles dress.

Even before she set eyes on him.

Jean. Jean. Jean. She hadn't been able to get the name out of her head.

She was going to fuck him, as simple as that.

And he knew it too. From the moment he levelled those dark eyes on her, they'd both known it. But she didn't give any sign, not in front of Ralph and Tim, the three of them celebrating their arrival in Marseilles in that tiny Rive Neuve bar, the first one they found as they staggered off the boat, first landfall since San Miguel.

He'd been sitting on a stool at the end of the bar. Caught her eye. Smiled when the brothers weren't looking. Seemed to know . . . Then he was gone, simply not there any more, and she'd been shocked, disappointed. Until the barman, delivering yet another round of beers to their table, discreetly passed her the card – the name, Jean, and a telephone number.

Result.

Jilly had called a couple of times before she got through. His voice was just as she'd imagined it. Black as molasses, smooth, a laughing kind of voice to match that smile. Of course, he assured her, of course he remembered her, so pleased she'd called, they must meet.

She'd changed into the Grenada dress in the Ladies' restroom at Café Samaritaine, applied her first make-up in weeks with an uncertain hand and stowed the knapsack in a left-luggage locker at Gare St-Charles. And now they were meeting. A little bar he knew. Back from the Corniche, he'd told her. They could have a drink. Maybe some dinner . . .

Except, she seemed to have got his directions wrong. Halfway down the Prado beach the cab driver said he must have missed the place and, circling the statue of David at the Prado *rondpoint*, he worked his way back along the strip and up onto the Corniche road. It was getting late and the sun hovered thickly over the distant ridges of the Frioul Islands.

Anxiously Jilly rubbed her hands together, still rough and sticky with salt. The first thing she'd done when they got their berth was find a *pharmacie*, some skin lotion, moisturiser, something to soften the hard ridges and salty lines that calloused her hands. But it didn't seem to have worked.

'Voilà, M'mselle. Là-haut!' said the driver and, swinging off the Corniche, he pulled up by a steep flight of steps almost hidden between a *tabac* and a launderette. On the wall of the launderette was a sign, the name of the bar they'd been looking for, a fist with a finger tilted upwards.

An hour later Jilly finished her second beer and looked at her watch. She couldn't believe he could have done this to her. She'd been stood up. The bastard wasn't going to show.

She beckoned over the waiter, asked for the bill and settled up.

It was dark by the time she got outside, which maybe explained why everything seemed so different. She stood on the pavement, looking up and down the street, trying to get her bearings. Everything was suddenly unfamiliar – the road, the houses, the shopfronts. She tried to remember the direction she'd come from, the steps from the Corniche, which way the cab had been headed. But she couldn't be certain. The darkness had changed everything.

Deciding to go left, Jilly set off along the street, glancing in shop windows, grateful for her reflection walking alongside and keeping her company. By the time she realised her mistake, she'd gone so far that she decided to carry on. Just so long as she kept heading downhill, she reasoned, she'd reach the Corniche and find herself another cab. She was wondering how she'd explain to the brothers her return from Nîmes so soon, when she heard a car coming up behind her, a cab.

And, truth be told, she really did think it was a cab, the low-gear prowling sound of it as though the driver was on the lookout for a fare. Squinting through the darkness at the approaching vehicle, Jilly tentatively raised an arm to flag it down – even if she couldn't actually see a cab light – and felt a jolt of relief as it pulled in ahead of her, the passenger door opening, the driver leaning across the passenger seat, face in shadow.

Of course she should have known better, just assuming it was a cab and the driver a cabbie, but she'd been at sea so long. She'd lost her land legs, her experience of city streets. And she was tired of walking, not knowing where she was.

'You want where?' asked a gruff voice and she bent closer to the cab's warm interior, tried to say 'Vieux Port' again, embarrassed by her poor French, and then felt a hand grab the front of her dress, fingers reaching for a grip inside the bodice and pulling her down. And her not resisting because, stupidly, she didn't want the dress to rip. Then that sharp prick in the neck, like a wasp sting, that she tried to brush away. Only her arm suddenly wouldn't operate the way she wanted it to, just like the rest of her body, which was now being bundled into the passenger footwell, wedged under the dash, the car door slamming shut, the dress pulled tight, so she knew it had caught in the door, dammit . . .

Then nothing, just a passage of time. The sound of a car wheel close by, drumming over cobbles, singing over tarmac. The warm, rubbery smell of the floor mat against her cheek. An absorption with the tangle of wires above her head, their colours, the way they bent and coiled, the little plastic box into which they disappeared. But no anxiety at her predicament, no real concern that her limbs refused to do what she wanted them to do.

Hey ho, she thought, and sighed contentedly, feeling a bubble of laughter work its way up her chest as the car turned sharply to the left. Or was it the right? Slowed and stopped. The engine died and she lay there in the ticking silence, heard the driver's door open and close and the sound of steps coming round the car. Then the passenger door opened, her dress loosened and she was lifted out.

The last thing Jilly saw that she could identify with any certainty was the domed roof of Aqua-Cité, the one she'd seen from *Anemone*'s deck the day they arrived in the old port of Marseilles. That, and the salty tang of the sea.

Part Two

24

Aqua-Cité, Marseilles, Wednesday

It was the constant, comforting sound of bubbles that Gabrielle liked. No silence here in this cool, watery place that smelt of the sea and the damp of buried concrete. Just that gentle bubbling. If the place had been silent, Gabrielle wouldn't have liked it at all. Below ground and all. Dark and shadowy. She'd have been spooked for sure. As it was, the playful sound kept her company, a light-hearted accompaniment to her humming.

Gabrielle Blanot arrived at her usual time, a little before six, making the journey from her home in Vieille Chapelle on her husband's Solex, letting herself in through one of the two service doors set into the perimeter of Aqua-Cité. In the staff changing rooms, she zipped up her overalls, made some coffee and, after her first cigarette of the day, set off for Block Seven – Reef Feeders and Open Sea – the first of the three areas she was responsible for. With only one row of tanks, a dozen in all, Seven was an easy job, an hour at most, a good way to start the shift.

The bubbling sound came to her as she unlocked the service door, entered into the cool, concrete bunker and felt for the light switch. Above her a line of neon tubes flickered and blinked on, one after another, casting an icy blue glow over the feeding gallery – a stepped walkway set above the tanks and concealed from the public's side. If Monsieur and Madame thought it was just fish that they were looking *at, they'd be in for a surprise. Above and behind the tanks was a real backstage area unseen by visitors, a concrete-walled space fretted with lagged pipes and stained with calcified leaks, where oxygen flow and temperature controls were located, where food supplies and cleaning equipment were stored and where Gabrielle Blanot worked.*

Climbing the ladder to the feeding catwalk she began her slow, methodical progress along the tanks. Gabrielle could have done the job in her sleep. Some mornings it felt like she did: checking oxygen and temperature levels at each station, measuring the feed into plastic hoppers before tipping it into the tank beneath, and then watching the hungry swirl of colours from the fish before moving on to the next tank. Then the next, until she reached the final tank, the food pellets spraying over the surface of the water like a sudden squall of rain. As she stowed the hopper and closed the food locker there was a slap and splash as one of the inhabitants in the tank below got a little carried away and broke surface.

Gabrielle smiled. Oscar again. She'd put money on it. The striped bass. The biggest mouth in the tank.

Making her way back along the catwalk to the ladder, she glanced at her watch. When she finished the next round – Block Six, Tropicals – and before she began Five – Crustaceans – there'd be plenty of time to stop for a coffee with her friends Tula and Corinne before the supervisor, Barzé, made an appearance. That Tula, thought Gabrielle, clambering down the ladder at the end of the catwalk – what a girl she was, what a riot. Married with three kids but she still managed to find the time and the energy to put herself about.

Leaving by a second service door, which led to Block Seven's public area, switching off the lights and locking up behind her, Gabrielle stepped out into the visitor walkway and started up the slope to the block's ground-level entrance. On one side were the tanks she'd just prepped, on the other a twenty-metre-long panel of glass set below the surface of the new open-sea aquarium. Gabrielle hummed as she walked, gazing idly through the glass, the sandy seabed stretching away into a blue-green distance.

This four-acre open-sea extension to the main aquarium had taken two years to build and though it had only been open a few months had already proved a massive visitor draw. It comprised two long concrete jetties, curving out from the shore, and set with viewing panels beneath the surface. Where the jetties ended, thirty metres apart, the mouth of the pool was secured with a Mylar steel web whose two-square-centimetre weave was large enough to allow shoals of smaller coastal fish to swim in and out freely, but narrow and strong enough to keep the larger fish in: the fat-lipped potato cod, the Napoleon wrasse, the barracuda and tuna, half a dozen rays, a couple of leatherback turtles and the pack of reef sharks whose white-tipped fins slicing the surface always brought a gasp from the crowd.

Set around the open-sea pool like a random pattern of stepping stones a half-dozen man-made islands broke the surface, built up from the sea floor to control storm surge and provide extra viewing possibilities from the bridges that connected them. Between two of these islands there was even a see-through plastic tunnel set thirty feet below the surface near the mouth of the pool, the deepest part of this open-sea feature.

Gabrielle never tired of this pool. Unlike her tanks, it required no cleaning and the residents no feeding. There was plenty enough food naturally provided to keep the inmates from going short, although Tula had told them that there were plans to introduce a midday feed from one of the bridges, supplying the larger, more aggressive inmates with buckets of fish and meat trimmings, creating a real-life feeding frenzy to entertain the crowds.

The other thing that Gabrielle loved about the pool was the way its residents changed from day to day, always something new to see. Beyond the glass a silvery bank of mackerel flitted here and there, looking for a way out before the reef sharks cornered them, a beady-eyed lobster on the sea floor waved off a curious wrasse with its antennae, a shoal of darting, bobbing sergeant majors patrolled their coral stronghold and there—

Gabrielle slowed, tried to focus on the new shape, distorted by the curve and density of the glass, suspended beneath the deck of a viewing platform maybe twenty feet ahead. As she came closer she wondered what the open ocean had brought them this time, without thinking about the Mylar net and how something so big . . .

And then, catching her breath, she stopped in her tracks, felt for the rail to steady herself.

25

Jacques Tarrou watched the two men walk towards him across the parking lot. Standing at his office window he'd seen their car pass through the gates and he'd come straight down. When Barzé, the supervisor, called with news of the discovery, Tarrou had phoned them himself, from home, then jumped in his car and driven in. He'd seen the body, had Security put up signs on the feeder road – *Aqua-Cité Fermé* – and now, here they were.

Stepping out from the foyer entrance, he held out his hand.

'Tarrou. I'm Aqua-Cité's director.'

The two policemen introduced themselves, showed their badges. Chief Inspectors Jacquot and Gastal.

'Please, Messieurs . . .' said Tarrou and, indicating that they should follow him, he led them back out into the parking lot and around the side of the administration building. 'It's this way . . . we can take the short cut,' he continued, over his shoulder, wondering at the pair behind him. Such an unlikely couple. The small, round one with that dreadful tie and pin, and his tall, heavily built sidekick – the boots, the ponytail, the lightweight suede blouson. Something familiar about the tall one, Tarrou thought; someone he'd seen before. But right then he couldn't think who or where.

And little wonder. A body . . . in his aquarium.

Tarrou pushed through a wicker door into an open-air service area and from there led them down a damp, dark corridor into Block Seven's feeding station. A line of blue neon tubes hummed in the

102

concrete ceiling. Another door was opened and he ushered them into the public walkway, the open sea held back by a curving sheet of glass.

'You can see her from here,' he said, leading them to the glass a few steps along the walkway, pointing upwards but keeping his eyes on the fat man's tiepin, then standing aside for them to take a look.

'Who found her?' asked the one called Jacquot, while his companion walked ahead for a closer look.

'One of the feeders – Gabrielle Blanot,' replied Tarrou. 'About seven this morning. She's in the staff canteen if you . . .'

'Can we see outside?' Jacquot continued, giving him a sympathetic nod.

'Of course. This way,' said Tarrou, hurrying past the body that floated like some grotesque coffee table, arms and legs hanging down.

Outside, a salty breeze caught at their hair, their clothes, dashed itself across the surface of the pool. Over Montredon, the morning sun passed behind grey cuttlefish clouds and the water in the pool darkened to a purple chop.

When they reached the decking above the body, the fat policeman, Gastal, went to the rail and peered down. His colleague, Jacquot, held back and turned to Tarrou. If he hadn't been a policeman, Tarrou would have sworn he'd seen him on television. Maybe he had.

But the man was talking to him.

'. . . And I'm afraid we'll have to leave the body where it is for our scene-of-crime team. So you'll need to keep those signs up.'

Tarrou nodded as though all this fitted in with how he'd read the situation. 'Of course. I understand. When do you suppose . . .?' he lifted his arms, his shoulders, his eyebrows in one single movement.

And then, suddenly, like a flash, Tarrou did know who the man was. The ponytail. Ponytail. And it was TV. A long time ago. Rugby. The Five Nations. One of the great tries. Jacquot. Of course. That run – unbelievable. Tarrou felt unaccountably excited.

'Hey, Danny.'

It was Jacquot's partner, Gastal, down on his knees and looking between the wood slats at the body below.

'There's something . . . I don't know . . . seems like the body's moving . . .'

Jacquot walked over, squatted down, took a look.

Tarrou followed, peering between their shoulders, not certain he wanted to see whatever it was they had found, but drawn somehow to take a look.

Three feet below them, the body jerked.

'There . . . see?'

Jacquot went to the rail and looked over. In the time that it had taken them to come up from the underground viewing gallery, a reef shark had spotted the body and come to investigate. Jacquot watched a blunt grey snout nuzzle the side of the body, the shark's scythe-like tail whipping through the water for purchase.

'Looks like we're going to have to start without SOC,' he said to Gastal. And, turning to Tarrou: 'Do you have any staff who could lend a hand, Monsieur?'

If it hadn't been a body that they were retrieving, Jacquot decided, it would have been funny. While Barzé and an assistant tried to get a proper grip on the woman and haul her aboard over the rubbery sides of an inflatable dinghy, another assistant attempted to beat off an increasing number of curious sharks with an oar that was far too short to be wholly effective. Between them, with the added assistance of a considerable chop and swell, the three men kept the boat rocking at an unhealthy tilt until it seemed almost certain that one or another of them was going to take a swim.

But then, with a final tug and grunt, Barzé and his chum managed to heave the body up and over into the dinghy and head back to the mooring slip where Jacquot, Gastal and Tarrou were waiting.

They all helped lift the body from between the plank seating – Gastal's shoes swamped by sea water when the inflatable lifted on a swell and pushed him sideways – and laid the body on its back, on the stone slipway, out of reach of the water. For a silent moment, Barzé, his assistants, Tarrou, Gastal and Jacquot all looked down at the naked body. Then, one by one, they turned away: Tarrou, walking a few steps off to make a call on his mobile, tugging self-consciously on his bow tie; Barzé, going off to look for something to cover the woman; his two assistants, close on his heels, dragging their eyes away from the pert breasts and the tangle of auburn hair between her legs, while Gastal found somewhere to perch so that he could wring the sea water from his socks.

But Jacquot didn't turn away. Instead he knelt beside the body and let his eyes roam.

She was tall and trim and well-muscled, the skin deeply tanned, right down to the toes, save for a white bikini-bottom triangle that showed the freckles the tan covered everywhere else. She looked to be in her early twenties, much the same age as the other victims. The eyes were closed but Jacquot guessed they'd be blue. A cap of red hair, not long enough to reach her shoulders, was slicked to her cheeks and neck.

He picked up an arm, felt the dead, cold weight of it, the limb loose, elbow still bending, hand drooping from the wrist. A strong hand, Jacquot decided, turning it in his own, workmanlike, square and squat, the palm deeply lined, fingers stubby and nails short but not bitten, a white band on the little finger and wrist where she'd worn a ring and watch. But no bruises anywhere. Just three parallel scratches between her breasts – someone with long nails? – and an angry graze down the length of her left shin, red and fresh, as though she'd stumbled or been dragged over some sharp edge.

He put down the arm, straightened the fingers. Their fourth victim. No doubt about it. Within the next twenty-four hours Pathology would confirm pronoprazone in the blood and signs of sexual abuse. Jacquot was certain of it.

He got to his feet just as Barzé returned with a blanket.

By the time they left Aqua-Cité an hour later, having questioned Gabrielle Blanot in the staff canteen – a pale face, trembling cigarette between her fingers and an ashtray full of butts by her elbow – and asked Tarrou for a printout of employee names and addresses, the scene-of-crime boys had arrived and set up camp.

There were four of them, three togged up in white boots and zippered Tyvek jumpsuits, the fourth pulling on a wetsuit and scuba harness. Before starting work, one of them began shooting off a roll of film, treading lightly around the corpse, careful not to disturb anything. Even in daylight, Jacquot noticed, the man was using a flash. Jacquot would see those same photos later that day, or the next, fanned out on his desk, then pinned up on a cork board in the squad room next to his office. He'd see them every day until they ceased to shock, or until the case was closed, the killer found. Big, glossy prints that missed nothing.

Jacquot walked over to Clisson, the senior forensics man. He was short, robust and businesslike, with a shock of ginger hair that shivered in the breeze. The two men shook hands. Like his colleagues, Clisson wore latex gloves snapped over his sleeves; his hand felt smooth, dry and powdery. And oddly warm.

'Well?' said Clisson, looking down at the body as though inspecting a hole in the road. 'What do you think? Number three?' Clisson had been in charge of the Grez and Ballarde recoveries but knew nothing of the body pulled out of the lake at Salon-le-Vitry.

'Looks pretty like it.'

'I'll get you an initial report as soon as I can,' said Clisson. 'Later today. Tomorrow, maybe. As for Valéry, I can't say.'

'Tell me something I don't know,' replied Jacquot. Valéry was the state pathologist, a man who liked to take his time whether the *Police Judiciaire* liked it or not. Sometimes it was worth the wait – tiny things that could make a case.

'Maybe this time we'll have more luck,' said Clisson. 'You never know.'

Jacquot nodded and left them to it. From here on in, he knew, it was nothing but grind – straightforward scene-of-crime forensic procedure. Hours bent over the body, here and at the morgue, searching the dinghy, the sandy floor of the pool, the jetties, the grounds, taking photographs, lifting prints. But with Clisson in charge, Jacquot knew that it would be a thorough job. The man would miss nothing, and he'd have that report on Jacquot's desk when he said he would. While the trail was still warm. Later would come the more complete pathologist's findings – when he'd find out about the pronoprazone, the confirmation of sexual abuse.

For now Jacquot had seen all he needed to see. There was nothing more for him here.

He gave Gastal the nod and they headed back to the car.

'So you reckon it's your man again?' asked Gastal.

'Has to be,' replied Jacquot.

'Could be an accident. Drowned some place and washed in here. Suicide, even.'

Jacquot got into the car and started it up. Gastal dropped in beside him, pulling at his trouser legs to make himself comfortable, pushing up off the seat and juggling his balls into place.

'You ready?' asked Jacquot.

Outside Aqua-Cité's main entrance, a crowd of reporters was waiting for them. Jacquot wondered how they'd found out about the body so soon; which of the Aqua-Cité staff had called it in. There was even a TV crew from TF1. A security guard opened the gate for them and Jacquot moved forward. He kept his window closed, hoping to get through without having to say anything. But Gastal had other ideas. When he saw the camera he wound down his window and put an arm on the ledge.

'Can you give us any details, Inspector?' asked the TV reporter, seeing her chance, pushing a microphone at Gastal. Beside her, the cameraman started shooting.

Gastal put on a grave face, adjusted his tie. 'It's difficult to be sure at this precise moment in time,' he told her, his non-committal reply releasing a wave of questions from the other reporters crowding round his window.

'Just the one body?' shouted one, from the back of the pack.

'Man or woman?' asked another.

'Did she drown?'

'Was it suicide?'

'Murder?'

'Weapon?'

'Was she shot?'

'Stabbed?'

'Raped?'

To which Gastal furnished the relevant answers, adding: 'As far as we can tell there appears to be no link yet with the other bodies found at Salon-le-Vitry and here in Marseilles.'

Jacquot couldn't believe his ears.

Nor could the reporters. They pounced, and Jacquot put his foot down.

'Salon-le-Vitry?' asked the first, running alongside.

'Marseilles?'

'What bodies?'

'Who?'

'When?'

26

S itting at a frail *secrétaire* that had once belonged to her grand-
mother, Madame Céléstine Basquet put down the phone and
made a note in her diary. Sunday. Dinner with the Fazilleaux and,
afterwards, a few hands of piquet. What fun. Such a lovely couple,
such good friends. But she'd have to keep her eyes open. That
Chantal was the most dreadful cheat. And Chantal's husband wasn't
much better.

When she'd done writing, Céléstine screwed the top on her pen
and wondered if Paul would accompany her. But she shook her head
as though she knew the answer all to well. An evening of cards? Not a
hope. Not her husband's kind of thing at all. Pigs would fly first.
Which was why she'd taken the precaution to warn Chantal that he'd
likely be busy, wouldn't be able to make it.

Which was a disappointment, in a long line of disappointments. An
embarrassment, too. Knowing what her friends must think. She
wished she didn't have to make these excuses. She would have liked
Paul to be there, with her and their friends. Without all this . . .
subtle, social subterfuge.

But she knew there was absolutely no point suggesting it to her
husband. All she'd get from him were those plaintive, pained eyes, as
though she ought to know better, but if she really wanted him there,
well . . . And then, an hour before they were due to set off, he'd get a
call, beg off, something had come up. It was all becoming just too
much to bear, the impositions on his time increasing rather than

diminishing. Meetings here, business there, lunch, dinner. Sometimes she didn't see him from one morning to the next. The weekends were just as bad – a phone call and he'd be off somewhere, someone to see. A peck on the cheek and their housekeeper, Adèle, ready to serve lunch, or friends about to call by. Not a word of warning, and he'd be gone. It made her so cross.

And sad, too. For the truth was that Célestine loved her husband and missed him when he wasn't around. She wanted him to be there, to be with her. She frowned at the unfairness of it all. They'd always talked about it, said the same thing: when the boys were old enough, when Valadeau et Cie was strong enough, he'd retire; they'd take a break, go travelling, see the world. And now here he was, fifty-nine last birthday, the kids grown up and ready to take over; surely the time had come to take it easy?

But still he kept on. Such a stubborn, stubborn man. Which was what, in the beginning, she'd so loved about him. His bullishness, his energy, the very strength of him. Despite herself, the thing she loved even now, thirty years on.

The first time she'd set eyes on him, she once told her daughter Amélie, her knees had wobbled. Really. That thick thatch of curly black hair, the big chest pushed out defiantly, the glint in his eye and the smile he gave her when they met. The builder's boy from Peyrolles winning his first contract to extend the Valadeau plant, the family business her forebears had started in Marseilles, the business which had made the family fortune. Savonnerie Valadeau, makers of fine soap – hard bricks rich in pumice for Napoleon's army, cheaply scented bars for *le gros public* and richly perfumed, prettily wrapped cakes for the aristocracy. A family business that, despite her parents' best efforts to find their only child a more suitable match, the Peyrolles builder had finally married into.

Taking over when her father's health had forced his retirement, Paul had steered the company through hazardous times but, after a shaky start, he'd begun to show profits his predecessors could never have imagined. Even though they'd have mightily disapproved of the means, moving away from the core business into property speculation and development, import and export – why, her husband even had his own fleet of merchantmen. An admiral in the family, no less. And though her father never gave him any credit, always putting him down, Célestine knew that Paul cared deeply about the family business. There was no one more loyal, more determined, more driven than he was. Take this morning, no different from any other – they'd hardly finished breakfast when he was up from the table and off into his study, making calls, arranging meetings.

But surely, she reasoned, the time was coming when he could safely start to delegate – Laurent, their eldest, a superb administrator, waiting patiently in the wings, and their second son, Lucien, finishing his MBA at Fontainebleau. Both boys born financiers, risk-takers too, just like their father.

A new generation, thought Célestine. Surely now it was the moment for Paul, like her father, to step aside. Their stake in the company was solid, the value of their stock secure. But still he kept going. One of these days, she feared, he'd have a stroke, or a heart attack, or he'd go and crash that fancy car of his, and it would all be over before they had a chance to start their future together.

Célestine got up from the *secrétaire* and walked to the fireplace. Carved above it, in a smoke-stained panel of stone, was the Valadeau coat of arms – three olive trees and a pair of millstones, the founding instruments of their wealth. And for five generations, since that shield had first been chiselled into the stone, the family had lived here, in this elegant, ancient *bastide* on the outskirts of Aix. Célestine loved its grandness, its airy, high-ceilinged salons and its worn stone floors. The family furniture and portraits. The gardens and the vineyard. For fifty-two years she'd lived here, with her mother and father, and with Paul. Yet now, suddenly, the place felt empty. Cold. Not just because Paul was never there, but because she knew it was just too big for them now; their time here had passed. There was simply no point in delaying further. It was time to move on. Time to let Laurent or Lucien and their families move in, just as she and Paul had done.

Except, for Paul, it was always business, business, business as usual. Either that, or . . .

At which point the study door opened and her husband jostled out, pulling on a jacket, transferring his briefcase from one hand to another to get his arms through the sleeves. Célestine went over to him and helped straighten his collar.

'Busy day?' she asked, following him across the room and out into the hallway.

'Like all the rest, *chérie*. No peace for the wicked.'

At the front door, Basquet turned to embrace his wife, the scent of *cachou* pastilles on his breath, the briefcase he carried slapping gently at her legs.

'I'll be back late. Dinner with the planning boys,' he said. 'I shouldn't wait up, if I were you.'

And he kissed her again.

'Paul . . .' she began, as he trotted down the steps.

'Yes?' he said, beeping open the locks on his silver Porsche, tossing his briefcase into the passenger seat and sliding in behind the wheel.

She came down the steps after him. 'It's just . . .'

The Fazilleaux. Sunday. Should she try to pin him down?

'Yes?' he said again, lowering his window and then leaning forward for the ignition.

But she changed her mind. 'Oh, nothing. Nothing.' And then, to cover: 'Just be careful, you hear? No going too fast in this, in this . . .'

'Porsche,' said her husband with relish. 'It's a Porsche, my darling.'

And, with a wink, he started the engine and she stood back, waved him down the drive.

'Please, God, look after him,' she prayed and, clasping her hands, she turned and made her way back up the steps.

27

The house was in the middle of one of three terraces, built on a slope of hillside and set around a dusty, sun-scorched square in the north of Hyères.

One of Jacquot's team, the stutterer Chevin, working through the phone directories, had found the name Monel, and an address, and phoned it through to Jacquot just as he and Gastal cleared the mob of reporters at Aqua-Cité.

'N-n-nothing in the Marseilles directory, boss. Nothing in Toulon. And according to D-D-Desjartes, nothing in Salon-le-Vitry either. But in Hyères. Just the one listing. Monel. Guilbert. Place Salusse. Number eleven.'

'He'll be at work,' said Gastal, sidling up beside Jacquot at the front door, glancing back at a game of boules going on in the square. 'We should have rung, coming all this way. Or got the local boys to pay a visit.'

Jacquot said nothing, still irritated by Gastal's inopportune comments to the press at Aqua-Cité. There'd be hell to pay for that slip of the tongue and the workload would quadruple. Dealing with the press, inundated with calls from people eager to confess, pass on useless information – all of which would have to be logged, looked into, followed up. Not to mention pressure from Guimpier and the office of the examining magistrate. The last thing Jacquot wanted was a toasting from Madame Solange Bonnefoy.

There was no bell on the door frame, so Jacquot knocked. He

breathed in deeply. The same gusting breeze that had ruffled the surface of the pool at Aqua-Cité blew here too and brought with it the sharp scent of salt from the *salines* at Étang des Pesquiers. He was about to knock again when the door swung open.

Standing in a singlet and shorts, tonsure tufts of hair springing out from the sides of his head, a man in his fifties looked at them through squinting eyes. There was a black bruise of stubble on his chin and sleep in his eyes. He was barefoot and looked as if he'd just got out of bed.

'*Oui?*' he said, looking from Jacquot to Gastal and back again. 'Help you?' From behind him came the sound of a radio.

'Monsieur Monel? Guilbert Monel?'

'That's me. Who wants to know?' The chin thrust out, hands went to hips. He wasn't looking sleepy now, noted Jacquot.

'*Police Judiciaire*, Marseilles,' he replied.

Monel rolled his eyes, let out a worn sigh. 'What's he done this time?'

'May we come in, Monsieur?'

Monel gave them a look and stepped aside, not allowing them as much room to squeeze past as he might have done.

The front door led straight into the front room. The floor was a polished concrete softened here and there with the kind of rugs old ladies make from used tights. A table and three chairs stood against the far wall, and two fake-leather loungers faced a TV and a two-bar electric fire. There were empty bottles of beer on the mantelpiece and a scatter of newspapers around one of the loungers, an ashtray balanced on one of its arms.

Closing the door and pushing ahead of them, Monel crossed the room and pulled out a chair, settling himself at the table with another deep sigh. He brushed at his two wings of hair, as if he knew they'd be sticking out, but the effort made little impression.

'Don't tell me. Let me guess . . .' said Monel, lowering the volume on a transistor radio but not switching it off. A breathy, excited woman was telling everyone to buy Aveda moisturiser. So soft, so rich . . .

'You said "he", Monsieur. Would that be your son?' asked Jacquot, taking a chair and joining Monel at the table. It was covered with a rumpled blue check cloth, stained a darker shade where oily food had fallen.

Monel reached for a tin, snapped it open and pulled out the makings of a cigarette. Across the room, with a rattle from the blinds, Gastal leant back on the windowsill, folding his arms across his chest.

'I need to tell you?' Monel pulled out a web of tobacco from the tin and palmed it onto a leaf of paper, rolled and licked it tight.

Jacquot shrugged, suggesting he'd like to know.

'Philippe. Crazy boy.' Monel shook his head, digging around in the pockets of his shorts and pulling out a Zippo. He snapped up the lid, flicked the wheel and put the end of his cigarette to the flame.

'He's been in trouble?' asked Jacquot.

'Isn't that why you're here?' asked Monel, whistling out a plume of smoke above their heads and pocketing the lighter.

'Actually, no. Not your son. It's about your daughter.'

The man squared up at that. Jacquot had his attention now.

'And?'

From his pocket, Jacquot took the photo they had of Vicki Monel and offered it to her father. It had been printed off from one of the gallery of pictures on the Internet, but cropped to a head shot. His daughter's eyes were set hungrily on something out of frame, black hair licking across her face, lips curled in a smile.

Monel took the picture, turned it to the light and scrutinised it. 'Yes. That's her,' he confirmed with a nod and a drag on his cigarette. He put the photo on the table.

'May I ask when you last saw your daughter?' asked Jacquot, picking up the photo and sliding it back into his pocket.

Monel gave Jacquot a long look. 'Four, five years,' he said at last.

'I believe she lived in Marseilles?'

'Well, that's where you're from, you tell me.'

'Her name is Vicki?'

'Vicki. That's right. So. What's the interest? What's she been up to?'

Jacquot broke the news as quickly and as gently as he could: how a body had been found in a lake near Salon-le-Vitry, how it had been identified as one Vicki Monel.

When Jacquot finished speaking, spreading his hands with regret, Monel took a last drag of his cigarette and dropped it into an empty beer bottle. He put a hand to his mouth, tipped back his head and lifted his eyes to the ceiling. Something seemed to go out inside him.

Monel took the hand from his mouth, wiped the side of his face with it, drawing down a bloodshot eye.

'Drowned, you say?' Searching for some way to get a grip on himself.

'I'm afraid it was not an accident,' said Jacquot softly.

Monel nodded, made another unsuccessful attempt to brush back his hair. 'Had to happen, I suppose,' he said at last.

'What makes you say that, Monsieur?' Gastal's voice across the room, leaving the man no space for his sorrow.

Monel took his time replying, as though he needed to gather himself before he risked speaking.

'She didn't leave five years ago,' he said at last. 'I threw her out. Nineteen and too much trouble, you know? Her mother leaving like she did. I just couldn't handle it on my own. You know how it is . . .?'

Monel leant forward, put his elbows on the table and lowered his head into his hands. He was trying to hold his composure, but Jacquot could see that it was a lost battle. The fight had gone out of him. A muffled sob from behind his hands confirmed it.

'I'm very sorry,' said Jacquot.

Monel raised his head, wiped a hand across his eyes and mouth.

'She was a handful, all right. Ask anyone round here. But she didn't deserve . . .'

He couldn't continue. Dropping his head into his hands once more, shoulders heaving, Guilbert Monel wept for his daughter.

28

Carnot loved Wednesdays. His favourite day of the week. This particular Wednesday he was where he always was, sitting in the middle of the bleachers at Plage Catalans with a newspaper on his knee, a styrofoam cup of espresso in his hand and his mobile in his pocket. He liked to think of the place as his office. It was mid-morning and the sun had shaken off a wreath of low clouds above Montredon and was blasting down from a blue, uncluttered sky, glittering off the sea and baking the wood plank he was sitting on.

Below him, twenty metres away, shifting on the breeze, came the shouts and screams of half a dozen girls, barefoot, bikinied, tanned and slim, three either side of the volleyball net, calling the shots. Wednesday morning, as per usual. Wednesday morning when the Seniors' team from Lycée Catalans left their classrooms for volleyball practice on the beach.

What a glorious city Marseilles was, thought Carnot, providing such unexpected pleasures for its citizenry. For Carnot was not alone. Plage Catalans was a favourite spot for taking the morning sun, getting a breath of fresh air, a scattering of old boys playing boules, dozing, reading their papers and, of course, like him, watching the Lycée girls. And no one seemed to mind. Certainly not the girls. It was as if they enjoyed the attention, the presence of spectators, making them yell all the louder, exert themselves just that little bit more, flinging their lithe, sun-browned bodies around that sandy court.

They were good players too, Carnot knew, worth watching. Two years earlier, a Lycée girl called Tanya had made the national squad and won silver at the last European Championships. Right now there was one player down there who had caught everyone's eye. Not because she was particularly good, just that she was clearly the prettiest girl there. Seventeen, eighteen maybe, with a glorious whiplash of brown hair that she'd refused to tie back, an aquamarine bikini highlighting her tan, long arms and legs. And the way she threw herself to the sand for that desperate point-saver, fingertips reaching for the ball . . . *Dieu*. He'd never seen her there before but he knew her name, shouted by her team-mates – Alice. Alice.

Carnot watched her pick herself up, patches of pales sand stuck to her elbows, her belly, the front of her long brown thighs, cream pools against brown skin. He knew exactly what he'd like to do to Alice, down there on the beach, all alone. Warm water, a hose, let the jet trickle across those sandy places, washing the sand away, revealing the warm, tanned skin beneath . . .

In his pocket, he heard his mobile ring. Carnot put down his coffee and paper, took off his sunglasses and flipped open his phone. He checked the name. This was one call he'd answer. It was Raissac. His main man.

As he listened, and spoke, Carnot kept his eyes firmly fixed on Alice.

'Doisneau, yes . . . That's right . . . It's the same one, I'm certain. Just got out of Baumettes. They've got him on work parole . . . Molineux's. In the kitchen . . . Usually nights . . . That's all I got. He's not easy to track, I can tell you . . . Yes, yes. He knows something's up, but he can't get out of Molineux's. That's where you'll find him . . . No problem, get Coupchoux to call me. Pleasure. Any time . . .'

Carnot slid his phone back in his pocket. Though he'd had his eye on court throughout the conversation, it hadn't registered that the game was over, that the girls had left the net.

Now for the best part.

Leaving his newspaper and empty coffee cup on the seat beside him, Carnot strolled along the bleacher, down the steps and out onto the sand, tan loafers sinking beneath him. Ahead of him, the six girls were showering, all in a line, the water pouring down their bodies, streaming through their hair. He slipped his sunglasses back on. Jesus, what a sight. And Alice, out on the end, twisting her hips this way and that, getting the water to slide and spatter down the back of her thighs, glistening on her skin, washing away the sand. What he wouldn't give . . .

It wouldn't have been the first time Carnot had scored on the beach.

29

An address. Guilbert Monel had given them an address. On the drive back to Marseilles from the Monel home in Hyères, Jacquot wondered what they might find there. A lead, a clue, something to follow up, something to point the way ahead?

It was Jacquot who'd asked if Monel knew where his daughter lived.

Dragging the back of his hand across his eyes, Monel had opened a drawer in the table, pulled out an envelope and handed it over. Inside, Jacquot could make out what looked like a greetings card, but printed on the back where the envelope had been sealed was a handwritten address, as though Vicki had wanted her father to know where she was.

Jacquot turned the envelope, but couldn't make out the postmark. 'When did you receive this?' he asked.

'Christmas, a few days before.'

'This year?'

Monel nodded.

'She send you a card every year?' This, from Gastal at the window.

Monel shook his head, sniffed.

Jacquot wondered whether the man was sad that he hadn't made an effort to visit his daughter, to see her, to put a future in place. But it was too late now.

Thanking him, handing back the Christmas card, Jacquot got to his feet and Monel had shown them out.

At the door, Jacquot asked gently about Vicki's body. What arrangements would he like to make?

'Can she be sent here? To be buried?' Monel had asked after a moment. 'It would be nice to . . . to have her close again.'

'I'll see to it,' said Jacquot and they shook hands.

An hour later, in Marseilles's first *arrondissement*, Jacquot and Gastal drew up outside a nineteenth-century block of apartments on Cours Lieutaud. The building had a new coat of *crépi* on its walls, freshly painted shutters on each of its five floors and new tiles and lead edgings on its roof. The front door had been painted a deep lacquered black and the entryphone panel with its nine buttons was a brightly polished plate of brass. It was a good address, on the border of Noaille and Thiers, with a rent, Jacquot reckoned, of easily twelve thousand francs a month. A lot more than he paid for his place on Les Moulins. He wondered too at the name, V. Monel, so clearly printed in the space beside the topmost bell. The place she'd lived. The place they'd been searching for. Here for all to see.

Without wasting any time, knowing that there'd be no reply from the top floor, Jacquot pressed for the concierge.

A woman's voice came over the intercom and Jacquot explained their business. A minute later, Madame Régine Piganiol swung open the door and ushered them in with a grave, disbelieving look on her face, knitting in one hand and a key in the other.

'Missing, you say? Oh dear me, no. And so young. Oh dear, oh dear . . .' Followed by much tut-tutting and whatever-nexts as she led them to the stairs. 'We would take the lift if it worked, Messieurs. They were supposed to be here yesterday, but you know how it is . . . ?'

Though she was around the same age, Jacquot guessed, as the Widow Foraque, Madame Piganiol was altogether more presentable, like the building she presided over. Carrying herself with a straight back and an imperious look, she wore her grey hair in a tight, tidy bun, a string of amber beads around her neck and a simple cotton shift that suggested a figure that Madame Foraque had lost years before, even if she'd ever had it. As she climbed the stairs ahead of them, answering their questions as she went, Jacquot also noted that Madame Piganiol wore no stockings, her feet shod in backless Moroccan slippers, her calves slim and gently tanned, with only a slight webbing of tiny blue veins around the ankles. Jacquot suspected she still went swimming, early morning before the crowds, maybe at Plage Catalans which was the nearest beach to the city centre.

The questions began as they climbed the first flight, their footfalls softened by a strip of plush red carpet running down the centre of the stairs, held in place by brightly polished stair rods.

'When did you last see Mademoiselle Monel?' Jacquot began.

'Ooh now. Last week. No, the week before.' Madame Piganiol started shaking her head. 'Something like that.'

'You see her every day?'

'Now and then, you know. Nothing regular.'

'And did Mademoiselle Monel have a job?' Jacquot continued.

'A job? Not that I know of. Her family had money, she said. One of those. The lucky ones, eh?'

Jacquot nodded, thinking of the tiny terrace house in Hyères. 'And how long has she lived here?' he asked.

Over her shoulder, Madame Piganiol told them a little over a year, last April, March maybe, she'd check to make sure.

'A good tenant?'

'Good as gold. Never a sound. Paid three months in advance when she moved in and after that always ahead of time. Not too many like her, I can tell you. I'll miss her. Car crash, you said?'

Jacquot smiled. The body might be better than Madame Foraque's, but the brain wasn't half as sharp.

'Murdered, I'm afraid,' he replied.

'So you said,' replied Madame Piganiol. 'So you said.'

'Many friends?' asked Gastal as they climbed on, tapping Jacquot on the sleeve and rolling his eyes.

Madame Piganiol stopped midway up the third flight, not to catch her breath, Jacquot noted, but to give Gastal's question some thought.

'Men friends? Or girlfriends?'

'Both, I guess,' managed Gastal, breathing hard, three steps below her.

She turned and carried on climbing. 'A couple of girlfriends who came regularly – pretty girls. I'd see them now and then. Always brought wine with them. Clinkety-clank, clinkety-clank they'd go, swinging the bags. I always thought it's a wonder the bottles didn't break. You can imagine. The mess on the stairs. And new carpet. Or in the lift. Ooo-là-là!'

'And men?'

Without looking back, Madame Piganiol shook her head. 'Lots of them. She liked a good time, you ask me. But respectable types, you know. Well-dressed. Always very courteous if we met in the hall.'

'Age?' asked Gastal.

'Like I said, respectable types. Professionals. Nice cars, nice suits.'

'Young? Middle-aged? Old?' asked Gastal with more eye-rolling.

'Middle-aged, I'd say. She didn't seem much bothered with the younger ones.'

'Anyone in particular?' asked Jacquot, as they started up the last flight.

'Not as you could say. No one, you know, regular-like.' Madame Piganiol sighed fondly. 'Playing the field, she was, taking her time, like. And no bad thing at that.'

When they reached the top landing the red carpet stopped at the last stair and Madame Piganiol's slippers slapped across the stone floor as she headed for Vicki's door. On each of the landings below there had been two doors, two apartments; here, under the roof, there was only the one.

'So, here we are,' she announced, fitting the key in the lock and opening up. '*Voilà.*'

The two men made to step past her.

'Should I wait?' she continued, flourishing her knitting, as though she'd be quite happy to sit there in Vicki Monel's apartment while they carried out their search.

'No need,' said Gastal, taking the key. 'We'll bring this down to you when we've finished. And any questions we might have . . . ?'

'Of course, of course, Monsieur. Just knock at my door on your way out. I'm here till three – when I go for my swim.'

Jacquot and Gastal watched her cross the landing and start down the stairs, then entered Vicki's apartment. Closing the door behind them, they snapped on the rubber gloves they'd brought from the car.

The apartment was large, about the same floor space as two apartments on the landings below. But the ceilings here were much lower and the outside walls set at a steep pitch, which gave the place a cramped, nestlike feel. There were five rooms in all – a sitting room with two windows looking over a narrow balcony onto the Cours Lieutaud, two bedrooms at back and front, with a bathroom and kitchen between. Whenever they'd done the make-over, Jacquot decided, the builders hadn't scrimped with the attic. The walls were roughly plastered in *faux* rustic style, the original floorboards, where they showed, had been carefully reset and sanded down, the slanting roof beams treated to a bright lime wash and the window frames were the insulated kind that kept out the sound of traffic. Not that you'd have the windows closed in the summer. So far as Jacquot could see, despite the finish and attention to detail – the units in the kitchen and bathroom, the built-in bedroom wardrobes, the alcoved shelving and subtle downlighting – there was no air-conditioning. The rooms felt close and stuffy, warmed by the sun beating down on the roof tiles overhead, the still, stagnant air laced with the gently rotten fragrance of an unemptied kitchen bin and decaying flowers. And beneath it, like a distant memory, the scent of a woman. Chanel, Coco – like Boni's, thought Jacquot with a wince.

After a quick reconnoitre, Gastal started on the bedrooms while Jacquot returned to the sitting room. It was the largest room in the apartment, occupying at least half the available floor space, but before he touched a thing Jacquot stood in the middle of the room, taking it all in: a pair of low, cream sofas either side of an open fireplace, a fringed Chinese rug between them, bookshelves stacked with magazines and ornaments but no books, a TV and hi-fi in a cabinet by the fire and, standing under a slope of roof between the two windows, an oval dining table furnished with a pair of brass candlesticks and six weave-seat chairs. A thick glass vase holding the wilted remains of some lilies of the valley stood between the candlesticks.

Had her killer been here, Jacquot wondered? Had he come to this apartment? Seen what Jacquot saw? Had he spotted Vicki Monel on the street, followed her on a whim, knocked at her door? Or was he a client? One of the 'respectable types' that Madame Piganiol had referred to? And if he *had* been here, had he left anything for them – a lead, a clue, something to follow up, something to bring them a step closer? There was only one way to find out.

Jacquot started with the dining table, flipping through the mess that covered it, the kind of random spread you'd get if you emptied out a handbag. A tiny bottle of bright red nail varnish lying on its side.

A pair of sunglasses. A hairbrush. A handful of crumpled receipts, a packet of Kool-wipes, some loose change, chewing gum. A biro. The stub of an eyebrow pencil. But no purse, no bag, no keys that he could see. Jacquot felt a jolt of disappointment. Whenever Vicki Monel last left the apartment, she must have taken them with her. Which meant, more than likely, that the killer hadn't been here, that he'd made his hit somewhere else in the city. At night, by the look of it, if the sunglasses were anything to go by.

Jacquot turned his attention to the scatter of mail. Bills, circulars, a membership-renewal form from a local gym, a couple of free-press newspapers, travel brochures still in their cellophane wrapping, a clothing catalogue and an envelope bearing the Credit Lyonnais logo. Jacquot pulled out a bank statement, unfolded it and whistled. Current account, a little over sixty thousand francs; deposit account, close to two hundred thousand francs. Sizeable assets for a twenty-five-year-old who didn't sound like she'd received a whole heap of education. Clearly the Internet paid well, in addition to what she made elsewhere. No wonder she could afford the rent.

Jacquot checked the date on the statement. It had been sent the last week of April. Which meant that Vicki Monel was still alive when the letter was delivered, say two days later. Given the ten days that Desjartes's boys reckoned the body had been in the water at Lac Calade, she'd probably died just a day or two after seeing how much money she had in the bank.

Getting up from the table, Jacquot heard drawers sliding open and snapping shut in the bedroom. Gastal hard at work, fingering his way through Vicki's underwear as though it might furnish some lead. Jacquot hadn't been entirely surprised that his colleague had opted for the bedrooms.

Making his way round the room, Jacquot noted the ornaments on the bookcase and mantelpiece, a velvet scarf on one of the sofas, three empty wine glasses on the coffee table, the hi-fi and flat-screen TV, Vicki's collection of CDs, stacked in a wooden rack. He slipped a few out, one by one. Clubbing music by the look of it, a beach scene on every cover. Ibiza, Ibiza, Ibiza. Then, halfway down, a rare live recording of Joao Gilberto and Oscar Peterson that he'd never seen before, never even heard of. Where on earth had she found that? For a moment Jacquot was tempted to slip it into his pocket, and might well have done so had Gastal not pushed through the door, snapping off his gloves.

'Nothing, in either bedroom. Though she's got enough clothes to start a frigging shop. But no men's clothing, no shaving gear. Looks like she lived alone, all right. Lots of toys, too,' said Gastal with a wink. 'If you get my drift.'

'And no purse, no key,' said Jacquot. 'She must have taken them with her.' He looked around once more and saw the telephone on the floor beside the sofa. He leant over. No speed dial. No names. No answerphone. But wedged underneath the phone Jacquot saw a small red book. He pulled it out and flipped through the pages. Names and numbers but nothing that caught his eye, nothing familiar. He waved the book at Gastal and slipped it into his pocket. Five minutes later, after checking through the kitchen and bathroom, Jacquot locked the apartment and they started down the stairs. Perhaps Forensics would have more luck with prints, find something they'd missed.

Back on the ground floor, Jacquot knocked at Madame Piganiol's door and asked if she would be kind enough to open Vicki Monel's mailbox.

'But it's the same key for both, mailbox and apartment,' the old lady exclaimed, tucking her knitting under her arm and taking the key from Jacquot. 'Look here, I'll show you,' she said and led them across the hall to the line of mailboxes just inside the front door. After much fiddling with the lock, she finally opened Vicki Monel's box.

Jacquot reached forward and pulled out a stack of mail, shuffling through it. Nothing personal, the same collection of flyers and catalogues that he'd found on her dining-room table. He pushed them back into the box and Madame Piganiol relocked it.

'Did you ever take her mail up to her?' asked Jacquot.

Madame Piganiol shook her head as she withdrew the key.

'Not now we have these,' she replied. 'I just put the mail in every morning and they come collect it themselves. Much easier.' She looked at Jacquot expectantly, as though she relished the prospect of more questions.

Jacquot obliged. 'Did Mademoiselle Monel have a car, Madame?'

'A car, you say? If she did, I never saw it.'

'There's no residents' parking here? A basement? Or back lot?'

'You live here, you take your chances on the streets, Monsieur. It's safe enough. I should know.'

'And you say Mademoiselle Monel's been here, what? A year or so?'

'Round that, I'd say. Near enough.'

'And before that? Before she moved in?'

Madame Piganiol frowned, gave Jacquot a puzzled look. 'Well, how could I possibly know that, Monsieur?'

Jacquot realised that she'd misunderstood. 'I mean other tenants, Madame. Upstairs. The top-floor apartment. Before Mademoiselle Monel arrived.'

'I see. I see. Of course. Well, there was . . . Let me see . . . Ah! Alina, such a lovely girl . . . and Nathalie . . . and Rose.' Her brow furrowed with the effort of recollection. Clearly there'd been others; she just couldn't remember the names.

'All young women?' prompted Jacquot.

'Always. Always girls. And all the prettiest things,' Madame Piganiol continued proudly. 'Never a dud. And the men; like bees to honey. Well, you're only young once, eh, Messieurs?'

Jacquot nodded, smiled his agreement, then asked if she could provide details of Vicki Monel's lease or rental agreement.

'Not kept here,' said Madame Piganiol, shaking her head and following them to the front door. 'You'll have to get in touch with the owners.'

'And they would be?' asked Jacquot, stepping out into the street and turning back to her.

Madame Piganiol pushed out her lip, squinted into the sun. 'I ought to know,' she replied. 'Seeing as they're the ones employ me.' And then, scratching the side of her head with the tips of her knitting needles as though this would somehow aid the process of recall: 'Valadeau. Of course. Valadeau et Cie. They're the ones. The soap people.'

30

S uzie de Cotigny slipped the straps of her leotard from her shoulders and peeled the costume down to her waist. She was still breathing hard from the circuit and repetitions, the muscles in her shoulders and thighs burning from the exertion, the wall of her belly aching with a gentle cramp. But she felt good. Pleased with herself. She turned and opened her locker, pulled out a towel and stripped away the rest of the leotard, tugging the tights with it into a bundle of damp pink and black lycra.

Wrapping the towel around her waist, she walked through the locker room to the showers, took the first stall she came to and turned on the water. Reaching for the controls she adjusted the temperature and, hanging the towel from a peg, stepped beneath the water. Perfect. It might not be the most chic, most expensive establishment in town, but Allez-Allez Gym had great showers: good wide heads, easy-to-adjust temperature controls and dependable water pressure independent of the dozen or so other cubicles in the shower room. Suzie closed her eyes, lifted her chin, and felt the rain-like stream spatter onto her face, sluice over her neck and shoulders and course down her body. Even more important, the gym was discreet. She was hardly likely to bump into anyone she knew here.

Twice a week Suzie came here, sometimes more often. Sometimes it was difficult to keep away. Such a temptation just to drop in, on the off chance. And always during the busy times, lunch hour or after work, when the secretaries and shop assistants stopped by for their

127

workouts and exercise classes. With no job to go to, Suzie could easily have come when the place wasn't so crowded. But the crowding was what it was all about, the reason she went there. So many young, pretty girls. It had been the same back home in the States. The gyms, the steam baths, the spas and exercise classes.

When Suzie told her husband she was thinking of joining a gym, Hubert de Cotigny warmed to the idea straight away, even suggesting that they hire a personal trainer to come over to the house.

But she'd said no. Better to go to a gym, she advised. So much more choice. A personal trainer was just that, always the same one, usually a man and maybe not up for what they had in mind.

Which was when he'd suggested Altius. Since Hubert's Planning Department had given it the green light two years earlier, Altius had become the city's most exclusive spa, gym and fitness centre, a sought-after membership amongst Marseilles's finest.

But again Suzie had shaken her head. It had to be discreet, somewhere she wasn't likely to bump into Hubert's daughter or any of their friends. Just imagine . . .

And again he'd nodded his head, understood immediately.

There always had to be a cut-off, she explained, between the two of them and their occasional 'companions'. Rather like a spy network. An arrangement that guaranteed that certain paths would never cross – at a dinner party or drinks someplace. Money, she said – that was the cut-off point. Somewhere not too expensive, somewhere anonymous, somewhere she'd just be one of the girls. With a nod, Hubert had acknowledged her reasoning, smiled at the prospect, and left it to her.

Just as she'd said, it had all worked splendidly – for both of them. In a little over a year, she'd gently seduced maybe a dozen different girls she'd met here. Sometimes she'd share them with Hubert, or take them to the small apartment she kept in town that Hubert didn't know about. Or go to their own homes. Their tiny flats and studios. Sometimes that was fun too.

Suzie eased the shower temperature down and felt the water chill in response, icy needles pricking at her warm skin, puckering her nipples. She shivered, gasped for breath, then turned the heat up again until her head spun.

Which was when she knew, just knew, that someone was watching her, there in the shower, head tipped back, playing the water over her face and breasts, hands clinging to the taps. So sure that she played the moment out, closing her eyes and turning her body this way and that, so that everything could be seen.

And she was right. The girl by the mirror, gently towelling her arms, the long arch of her neck, her breasts, not bothering to look away when Suzie stepped from the shower and caught her eye. She even smiled.

A sure thing, thought Suzie. A done deal. And a honey too. Hubert would love this one. Not like the last one she'd picked up here. She'd got it wrong with that one. Suzie had been stunned by her but Hubert had taken against her from the start. Couldn't bear the tattoo, simply couldn't tolerate it, he said. A couple of sessions and that was it.

Not a problem with this one, though, judged Suzie, the girl's skin lightly tanned, lithe and, so far as Suzie could see, neither tattooed nor pierced.

Then again, maybe she'd keep this one to herself. Keep Hubert out of the loop. Maybe tomorrow night, while Hubert was having dinner with his mother. Perfect.

Wrapping the towel around her waist, Suzie returned the girl's smile.

It was as easy as that.

31

With Gastal at the wheel, driving back to police headquarters from Cours Lieutaud, Jacquot flicked his way through the address book that he'd taken from Vicki Monel's apartment. It was an expensive make, leather-bound, with gold edging and thin ruled pages, but too bulky to fit comfortably in a purse or pocket. In the days to come they'd check every name, every telephone number, every address – any one of which might bring them closer to her killer – and try to decipher every scratch and doodle that Vicki Monel had made. Just as they'd done with the address books of the teacher Yvonne Ballarde who had lain undetected in her bath for more than a week, and Joline Grez whose naked body had choked one of the overflow outlets in the cascade at Longchamp.

By the time they reached Headquarters, Jacquot had found only one name he recognised. Under V. Vrech, the tattooist. Maybe Mademoiselle Monel was considering another tattoo? Or maybe she'd taken a fancy to the throaty-voiced Dutchman? But so far as Jacquot could see, no mention of Jean Carnot, the one name he'd expected to find. Then, as Gastal rolled down the ramp into the underground parking level beneath police HQ, Jacquot found it. On the inside back cover. Outlined in biro, a thick rectangle of single strokes, 'JC' and a mobile phone number.

Up in the squad room on the second floor, the team had gathered for their weekly briefing, just as they had every Wednesday since the second body had been found and confirmed as a homicide. At first

130

there'd been just Jacquot and Rully, with Claude Peluze and Al Grenier working back-up. Now there were three more units roped in from other duties and reporting directly to Jacquot as the senior officer in charge of the investigation. Pierre Chevin and Luc Dutoit, Etienne Laganne and Charles Serre, Bernie Muzon and Isabelle Cassier, the only woman on the squad. And not a single one of them, Jacquot knew, with anything significant to report since the last meeting, just the usual jumble of possible leads and dubious theories that might, just might, add up to something.

Even with the blinds angled against the afternoon sun, and a thin draught of air-conditioning, the squad room was still uncomfortably hot. Were it not for the dust and the jackhammering of drills at work on the Metro extension, Jacquot would have had someone open the windows. Instead he slipped off his jacket and made his way to the far end of the room where a large-scale city map had been pinned to the wall. Three smaller maps – of Salon-le-Vitry and the coastline east and west of Marseilles – were set around its edges. On the city map, within half a dozen blocks of each other, were two red flags indicating where the bodies of Ballarde and Grez had been found. On the Salon-le-Vitry map was a third red flag for Vicki Monel and on the remaining two maps four blue flags – two apiece – sited along the coast where bodies had been washed up but where no evidence of foul play could be confirmed.

Around the border of the larger city map were three groups of photos – head shots of three young women, alive and smiling, taken from parents, friends, apartments or, in Vicki's case, from the Internet – each with a thread of red cotton reaching to the red flag where the body had been found. Beneath each head shot was a collection of glossy pictures taken by the boys on scene-of-crime. Certain images were stronger than others: an arm hanging over the edge of a bath, a skein of hair across a bloated face, a foetal-like bundle of limbs jammed into an overflow vent. Within the next few hours, a fourth set of pictures would be pinned to the board, a fourth victim to play on their consciences and keep them alert.

Jacquot reached for a red flag and pinned it on the city map where a tiny blue square denoted Aqua-Cité. Perching on the edge of a desk he got right to the point.

'As you'll have heard, another body's been found at Aqua-Cité, out on Prado. Victim in her twenties, naked, drowned. We don't yet know for certain when she died, but it's pretty clear the body must have been dumped sometime last night. With the park so well patrolled there's no way our man could have done it during the hours of daylight. Or got the body in from the land side. My bet is that he used a boat, under cover of darkness. Either he heaved her over the netting at the entrance to the pool, or a swell washed the body over. It's the only other way in.'

'How high's the n-n-net at the entrance?' asked Chevin.

'Looks about half a metre above the surface, so no big deal getting the body over.'

'Drugs? Rape?' called out Peluze from the back, rubbing his five o'clock stubble with an audible rasp. He was a big man, an ex-Legionnaire, with a suitably military buzz-cut and a parachute tattooed on his forearm.

'Can't say yet about the presence of any drugs. Or if there was a rape involved. We'll have to wait for that.'

A chair scraped as Gastal tried to make himself comfortable, his legs too short and fat to cross comfortably.

'Restraint marks? Was she tied?' This from Isabelle Cassier, the youngest member of the team. She'd been at Headquarters nearly a year, starting with Vice and moving to Homicide just a few months earlier.

Jacquot shook his head. 'A graze on her leg, down the shin, and a couple of scratches on her chest – looked like fingernails to me. Like someone made a grab for her. But that's all . . .' He paused, looked around at his team. 'But I'd say it's the same guy. No doubt. Number four.'

There were resigned expressions around the room, a few uncomfortable coughs. None of them liked the idea that there was someone loose in the city who was getting the better of them. A new body made it even more dispiriting.

'So here's where we go from here. Bernie, you and Isabelle go back to Aqua-Cité. Nose around, talk to a few people. Nothing formal. No statements. Just show your badge and chat.'

'Should we check in with anyone first?' asked Bernie, pushing back a fringe of black hair. He was dressed in his usual uniform – blue jeans, black T-shirt and scuffed trainers. A linen jacket hung from the back of his chair.

'The man in charge is called Tarrou,' Jacquot replied. 'It'd probably be a good idea to introduce yourselves first.'

Bernie nodded, reaching back for his jacket.

'Etienne? Charlie?' Jacquot looked at each man in turn. 'I want you to check the harbours.'

The two men groaned, Etienne Laganne pulling a toothpick from his mouth, his colleague Charlie Serre stubbing out a cigarette.

'I'm sorry, but it's got to be done. Monel ended up in a lake and this one in the sea. So someone must have access to a boat or at least knows how to handle one. Start with the Vieux Port, Malmousque, the docks . . . anything suspicious. Late-night departures or arrivals, that sort of thing.'

'Da-da, da-da,' said Etienne with a sour grin, snapping the toothpick in half and tossing it into a bin. 'We get the picture.'

'Pierre, Luc, keep chasing other bureaux outside Marseilles – any similar water-related deaths, anywhere in the country. If our man's not Marseilles born and bred, and this is the way he likes to do things, he may have left a trail elsewhere. Again, we might find some links. Also . . .' Jacquot pulled Vicki's address book from his pocket, waved it in the air and tossed it to Peluze. 'Get copies of every page and divide them up between you – start doing the rounds. And all of you keep on looking back to Ballarde and Grez. Maybe there's something we missed. Maybe there's some connection with Monel.'

Jacquot glanced across at Gastal, picking at his fingernails. There was something else he had to tell them. 'You should also know that the press have got hold of this. So over the next few days you can expect the usual raft of callers phoning in to confess, finger their neighbours or send us off on some wild-goose chase. All I want to say is: don't let anything slip through the net. Just keep aware. Keep it open.'

Outside, the jackhammers fell silent.

'And one last thing. Our man seems to be upping his hit rate. Two in two months and now two in as many weeks. Maybe he's getting cocky. Maybe this is when he makes a mistake. Let's just be sure we're on to him before he makes it five. Anything else?' he concluded, scanning the faces, knowing that there wouldn't be.

The squad looked at one another, shook their heads, started to get themselves together.

'Okay, let's get busy, please. Four bodies as of today and so far not a single lead. All hell's going to break loose if we don't move on this. And move fast.'

Down in the street, the jackhammers started up again.

It was reminding his colleagues to stay alert that gave Jacquot pause for thought. He knew that he should be doing the same himself. And yet he wasn't. There was something he'd seen that morning but missed, some small connection he'd taken in but failed to process.

Back in his office, a glass and wood-panelled cube at one end of the main squad room, he went to the window and split the blinds. Two floors below, between police headquarters and Cathédrale de la Major, a deep trench had been gouged out of the earth, the latest phase of the Metro extension connecting La Joliette and the Vieux Port. As he watched, a sheet of corrugated steel the size of a cinema screen was being lowered into the pit by crane, while a massive yellow piledriver was manoeuvring into position to hammer it home.

There were a hundred things that Jacquot should have been doing, but he sensed he wasn't wasting time, gazing distractedly out of the window. Without really knowing why, it struck him that whatever was niggling away in the back of his mind had something to do with what was going on beneath him, in the dusty wasteland between police headquarters and the cathedral. Workers in hard hats, the spiralling dust from jackhammers caught in the breeze and hoisted aloft, the scarred and dented bodywork of the diggers and tractors lumbering around the site, the rusting stacks of steel rods and hoops of cabling, all of it set within a meshed fence that marked the boundaries of the site.

Construction. Construction.

Whatever it was, whatever was clamouring in his head for attention, it had something to do with construction.

Jacquot squeezed his eyes shut, then opened them, focusing on the scene below him, and his attention was drawn to the perimeter fencing and the billboards fixed along its length. The names of the major contractors – FranCon, Martco, TerrePlus. After weeks of construction Jacquot knew the names by heart.

Then, from out of nowhere, he had it.

The boards at Aqua-Cité, sited along the access road. The names of the contractors and building companies involved in the construction of the new open-sea extension. FranCon again, SeaWayCo, Siemens . . .

And Valadeau-Basquet.

Valadeau.

Valadeau et Cie.

Soap people, Madame Piganiol had said. But suddenly it seemed they were more than that. Not only did Valadeau own the building on Cours Lieutaud where Vicki Monel had lived, it also looked like the same company had been involved in construction work on the open-sea extension at Aqua-Cité where the latest victim had been found. One company, two bodies. It was a link, but a tenuous one. Maybe something, maybe nothing. But in Jacquot's book far too much of a coincidence to let pass.

He turned from the window, picked up the phone and called through to the switchboard.

'Could you get me Valadeau et Cie, please?'

While Jacquot waited for the connection, Gastal came into his office. He yawned, took a chair and made himself comfortable. He seemed about as interested in their investigation as one of his snails, thought Jacquot, giving him a nod. He was about to say something when he heard the ringing tone break off and a young woman's voice.

'Good afternoon – Valadeau et Cie.'

'Yes,' said Jacquot. 'I wonder if you could put me through to Monsieur Valadeau?'

There was a brief silence at the end of the line.

'I'm sorry, there is no Monsieur Valadeau.'

Jacquot frowned.

The woman's voice came back again. 'Unless you mean Monsieur Basquet? Our chief executive. I believe he is married to old Monsieur Valadeau's daughter.'

'That's the one. How silly of me. Thank you.'

'Please hold, Monsieur. I'll put you through to his assistant.'

Across the desk from Jacquot, Gastal looked at his watch, pointed to the time and made signals that he was off home, or out of the office at any rate, two pudgy fingers walking through the air. It was not quite late enough to call it a day, but nor was there much time to get anything useful done.

Jacquot nodded and Gastal mouthed the word 'tomorrow'.

Another woman's voice came on the line. 'Geneviève Chantreau speaking. How may I be of help?'

'I'd like to make an appointment to see Monsieur Basquet,' replied Jacquot, watching Gastal waddle out of his office.

'I'm afraid Monsieur Basquet is a little tied up at the moment. May I ask what this is in connection with?'

Jacquot recognised the tone of voice – cool but impenetrable. A barrier between her boss and unknown individuals like Jacquot who rang up imagining they could just walk in and see the man himself whenever they felt like it. The message was clear: Monsieur Basquet was a very important man, a very busy man.

'This is Chief Inspector Jacquot from the *Police Judiciaire*,' said Jacquot curtly. At five o'clock in the afternoon, with another body laid out on the slab in the city morgue, he wasn't in the mood for pandering to corporate types, or to their snotty assistants for that matter. Not with a killer stalking his city. 'I'd appreciate a moment of his time.'

'Of course, Chief Inspector,' came the reply, her voice a little more conciliatory. 'Now, let me see . . .'

'Perhaps you could tell me where your offices are?' asked Jacquot, wanting to speed things along.

'Down on La Joliette, the old docks, Chief Inspector. But . . .'

Jacquot looked at his watch. 'I could be with you in ten, twenty minutes? I'll only need a few moments of Monsieur Basquet's time.'

Just enough for me to get a look at the man, thought Jacquot, decide whether the lead was worth pursuing. Or whether it was just coincidence, pure and simple. One of those strange conjunctions that sometimes crop up out of nowhere, and end up headed in the same direction.

'As I was about to say,' the assistant continued, 'I'm afraid it would be a wasted journey. Monsieur Basquet is out of the office right now. But I could get you in to see him for a few minutes, let's see . . . early tomorrow afternoon? Say . . . two-twenty?'

'That'll do fine,' said Jacquot and put down the phone.

32

At the offices of the planning department in Marseilles's Préfecture, Paul Vintrou, one of the city council's assistant planning officers and Hubert de Cotigny's acting deputy, could hardly believe his ears.

'The Calanques plans?'

'When you have a moment, Paul,' said de Cotigny over his shoulder, watching the breeze ripple through the trees in the square beneath his office window, a lowering sun catching on car windscreens and winking through the branches. Already the afternoon's rush-hour traffic had started to build up.

De Cotigny didn't need to be told why Vintrou sounded so astonished. He'd known this was how his deputy would respond. The Calanques proposal? It had been up before the planning committee on three separate occasions and each time it had taken only a few moments before the plans were voted down, de Cotigny always the first to voice his concern and signal his disapproval.

But then, Vintrou didn't know about de Cotigny's late-night caller; Vintrou hadn't seen the tape; and there was no way Vintrou could comprehend the immense pressure being brought to bear. Nor would he, nor anyone else, if de Cotigny had his way.

Of course, de Cotigny could have gone to the library and asked for the plans himself. But he sensed there was something furtive about that kind of approach, something that might suggest some personal interest, possibly something underhand. And anyway, making visits to the library – where unsuccessful planning proposals were kept for three months pending appeal – was not what the chairman of the Marseilles planning committee would do. Instead he'd decided to have Vintrou fetch them for him, late afternoon, when everyone was going home. Everything above board.

'But it didn't even make it past conditional approval,' said Vintrou, wondering what could have started de Cotigny thinking about the Calanques, wondering how long it would take him to get what his boss wanted from the planning library.

De Cotigny sighed, as though the effort of explanation was really too much to bear. But he did it anyway, just as he'd planned, his eyes still fixed on the square below.

'I had a call from a magazine. Some American publication,' he replied, as if somehow that gave his request more substance. 'Said they'd heard something about the Calanques project and could I give them more information. Something to do with sustainable energy . . . the way ahead, that sort of thing. I couldn't remember the details, so I thought I'd better get up to speed on it. I know it's late, but if the press start asking questions I'd better have some answers . . .'

De Cotigny tailed off. It was a lie, of course. But plausible.

'Why don't you just tell them it was a no-go? Which it is. Protected site. Possible national park.'

At which de Cotigny finally turned from the window and smiled indulgently at his deputy.

'Paul, really.'

Which made Vintrou blush.

'And what do you suppose the mayor will say when the magazine phones him?' de Cotigny continued, pulling out his chair and sitting down. 'As they surely will, if they don't get what they want from me.'

'He'll call you.'

De Cotigny nodded. 'Correct. So why don't we prepare ourselves? Who knows what's going to happen?'

Striding down the corridor from de Cotigny's office, on his way to the planning library, Vintrou decided the time had finally come to join the architectural firm that had sounded him out about the job in Avignon. Good salary. Excellent prospects. A partnership if everything went okay.

And no politics.

Vintrou knew he'd never get the hang of it, the way local government functioned.

Not like de Cotigny.

33

A nais Cuvry worked the moisturiser into her skin, from between her toes to the line of her jaw, sitting on the edge of the tub to work on her feet and calves, standing for her thighs, then turning to the bathroom mirror as she soaped her belly and breasts, feeling as she did so an unfamiliar ache of sensitivity as the brown button nipples slid past her fingers.

Every day, for fifteen years, Anais had followed this same routine, keeping her skin as smooth as glass. Back in Martinique she had used aloe cut from the plants along the Plage Grande Anse. Now it was Chanel or Dior, or whatever else her clients sometimes thought to buy her. She had enough supplies to last a lifetime. Even if she gave up the job tomorrow. Which, if all went according to plan, she might just do; well, if not actually tomorrow, then certainly, all things being equal, by the end of the month. It was a prospect that made her insides flutter.

Working the last of the moisturiser in between her fingers, Anais parted the bathroom drapes and looked into the garden. The Aleppo pines on the hillside no longer wore their midday skirts of shadow. Now they cast a slanting rail across her lawn. It was a few minutes before six at the end of a sweltering Marseilles afternoon, the first really hot day of the year, a white-sky day when the sun was just a glare of squinting light beating down on the city. Now, at last, the air that had crackled at lunchtime was turning gentle.

She let the curtain drop, then went through to the bedroom,

picking up the watch he'd given her from the bedside table. He'd be here in minutes, she thought. Always punctual. Exactly an hour after the first phone call. That's all she had. The hour. If she was free and answered the phone. Which she'd done exactly fifty-three minutes earlier. She replaced the Rolex a little behind the bedside lamp, arranging its coils so she'd be able to see the time without too much manoeuvring.

Anais went to the wardrobe, flicked impatiently through a line of clothes, then turned to the bed. Still too hot for clothes, she decided. And what was the point, anyway? When they wouldn't be on her for longer than the time it took him to pour a drink.

She bent down and picked up a silk wrap from the bed. Wasn't this the very one he'd bought her? She held it out, trying to remember, then slipped it on with a nod of recognition, reaching for the ties, pulling them tight till the material stretched. At least he'd been a generous lover. All the clothes, trinkets and little treats. Not like some of them . . . Which was a comforting thought.

At the dressing table Anais adjusted the lapels and sprayed her wrists with scent, raking them across her throat, neck and between her breasts.

A minute or two still to go.

For the first time, she admitted to herself that she was nervous. This was not a man to fool with. While she'd been his mistress she'd seen and heard enough to know that he had a nasty little temper. But so what? She'd done it before and it had worked, and with bigger fish than him. So why, she reasoned, shouldn't it work again?

Except, of course, these were higher stakes.

This time she really was pregnant.

Anais shook her head crossly. Don't be sentimental. Right now she had to be strong.

Just take the money. A reasonable amount – something he could easily manage, but which she would take years to earn. Then run. Disappear. London, perhaps. Maybe Geneva. No, no, she thought. Too cold.

She'd started thinking about going home to Martinique when the door bell sounded.

Her lover.

Paul Basquet.

34

B y the time Jacquot retrieved his car from the underground car
park it was a little after six and, as usual, he was thinking of
something to do rather than go home to Moulins.

For the last three nights he'd half-expected – maybe half-hoped
was more accurate – to open the door of his apartment and find Boni
there, hanging her clothes in the wardrobe, putting the curtains back
up; contrite, apologetic, wanting to start again. Smiling at him the way
she used to. Reaching for the zip on her skirt, or just wriggling it up
around her hips. But every night the apartment was just as he'd left it
– cool, empty, reproachful. Which was why, save for Madame
Foraque's rabbit on his return from Salon-le-Vitry, he'd eaten out. It
looked like he'd be doing the same again this evening.

Not that he hadn't had a chance to do something about it. He'd
been about to leave the office when Isabelle Cassier knocked at his
door with a report on the Internet company she'd been tracking
down, the company that had bought and displayed Vicki Monel's
photos. According to their records, she told Jacquot, they'd secured
the last set of images a month earlier, from an agent in Paris. 'So I
chased him up and got him to give me the photographer's name.
Some guy in Toulon,' said Isabelle, looping a curl of black hair behind
her ear. 'And the names of the models she . . . appeared with. Maybe
one of them . . . ?'

Jacquot had been impressed, and had told her so.

She'd smiled, and then, right out of the blue, suggested a drink, said in such a way – an eyebrow lifting, a smile on her lips, a soft brushing of the file against her hip – that there could be no mistaking her intent, that this was more than a drink-with-a-colleague-after-work sort of situation.

For a moment Jacquot hadn't quite known how to respond. She was a good kid, Isabelle, hard-working, conscientious, and pretty in a cheeky, gamine sort of way. It was also clear that she had some nerve . . . coming on to him like that. Her boss. And though he couldn't be certain, Jacquot had a feeling this wasn't the first time she'd tried something, made a play; though nothing quite so forward, so . . . unambiguous.

Not wanting to offend her, or reprimand her, Jacquot had taken the easy way out, telling her that he couldn't manage it, had someone to see. But thanks all the same. Maybe another time. As though he'd completely missed her clear intent.

She'd taken it well: 'Sure, no problem,' she'd said, as though she'd been expecting it. But Isabelle Cassier wasn't so easily put off. When she got to his door she'd turned, raised the corner of the file to her lips and given him another mischievous little smile that said, 'I know you'll crack one of these days.' And then she was gone.

Now, ten minutes later, coming up the ramp from the underground car park, Jacquot rather wished he'd taken her up on the invitation. It would have been good to have the company, someone like Isabelle to pass the time with, and as he joined the evening traffic on rue de l'Evêché he had little trouble persuading himself that he'd never have allowed it to go too far. Just a couple of drinks. Maybe supper somewhere. What was wrong with that? Better than going back to an empty apartment. And if it had gotten difficult, why, he'd just show her the ring, the wide silver band on his wedding finger. To deter her, let her down lightly. The ring Boni had given him. Not a real wedding ring, but a token, she'd said. Of her love. She'd slipped it onto his finger just a month after they'd met and he still wore it, hadn't thought to take it off.

Turning out of Le Panier towards the Vieux Port, Jacquot headed back to town, away from the apartment on Moulins. Rue Haxo, he decided. Dinner at La Coupole, followed by a few drinks at Gallante to finish him off. Then, when the focus started going and the tiredness kicked in, he could safely head back home, alone, to bed, and deep, blackout sleep.

Which was when Jacquot saw the sign, screwed onto the inside column of a doorway on rue St-Ferréol, a small glass panel with the words *Allez-Allez Gym* painted in racy italics across its surface. He tried to place the name. Where had he seen it? What was the connection? Why had it caught his attention? It was like the building site earlier that afternoon. The contractors' billboards fixed to the perimeter fence.

Something . . . something . . .

Then he had it.

The very same name on the membership renewal form on the table in Vicki Monel's apartment.

Mer-de.

Two blocks further on, Jacquot found a parking space in a side street off St-Ferréol and went back to investigate. At first, coming at it the other way, Jacquot couldn't see the doorway or the sign. But then he recognised the café-bar on the other side of the road and remembered that it was directly opposite the gym.

And there it was. The glass plate. Allez-Allez Gym. And inside, a flight of stairs leading up to the first floor.

A couple of girls, tote bags over their shoulders, passed him in the doorway. One of them gave him an odd look as he made room for them, as though he shouldn't have been there, loitering. Then he realised why. In small letters beneath the *horaire*, the times when the gym was open, were the words *Femmes Seulement*.

By the time Jacquot reached the first floor, the two girls were signing in at a reception desk. It gave him a moment to get his bearings, look around – potted palms in every corner, a square of sofas, low tables set with fashion and fitness magazines, the walls hung with blurred, blown-up photos of women athletes arching their bodies over bars, breasting tapes, slicing goggled and capped through Olympic pools – and, overlaying it all, the warm, sinuous scent of liniment and perfume, steam and bodies.

Jacquot was breathing in this scent when the two girls in front of him stepped away from the desk and disappeared through a side door. The receptionist looked up and smiled at him. She was young, pretty, healthily tanned and wore a tight T-shirt with the club's name branded across the front.

'Can I help you, Monsieur?'

He showed her his identification and told her that he hoped so.

The smile disappeared. She frowned, grew serious. 'Of course, anything I can do.'

'You have a member here . . . the name of Monel?'

The girl turned to her computer and tapped in the letters.

'Monel . . . Monel . . . Yes. Here. Victorine Monel.'

'How long has she been a member?'

The girl consulted the screen. 'Two years. She takes . . . Steps, aerobics and yoga.' She looked back at him, a little concerned now. 'I hope there's nothing wrong . . .'

Jacquot shook his head. No, nothing wrong.

'Can you tell me when she was last here?'

The girl turned to the screen again, scrolled it down.

'The seventeenth. An evening session. Yoga.'

Jacquot nodded. And then, he couldn't say for certain how the idea came to him, he asked: 'And Grez? Joline Grez. G.R.E.Z. Is she also a member? And Ballarde. Yvonne Ballarde? With an "e"?'

The girl's fingers danced over the keyboard again, her eyes scanned the screen. '*Oui*, both ladies. Swimming and circuits. Though they have not been here in some time.'

'Thank you,' said Jacquot.

'Do you need their addresses? I have them here if you want . . .'

'No, no. That's fine.'

Fine for now, thought Jacquot as he went back down the stairs and into the street, heart hammering at his discovery. Tomorrow would be different. Tomorrow he'd have someone in there with photos of Grez, Ballarde and Monel. The latest victim too, from Aqua-Cité. Talking to anyone who might know them. The steps teacher, the aerobics teacher, the yoga teacher, whoever monitored their circuit training and, given the girls' respective ends, thought Jacquot grimly, whoever worked in the pool – swimming instructors, cleaners. All of them. Employees. Members. The works.

A job for Gastal, thought Jacquot as he waited for a gap in the traffic and crossed the road. Something he could get his teeth into.

Which was when a woman, tugging a blue cotton mackintosh over the shoulders of a white pants suit, came out of the café-bar opposite the gym and almost collided with him. The two of them wrong-footed each other for a moment, exchanged appropriate smiles and apologies, and Jacquot started off again.

Then, as he turned into rue Haxo, he stopped in his tracks.

The café-bar. The row of stools set up against a wooden shelf that ran the length of the window.

Directly opposite the entrance to the gym.

A perfect vantage point.

Jacquot felt a shiver of possibility. A satisfying sense of movement. He'd put money down that this was where the killer had spotted Ballarde and Grez and Monel. And maybe even the latest victim, the one at Aqua-Cité.

He'd place someone there as well, but discreetly. Someone like Isabelle Cassier.

35

Céléstine stood at the terrace doors looking out into the night. All she could see were her drawn features reflected against the darkness and, distantly, the room behind her. She finished her drink and glanced at her watch. A little after nine and Paul still wasn't home. What was it he'd said that morning? Dinner with the planners? How long did that take, for God's sake? Surely he should be back by now.

Céléstine turned and walked to the fireplace, her shoes tapping on the tiled floor, then muffled by the rugs that covered it. On the coffee table she put down her empty glass, took a cigarette from a silver box, and lit it.

And then, for the first time that day, she let herself acknowledge it, accept it, think the things she'd refused to entertain all day.

Paul wasn't having dinner with his planners. He was having dinner – or whatever – with his mistress. Whoever she was. The one who knew how to get him running, the one who had only to lift a finger to have him cancel all their plans. The storm cloud on the horizon, the threat to their future. What a fool he was making of himself. If the children should ever find out . . .

And then: how could he do such a thing? Put their lives on hold. Jeopardise everything. She should just divorce him, throw him out. Enough.

The problem was, of course, that she loved him too much, that she minded. Other wives, she knew, just shrugged their shoulders, relieved that there was someone else to share the load, someone else to put up with their husbands' boorish demands. And Céléstine marvelled at it. The way they gloried in their betrayals. For that was what it was, thought Céléstine. Betrayal.

But now she had had enough; things were going to change. It was time for ultimatums, time for a settling of accounts. Time to get on with the rest of her life, what was left of it, with the man she loved.

Behind her, the door to the salon opened and Adèle appeared. 'Shall I serve dinner, Madame?'

'In here, please, Adèle. It'll just be me tonight.'

Adele nodded and withdrew.

Céléstine stubbed out the cigarette, and gritted her teeth.

But not for long, she thought

36

Thursday

By the time Jacquot arrived at police headquarters the following morning, the latest set of glossies had been pinned on the incident board in the squad room. Black and white, and colour. A length of thread connected them to the flag he'd jabbed into Aqua-Cité the day before. He paused to look at them. The body laid out on the stone ramp. The cap of red hair slicked back by the water off the victim's forehead. The unresisting, useless limbs, laid straight. Eyes closed. Lips slightly open. A close-up of the scratch between her breasts, the angry red of the colour photos reduced to three grey stripes in the black and white images. Another unidentified body. Jacquot wondered how long it would take them to find the victim a name.

Somewhere, he thought, going into his office, somewhere out there you're up to no good. And I am going to catch you.

Gastal wasn't around so Jacquot dialled up his mobile.

'Yes?' Gastal's voice came through with a backing soundtrack of traffic. He was out on the street somewhere.

Jacquot told him about Allez-Allez Gym and the three victims all having been members there.

Not bad, Gastal told him. Not bad.

There was something odd about the man's voice. And then Jacquot knew what it was.

149

'Where are you?' asked Jacquot.

'On République,' replied Gastal. 'Thought I'd walk in.'

And stop for a slice of pizza on your way, thought Jacquot, or a sugared length of *churros*. The man was always eating, always something in his mouth or his hand, or on his chin, or his tie.

'Can I leave it to you? The gym? You're close.' Jacquot didn't imagine there'd be any complaints.

'You got it,' came his partner's muffled response and then the line went dead.

Next Jacquot called in Isabelle Cassier and told her about the gym, the memberships and the bar opposite. Her eyes lit up at the possibility of a lead, not a sign of her interest from the night before. Thoroughly professional. Jacquot was impressed – and relieved.

'I'd like you to spend some time in the bar,' he told her. 'Lunch-times. And after work. But low profile. Crossword, classified, cup of coffee, you know the sort of thing. If someone's watching the gym, maybe you'll pick them out.'

Isabelle nodded.

'Start right now, and while you're about it, take a photo of the Aqua-Cité girl down for Gastal. He's working the gym. She might have been a member too. Someone might recognize her.'

'Good one, boss,' she said and was on her way out of his office when the state pathologist's assistant arrived.

'Chief Inspector Jacquot?' he asked, making room for Isabelle to pass in the doorway and eyeing her up as she slid by.

Jacquot nodded, waved him in.

'Doctor Valéry asked me to drop this in to you.' He handed over a slim blue file. 'Preliminary findings on the body retrieved from Aqua-Cité. He says he'll get you a full report tomorrow, but that this should keep you going for now.'

'Tell him thanks,' said Jacquot and flicked open the file.

'No problem,' replied the young man. When the door closed behind him, Jacquot made himself comfortable and started reading:

Blanche inconnue – white, unidentified female; sixty-one kilos; medium height; aged between twenty and twenty-five; short, auburn hair, blue eyes. Cause of death: drowning. Signs of a brutal sexual assault, like the other victims, but no initial evidence of semen, spermicide or lubricant. Further tests would be made. Also a blood sample had been taken to check for the presence of drugs, which was when they'd find out if pronoprazone had been used and thereby establish a link between the victims.

Jacquot turned to the second page where Valéry had added the usual additional remarks and observations – the tiny details that Jacquot loved, stored away.

According to their dental expert, Valéry reported in his spidery handwriting, the victim was not French. Unless she'd had all her fillings done while she was visiting England. Apparently they used different techniques, amalgams, something like that.

Also, just as Jacquot had done, the state pathologist noted that the victim had rough hands. At first he'd thought that the skin was simply wrinkled from her time in the water. But it wasn't. The skin stayed rough. Whatever she did, the victim worked with her hands.

And there was something else that Valéry had found. Salt crystals in her hair. Looked like dandruff. Really stuck to the skull like they'd been there a long time.

Jacquot closed the report and smiled to himself.

A yachtie. Had to be.

It was Jacquot's first call of the day. The harbour master's office. 'Permission to come aboard, *Capitaine*?'

The old harbour master was doing what he did best. Feet on the table, ankles crossed, a thick roll of charts crumpled under the heels of his blue sail shoes and a copy of *L'Equipe*, folded into paperback size, held in a meaty fist. Outside the morning sun gilded the stone flanks of Fort St-Jean across the water and a breeze ruffled the blue-glass surface of the Vieux Port.

'You,' said Salette, looking over the top of his paper as Jacquot closed the door behind him. 'Can't you see I'm busy right now?'

The words were short and sharp but the tone was affectionate. If there was one policeman for whom Salette had time it was Daniel Jacquot, the son of a man he'd sailed with more times than he could remember, a man who'd saved his hide on and off the water just as often.

Jacquot helped himself to a coffee from the electric plate and wandered over to Salette's desk. The old man had returned to his paper.

'Help yourself to some coffee, why don't you?' he grunted.

'Already did,' replied Jacquot and put his cup on Salette's desk.

Picking up a pair of binoculars, he went to the window and aimed them at the port. Boats, hundreds of them, sailboats, motor cruisers, fishing skiffs, tied to their respective *pannes*, the metal slipways that stretched out into the Vieux Port from Quai de Rive Neuve on the south side and Quai du Port on the north like a set of ribs. From his vantage point above Marseilles's Vieux Port, Salette could see an eel squirm on the fishmonger stalls of the Quai des Belges.

'So what can I do for you, Chief Inspector?' Salette tossed the paper onto his desk and swung round to face his visitor.

'A glance at your records, old man, nothing more,' replied Jacquot, setting the binoculars back on the desk.

'What is it this time?'

'New arrivals in the last week. And any significant departures in the last forty-eight hours.'

'No need to look,' said Salette, folding his hands behind his head and leaning back to inspect the ceiling as though the information that Jacquot wanted was to be found there. 'Let's see. Thirty-two craft total as of this morning, either moored in the port or the Carénage.'

The Carénage, Jacquot knew, was the small marina directly below the crenellated towers of the St-Victor basilica and the battlements of Fort St-Nicolas. Old hands knew it was the better berth. Not so public and you didn't have to cross the busy Rive Neuve to get to the chandlers and repair yards. The only downside was the encircling belt of dual carriageway leading to the harbour tunnel and the endless drone of traffic.

'And departing?'

Salette shook his head. 'Nothing since Sunday afternoon. The *Rémy* bound for Antibes. Everything else accounted for.'

'How many in the Carénage?'

The harbour master swung round to his computer screen and tapped in a command.

'Five,' he said.

'I'll start with them,' said Jacquot. 'Maybe you could print out a list for me, if your busy schedule allows.'

Salette snorted. 'For you, Chief Inspector, I'll make an exception.'

The first two yachts that Jacquot visited on the Carénage, tied stern to slip, were French-crewed, their *tricolores* shifting and settling in the breeze. All hands accounted for. The third had its deck-way secured and was closed down tight as a clam. The fourth, with the name of its home port, Toulon, painted on the transom, looked as if it had never put to sea, or at least had never strayed further than the sea lane between Marseilles and its registered port. Jacquot knew the type who owned boats like these, rarely doing anything more energetic than popping a cork, inviting friends on board for a drink – that sort of thing. He wondered if the sails had ever been unfurled. More likely they motored everywhere, keeping the batteries charged for the fridge and chill cabinet.

But the last vessel Salette had listed for the Carénage, further along the *quai*, looked like it had been through a hurricane. It was a mess: the sails untidily wrapped around the boom, the deck crowded with carelessly wound rope, its waterline hung with a green border of seaweed crisping in the sun and the wheel strung with clothing set out to dry. Jacquot noted a bikini top among the T-shirts and cut-off jeans. On the transom was the yacht's name, *Anemone*, and its home port, BVI. The British Virgin Islands.

'Anyone home?' called Jacquot, tapping his boot against the gangway handrail.

From below deck came the sound of someone moving around, something knocked over, the smash of china – a mug, a plate – and a muffled 'Shit!' A moment later a head appeared from the galley hatch, all tousled hair and suntanned features.

Jacquot reckoned the man was somewhere in his mid-thirties. He wore a hefty sea-going watch and had a piece of braid tied around his neck and right wrist, the colours long faded. He scratched his head, tried to flatten down a mat of curling blond hair and squinted painfully in Jacquot's direction. He looked like he'd just woken up after a heavy night along the Rive Neuve. Jacquot knew how he felt.

'*Oui?*' he asked, returning Jacquot's once-over with one of his own.

'Chief Inspector Jacquot. *Police Judiciaire.*' Jacquot dug for his wallet and held out his badge.

The man peered at it, nodded, and hauled himself onto deck. He was wearing blue cotton shorts and was barefoot, his shoulders heavily freckled and his chest, arms and legs well muscled, not an ounce of superfluous flesh. He looked like he'd spent a lot of time at sea.

'You speak English?' the young man asked, swinging round the wheel and taking a seat in the cockpit.

Jacquot nodded. 'If I have to,' he replied.

'Then come aboard. You want a beer? Coffee?'

'Nothing, thank you,' replied Jacquot, pulling himself up onto the walkway and then stepping down into the cockpit.

'So what can I do for you?' asked the Englishman, rubbing his eyes and yawning.

'Just a few questions, Monsieur . . .?'

'Wraxton. Ralph. Go ahead.'

'According to the harbour master you got in . . .' Jacquot checked Salette's list. 'Tuesday?'

Ralph nodded. 'From St John's, Antigua. Thirty-one days out. A real slow crossing till the end.'

'Crew?'

'My brother Tim, and Jill. Jilly Holford. Just the three of us.'

'And they are where, exactly?'

Ralph shrugged, pushed out his bottom lip.

'Your brother? Tim Wraxton?' prompted Jacquot; he had a problem with the surname. It came out missing the 'r'.

'Last seen at Bar de la Marine,' reported the Englishman. 'Late last night. Not back aboard yet.'

'And Mademoiselle Holford?'

'Left the boat late Tuesday afternoon. Meeting up with her sister somewhere. Nîmes?'

'And you're expecting her back when?'

Ralph shrugged.

'Today? Tomorrow?' prompted Jacquot.

'She said a couple of days, but it could be longer, I guess . . .'

Then Ralph sat forward, brows knitting. 'There's nothing wrong, is there? I mean . . . Tim? Jilly? Has there been an accident?'

If Ralph had been a suspect, Jacquot would have played this a while longer. But he wasn't. Couldn't have been. Holford – for Jacquot was now certain that this was who their victim would turn out to be – had been murdered by the same man who'd drowned his last three victims in a lake, a bath and the lowest level of the Palais Longchamp fountains. At exactly the same time that the *Anemone* and her crew were sailing in the Caribbean or halfway across the Atlantic. There was no way that Ralph, or his brother Tim, could be the killer.

Jacquot reached into his pocket and pulled out the photo he'd taken from the incident board on his way out of the squad room. He looked at it briefly before handing it over.

It was a black and white photo. A head shot, taken in the morgue. If the photographer had moved back half a step you'd have seen the scratches between the victim's breasts. The hair was dry, and lighter in colour, the eyes closed. The black and white image, Jacquot had decided, was kinder than colour. The bluish lips, pallid skin and bruised eyes didn't show so strongly.

Ralph leant forward to take the photo, turned it the right way up and his head just snapped back. If he'd been acting, it was a very convincing response, a masterful performance.

'Jesus,' he snorted, covering his mouth.

'I'm very sorry . . .' said Jacquot gently, wondering whether Ralph and Jilly were more than shipmates. Or maybe it was the brother, Tim?

Ralph shook his head from side to side, eyes squeezing shut. 'Jesus. Jesus. What happened? Where is she?'

'So you can confirm that this is your crewmate, Jilly Holford?'

Ralph nodded, unable to drag his eyes from the picture.

Jacquot waited a few moments before speaking again. 'I'm afraid there are certain procedures, Monsieur. We'll need a formal identification and we'd be grateful if you could let us have the names of next of kin – if you have that information?'

Ralph took a series of deep breaths, trying to gather himself. 'I haven't known her long. We met in Grenada. She was working there, in a bar. Her parents are dead. I think they lived near London somewhere. That's all I know, I'm afraid. But tell me. What happened?'

'Her body was found yesterday morning. Near the Prado beach. It's along the coast from here.'

Ralph looked confused. 'You mean she drowned?'

'She was a good swimmer?' asked Jacquot.

'Like a fish. It's not possible she could have drowned.'

Jacquot held out his hands as though to suggest he didn't know, to see what else Ralph might come up with.

'No, no. Not Jilly. There must be a mistake . . .'

'I'm afraid not, Monsieur Wraxton.'

Ralph gave Jacquot a long hard look, drawing the only possible conclusion.

'You mean someone did this? Someone killed her?'

Jacquot raised his shoulders, spread his hands. 'The evidence suggests . . .'

'Shit . . .' Ralph covered his mouth and nose with his fingers, as though he was about to sneeze. He took another deep breath.

'Tell me, if you please, did she leave any belongings on board?' asked Jacquot.

Ralph didn't seem to understand what Jacquot was saying.

'Is there a suitcase of hers, a bag . . . Could I see where . . . ?'

'Yes. Yes, of course,' he said, getting to his feet, still holding the photo. 'I'm sorry. Follow me.'

Jilly's cabin was in the bow of the boat, hot and airless, a low, curving, triangular space filled with a roughly cut wedge of foam mattress whose edges curled up the cabin's sloping sides. There were no sheets, just an unzipped sleeping bag and slipless pillow.

Ralph leant in through the doorway and opened a cupboard, then stepped aside to let Jacquot pass.

The cupboard was hung with wet-weather gear, a quilted jacket, jeans, and cotton trousers. Beneath these, under a pile of dirty clothes – a tangle of T-shirts, sweats, sarongs – Jacquot uncovered a black holdall, pulled it out and took it through into the main cabin, Ralph backing down the passage ahead of him to make room. Placing the holdall on the chart table, Jacquot tugged open the zip and started going through the contents: a wad of clean clothes – T-shirts, shorts, knickers, bras and long wool socks rolled into balls – nothing ironed but everything dry and neatly folded. Jacquot hauled them out and laid them on the galley table, behind which Ralph lay curled up on a strip of cushioned banquette, Jilly's photo face down in front of him.

Looking back into the holdall, Jacquot tipped it to the light and pushed his arm into the opening. From the bottom of the holdall he retrieved a roll of American dollars secured with a rubber band, a packet of batteries, a sure-shot camera and a pair of sneakers. Placing them beside the clothes, he reached back into the bag and pulled out a pen, some blank postcards and a crumpled bundle of currency-exchange receipts. Jacquot smoothed them out. The latest was dated the end of March, just before the *Anemone* set sail for Europe.

The passport that Jacquot was looking for was in a zip-up side pocket. He flipped it open. A bright, freckled face stared out from the photo, hair tied in plaits, braces – a schoolgirl. Jacquot checked the date of issue. Eight years earlier. Her birth-date was registered as 12 September 1973. Place of birth – Windsor. He flicked through the pages. A good half of the passport was filled with various immigration visas: blurred red and black stamps from Trinidad and Tobago, Grenada, Dominica, Guadeloupe, St Vincent, Jamaica, dating back to the States in September the previous year, ending in early April with a blue hexagonal exit stamp for Antigua. The American visa had been issued in London fourteen months earlier.

At precisely that moment the yacht seemed to dip and sway and footsteps could be heard coming up the gangway. Someone jumped down into the cockpit and a voice called out:

'Rafe? You about?'

A younger, blonder version of Ralph peered through the hatch.

Ralph looked at Jacquot. 'My brother.'

Then, turning to the figure stepping down into the galley: 'Tim, this is someone from the French police. It's Jilly . . .'

37

I t had not been the best of mornings and Paul Basquet was not in
the best of humours. First of all he was well behind schedule. And
Basquet hated falling behind schedule. Time was a valuable commod-
ity in any language and not to be lightly squandered.

It had started first thing that morning. What should have been a
brief on-site meeting with his architect had taken twice as long as
planned. The proposed development was two kilometres the other
side of Marignane airport, twenty hectares of farmland that Basquet
had acquired through a subsidiary and planned on turning into a
freeze storage facility for an in-flight catering operation. Two hundred
planes, under the banners of twenty-seven airlines, touched down at
Marignane every day, a six per cent increase on the previous year
with, according to his planners, probably twice that percentage
increment in the twelve months to come. Already he'd heard talk of
extensions to the airport's runways and terminal buildings. The
purchase of that scrubby field of olives and stony soil between
Marignane's runways and the Fos-Martigues road would prove a real
money-spinner. And if the catering company and freezer storage
facility didn't work out, why, he could always cover the plot with
tarmac, turn it into a car park and still make back his original
investment many times over.

It was the first time that Basquet had visited the site in person and
he hadn't been prepared for the state of the access road. If he'd
known how bad it was going to be, he'd have taken the Cherokee Jeep

and left the Porsche at home. Instead the belly of his beloved Carrera scraped frighteningly over the sun-hardened ruts that made up the approach. By the time he arrived on site his nerves were stretched to snapping, wincing every time a wheel sank into a pothole and his cherished Porsche made grating, jarring contact with the ground. He'd have got out and walked if it hadn't been so damn far.

Then, when he finally arrived on site, the man waiting for him was not the man he'd been expecting. Apparently the architect he'd contracted was down with toothache and the colleague he'd sent in his place was woefully under-briefed. Instead of the thirty minutes that his assistant, Geneviève Chantreau, had allowed for, the meeting had taken closer to an hour, with no significant progress made.

Basquet then made the mistake of letting the architect's deputy, who did have a four-wheel drive, leave the site first, so that his return journey along the access road was conducted in a billowing cloud of dust. By the time he nursed the Porsche back onto the main road the windscreen was covered in a fine, chalky gauze and he was well behind schedule, which meant that he'd have to postpone his quarterly meeting with Valadeau's finance director and trustees.

Not that the meeting was in any way important. Basquet just wanted to get it over with as soon as he possibly could. All the usual cautious, corporate guff about unfamiliar investments, possible shortfalls and the threat of being too highly leveraged. He knew their line by heart: Savonnerie Valadeau was overextending itself, they'd warn him; it was time to sell off some of the associated companies that Basquet had set up since the old man's death. (Like hell he would.) They were soap people, the trustees would argue, not market speculators, property developers, construction engineers or maritime traders. Their business was the manufacture and retailing of soap, and soap's increasingly profitable derivatives – shower and bath gels, shampoos, bath oils – all this from a bunch of tedious family lawyers and accountants whom his father-in-law had put in place as board members to represent his interests. That old bastard had never trusted him an inch, but at least the most recent shake-up Basquet had orchestrated at Valadeau had seen them relegated to non-executive positions.

After they'd said their piece and looked pleased with themselves, and concerned at the same time (bastards, the lot of them), Basquet would then make his usual plea for the need to diversify in an increasingly competitive market.

The point he was always trying to get across to these *cons* was this: if he wasn't worried, why should they be? This was a family business, after all, and he wanted the business to stay that way for his sons. And his sons' sons. Why would he jeopardise their future? It was surely in everyone's long-term interests for Valadeau et Cie to provide the family with a corporate future worth investing in, and the best way to do that was to make Valadeau bigger and stronger. Which meant that relying solely on the manufacture of fancy bubble baths, pretty packaging and miscellaneous bathroom sundries was no longer a realistic option.

At which there'd be the usual dark mutterings and whispered disapproval from the other side of the boardroom table, under the brooding portraits of past Valadeau patriarchs, until the meeting ground to an end with no real agreement reached. It was the same every time. The only thing it achieved was to make the trustees feel that they were remaining faithful to the letter of their trusteeship while still enjoying the increased fruits of their dividends. And waste more time when he, Basquet, had more important matters to attend to.

Like the *calanques* project. His latest baby. According to Raissac at Tuesday's offshore meeting, the whole thing was as good as a done deal, and everything nicely at arm's length. Untraceable. Nothing to tie him in. All Basquet Maritime, registered in Senegal, had had to do was have one of its tankers call in at Maracaibo twice a year, pick up a cargo of kaolin and sail it back to Marseilles, the first consignment due in port any day now. Much to Basquet's relief. Their ship, *Aurore*, had been held up a nerve-racking extra day in Accra, but according to his agents she'd finally put to sea, coming north at a good clip.

As he eased off the rutted farm track and made the smoother surface of the main Fos-Martigues road, Basquet put his foot down and felt the Porsche surge forward. He began to feel a little cheerier. This was what it was all about. Having the power, on tap, and knowing how to use it. All he had to do was press down with his foot, like so, and the engine responded. Without delay or hesitation, and no family trustees poking their fucking noses in.

It was what Basquet so loved about Raissac. The way he waved aside problems, uncertainties. Nothing seemed to faze him. *Now,*

Raissac liked to say. Not tomorrow. Not the day after. But *now*, slapping his hands together like a hypnotist bringing you out of a trance. It was the kind of talk Basquet liked to hear – fighting talk.

They really were two of a kind, Basquet decided. They shared the same background, knew what hard graft was all about and had learnt early on that business was as much about luck as legwork. The other thing that Basquet liked about Raissac was the fact that he always delivered – effectively, discreetly. He did what he said he was going to do, and no half measures.

He was also a chancer, no doubt about it. You only had to look at him to know that somewhere along the line he'd probably been up to no good. The scarred, cratered face, those hard, dangerous black eyes, and that startling splash of claret across the side of his cheek and jaw. A *tache de vin*, they called it, like a spill of blood, its livid, ruby fingers reaching to the bridge of Raissac's nose and deep into his collar.

But the man was kosher; he was what he said he was. Basquet had checked. Alexandre Majoub Raissac. Joint Chairman of Raissac et Frères. A private construction company forty years in business, with interests in Switzerland, Sicily, North Africa, West Africa and, most recently, Venezuela. Mining, drilling, mineral-resource development, tourism even. Raissac's interests were almost as varied as Basquet's own. But his net worth, according to the records that Basquet had managed to dig up, was clear and unleveraged, and substantially higher than Valadeau's. The man ran a tight ship and though he'd probably bent a few rules getting there, he was unquestionably a player. A player whom Basquet was delighted to have on his side.

Their first meeting, Basquet reflected, had been a piece of outrageously good fortune. The way it sometimes goes. The right place, the right time – and the right man. A couple of years earlier, in the middle of an ambitious residential redevelopment programme that Basquet had undertaken in the centre of Marseilles, he'd hit a problem with his construction teams. Suddenly the unions were giving him a hard time – overtime quotas, on-site insurance, working conditions – and every day the delay was costing him money. Basquet's problems were twofold. He didn't have any further funds to renegotiate with the unions, even if he'd wanted to, and the more he delayed the more likely it was that agreed deadlines would be exceeded and penalty notices invoked. All this at a time when the Valadeau family trustees had had more power than they did right now.

When in steps this Alexandre Raissac. An introduction from Fouhety, one of Basquet's suppliers in whom he'd confided, trying to extend credit terms to cover the workforce hold-up.

'Leave it to me,' Raissac had said breezily when Basquet explained the problem, admitting how badly overextended he was. And the following week everything returned to normal, the construction crews back at work. A month later, thanks to Raissac, the development was completed in time and on budget.

For which small service, all Monsieur Raissac wanted was a top-floor apartment in one of the redeveloped properties. As simple as that. He even showed Basquet how to do it without cutting his margins. Masterful.

A few months later Basquet got in touch with Raissac for a second time, when he was negotiating building costs on a two-hundred-unit housing project in Valmont. As Basquet had hoped, a word from Raissac and the initial supply estimates that had caused him such a headache were re-presented in far more favourable terms.

And the price? A Bentley Arnage. Purchased in Brussels and driven south. Small change for such big returns.

But what really sold the man to Basquet was that Raissac never followed up on these 'arrangements', never called him back with a favour to ask. Once Raissac had received his agreed 'fee', there was no sense of obligation, of something owing. The matter was at an end. A one-off. What Basquet also liked was the fact that the two men only ever did business when Basquet sought him out, when Basquet needed something. Never the other way round.

Like the *calanques* deal. Did Raissac's sphere of influence, Basquet had asked after his plans for the development had been dumped for a third time, extend as far as planning permits?

At which Raissac had questioned him closely on what this planning permission might be in relation to, before assuring him that, in his experience, no planning *permis* was too difficult to acquire – so long as you knew the right people. He'd said it with that glint in his eyes, that careless, dismissive wave of the hand, and Basquet had known better than to inquire further. The less he knew, the safer he was. But he'd given Raissac the nod and, by the sound of it, Raissac had as good as guaranteed that next time Basquet's proposals were presented to the planning authorities, the chances were that he would find his way clear.

Which was the one time Raissac did take that extra step. How, he had asked, did Basquet plan to finance this ambitious development? Such an undertaking would surely run into hundreds of millions of francs. If Basquet hadn't yet arranged his finances, perhaps he, Raissac, could be of some assistance?

At first Basquet had imagined some kind of corporate investment, maybe a short-term, low-interest loan facility from Raissac et Frères. But it was nothing like that. What Raissac proposed was some cargo space on a Basquet Maritime vessel twice a year and a new port of call. That was all Basquet needed to do. Raissac would handle the rest – dismissing Basquet's objections with that thin smile and that careless toss of the hand.

Of course Basquet knew what Raissac was up to. There weren't many cargoes from South America that generated the kinds of profits his associate was talking about. And it certainly wasn't kaolin. But Basquet had managed to put this out of his mind – what he didn't know, he persuaded himself, couldn't harm him – and two days later he'd agreed to the deal. How could he not? It was the perfect arrangement. With Customs dealt with, distribution in place and unbelievable profits, all Basquet had to do to access his share of the proceeds was draw down whatever funds he needed from a new-found offshore capital investment source set up for him in Morocco. A straightforward 'non-repayable' loan which the Valadeau trustees couldn't do a thing about. Wouldn't even need to know about. And everything at arm's length. Just brilliant.

If only everything else in his life was so fucking straightforward, thought Basquet as the Porsche roared out of the tunnel above L'Estaque, the coast and the city spreading out in front of him.

Anais for starters. His mistress Anais. Pregnant, for Christ's sake. What in hell's name did she think she was up to? She was supposed to be a professional, goddammit. Didn't anyone ever tell her that mistresses don't get pregnant?

Basquet still hadn't properly got to grips with this bombshell. All the way home the night before, after Anais had broken the news, his mind had just ceased to function at any rational level, his analytical powers reduced by a combination of shock and fury at the news to a kind of inoperative mush. All he could think was pregnant-pregnant-pregnant . . .

The picture didn't look any more promising this morning.

Fifty-nine years old, with the biggest deal in his career looming, and the ungrateful little bitch gets pregnant. Worse still, she wanted to keep the child. There'd been no persuading her otherwise. God help him, he'd tried, but her mind was made up. Beneath that silky skin of hers lay cast-iron resolve.

Of course she'd sworn to him that she'd leave town, go somewhere far away, he'd never hear from her again . . . But Basquet knew with an absolute clarity that any settlement they agreed would be renegotiated whenever Anais felt like it. The child guaranteed it.

If, indeed, the child was actually his.

If, in fact, Anais really was pregnant.

Goddammit . . . Goddammit . . .

As he parked the Porsche in the secured underground car park beneath the Marseilles offices of Valadeau et Cie, Basquet wondered if he should say something to Raissac. Raissac would know what to do. But by the time the lift reached the top floor, Basquet had decided against it. Business was one thing, personal was another. Stepping out of the lift, he strode down the corridor to his corner office, acknowledging that, whether he liked it or not, this was one problem he'd have to deal with himself.

As he pushed through the door into his outer office, his assistant Geneviève rose from behind her desk and followed after him, appointments book in hand, telling him brightly that, amongst his other meetings that afternoon, she'd shoehorned in some policeman from the *Judiciaire*.

Basquet didn't like the word *policeman*. It had the same ring to it as trustee, only not so malleable. Not that there was anything he needed to worry about. He donated generously to *Judiciaire* charities and benevolent schemes, and he'd employed a number of *Judiciaire* retirees as security consultants. Which was likely what this was all about. Someone retiring. Someone looking for employment. But the call on his time was an irritating intrusion all the same, when he had so much else on his mind.

'What does he want?' asked Basquet, tugging off his jacket and dropping into his chair.

'He didn't say, sir,' replied Geneviève, the appointments book clasped to her chest. 'He called last evening after you'd left to visit your aunt. Just said he'd appreciate a few moments of your time. I could always reschedule . . . ?'

'No, no. It doesn't matter now,' said Basquet, unbuttoning his shirt cuffs and rolling up his sleeves. 'But no longer than ten minutes. Just knock and come in, say I'm needed somewhere else. You know the drill.'

Geneviève Chantreau nodded and withdrew. She knew the drill.

When the door closed after her, Basquet went to the drinks cabinet and poured himself a brandy. He winced as the first mouthful burnt its way down, scorching the sides of an empty stomach.

Then, hammering its way back into his consciousness, came that deadly, dreadful word: pregnant-pregnant-pregnant . . .

38

'So tell me something I want to hear, Chief Inspector.'
It was clear the moment Jacquot opened her office door that Solange Bonnefoy, Marseilles's formidable examining magistrate, was in no mood for the easy banter that usually characterised their working relationship. After Gastal's comments at Aqua-Cité the previous day, published in the papers that very morning, Jacquot had known it could only be a matter of time before he got a call from her office – and a frosty reception.

'We're making progress,' he replied, closing the door behind him.

'And so, it seems, is the killer,' Madame Bonnefoy shot back, holding a copy of that morning's paper rolled up like a cosh. She was standing at her desk, dressed for court in a black gown and white advocate's collar. She was forty-nine, single and six feet tall, with a long face set beneath wavy curls of prematurely grey hair. There was a grim set to her mouth and her chin was lowered disapprovingly into her neck, bringing her eyes to the parapet of her bifocals. 'You've seen this, I presume?' continued Madame Bonnefoy, waving the newspaper at Jacquot.

'Actually, no. I haven't,' he replied lightly, leaning across the desk and plucking the paper from her hand. He unrolled it and glanced at the 'Serial Killer At Large' headline and below, in smaller type, 'Police Deny Cover-Up'. Beside the headline was a picture of Gastal, leaning out of his car window, taken as he and Jacquot left the Aqua-Cité compound. Front-page news. Good old Gastal.

'Do you mind . . .?' Jacquot indicated the chair.

Madame Bonnefoy nodded. 'Well?'

'I'm not sure about the cover-up,' he said at last, making himself comfortable.

'Daniel, play straight with me or . . .'

'We have four bodies so far,' he began, pushing the newspaper back onto her desk.

'And a single killer?'

Jacquot nodded. 'It looks that way. Victims drugged, assaulted and drowned.'

'And why wasn't I told that you suspected a connection between them?'

'We didn't know ourselves. Not until this last one. Not for certain.'

'And? Leads? Suspects? When can we expect an arrest?' Gathering up her gown, Madame Bonnefoy settled in her chair and set her arms on her desk. She knew what Jacquot was going to tell her, but she adopted a hopeful, expectant look. She'd worked enough cases with him to know that he was never less than thorough and resourceful and it was a rare case when he didn't bring in a player with enough evidence to convict.

'There have been developments . . .'

'Arrest is what I want to hear. Not developments. Arrest.'

'We don't have enough, Madame.'

'Well, let's start with three young women brutally raped and murdered within a two-mile radius of this office,' said Madame Bonnefoy, tapping the newspaper with a fingernail. 'And a fourth only an hour's drive away. Wouldn't you call that enough?'

'The killer leaves no prints, no evidence. And so far there are no witnesses and no motive.'

'Don't tell me no prints, no evidence, no witnesses. The press are going mad. Doubly so because they think they've been kept out of the loop. As I am, I hasten to add. And it's me on the spot here. I want results, Daniel. Fast.' She pushed the newspaper away from her and leant back in her seat. 'You said "developments"?'

'I was hoping you wouldn't ask.'

Madame Bonnefoy frowned.

'Apart from their age, sex and the way they died,' Jacquot continued, 'all we've been able to establish is that three of the victims were members of the same gym.' He decided not to mention that they had only made that connection the evening before.

'They probably all paid tax as well, and knew how to ride a bicycle.'

Jacquot pretended that he hadn't heard. 'There's a bar opposite the gym. We think the killer uses it as an observation post.'

'The girl you found yesterday. Did she use this gym?'

It was clear that Madame Bonnefoy still had her eye on the ball.

Jacquot shook his head, but hedged. 'Maybe. We don't know yet for sure . . .'

'So not what we could call a rock-solid development, then?'

'We have someone there, keeping an eye on the place. Staff. Customers. Something might turn up.'

Madame Bonnefoy gave him a pained but sympathetic look, as though to say: it's a long shot, but what else can you do? 'And? Anything else?'

Jacquot noted the implied whisper of understanding but didn't reckon he could stretch the examining magistrate's patience as far as the link between Vicki Monel's apartment and Aqua-Cité. The same company, Valadeau et Cie, involved with both. He'd keep that to himself for the time being. Instead, he gave a helpless shrug.

'What about a profile?'

'The usual. Loner. Mummy's boy. Single. Aged between twenty-five and forty. Familiarity with, and access to, drugs – the prono-prazone found in the first three victims and possibly in the latest victim. A hospital worker, maybe? Nurse? Doctor? But that hardly narrows it down,' added Jacquot when he spotted a flicker of interest from Madame Bonnefoy. 'There are thousands of people working in health care in this city. Bring in the single angle, age, gender, and you're still left with, what? Maybe fifteen thousand possible suspects?'

'And of course we don't have the resources . . .'

'You said it, Madame, not me.'

'And? What else?'

'Our profiler thought there might be a religious angle. The water. Cleansing. Some wild theory about baptism.'

Madame Bonnefoy sighed. 'So, we add the city's religious commu-nity to our list of suspects,' she said with a grim chuckle, then shook her head, exasperation fretting her expression. She gave Jacquot a steady look. 'What's your instinct?'

'Loner? Yes. Single? Probably, but not definitely. Age? It's a wide enough span to be a good bet, given the fact that the killer can handle a boat and lug bodies around.' Jacquot paused. 'I also believe he may be an out-of-towner. Not a local.'

'What makes you think that?'

Jacquot spread his hands. 'You asked for instinct.'

'Okay . . . Go on.'

'Well, look. If he's a local, chances are we'd have heard of him before. Four deaths in the last three months? I mean, what was he doing before that?'

'Well, he certainly knows his way round.'

Jacquot cocked his head.

'The Longchamp fountain,' said Madame Bonnefoy. 'He knew he could get access to the fountain after dark. That a part of it extends beyond the railings. And faces a small parking area. Easy to back up a car, and lift a body from the boot into the water. He also knows there are no security cameras on the perimeter. And with the cascades and overflows, you'd never hear the splash.'

'You've been doing your homework.'

'I try to keep in touch.'

'Well, you're right. He does seem to know his way round. But that doesn't necessarily make him Marseillaise. Take the first murder. The teacher Ballarde. He kills in the privacy of the victim's home, drowning her in the bath. He doesn't move the body from there. That's where he kills her and that's where he leaves her. Because that's the easiest option. Then, a month later, there's Grez, turning up at Longchamp. But she didn't drown there, remember. It's my guess he used his own place, then dumped her. But by now he's had time to look around. Choose his spots. Somewhere to take his pleasure where he won't be disturbed. Like the lake at Salon-le-Vitry. Like Aqua-Cité.'

'So if you think he's an out-of-towner, I assume you've put in a request to other *départements*? Similar cases?'

Jacquot nodded. 'We started with other coastal cities – Nice, Toulon, La Rochelle, Cherbourg, Le Havre. Same with places on rivers and lakes – Bordeaux, Nantes, Annecy. Pretty well anywhere with access to water.'

'And? Any luck?'

Jacquot spread his hands. 'You know as well as I that you never get the full story. One police authority rarely likes admitting to another authority that they might have overlooked something, that their inquiries were not thorough and professional. But having said that, there are five or six cases we've come up with that could support the theory that the killer moves around. In Cherbourg, for example, three bodies washed up in a five-week period – during winter, so they weren't out swimming. But then nothing. The trail dried up. But four months later, the same thing starts happening in La Rochelle, then stops again.'

'And these bodies, in Cherbourg, La Rochelle – they were all women?'

Jacquot nodded.

'And drugged?'

'Hard to say, Madame. The longer a body stays in the water, the more difficult it is to detect certain drugs, to confirm foul play. Potential evidence becomes . . . contaminated.'

'And potential homicides have a way of ending up filed away as accidental deaths. A whole lot easier than launching an investigation that'll tie up manpower and possibly go nowhere.'

'I'm afraid that could sometimes be the case. But you can't blame anyone for not—'

Madame Bonnefoy held up her hand. She knew what Jacquot was going to say and she didn't need to hear it.

'What's the drug again?'

'Pronoprazone.'

'And?'

'And it's extremely effective, shutting down the central nervous system in seconds. Even a small dose, say ten milligrams, would put you out for close to six hours. You'd be conscious, eyes open, but you couldn't defend yourself. According to the pathologist, about the only thing the victims can do is giggle. Even when they're drowning.'

'I think we'll keep that one back from the press, don't you?' Madame Bonnefoy gave him a look. 'Is it easy to get, this pronoprazone?'

Jacquot spread his hands. 'Easy enough if you know where to look. But it's not over-the-counter or prescription. Hospitals and medical centres only. And some of the larger surgeries. Or there's the pharmaceutical company, Wilzer, that makes it.'

'So you'll have checked . . . ?'

'. . . Their company records for firings, disgruntled workers, theft.

You name it, all accounted for. As for hospitals and surgeries, it's staff access only. But like I said, if you know what you're looking for, and you're prepared to hang around until someone forgets to lock the dispensary door . . .' Jacquot shrugged. It could be anyone. What more could he do?

'What about the sex?'

Jacquot leant forward. 'Pretty brutal. With a lot of bruising.'

'Bruising?'

'Arms, shoulders, suggesting a struggle before the drug takes effect. The genital area. Plus bruising between the shoulder blades, consistent with a knee or hand pressed between them, most likely during the drowning itself. And he's strong. On one victim he dislocated a vertebra. Another, there's a clump of hair missing at the top of the forehead.'

'How come?'

'It looks like he pulls their heads back, by the hair. Under the influence of the pronoprazone, the jaw just springs open. No control. No ability – no will – to close it. The water just pours down their throats.'

'Blood? Saliva? Semen? Any DNA route?'

'Not a thing.'

'Fibres? Fingernails?'

'All we have is neoprene. From the victim at Salon-le-Vitry.'

'He wore a wetsuit?'

'It gets cold in the water, Madame.'

Solange Bonnefoy sighed, looked around her office. 'So, if we assume this lunatic is an out-of-towner, where's he holed up?'

'Hotel registrations in the city for periods longer than a month threw up a hundred and sixty possibles. All long-term residents, none of them likely suspects. And no name cropping up for shorter stays but moving consecutively from hotel to hotel.'

'Rentals for the same time period? Villas, houses, apartments?'

Jacquot shrugged. 'Maybe. But . . .'

'Don't tell me. Resources.'

'It's too much of a long shot, Madame. Checking hotels took ten days. Rentals would take much, much longer. And that's assuming our friend is even renting. Like I said, we simply don't have the time or the manpower.'

'So what next? What can I tell the press? The mayor? The chamber of commerce? Not to mention my boss.'

'You can tell them—'

Which was when Madame Bonnefoy's assistant buzzed through.

'You're due in court in five minutes, Madame.'

Solange Bonnefoy looked at her watch and pushed away from her desk. 'I'm afraid we'll have to leave it there, Daniel,' she said, getting to her feet, gathering up her papers and packing them into a briefcase. 'Although I doubt that worries you too much.'

She gave Jacquot a comradely smile.

'It's always a pleasure to see you,' replied Jacquot. 'I'll admit it's a difficult one, and I'm sorry I can't give you anything more . . . positive. But I do promise that we will get him, Madame.'

Solange Bonnefoy came round her desk and headed for the door.

'Believe me,' said Jacquot as he pushed it open for her and stood aside. 'Our man will make a mistake.'

Madame Bonnefoy breezed past him and, over her shoulder, said:

'Then let us hope he makes it soon.'

'Let's hope so, Madame.'

It was only later, in the lift, that Jacquot remembered Doisneau. He'd meant to ask Madame Bonnefoy a favour.

39

With no one to cook for her, Suzie de Cotigny prepared her own lunch. In the kitchen she whisked up a couple of eggs, melted butter in a skillet and found the makings of a salad in the fridge. Returning to the stove she took the pan off the flame, rubbed its bubbling surface with a stub of garlic, then poured in the beaten eggs. Tipping the pan and adding a pinch of salt and pepper, she worked the mixture into a roll and slid it onto a plate. As easy as that. Plain omelette with a *frisée* side-salad. Breathing in the warm garlic, she set her lunch on the kitchen table, took a bottle of Provençal rosé from the fridge and poured herself a glass, recorking the bottle and placing it back in the rack. A single glass wouldn't hurt.

Thursday was Suzie's favourite day. The house to herself. Hortense, the maid, and Gilles, the gardener, both had the day off and Hortense had left earlier than usual to visit her sister in L'Estaque. When Hortense did this she always stayed overnight so she would not return until the following morning.

Thursday was also the day that Hubert had supper with his mother, going to her apartment in Castellane straight from work, rarely getting back to the house before ten. The old dame liked her suppers early – and her son alone. Suzie had long ago been excluded from these soirées, meeting up with the dragon only when some formal or family occasion demanded it, so that most Thursdays, from mid-morning until a little after ten at night, Suzie was on her own.

Days off were rare treats for her. She might not have needed to work – her own trust fund from the States and Hubert's small allowance saw to that – but she was always on the go. Not necessarily of her own choosing. There were the dreary business dinners to arrange for Hubert's colleagues from the Préfecture or State Legislature, or family dinners with his atrocious daughter and her weedy husband, or receptions for visiting dignitaries, charity balls, cocktail parties, or gallery openings, the Opera or theatre. But thursdays she always kept clear. Her day. A day to herself.

Normally Suzie went shopping, called in at the gym, or curled up in her own little apartment off rue Paradis with whoever it was she had on the boil. She'd rented the place soon after moving to Marseilles and she'd taken as much care in its refurbishment as she had in the restoration of Hubert's dark and gloomy residence in Roucas Blanc – as soon as they'd managed to lever out the old lady and send her packing to Castellane. One of the many reasons why Suzie was not welcome at Thursday supper. Not that it bothered Suzie one jot.

Suzie liked having her place on rue Paradis and used it frequently, as though she actually lived there. There was a TV, a hi-fi, a stack of discs, a stocked kitchen, loaded bookshelves, odd bits and pieces that she'd taken a fancy to at the markets – which Hubert would never have given house room to – and, in the bedroom, a packed wardrobe. Clothes she'd bought in town and brought back to the flat, clothes she never wore at home, that Hubert had never seen. It was all hers and she loved it. The independence of it all. Another life. She'd done the same in New York, briefly married to that investment banker Brad. Twenty minutes downtown from their Park Avenue duplex was her own little roost. The place she'd had as a student and kept on without Brad knowing. Not much different from her bolt-hole on Paradis.

She finished her omelette and salad and pushed the plates away. She might cook for herself, but Suzie had no intention of clearing up, even if there was a dishwasher. Didn't even think about it; that was what maids were for.

Of course the rue Paradis place was different. There Suzie gloried in her homekeeping, the apartment always scrupulously clean. At the de Cotigny residence she'd never dream of lifting a finger, but at Paradis she dusted, she hoovered and she cleaned the bathtub even when it didn't need doing. As though the effort suited the space, as though that was how it was done in such close, intimate quarters, in the lives lived in such places. And on those occasions when Suzie had company on Paradis, she never left without changing the sheets, making the bed, and filling the airing cupboard with fresh towels.

But this Thursday she was going nowhere. Suzie was staying put.

She'd got up late, made herself coffee and toast for breakfast – the empty cup, percolator and toast crumbs left untouched by the stove – and spent what was left of the morning by the pool. But now it was too hot to be there, the sun too fierce, the wasps that hummed around the pool too numerous and irritating. The best time was evening, when the sun slanted through the stand of pines lining the boundaries of their property, the air cool and the light that fabulous dusky gold.

She looked at her watch. It would be another hour or more before the terrace was bearable. Even in the shade.

Time to freshen up, she decided, time to get herself ready.

She had a visitor coming by.

Her new friend from the gym.

40

The call came through on his mobile as Jacquot pushed through the doors of the Palais de Justice and stepped out into the bright midday sunshine, eyes squinting against the glare.

It was Luc Jouannay, Clisson's number two on the forensics team, calling from Vicki Monel's apartment. They had gone in there that morning to give the place a proper going-over, looking primarily for prints to see if they could turn up any matches with Records.

'How's it going?' said Jacquot, pressing the mobile to his ear. The lunchtime traffic on rue Grignan was loud with the beep of horns and the gunning of engines.

'Plenty of prints so far, coming on for thirty separate sets the last count.'

'Good, good,' replied Jacquot, crossing the road to his car, wondering why Jouannay should be calling him.

'But there's something you should see,' said Jouannay. 'It could be important.' Taller and younger than his boss, with thick black brows and lazy grey eyes, Jouannay was far less bothered by scene-of-crime protocols. When he came across something interesting, he called it in straight away, rather than waiting and typing it up like Clisson.

'I'll come right over,' said Jacquot.

'We'll be here,' replied Jouannay and the line went dead.

Twenty minutes later, Jacquot arrived at Vicki Monel's apartment building. This time he avoided Madame Piganiol's bell and rang the one for Vicki's apartment. It was Jouannay who buzzed him in. On this visit the lift was working, the sign forbidding its use no longer strung from the door handle. By the time he reached the top landing, Jouannay was waiting for him in the open doorway. He was dressed in his usual kit, a white zip-up Tyvek suit and white booties, with a face mask loose around his throat.

'Thought you'd like to see this,' said Jouannay with a grin, leading Jacquot into the apartment.

There were four of them, including Jouannay, in the apartment, all dressed in zip-ups. Jouannay's three colleagues were patiently dusting down every door frame, door handle and light switch they could find, taps and cooker knobs, TV and hi-fi controls, picking fibres off the sofas and carpets, working their way silently and thoroughly through the apartment.

'Christian here found it by accident.'

Christian, in the kitchen, was going through a bag of rubbish, its contents spread across the kitchen table. He was masked. He looked up and nodded as they stepped past him into the bathroom.

'And?' said Jacquot.

'There,' said Jouannay, pointing at a built-out panelled corner at the head of the bath. It would have made a perfect space for an immersion heater, or for storing towels and linen. But there was no handle, no evidence that this was anything other than a wall, possibly concealing a chimney flue from the floors below. 'Just push your fingers there,' said Jouannay.

Jacquot pushed where Jouannay indicated and, with a click, the entire panel opened up from ceiling to floor. Inside the 'cupboard' Jacquot reckoned there was room for two people standing side by side. So far as he could see there was no light, and with the door closed this cramped space would have been pitch black. Except for three square apertures set at about shoulder height. One looked down on the bath and shower unit, the second into the larger of the two bedrooms, while the third looked straight ahead into the sitting room where one of Jouannay's team was numbering a sample bag and dropping it into his case.

Jacquot stepped out of the cupboard and looked at the wall at the head of the bath. A square of mirrored tiles. He left the bathroom and looked into the bedroom and sitting room. Two more mirrors screwed to the walls. A perfect way to watch whatever was going on in most of the apartment without being seen. Or, Jacquot reflected, the perfect place to set up a camera. In one easy sweep, someone with the right equipment could film or photograph anything going on in all three rooms.

Well, well, well, Jacquot thought to himself. A change of gear. Things were beginning to move.

41

The phone hadn't stopped since Basquet arrived back at the office. An apologetic call from the architect whose teeth had played up, his voice appropriately muffled with novocaine; a call from his finance director telling him that the trustees' meeting had been rescheduled for the following week; and a dozen others.

At a little after one o'clock, Basquet had Geneviève order him up some lunch from the Jardins de Clémence on rue Dunkerque and he'd eaten it at his desk, a steak baguette with a side-order of their fabulously crisp *frites*, washed down with a half-bottle of claret from his own drinks cabinet. By the time Geneviève put her head round the door to announce a Chief Inspector Daniel Jacquot, the remains of the meal and the empty bottle had been spirited away, Basquet working his way through a stack of that morning's flagged communiqués. He'd been kept so busy since getting back to the office that he'd not had the time to ponder any further the reason for this visit from the *Judiciaire*.

Getting up from his desk and brushing crumbs from his lap, Basquet came round to greet his visitor who was even now being ushered into his office.

The man was not what Basquet had expected. Tall, early forties, with a leather jacket, bright blue jeans, tasselled loafers and, of all things, a ponytail. The eyes were a light green and sleepy and the nose oddly bent – no doubt broken in the line of duty, thought Basquet. They shook hands and Basquet indicated a chair, returning

179

behind the desk and making himself comfortable.

'So, Chief Inspector. How can I be of help?' Basquet began.

'It's kind of you to see me at such short notice, Monsieur,' the policeman replied.

'Of course. Anything I can do.' Basquet put on an expectant face. He noticed that the policeman looked uncomfortable. Embarrassed at what he was about to ask? Or just intimidated by the power? The wealth? Being in such a luxuriously appointed office?

'It's really just a formality,' the policeman began.

Basquet nodded. He reached forward for the Lajaunie pastilles, tapped one out into his palm, closed it in a fist and tossed it into his mouth.

'I believe your company was involved in the new open-sea development at Aqua-Cité?'

'One of my companies. That's correct.' Basquet nodded, rolling the pastille round in his mouth. 'An incredibly complex undertaking,' he continued, unable to resist the chest-beating. 'Nothing like it anywhere. Admissions up seventy-eight per cent because of it.'

The policeman looked suitably impressed. 'And I believe you also own a residential redevelopment at 44–48 Cours Lieutaud?'

'Cours Lieutaud? That's right,' he replied, sucking at his pastille. 'Our property division. Along with a number of other similar developments both in and outside the city. Commercial and residential. Soap'll get you just so far, Chief Inspector,' continued Basquet, leaning back in his chair. 'But nowadays you've got to diversify or drown. Simple as that. Which is why we also have interests in leasing, insurance, mortgage refinancing. We even have our own import and export arm, maritime trading . . .' Basquet spread his hands expansively.

The policeman nodded, said nothing, seemed uncertain how to proceed.

Basquet watched the man's eyes wander over the honey-coloured herringbone pattern of the parquet, the thick pile of the Persian rug on which his desk stood.

'And?' prompted Basquet, feeling comfortably in control of the situation, even if he couldn't see exactly where this line of questioning was headed.

'It's just . . . Well, you may have read, seen something on TV . . . a body was recovered from the open-sea pool at Aqua-Cité yesterday morning. A young woman. She'd been murdered.'

'How dreadful . . .' Basquet tried a suitably concerned look. 'But I can't see . . .'

'And then, just last week, a resident at Cours Lieutaud, at number forty-six, was found drowned in a lake in Salon-le-Vitry.'

'And?' Basquet might have looked confused at this information, but he recognised it immediately for what it was. The police were investigating a coincidence, nothing more nor less, simple procedure, groundwork, in the absence of anything more substantial to follow up.

'It just seemed something of a . . . well, coincidence. I'm sure you'll agree . . .'

Basquet looked patiently at the man across his desk. You could almost hear him think.

'Yeeeeesss . . . and . . .?'

'Well, Monsieur, it's just that your company being the owner of Cours Lieutaud, and also involved in construction at Aqua-Cité...'

Basquet noted the words tailing off. His visitor was now clearly unsettled.

'Chief Inspector. Chief Inspector . . . What was the name again?'

'Jacquot. Chief Inspector Jacquot.'

'So. Chief Inspector Jacquot. *Bien sûr*, I can see how these facts might appear to have some relevance, given the coincidence, if not any particular significance, but really . . .' Basquet turned to his desktop and began to shuffle at his papers as though he had more pressing matters to occupy him.

'It just seemed worth a call . . . To see if you could help us in any way. Something we might not know . . .'

'Chief Inspector,' said Basquet patiently. 'Tell me . . . If two people are run over by Peugeots in a single week, do you pay a call on Monsieur Peugeot? If a Laguiole knife is used in a stabbing, do you contact Monsieur Laguiole? If a . . . if a . . .' Basquet spread his hands, trying to think of an equally appropriate analogy, but suddenly he couldn't be bothered. This was all too ridiculous. Wasting his time like this. Really.

Across the desk, the policeman nodded his agreement. Of course, of course . . . A silence fell between them, save for the shuffling of papers.

Basquet took his cue. 'Well, if that's all, Chief Inspector?' he said, managing to squeeze out a weary smile.

And then:

'I wonder, Monsieur . . .' began the policeman, pulling gently at his ponytail. 'How did that particular property, Cours Lieutaud, come into your possession?'

'Like most of our acquisitions, we probably got it from the City Council. Usually those places are in terrible condition. Overcrowding, poor sanitation. We simply turn them around. Relocate the families in residence and take the properties in hand. Redecorate. Refurbish. Put in proper plumbing, a lift, things like that . . .'

'And does your company own all the apartments in Cours Lieutaud? Or just some of them?'

'Most of them, I believe, though we don't like to keep the places too long. Get shot of them. Loosen up some capital, you understand?' added Basquet, suspecting that the policeman probably wouldn't.

'So as well as holding rentals, you also sell leases?'

Basquet nodded. 'When the market's right. We have a division, Basquet Immo, that deals with that side of things,' he explained, wondering where all this was leading. The policeman, Jacquot, seemed to have found a rhythm, a line, and no longer appeared as hesitant, as uncertain as Basquet had first imagined. There was something steely about the eyes . . . a confidence. As if somehow – though Basquet couldn't say how – he'd been seen through. It was an unsettling moment.

'And you'd have records of leases and rentals in that particular block?'

'Of course. But not here, you understand. Not in this building. As I said, that would be Basquet Immo, our property division over in Valmont. But I don't see—'

At that precise moment Geneviève knocked and leant round the door to remind Basquet about his two-forty meeting with the finance committee.

Basquet got to his feet. The policeman got to his. The meeting was at an end.

'Thank you for your time, Monsieur,' said the policeman. 'I'm sure you'll understand that in this kind of investigation we have to cover all the bases, chase everything up . . .'

'Of course, of course,' replied Basquet, coming round the desk and shaking Jacquot's hand. 'If you call Hervé Thierry at Basquet Immo, I'm sure he'll be able to help you with the names of leaseholders.

Geneviève, my assistant here, will give you the number. And now, perhaps, if you'll excuse me?'

It was only when the door closed and Basquet returned to his desk that the name Raissac suddenly sprang into his mind.

One of the apartments on Cours Lieutaud was his.

42

For a month now the Waterman had been watching her. Not every day, you understand, but as often as possible: when shifts allowed, at weekends, the end of the day. Following wherever she went: on foot, in the car, jumping on a bus after her. Learning about her, gradually closing in.

After all this time, becoming so familiar with her routine, there was never any problem finding her. Hang around long enough and there she'd be: at the beauty salon on rue Sibié where she worked; or at the bar off Place Jean-Jaures where she sometimes went for lunch; at the café on rue des Trois Rois where she stopped every morning for a croissant and latte, or at the gym on St-Ferréol where the Waterman had first set eyes on her, a bag slung over her shoulder, skipping down the stairs and out onto the street.

It was something to do with the way she moved, the Waterman would have told you, that caught the attention, marked her out from the rest. That nonchalant twist and swing of the hips as she slipped between the traffic, the breezy toss of her hair as she hopped up onto a sidewalk, the way she rolled her shoulders as she walked through the crowds, digging her hands into her pockets. So full of life, so confident, enthusiastic. And pretty. That dark skin, the blue eyes, that tiny mole on the side of her chin that made her lips look fuller than they probably were, the cheeks more sculpted. A true beauty spot, just tilting every feature tantalisingly out of kilter.

The gym, of course, had been a real discovery. *Femmes Seulement.*

Could there be any two words more alluring than those? The Waterman didn't think so. Irresistible. And there, right across the street from its entrance, stood the Café-Bar Guillaume. Just the perfect observation point. A convenient place to stop after work. A stool at the narrow wood bar that ran the length of the picture window. All you had to do was sit there and watch, glancing up from the paper, sipping your beer, lighting a cigarette. All their comings and goings. Take your pick.

Like sweet little Joline with her bee-stung lips, short blonde hair and big, imploring brown eyes; or the teacher Yvonne, with bitten fingernails and chalk from the classroom blackboard on her finger-tips; and that Vicki, a real handful, tough as they come, desperately trying to get away. The Waterman should have known that she'd be difficult. She might live in a fancy apartment but she was street trade, pure and simple – the clothes she wore, that sassy walk – all of a sudden kicking out, swinging her fists and elbows, and scratching like an alley cat, finally pulling free on that sandy strip of beach and trying to make a run for it.

But she'd gone the wrong way, hadn't she? Heading for the water instead of making for the track and the cover of the trees, trying to scream out for help but never quite managing to get a sound from her throat. The drug, of course – made the tongue and the throat as dry as sandpaper. Of course, if she'd stayed still out there on the lake – if she hadn't splashed around, broadcasting her position, trying to keep above the surface – she might just have made it. But that didn't happen. Instead the Waterman had come from below, grabbed her ankles and dragged her body into the depths. Pulled her down into the chill, black water where they'd taken a dance together, the two of them, until the breath was finally gone from her body.

Now it was Berthe's turn.

Like the others, the Waterman knew her name, knew where she lived. A couple of weeks before, she'd parked her beaten-up brown Renault on a meter, right outside the beauty salon on rue Sibié. And there, as the Waterman passed and paused to light a cigarette, on top of the dashboard for all to see, was an envelope, a letter. Name and address. As easy as that. Mlle Berthe Mourdet, 14 Place du Bois. Two in one. A sign if ever there was one.

But Berthe Mourdet, as the Waterman discovered a few nights later, did not live alone. Not like the others. A shared apartment, two other girls. Which made things trickier, a little more demanding. Not that it presented any real problem. Indeed, it added to the pleasure, having to work out a way to isolate her, draw her in.

That afternoon, a Thursday, the Waterman watched Berthe leave the salon early. Tossing her bag onto the back seat of the Renault, she opened up the roof and set off towards the harbour. As usual the Waterman stayed a few cars back, wondering where she was headed. Certainly not home. That would have been a right at the last set of lights. Nor was she visiting her mother, up past the cemetery in Saint Pierre. Instead, skirting the Vieux Port, Berthe made a left off Boulevard de la Corderie and set a course for Roucas Blanc.

With the Waterman following close behind.

43

Nearing his mother's home on Place Castellane, Hubert de Cotigny tossed his mobile phone onto the passenger seat and concentrated on his driving. In the rear-view mirror he saw the car behind him, whose driver had been flashing his lights and sounding his horn the length of rue d'Italie, turn finally into rue Berlioz and accelerate away to make a point. De Cotigny sighed with relief.

As usual the rush-hour traffic had been atrocious, the streets steaming in the evening heat, cars bumper to bumper, pedestrians weaving through wherever there was space, drivers smacking their steering wheels in frustration, pounding horns. Metro buses slowed, stopped, started again, seeming to sway at the end of their connector rods, every passenger crammed inside wondering whether they could walk faster than the bus moved, but unwilling to take the risk, relaxing every time it inched forward, tightening at every hissing hydraulic stop.

Not that the delay bothered de Cotigny. There was too much on his mind for him to worry about traffic flow. He would get where he was going either sooner or later, and it mattered little to him which it was. As he sat there in the leathery, air-conditioned cocoon of his BMW he considered how best to extricate himself from the mess in which he found himself.

As requested, his assistant Vintrou had brought him the Calanques brief and he'd taken another look at the proposed development. It was, just as he remembered, an unbelievably ambitious − not to mention outrageous – project. A dozen super-de-luxe villas jutting out from the walls of Calanque Papiau, a club house and marina, tennis courts, golf course and access roads. It didn't take a genius to see that there'd be no chance of the proposals going through. Protected land, a pair of nesting ospreys (also protected), not to mention a raft of similar plans vetoed in the past. It was absolutely a no-go, although de Cotigny recalled that the planning committee's resident architect had gone out of his way at the last presentation to talk up the designs. A *grand projet* of spectacular proportions, he'd called it, something that would put Marseilles firmly on the architectural map, citing the much smaller development at Morgiou as precedent. Probably on Basquet's pay-roll, concluded de Cotigny.

Because Basquet was the man behind all this – behind the videotape he'd been shown, the deal he'd been offered. It couldn't be anyone else. Paul Basquet, chairman of Valadeau et Cie, who'd come before them on three separate occasions with this totally preposterous plan for developing one of the *calanques*.

The problem was, how to take it from here? How to persuade his fellow committee members that, on reflection, maybe it was time to use Calanque Papiau more profitably, more imaginatively, than just free mooring for yachts and a happy-hour destination for tourist cruise ships? There were enough of them to spare, after all, he could argue, at least a dozen similar inlets between Marseilles and Cassis.

But time for inspiration was limited. The next planning meeting was scheduled for the following week and de Cotigny was going to have to come up with a very persuasive argument if he didn't want that videotape falling into the wrong hands. Which would be nothing less than *une catastrophe*. His career would be finished and his family shamed. The consequences were simply too dreadful to contemplate.

As he sat at the lights on Boulevard Baille, de Cotigny tried to think of favours he could call in, members of the committee who might appreciate the loan of the de Cotigny summer house on Guadeloupe, their winter chalet in Tignes. He knew who they were – Lebarne, Pilou, that fellow Missoné from Works – but it was still a galling prospect. Having to join their number, having to lower himself to their level. In all his time at the State Legislature, de Cotigny had never greased a palm, never accepted a bribe. Never even been offered one, either. The de Cotigny name saw to that. Purer than the driven snow. Incorruptible.

If only they knew, he thought.

By the time de Cotigny reached Place Castellane, the traffic had started to ease up and after only two circuits of the fountain, peering down each side street, he spotted a gap and went for it, reversing untidily into the space but altogether too distracted to do anything about it.

Locking the car, he set off for his mother's home, a top-floor apartment overlooking the Cantini Fountain and the rush-hour bustle. Going up in the caged lift, he wondered whether he'd be having the lamb, the lasagne or the *morue*, all of which were favourites of his mother's and, judging by the frequency with which they were served whenever he came to dinner, the only thing her housekeeper, Luisa, seemed able to cook.

It was Luisa who opened the door. De Cotigny smelled rosemary and garlic. Lamb.

'Good evening, Monsieur Hubert,' she said, taking his briefcase and coat. 'Your mother . . .'

'Hubert, Hubert? Is that you?' His mother's voice shrilled from the salon.

'It's me. It's me. Sorry I'm so late . . . The traffic . . .'

Madame Murielle de Cotigny, a jangle of bracelets, rustling silk and clicking pearls, came bustling down the corridor, arms outstretched. Luisa ducked out of her path and a second later de Cotigny was clasped tight, enveloped in a cloud of eau de toilette, hairspray and whisky breath, his mother's rouged lips reaching for his cheeks.

But tonight she was in no mood for extended hugs or pleasantries. She stepped back, holding his shoulders at arms' length, her eyes glittering with the news that she was bursting to tell him.

'Have you heard? Have you? You have?'

De Cotigny frowned, shook his head, not understanding.

Which delighted her. He hadn't heard. It was for her to break the news. The magnificent, the wonderful news.

'Daudet. The mayor. He's had a stroke,' said Madame de Cotigny breathlessly, taking his hand and leading her son into the salon. 'A bad one. He's in Témoin. Gaga, they say.'

Making himself comfortable, Hubert took his drink from Luisa and tried to get a grip on what his mother was telling him. Daudet. A stroke. He listened as she delivered the details.

She'd heard the news that morning from Virginie Lejulianne,

who'd heard it from Clotilde Rollin, who'd actually called by at the Daudet residence only minutes after the discovery. They'd rushed to the hospital together, Madame Daudet and Clotilde, following the ambulance, Madame Daudet too overcome to drive herself.

'First thing this morning. In bed. At first Madame Daudet thought he was sleeping, so she tiptoes out of the bedroom, lets him sleep on; she's always complaining he works too hard, needs his rest . . . you know Madame Daudet. Likes the perks, but not the hours. Hah!'

Madame de Cotigny reached for a cigarette and tapped it on the lid of the box. Hubert leant across and lit it for her.

'So after breakfast, just before Clotilde comes calling, she goes back to the bedroom, to wake him. And he's in the same position, hasn't moved an inch. So she goes round his side of the bed and his eyes are wide open, mouth all scrunched up, drooling, a panicked look. Paralysed.'

'Who knows about this?'

'Well, if you don't . . .'

Hubert's mind went back over the events of the day – the meeting with Goulandre from the Préfecture, lunch with the British consul, phone calls from Massen at Justice, Missoné at Works, a dozen others. But not one of them had said a word, not one of them sounded as though they might have heard something. Not a hint, a squeak. Somehow the mayor's office had managed to keep a lid on it, but that wouldn't last. A year to go before the next elections and Daudet was gone. Or as good as.

Hubert's blood chilled. He knew at once what was on his mother's mind. She wanted him to step into Daudet's shoes. Put himself forward as a candidate, start planning an election campaign . . .

'So?' she said, shuffling herself to the edge of the sofa, plunging the half-smoked cigarette into an ashtray. 'Now's your chance, Hubert. Who else is there? Tell me. You see, you can't.'

'I don't want it, Maman.'

'Nor did your father,' she shot back.

This was followed by a silence, save for the steady tick of a grandfather clock and a distant murmur of traffic from the street below.

'My darling, it's your big chance,' she began again, softer now, changing tack but not direction. 'Of course,' she continued, 'if you really don't . . .'

Madame de Cotigny didn't finish, latching her attention onto a thread in her skirt, brows raised. Deeply hurt, deeply disappointed, but understanding.

Always her first move, Hubert knew from experience. But never her last.

He waited for her to continue. She didn't disappoint.

'Your father never regretted it for a moment. Did you know that?' There was almost a sob to accompany the recollection. 'He thought he'd hate it, but he loved it. It's in the blood, you see, and there's no getting away from that, my darling . . .' She was admonishing now, but gently, quietly.

Then, dismissively, almost icily: 'But, as I said, if you really want to stay on in . . . what is it? Planning, for the rest of your career . . .'

Madame de Cotigny knew precisely what it was that Hubert did. Hated the very thought of it. Could hardly speak the word. Planning? A de Cotigny? *Mais non.* Nothing more than a backwater posting. Political stagnation. Useful as a step up, of course, but not for five years. In Marseilles there was only one job worth having – conveniently vacated that very morning – and she wanted it for her son. Mayor. It was time for Hubert to start moving up in the world. With their connections, they couldn't go wrong. If only her son was more forceful, more . . . more . . . in touch with real politics.

'Look at Chirac,' she said. 'He was mayor.'

'Of Paris, Maman.'

'Marseilles. Paris. *Quelle différence?*' she retorted, fingers fidgeting with her string of pearls. 'It's the first step. The important one. Here or there, doesn't matter a fig.' Then, softer, almost hesitating to say it: 'I know it's what your father would have wanted. He'd be so proud.'

With a soft knock on the door Luisa bobbed into the salon and announced that dinner was served. Madame de Cotigny drained her whisky glass and Hubert stood to accompany her through to the dining room.

Of course the news about Daudet was staggering. But as he pulled back his mother's chair and helped her into her seat, de Cotigny knew one thing for sure. Even if he'd wanted to, there was no way that he could possibly run for mayor. Certainly not now. Not after seeing that videotape.

Over dinner, his mother laid out her plans for his succession but Hubert only half listened, his mind always finding its way back to his

191

study, three nights earlier, and the honeyed demands of his guest. Hubert could see him now, tall, dark complexion, the curl of floppy black hair, the sharp clothes, the knowing smile and gentle explanations. A familiar face, as though he'd seen him somewhere . . .

Then the cassette pushed into the video-player – that place in Cours Lieutaud. He recognised it immediately. That and the lapping of bodies, the swipe of the cane, the harsh grunting of the soundtrack – accompanied by a simple request, what the man wanted, as the images unreeled on the TV screen. As though he, de Cotigny, had any alternative, watching his performance with a rising, chilling horror. If only his guest knew the whole story, thought de Cotigny. But who was to say he wouldn't find out?

And now, if his mother had her way, it wouldn't just be the Head of Planning his late-night visitor had in thrall. If Hubert did what she wanted – run for mayor and get elected – the man would have an even bigger fish to fry. The whole thing was simply, horribly, out of the question. But how in God's name would he ever be able to break the news to his mother?

Later, after Madame de Cotigny had helped him on with his coat, passed him his briefcase and kissed him goodnight, she reached up a hand to smooth his cheek, fondly, proudly. She didn't have to say a thing.

But he did, and as he buttoned up his coat he promised her that he'd think about it.

As expected, tears welled in his mother's eyes.

On the way home, Hubert de Cotigny pulled over in Endoume, opened the driver's door and threw up his dinner in the gutter.

44

'You haven't forgotten, have you?'

The voice on his mobile, as Jacquot headed for home, had been immediately familiar. Dark, with a syrupy hint of accent.

Sydné. Sid and César Mesnil. Dinner. Thursday. A few friends . . . a bottle or two . . . maybe a couscous . . . nothing special . . . That was the brief. That was what Sid had said when she'd called to invite him the week before.

But Jacquot had forgotten. Though he didn't say that.

'Would I forget?'

'It's been known,' replied Sid suspiciously. 'I know you . . . remember?'

'Except it'll just be the one.'

'Boni on call?'

'You could say.'

There was a sharp intake of breath on the other end of the line. You didn't need a sledgehammer with Sydné Mesnil.

'And?'

'And nothing, Sid. It'll just be me.'

'Are you all right? Tell me, Daniel.'

'Later maybe. Right now I'm trying to get home. And the traffic's murder. See you at . . . what . . . ? Eight, wasn't it?'

'Eight-thirty,' she replied.

'Eight-thirty? No problem,' he said, then hung up before she could ask anything else.

★   ★   ★

It was a typical Sid and César evening. Nothing formal, no *placement*.
A dozen people – colleagues of César's from the University, friends of
Sid's, people they'd known for years, people they'd only just met but
taken a liking to – spread around the Mesnils' top-floor apartment in
St-Victor, sitting and standing, drifting from one room to another,
smoking, drinking, helping themselves to the food when they felt like
it – couscous as advertised and a dozen different salads, plates of
mezes, warm pastries, fruit, cheese, trays of honey-sweet baclava from
the market in Belsunce – set out on a long trestle table on the loggia,
John Coltrane playing in the background.

It was the way Sid and César did things. The way you did it if you
grew up in Istanbul, as Sid had done, or Tunisia, as César had done.
This odd couple who'd been Jacquot's friends since Sid, an osteopath,
had sorted his shoulder, a recurring discomfort from the rugby pitch.

Despite instructions Jacquot had come late – the last to arrive,
judging by the crowd inside. As Sid took his jacket, flung it on a pile
by the door, leant up to kiss, hug him, tell him off as she always did –
he was working too hard, he should learn to relax – Jacquot wished
that he hadn't forgotten the prospect of this evening; it would have
been something to look forward to, something to ease him through
the days since Boni's departure.

Then César was there, tugging Jacquot's ponytail from behind like
a bell pull, coming round to clasp him tight, big grey beard rubbing
against his cheeks, a gurgle of wine splattering into a glass, shoved
into his hand, before Sid tugged him away, hauling him around the
room to make the introductions: Chloé – a masseuse at Sid's practice
('You don't look like a policeman'); Freydeau – a lecturer in maritime
law from Aix ('Of course he does, don't all cops wear ponytails?');
someone called Janine in PR with a swelling, low-cut cleavage; a
thickly spectacled cartoonist called Alf whose work appeared on the
front page of *Le Provençal*; a goateed Russian violinist called Ig from
the city orchestra; a portly documentary maker called Gustave and his
girlfriend Uta – all kinds. Until Jacquot had met just about everyone
there – tall, short, young, old, solemn, flirty, witty and pretty, all of
them interesting, interested, good company, smiley faces – finally
ending up in a corner, with a plate handed to him by Sid piled with
the savoury pastries she knew he loved, talking to a woman called
Delphie, a journalist from Paris who was down in the city for her

sister's first show. ('She's an artist, Claudine Eddé, really talented, even if I am her sister. You must come, the more the merrier. Saturday evening at the Ton-Ton. You promise?')

For the next few hours, as though washed away like dust after a fall of rain, all thoughts of the killer the newspapers were calling the Waterman were put on hold, along with the squad room, Gastal, Madame Bonnefoy, the victims in the morgue, that dreadful patronising little crapaud Basquet ... Which was another reason why Jacquot liked coming here. At Sid and César's, you didn't just leave your coat at the door.

Later, after the guests had gone, Jacquot invited to spend the night, the three of them sat out on the open loggia, its trellised sides laced with honeysuckle, its beamed roof hung with flickering hurricane lamps. Below them, across the stepping levels of descending rooftops, lights shimmered over the oily black surface of the Vieux Port, the seven-sided spire of St Accoule and the façade of the Hotel de Ville were gaudily floodlit, and Le Panier's street lights winked mysteriously on the opposite hillside. Somewhere behind them, up in the mountains of Sainte-Baume, a roll of thunder grumbled over the peaks and a chill breeze whispered through the loggia, making the hurricane lamps squeak on their nails.

'I told you all along she wasn't right for you,' Sid was saying, pulling a shawl round her shoulders.

'You did no such thing, Sydné. You liar.' César gave Jacquot a look through their cigar smoke as if to say: 'This is what you get when you marry a woman like Sydné; be warned. You're well out of it, my friend.'

'Well,' she conceded, 'if I didn't actually say it, then I thought it – all the time. Right from the start.'

'Well, she's gone,' said Jacquot, telling them about the weekend, the lead-up, everything save for the miscarriage.

'And good riddance ...' said Sid, draining her glass.

'Sydné! Really.' And then to Jacquot, waving his hand on his wrist: 'But she was a sexy beast, my friend. Wasn't she just? Ooh-là-là.'

Sid struck out and hit César playfully on the arm, tipping a column of cigar ash into his lap. 'Serves you right,' she said, pretending to look put out.

'It's still the truth, *chérie*,' said César, brushing the ash from his cords. 'A very, very sexy woman.'

'Like I say, she wasn't right for you, Dan. There was something . . . hungry about her . . .'

'Exactly,' said César.

'I mean, she wasn't the settling-down type. She had things to do, places to go. You could see it.'

'As you know, my friend,' said César, leaning towards Jacquot. 'Women don't always see what we see. They think with their hearts. Men, we think with—'

'. . . With your dicks, you don't have to say it,' interrupted Sid with a flourish.

'. . . With our *heads*,' finished César.

'Is there a difference?' countered Sid, determined to have the last word.

And so it had gone, Jacquot contentedly smoking his cigar, savouring the brandy and badinage, forgetting altogether what time it was, what city he was in.

45

Sardé parked the Piscine Picquart van a couple of blocks from the house, on the corner of Allée Jobar and rue Mantine, and switched off the engine. The hot shuddering and juddering of its metal frame ceased with a final, uncertain shiver. The grinding of its gears, the blackboard screech of its brakes and the rattle of Sardé's toolbox on the warped metal floor, all the sounds that characterised movement for the Citroën, were reduced to the creak of its springs settling against the incline and the hot ticking of its corrugated flanks. As a precaution, Sardé set the offside front wheel against the kerb. The last thing he wanted was a runaway to deal with. Not this evening. Not here in Roucas Blanc.

He folded his arms over the steering wheel and looked up through the windscreen. Across the street, maybe fifty metres along Allée Jobar, peeking through a rambling palisade of hibiscus, he could see a corner of the house, a jutting prow of white stucco and rust-coloured tiles set against a darkening blue sky.

Sardé pulled a handkerchief from the pocket of his shorts and wiped his brow and neck. Even with both windows down, it was stifling in the van. He dipped a hand into the mess of the door pocket, felt around, then pulled out the bottle of aftershave that he kept there. He flipped up the cap, found the nozzle and, tipping his head back, gave himself a couple of generous squirts. Even the spray felt warm as it settled onto his skin.

But at least it killed off the reek of hot oil and diesel that seeped up from the engine. This evening the fumes were worse than usual, thanks to a pair of jerrycans secured in the back of the van. Picquart had asked him to drop them off at the marina on his way home, along with a roll of tarpaulin, plastic bucket and a brand-new deck brush. A deck brush, decided Sardé, was surely pushing it; there was hardly enough deck on Picquart's twenty-footer to brush. Not that he'd ever say anything. You didn't say anything to Picquart about his boat, unless you had a half-hour to spare. At Piscine Picquart you knew it was a Friday because the old boy always arrived at the showroom in his skipper's hat, its peak braided with gold. His wattled ears were too large for him to wear it with any dignity, but at least it covered the toupé.

Sardé checked his fingernails – about as clean as he could ever get them – and glanced at his watch. A little after six, the shadows starting to lengthen. Winding up both windows, he climbed out of the van, closed the door and locked it. At the back of the Citroën he tested the lock on the doors, then came round to the passenger side, pulled out his bag and slung it over his shoulder. He glanced around casually – not a soul – and started down the street, the key he'd taken from Picquart's office patting against his thigh with a pleasurable beat. He put a hand in his pocket and wrapped it in his fist.

Two minutes later, Sardé looked around one last time, up and down the street. In this area you didn't get too many windows overlooking the road, which was a good thing, but the cars that drove around here did so with a whisper. They came up behind you just like that, and went past with hardly a hum. You had to watch out for that. One minute the street was clear, the next you got some limo purring its way home.

All clear.

Quickly now, Sardé slipped the key into the lock and turned it. Pushed his shoulder against the garden gate and slid inside.

The lowest terrace was in shade and oddly chilled. Crickets still chirruped in the tangle of branches that clung to the wall, but the heads of the frangipani were already drooping, closing into tightly twisted pink fingers. By morning the lawn here would be littered with their fallen husks. Keeping to the boundary wall, the bag bouncing against his elbow, Sardé made his way round the lawn. When he reached the steps to the second terrace he sprinted up them, keeping low. By now the windows on the topmost floor of the house were in view, but the shutters were closed. Still, he kept low and didn't hang around, following the terrace balustrade to the right, making the first stand of pines with a beating heart and catching breath. From here the ground rose sharply, a steepish slope of crumbling red earth webbed with a snarl of tree roots. He swung the bag around his neck so it wouldn't slip from his shoulder and reached up for a handhold. This was the only way to reach the top terrace with its sweep of lawn and swimming pool without being seen. If he'd been visiting for professional reasons, he'd have trotted up the steps and made his way directly to the pool. But this was no professional visit. Not with a camera, binoculars and a long-bladed hunting knife in his bag. Once again, looking for the next handhold, Sardé wondered about the knife.

He always carried it, just in case, but so far he'd used it just the once, over Borély way, when the woman he'd been after had tried to push him away and make a run for it. But he'd caught her and, without thinking, reached into his pocket and brought the blade to her throat. She'd frozen, like a statue. He'd let go her arm and she didn't move, not a muscle, the knife pressing against her skin.

He'd liked that. The look of it. What it did. The silver, curving sharpness of the steel whitening the woman's tan in a thin line, the sound of her small sobbing breaths. The low moan when he eased the knife from her neck, a slight flinching as he ran the blade to her shoulders and cut through the straps, easing down the top of her swimsuit with the tip of the knife, loosening the wrap she wore round her waist with a single slice. She'd done everything he'd said, everything the knife indicated. And when it was over, he knew she'd never say a word. Wouldn't risk it. Not a woman like that. Too much to lose.

Pulling himself to the top of the slope, Sardé brushed the dirt from his shorts and T-shirt and looked around. It was just as he'd hoped. A high stone wall covered in a tangle of hibiscus and honeysuckle shielded him from the neighbouring property and the grey flaking trunks of the pines and a bank of spiky aloe and pink-tipped oleander concealed him from the de Cotignys' terrace. Slowly he pushed himself up and peeked between the trees. Beyond the aloe and oleander, the lawn stretched out across the front of the house. Fifty metres away he could see the stone lip of the pool, the diving board, a slice of blue water and a scatter of cane-woven loungers, the kind that came with padded footstools and cost more than he earned in a week. Keeping low, Sardé scuttled along between the pines and the boundary wall, the land rising more gently now, the carpet of pine needles springy underfoot, until he reached what he had judged on his last visit to be the best vantage point, where the slope flattened for twenty feet before rising away again, up past the side of the house.

Pulling off the shoulder bag, he lay on his back and looked up at the darkening sky through the lacy branches of the pines, waiting for the thumping in his chest to settle. The smell of resin was strong after the heat of the sun and the earth was warm on his back and legs, the needles tickling his elbows, thighs and calves with tiny pinpricks. He turned over onto his stomach and slithered up the bank that concealed him from the house, finding as comfortable a position as he could amongst the elbowing tree roots.

Loosening the tie-top of his shoulder bag, Sardé felt inside for the binoculars, pulled them out and trained them on the distant terrace. He worked the focus and a blur of shapes and colours suddenly cleared and steadied – the diving board, the loungers, a wine bucket and glass.

Then, away to the right, came the cut-crystal glitter of a laugh. And then another.

Sardé moved the binoculars and saw the two of them come out of the house, stepping through a set of terrace doors, Madame de Cotigny first, wrapped in a silk gown, barefoot, the woman behind her draping a sweater over her shoulders. The lady of the house turned, slid an arm round her companion's waist and drew her forward, letting her lips graze her cheek, whispering into the woman's ear. Another peal of laughter.

Thanks to the binoculars, Sardé could have been standing right there, next to them, close enough to run his fingers over their breasts. If he'd got there an hour earlier, he reckoned, he'd have seen more than he'd bargained for. He was certain of it. A couple of dykes, he thought hungrily. He'd have liked watching that. But it was too late now, since the younger woman was clearly leaving. She picked up her bag from one of the loungers, let Madame take her hand and the two of them, weaving their arms together, stepped back into the house through the terrace doors and disappeared.

In their absence Sardé scanned each window with his glasses. Not a light. Not a movement. Not a sound. Not that he was expecting any.

There'd hardly be anyone else around, he reasoned, with the lady of the house entertaining like that.

From the front of the house, Sardé heard the cranking of an engine starting up, a rasp of gravel and a tinny beep-beep. He swung the glasses back to the terrace and pool. A few moments later, Madame de Cotigny reappeared, stepping into the overlapping circles of his binoculars, tantalisingly close. She came around the pool to the side nearest to him, turned her back and slid off the wrap. His breath caught and he dropped the glasses to take in her arse. But he wasn't quick enough. She'd dived in and the image was gone, just the tiles and lapping water.

Sardé took the binoculars from his eyes and wiped the sweat away.

Camera or knife? Camera or knife? Was this the night he made his move?

He could feel himself pressing uncomfortably against the material of his shorts. Jesus, what a boner. He pushed a hand under the waistband and tried to rearrange himself. More comfortable now, he brought the binoculars back to his eyes in time to see Madame de Cotigny haul herself from the pool, standing at its edge to wring out her hair, water spilling down her body, the last of the sun licking out a cube of gold across her breasts.

Not bothering with the wrap, she strolled towards him, to one of the loungers, and picked up a pack of cigarettes from its seat, tipped one out and lit it.

She smoked. Sardé hadn't known that.

He gritted his teeth. He wouldn't be able to kiss her now, the bitch. The inside of her mouth, her tongue, all sour and acrid. But there were other places where the taste would still be sweet. And thinking of that Sardé decided against the camera. Pulling himself into a crouch, he pushed the binoculars into the top of his bag and made his way forward, calculating the distance between them, still not certain what form of approach to make, how to play it.

That would come to him, he knew. The way to play it.

And if things went wrong, there was always the knife.

46

S uzie de Cotigny watched the beat-up Renault turn out of the drive. A long brown arm snaked up through the sunroof and waved, a farewell beep-beep from the horn, and the next moment the car was gone. Suzie listened as the Renault's engine faded into the silent evening streets of Roucas Blanc, then turned and made her way back to the terrace.

It had been, she supposed, a good afternoon. Certainly everything had gone according to plan. But there'd been something missing, something absent in the encounter, which she hadn't anticipated.

Usually Suzie arranged her solo assignments for the apartment on Paradis but, having Roucas Blanc to herself, she'd told the girl from the gym – Berthe was her name – to come out to the house. It was the first time Suzie had invited someone to visit without Hubert being there to join in, and the idea appealed to her. In his absence, there would be something illicit about the encounter which might add to the thrill, and it would be fun to show the place off. For the de Cotigny residence was certainly something to see. Suzie had worked hard on it: cajoling Hubert's approval as she tore out this and that, persuading him gently for the smaller changes, imploring for the larger, bigger, more ambitious takes, until the makeover was complete. The kitchen, the bathrooms, the bedrooms, the tessellated entrance hall, the lofty, panelled salons, the dark Edwardian style of the house modernised, minimalised. Americanised.

Berthe, as expected, had been entranced, twirling around the grand hallway like a ballet dancer, opening all the cupboards in the kitchen, and exclaiming at the salon with its Warhol silk-screens, its cool, designer shades and plump Neime upholsteries. But then, how could she not have been entranced, the little *gitana* who probably lived in a walk-up in Belsunce or some such place?

Yet none of it had quite . . . worked, or not as Suzie had hoped. The girl from Belsunce – or wherever – might have been in heaven, but Suzie had soon tired of her companion's ooh-là-là-ing enthusiasm. This, she realised, as she lay back on the bed and let her thighs be opened, was not what she wanted. Not this house. Not this life. And certainly not this pert-breasted gypsy whose hands searched her out, too young, too keen to give anything but the most rudimentary, amateurish pleasures. Even though, Suzie conceded, there had been a satisfaction of sorts to be had from it.

Coming through the trees at the side of the house, she stepped out onto the terrace. The pool lights were off and, in the evening shade, the water lay greasily still, sucking softly at the overflows. She slipped the wrap from her shoulders, took a deep breath and dived into the water, pulling herself the length of the pool, through its warm thickness, before surfacing in a wash of water that slapped against the edge of the pool and flooded across the flagstones. Flipping onto her back she set her toes against the tiles, bent her knees and pushed away, paddling her feet gently, thigh rubbing smoothly against thigh, water sluicing past her cheeks, bubbling across her lips and streaming down the length of her body. Above her the sky was darkening fast, a few early stars twinkling down and a scent of rain in the air.

Three more hours, maybe. Ten-thirty. Eleven. She had until then, on her own, before Hubert was back.

He'd called while she and Berthe were playing in the bedroom, leaving a message on the answerphone in the salon downstairs. She'd only picked up the guest-room extension when she recognised his voice, not wanting her companion to be privy to anything personal. He still hadn't got to his mother's, he told her. The traffic was *affreuse*. He . . .

On the other end of the line, she heard a car horn sound angrily. She guessed it was aimed at Hubert – not realising the traffic lights had changed, or getting himself in the wrong lane, or stalling the engine, or not using his indicators. Hubert and cars did not go well together.

Suzie was sure she was right; he sounded flustered when he came back on the line. She listened a moment, then told him that she had a headache, had fallen asleep in the sun and felt dreadful – shushing her companion who'd started to giggle again, instead of concentrating on what she was supposed to be doing, down there between Suzie's legs. 'I'll sleep in the spare room, if you don't mind? But I'll make up for it tomorrow, darling. I promise. Would you like me to wake you?'

Flipping over again, Suzie headed for the side of the pool and hauled herself out, water cascading off her, arms locking at the elbow to bear the weight of her body rising up out of the water. She stood, slicked back her hair with lifting hands and, not bothering with the wrap, walked over to the loungers, picked up cigarettes and lighter. Perching on the footstool, she lit up and took a deep drag, funnelling the smoke from her lips to drift out across the lawn. She watched it till it disappeared then, judging the conditions right, tried some smoke rings.

One. Two. Three.

Perfect. Rolling away into the night like tiny grey lifebelts.

Time. To. Move.

As the last smoke ring coiled and knotted and disappeared Suzie acknowledged the fact, admitted to herself, that she was suddenly fed up. Fed up with the house, and fed up with Marseilles. So provincial, so small-town, so . . . out of the loop. And, increasingly, fed up with Hubert and his snobbish, exasperating family. They pretended they were *le tout gratin* – the 'toot cretin' as she liked to call it – the upper crust. But they were as narrowly self-interested as any *petite bourgeoisie*. What really riled her was how Hubert always pandered to them – his mother particularly, the self-centred old crone.

Grasping. Greedy. Self-absorbed.

Suzie blew three more smoke rings.

At first, when she and Hubert met in the States, she'd been awed by him. Twenty years older, he'd seemed so self-assured, so suave and cosmopolitan. So French. The fact that he shared her . . . exquisite tastes, that he understood them and took pleasure in them, only served to increase the attraction, and the wild unpredictability of the affair that followed. By the end of his stay she was his, falling for him like a silver dollar dropped into water.

But somewhere along the line the balance had changed. The more Hubert fell for Suzie, the less she felt for him; the greater his dependence, the greater her independence. Five years on, the glow was fading. He was now fifty-eight. She was thirty-seven. Of course she was fond of him, of course she still loved him, but it was different now. She'd outgrown him, outgrown the house and the city he'd brought her to, and the life they lived. Not to mention the girls, girls like Berthe. Increasingly, their easy, peasant charms had started to run thin. Their manners were appalling, their skin was coarse and their sweat reeked of garlic. Even the lone pleasures of her apartment on rue Paradis had started to pall.

Suzie sucked in a last lungful of smoke and dropped the cigarette into the ice bucket – a swift hiss as it extinguished. She stood and looked across the lawn. Private, no windows bar their own to intrude on her, a conspiracy of pines and high walls, battlements of hibiscus and frangipani and the subtle, sloping contours of the land to protect each residence from its neighbour. Suzie stepped off the stone flags and felt the grass give beneath her feet. It was still warm enough to be naked she decided, the water from the pool almost dry on her skin, just a coil of moisture leaking between her shoulder blades and down her back from the fall of her hair. She raised her hands, leant back and squeezed the water from it, twisting it out.

She wondered what she'd miss, when the time came to move on. Not France, certainly. And increasingly not the French. Not Hubert's interfering mother, nor his spoilt, self-opinionated daughter. If she never set eyes on the two of them again, it wouldn't be too soon for Suzie. As for Hubert, he'd be heartbroken, of course, but *tant pis* as the French would say. He might plead with her to stay – in vain, of course – but he'd survive, he'd get over it.

But where to go, thought Suzie? Where to move on to? Strolling across the lawn she considered the possibilities, the grass prickling underfoot, not a whisper of breeze to whip away the day's sultry, leaden heat. There was the Caribbean, of course, but that was way, way too close to home. North Africa, maybe? Or Spain, perhaps? Or further afield? Bali, Malaysia, the tropics? Somewhere hot. Somewhere exotic. Somewhere her parents would disapprove of. She liked it when they disapproved. Even now.

And then, in the middle of the lawn, Suzie paused, aware of a sound, a movement, at the far edge of the terrace, among the pines.

Her first thought was a cat or dog chasing through the undergrowth. But then there was a voice. Someone calling out. Someone on her side of the boundary wall.

Realising that she was naked, Suzie turned back to the pool for something to cover herself. She picked up her wrap from the flagstones, belted it around her, then retraced her steps across the lawn.

And there, from the darkening shadows at the far edge of the property, where the pines twisted up into the night sky, was a figure, coming towards her.

Berthe? Hortense? Their neighbour, Madame Deslandes? But then she saw trousers. Gilles the gardener? Hubert home early? She peered into the gloom, but couldn't make out any feature, save that the figure was tall. Taller than Berthe, but about right for Madame Deslandes. Or Gilles. Or even Hubert.

'Who's there?' she called out, noticing for the first time the citrus scent of aftershave. 'Hubert? Is that you, honey?'

The figure approaching across the lawn spoke again, sounding concerned, as though something had happened of which Suzie was unaware, and she knew at once it wasn't Hubert.

'Madame, Madame, are you all right? I thought I saw something . . .'

And before Suzie could do anything about it, before she had time to react or defend herself, the figure was leaping at her, toppling her to the ground. And then . . . something hitting the side of her head, stars springing into her eyes, more stars than she remembered in the night sky, spinning through her vision, the breath crushed from her body . . . a weight on her chest, her arms and legs pinned down and a prickling of grass on her neck . . .

And up above . . . The sky darkening, the stars still there but blinking out, one by one, fast . . .

Until . . . just an irresistible urge to giggle. To laugh at the . . . And then . . .

Nothing . . .

Part Three

47

La Résidence Cotigny, Marseilles, Friday

It was early morning when Gilles, the de Cotignys' gardener, arrived for work, the sun still to breach the peaks above Montredon, the white stucco of the house the pale gold of a chamois cloth, its cornered recesses chill and angled with shadow.

He entered the grounds where he always did, at their lowest level, through the garden gate on Allée Jobar, a panel of weathered grey wood set into a boundary wall that rose nearly twelve feet above the pavement, so that only the crowns of the garden palms and pines could be seen from the road.

Closing the gate behind him and pocketing the key, Gilles made his way up to the house, taking the long route around the bottom lawn beside the chip-bark path of the flower beds, then up the steps to the middle terrace. There'd been a blow the night before, down from the mountains, only now heading out to sea, chopping the water in the bay. It had been strong enough to strip away palm fronds and loosen pine cones, which now lay scattered across the grass. They'd need picking up, tidying away.

Halfway across the terrace, Gilles paused, his attention caught by something else on the grass. And nothing brought down by last night's blow.

Damn dogs, he thought, kicking a sun-dried crotte out of his path. It looked like a shrivelled brown finger. Now he looked, he could see *half a dozen more that would need shifting before he mowed the lawn. They might be hard on the outside, those* crottes, *but there was always a soft-centre core to them. And when the blades caught them and spat them out . . . well, the smell was enough. Clung to his trouser legs and all. They weren't even good manure.*

Of course, he knew the culprits. Deutsch, the big old German shepherd that belonged to Doctor Crespin along the road, and those three little yapping monsters of Madame Deslandes's. By the look of the crottes *this morning, it was the mutts from next door that were to blame. Deutsch always left far more substantial calling cards. If only Madame remembered to close the front gates, it wouldn't have been a problem. He'd mentioned it to the boss a hundred times, but the message had failed to filter down to her. Or, if it had, it didn't seem to make any difference.*

Gilles climbed the steps to the top terrace and started off across the lawn, the house rising above him, the pool away to his left, the land banking up to his right, where he was headed, rising gently to a border of pine, oleander and aloe. It was round this side of the house, near the service entry, that Gilles kept his work shed, stored the spades and shovels, rakes and secateurs, all the things he needed to keep the place in order. It was also, in the middle of the day, a cool spot to stop for his lunch and the eau de vie *he kept amongst the seed trays. As for the mornings, a nip of* calva *from a weedkiller bottle was all it took to get him motivated.*

The first hour was always the best, early enough to be on his own, trundling the wheelbarrow back down to the bottom terrace, dropping off tools as he went: shears and canvas sheet on the top terrace for clipping back the bougainvillaea on the balustrade; a rake and shovel on the middle terrace where he'd seen the dog crap; his secateurs and a trug by the climbing roses; and a hoe by the fruit beds on the bottom terrace. Anyone walked round the garden and they'd think he was the hardest worker in the world – four jobs on the go at once. But they'd be lucky if he finished one.

It was around six, while wheeling a lightly loaded barrow of palm fronds and pine cones to the compost heap beyond the pool, that Gilles saw her first. Or rather her outline, and the jet-black hair, through the back of the see-through inflatable pool chair she liked to use – high enough out of the water to keep her books and magazines dry, and easily manoeuvrable when the sun got too hot and she needed the shade. What surprised the gardener was the fact she should be up and about so early.

But there she was. Madame. And yet, as he steered his barrow along the edge of the terrace so as not to disturb her, Gilles was aware of something not quite right, his eyes seeking her out almost against his will. And it wasn't just the possibility she was topless. Great tits, Christ . . . Something else altogether. But no, not her tits. Something in the way she sat in the chair; she looked . . . uncomfortable. Slumped.

As he drew parallel, maybe ten metres from the edge of the pool, Gilles slowed his pace and peered cautiously in her direction. She seemed to be asleep, head lolling, an arm slung out, fingers trailing in the water. He lowered the barrow handles, ready to stoop and pick something up if she sensed him there and turned in his direction.

Which she proceeded to do, a whisper of breeze moving the chair and bringing her round to face him, head tilted, eyes fixed on him, as though surprised that there should be anyone there that early.

And very pale, it seemed to Gilles.

Madame always had such a good colour. But not this morning. As pale as the stucco on the house that rose above them.

It was only when he stepped onto the flagstones edging the pool that Gilles saw what was wrong.

48

'Whose mobile?' It was César's voice, calling from the kitchen. And then, after checking his and Sid's: 'Daniel, it's yours.'

Jacquot roused himself. Squinted at his watch. Six-thirty. Jesus. His head ached. The brandy. The joint César had rolled after Sydné had gone to bed. He looked around, tried to get his bearings. A tented room, painted furniture and terracotta colours. A Moroccan feel. Sid and César's spare room. The smell of patchouli and coffee percolating.

He tried to remember where his jacket was, his mobile. Out in the hall. Bleating away.

It was Gastal, chewing on something. 'We got us another one.'

The address Gastal had given him was in Roucas Blanc, at the end of a cul-de-sac off Avenue des Roches. Jacquot had to use a street map to find it, hidden away in a fold of hills closer to Prado Plage than the Vieux Port. Exclusive territory. When he saw the squad cars, the Forensics van, and an ambulance all drawn up in a semicircle under a stand of pines at the end of the lane, Jacquot knew that he'd arrived.

They were all there. Peluze and Grenier, Chevin and Dutoit, Laganne, Serre, Muzon and Isabelle Cassier, each marking out their own area of inquiry: Peluze and Grenier with Gilles, the gardener, working him through the discovery of the body, the last few days . . . anything suspicious? Isabelle Cassier sitting in the kitchen with a tearful Hortense; Chevin and Dutoit sweeping the gardens; and Laganne, Serre and Muzon, according to Dutoit, waking the neighbours, asking questions, getting statements.

Jacquot went straight for the victim, settling himself on a lounger at the side of the pool where three of Clisson's men worked on the body, laid out on the flagstones in a shadowing puddle of water. Crouched around it like worker ants attending a queen, gloved and zippered, they combed through her hair, secured her hands in plastic bags, moved her head from side to side, opened her mouth, peered into ears and nostrils. Three more, on hands and knees, scoured the surrounding flagstones.

'Is this where she was found?' Jacquot asked Clisson, who was unloading a film from his camera. His ginger hair was still slick from his early-morning shower.

Clisson shook his head, bagged the roll of film and fitted a new one into the camera. 'In the chair,' he replied, nodding at a plastic inflatable armchair tethered to the diving board. He closed the back of his camera and an electric motor wound the film on.

'And?'

'Same as the others, you ask me. Drowned, no question. Drugged? Possibly. We'll know later. Sex? This one looks pretty brutal to me. And, like the others, the same pattern of bruising between her shoulder blades and on her upper arms, as though she was held down . . . restrained. Also, she's got a lump on the left temple the size of an egg,' continued Clisson, taking up a position to photograph the victim's feet and legs. His colleagues stopped their work on the body and moved back, giving him room. 'If she wasn't drugged,' continued Clisson, sighting through the lens, 'the chances are she was unconscious the whole time.'

Jacquot looked at the body. He could see a shiny swelling on the side of the head by the hairline, a soft bruising above the elbows and angry red rub marks between her upper thighs. Like the other Waterman victims, there was no jewellery on the body.

'Time of death?' asked Jacquot.

Clisson adjusted the focus and shot off a couple of frames, then moved to another position. 'Eight, nine, maybe as late as ten p.m. At a guess.'

'When did they find her?'

'About an hour ago. The gardener . . .'

'You seen Gastal?'

'The fat guy at Aqua-Cité?'

Jacquot smiled. 'That's the one.'

'In the house somewhere. With the husband.'

Jacquot got up from the lounger.

'Looks like your man's moving upmarket,' said Clisson over his shoulder.

'You mean the house?'

'And who owns it.'

'Yes?'

'Family called de Cotigny. Old Marseilles money. Very influential. Big political clout. The husband, Hubert de Cotigny, is head of planning and development at the Préfecture. Nothing, absolutely nothing, happens in this city without his say-so. And his mother, whoa . . . a real political player, *grande dame* of the old school. When the press get hold of this . . .'

'Don't,' said Jacquot. 'I don't want to hear.'

Clisson shrugged and gave him a tiny, satisfied smile as though he was glad it wasn't his job to find out who was responsible.

On Jacquot's way to the house, Chevin called him over. 'B-b-boss, you want to take a look?'

Jacquot changed direction, stepped out onto the lawn.

Pierre Chevin was squatting on his heels, pointing to something on the grass. Jacquot crouched down and took a look. A scuff of red earth showed through the turf.

'And there,' said Chevin, pointing to another. 'L-l-looks like this was where it started.'

Jacquot and Chevin got to their feet.

'You ask me,' said Chevin, turning to point, 'the k-k-killer came up the steps, or more likely from the trees. Maybe hiding out, waiting for the right moment.'

'Anything over there?'

Chevin shook his head.

'Ways in?'

'Walled right round. They all are up around here. Front gate. Electronic. You need a b-b-buzzer to open it. The railings are too narrow to squeeze through, but you could get over the front w-w-wall if you wanted. It's quiet enough round here so no one would see you.'

'Who gets the buzzers?'

'There are three. The maid, husband and victim. K-k-kept in their cars. All accounted for. Deliveries ring in through the intercom. The gate can be opened from the f-f-front door.'

'Any other way in?'

'Garden door down the bottom terrace. Opens on to J-J-Jobar. According to the gardener, it's always locked.'

'Keys?'

'I'll check with Al.'

'Let me know,' said Jacquot and he turned back to the house, wishing he'd drunk a little less of César's brandy.

After looking in on Isabelle in the kitchen, consoling the maid, Jacquot found Gastal in the study with Hubert de Cotigny. Wrapped in a silk Paisley dressing gown – striped pyjama trousers and worn Moroccan slippers showing beneath its hem – de Cotigny was slumped in an armchair, his thin grey hair awry, eyes red and vacant, cheeks drawn and unshaven. Jacquot judged him somewhere in his late fifties, old enough to be the victim's father. Gastal introduced them.

De Cotigny looked up, gave Jacquot a brief nod.

After the formalities of sympathy and condolences to which de Cotigny responded with another brief nod and a tightening of his lips, Gastal brought Jacquot up to speed.

'Monsieur de Cotigny here was out last night, having dinner with his mother in Castellane. He got home round ten-thirty, ten-forty-five.'

'Did you see your wife, Monsieur? When you got home?'

De Cotigny didn't seem to have heard the question.

Jacquot was about to repeat it when de Cotigny shook his head.

'I've told your colleague everything I know, Chief Inspector.'

Jacquot turned to Gastal.

'Apparently Monsieur de Cotigny called the vict— his wife, Madame de Cotigny, round six-thirty last evening, on his way to his mother's. She told him she wasn't feeling too well and was going to bed.'

'She said she'd sleep in the guest room. Asked me not to disturb her,' added de Cotigny.

'She actually said that? Not to disturb her?'

De Cotigny frowned. 'Not exactly. She said . . . she said she would see me in the morning.'

'And when you got back, after dinner with your mother, the place was locked? Secure?'

'The front gates were open, but that's not unusual. Inside I closed the doors to the terrace and activated the alarm.'

'The front gates and terrace doors were open?'

'My wife was not good with locks, doors. Always leaving them open. She didn't think. Like I said, it wasn't unusual.'

'And did you go out on the terrace, to see if she was there, before you locked up?'

'I didn't think to. It was late. There were no lights on out there. And, anyway, she'd said she was going to bed early. I assumed she was already upstairs. Asleep.'

'And you didn't look in on her? To see if she was all right?'

De Cotigny shook his head. 'I didn't want to disturb her. My wife . . .' He paused for a moment, squeezed his thumb and forefinger into the corner of his eyes.

'Yes, Monsieur?'

De Cotigny sighed, got to his feet. 'My wife is . . . was . . . a light sleeper. She would not have appreciated my waking her up.' He walked to the study door. 'And now, Chief Inspector, if you don't mind, I would like to get dressed.'

'Of course, Monsieur. And . . .'

De Cotigny turned at the door.

'. . . Perhaps you'd be kind enough to show us the room where your wife slept?'

'You mean, where she *would* have slept?'

'If you wouldn't mind.'

Exchanging looks, Gastal and Jacquot followed de Cotigny from the study. He led them across the hallway to the stairs and started climbing, hand on the rail as though to steady himself, laboriously, like a mountaineer on some demanding summit slope. When he reached the landing, de Cotigny pointed down the corridor.

'Third door down,' he told them, then turned to his own room directly opposite the stairs, closing the door quietly behind him.

For a bedroom that hadn't been slept in the place was a mess. The first thing that Jacquot and Gastal noticed was the bed. The duvet had been thrown to the floor, the bottom sheet was crumpled and the pillows were dented.

'Not the most comfortable way to sleep,' said Gastal, nodding at a lone pillow doubled over and deliberately placed in the middle of the bed. He picked it up, buried his face in it, sniffed deeply. 'Looks like afternoon delight, you ask me.'

'Fun and games all round,' replied Jacquot, nodding at a mirrored square on the dressing table. Its surface was smeared with white, and a length of straw and a platinum American Express card lay beside it. He bent down, read the name: Suzanne de Cotigny. 'We better get Clisson up here,' he said, going to the window.

Pulling up a blind, Jacquot looked down into the garden. By the pool, the Forensics boys had bagged the body and were lifting it onto a stretcher. Clisson had stepped off the flagstones and was taking some long shots of the pool. Down below, on the far side of the middle terrace, Chevin and Dutoit were diligently working their way through the flower beds. Jacquot tapped on the window, signalled to Clisson.

The Forensics man looked up, saw Jacquot and nodded.

'What do you think?' asked Gastal, sliding open a panelled wardrobe door and peering inside. 'She got herself a bit of *cinq à sept*?'

Jacquot came back to the bed, tipped one of the pillows, then turned his attention to an ashtray on one of the bedside cabinets. He pushed his finger through the ash, picked out two cigarette ends, turned them in the light.

'Looks that way,' he replied. 'But a lover who wears lipstick.' He held up the stubs. 'Different colours.'

'Dirty cow,' smirked Gastal.

They passed Clisson on the stairs, lugging his box of tricks.

'Third door,' said Jacquot. 'Cigarette ends in the ashtray and hair on the pillow. Coke, too. On the dressing table.'

Clisson nodded and carried on up to the landing, his sterilised Tyvek suit swishing with every step.

Downstairs, Jacquot and Gastal made a tour of the ground floor.

'Some place,' said Gastal, taking it in.

Jacquot nodded. It certainly was. Though the house clearly dated from the turn of the century, probably one of the first to be built in this part of the city, its interior was resolutely modern, the kind of spotless set-up you might see in *Elle Decoration* or *Architectural Digest*. While the original cornicing, marble fireplaces and marquetry flooring were still in place, the walls and doorways that had divided and connected the various ground-floor salons had been stripped away, creating an open-plan space painted in soothing pastel colours, filled with gleaming tubular steel furnishings and hung with bold modern artwork, golden slants of morning light spilling through a line of terrace doors running the length of the room. Between two of the doors was an ancient Balinese chest set with a tub of orchids and a telephone.

Gastal stopped by the phone. 'We got ourselves a message.'

Taking a pen from his pocket, he pressed the playback button. The tape rewound with a whirr, then connected.

'You have one caller,' came the recorded message. 'Timed at eighteen seventeen.'

And then: 'Darling, it's me.' There was no mistaking de Cotigny's voice, harassed, a little frantic. 'Just thought I'd call to let you know . . . I'm not at mother's yet, the traffic, you wouldn't believe . . . oh hell . . .' There was the sound of a car horn in the background. 'Hold on . . .' said de Cotigny, and then there was a click as Suzie de Cotigny came on the line, her French good but the American accent unmistakable.

'Honey? Honey, you okay? Where are you?'

The conversation that followed was exactly as de Cotigny had described it to Gastal. The traffic was dreadful and he still hadn't got to his mother's place. He'd likely be late back. And then Suzie telling him not to rush home; she wasn't feeling too well; she'd sleep in the guest room, wake him in the morning. Then their goodbyes. The connection broken. The last time they'd ever speak to one another.

'Play it again,' said Jacquot.

Gastal rewound the tape, and pressed *play*.

The voices started again, sharp and clear. Suzie de Cotigny was speaking.

'There. You hear it?'

Gastal turned to him, looked perplexed.

'Again,' said Jacquot. 'After she says not to rush home.'

They played the tape again and Gastal leant forward, straining to hear whatever it was that Jacquot had heard.

And there it was. Unmistakable.

But not the sound of traffic. Not their voices. Something else.

A sniff. A girlish giggle, followed by a shushing sound. You could almost see a hand over the mouthpiece.

Gastal's eyebrows shot up and a smile licked over his lips.

★ ★ ★

'So. What have we got?'

It was mid-morning, the sun climbing above the rooftops of Roucas Blanc, the trees throwing down a cool, slanting shade. Suzie de Cotigny's body had been taken away by ambulance twenty minutes earlier, Monsieur de Cotigny's mother and daughter had arrived shortly afterwards and Jacquot's squad had left the property and were now gathered by their cars.

Jacquot perched on the bonnet of his Peugeot, boot hooked onto the fender, looking at the faces grouped around him.

Luc Dutoit, Chevin's partner, was the first to speak. 'The gardener, Gilles Therizols, arrived sometime around five this morning,' he told them. 'Found the body about an hour later.'

'He a regular?' asked Jacquot.

'Been working for the family the last eleven years. Yesterday was his day off.'

Jacquot nodded.

'Same with the maid,' said Isabelle Cassier. 'Her day off, too.'

'So whoever did this knew the house would be clear Thursdays,' said Jacquot. 'Or was it just chance?'

'Too much of a coincidence,' said Claude Peluze, who looked like he hadn't had time to shave that morning, his stubble bristling black and shadowy around his jaw.

'So?'

'It was planned,' continued Peluze. 'The Waterman scoped the place . . .'

'So you say it's our killer?' asked Jacquot.

'Who else, boss?' said Isabelle. 'The maid says nothing's been taken from the house, just the victim's jewellery – big fat diamond and a gold bracelet.'

Her partner, Bernie, pushing back a wedge of hair from his brow, nodded agreement. 'Naked. Drowned. Then propped in the chair. It's got to be.'

Jacquot didn't comment. Until Valéry, the state pathologist, confirmed pronoprazone, he'd try to keep his options open.

'So, sometime between, say, seven-thirty and ten-thirty latest, Madame de Cotigny gets taken out. Now. The husband . . . Could we be talking a domestic here?'

Gastal, unwrapping a coil of *churros* from a paper bag but making no effort to offer it around, shook his head.

'He couldn't squash a bug, that one. And, anyway, he's alibied up to his ear hair. Plus the time frame doesn't give him much opportunity . . .'

'So not a domestic?'

A shake of heads all round.

'So . . . another Waterman? Second in a week? He's speeding up if it's him.' Jacquot looked around the faces. 'Anything anyone's found that gets us any closer?'

At that moment Etienne Laganne appeared round the corner and joined the group. He was near enough to hear what Jacquot had said and a big smile creased his face.

'Something you'll like, boss,' he said, chewing on a toothpick.

Everyone turned in his direction. Laganne kept them waiting, opening his car door and tossing his notebook onto the driver's seat.

'And . . .?' asked Jacquot. It was the first time since he'd tracked down Carnot that he'd felt that tiny buzz of excitement, sensed a way forward.

'Guy at the top of the street,' continued Laganne, taking the toothpick from his mouth and flicking it away. 'A doctor. Jules Crespin. Lives alone. Well, seems he was walking his dog yesterday evening, when this car exits the property. Turns out of the drive here, toots a horn and goes right past him.'

'Time? Driver? Make? Number?'

'Round six-forty, six-fifty. Before seven, anyway. An old Renault, he said. Brown. Rust bucket. Engine like a meat grinder. Couldn't say for sure if the driver was a man or a woman.'

'And . . .?'

'He doesn't make the number, but there's a sticker in the rear window. You know the kind . . . All he can remember is . . . wait for it . . . *Allez-Allez* . . .

'*Gym*,' said Isabelle, with a whoop.

Jacquot took a deep breath. The gym. He couldn't see how yet, but it was all, somehow, falling into place. Gastal might not have had any luck with Holford, which was no surprise given that they'd established she'd just arrived in town, but Ballarde, Grez and Monel had all been members. And now, someone visiting the latest victim had the gym's name flagged on the car's rear window. Could the Waterman be someone who worked there, or another member? Another woman?

Four confirmed victims and they still hadn't found any trace of semen despite evidence of penetration.

There was a stir in the group, a few smiles. It was clear that Jacquot wasn't the only one feeling the way he did, but he needed to contain it.

'Hold on, now – let's not get too excited,' he began. The group quietened. 'For starters, we shouldn't assume this Renault driver's the killer. Could have been just a friend visiting, then leaving, tooting the car horn to say goodbye. And you don't toot a horn to say goodbye to someone you've just killed.'

In the middle of the group, the old-timer Grenier nodded his head. It made sense. Jacquot looked at the other faces and he could see that the possibility had registered.

'Okay,' he began. 'This is what we do. Isabelle, get down to that bar and stay there. Get a make on everyone. And this time speed things up. Who owns the place?'

'Old man, Patrice Carré, and his wife, Nadine. Both in their sixties. They rent the place, live upstairs. Been there twenty years.'

'Up front with them. Show the badge. But don't let them know what it's all about. Names of regulars, new faces, that sort of thing.'

Isabelle nodded.

'By the way,' said Jacquot, his mind racing. 'Any word on the Internet boys you were chasing?'

'Clean as a whistle,' she replied. 'Photographer. Models. All of them watertight alibis.'

'And the aquarium?'

'Not a thing.'

Jacquot took this in. He'd been hoping for a lead, either at Aqua-Cité or with the Internet site, but now it looked like they'd have to close those avenues down. Maybe Isabelle would have more luck with the bar . . .

'Okay, then,' he continued, getting back to business. 'Bernie, Luc. Chase up that guy Carnot. Where was he last night, blah, blah, blah? And don't be worried about applying some pressure. Also, pay a call on those English lads down at the Carénage. The brothers. I know they're not on our list, but it won't hurt to check their whereabouts last night. We don't want any loose ends here, okay? Etienne, Charlie – give the harbours a rest . . .'

A look of relief spread over their faces. It had been an impossible job to get landed with. A lot of shoe leather and no answers.

'. . . Get together with Pierre, Al and Claude and start going through the victim's diary, address book, correspondence. Anything you can find . . . and Alain.' Jacquot turned to Gastal.

'I hear you. Back to the gym and check Madame for membership, like the others. When was she last there? Who was there at the same time? Say, the last two weeks?'

Jacquot nodded. 'And . . .'

'. . . And find out which member drives an old Ren—'

'In one.' Jacquot was impressed. Gastal was starting to pay attention.

Jacquot turned to Chevin. 'What about the keys? You find out about the garden gate?'

'Five in all,' he replied. 'One key, with a spare, in the k-k-kitchen; one with the gardener, and another in de Cotigny's study.'

'And the fifth?'

Chevin flipped open his notebook. 'P-P-Piscine Picquart. Pool supply company out on L-L-Ladollié. They didn't install the pool but according to the gardener they've got a service contract. Call in every couple of weeks.'

49

B asquet had not slept well, his brain refusing to settle, his body refusing to find comfort, the bedlinen wrapping around him like a hot, sweaty shroud. Yet when he finally dredged himself awake, eyes squinting, neck stiff from the bolster, his shorts rucked up between his buttocks, he could see from the morning sunshine that he'd somehow managed to oversleep by a couple of hours. He also discovered that he'd woken up alone.

And that meant one thing. He'd been snoring. The few times he'd actually fallen asleep, he must have bellowed, could even remember Céléstine elbowing him quite firmly, trying to coax him off his back and onto his side. But clearly, at some stage in the night, she had given up the struggle and taken herself off to one of the kids' rooms. She always did that when he snored.

And if he'd been snoring, Basquet reasoned, he must have been drinking. The two went together like bricks and mortar, explaining the muscly press of pain behind his eyes and the tight clench of his cranium. It hadn't been an epic outing, so far as he could recall, but it had clearly been enough. It had started with the two large tumblers of Scotch and soda that he'd poured himself when he arrived home the evening before, early enough to have Céléstine greet him with surprise and delight. And after the Scotches, the half-bottle of white Rhône with Adèle's *poivrons* and the bottle of Vosne Romanée with her *daube*.

And then, as if that was not enough, he'd gone and fixed himself a couple of brandies in the salon, sitting in front of the fire after his wife went to bed. He hadn't been there that long, still nursing the first, when Célestine made a point of coming down from their bedroom to say goodnight, dressed in a long, lacy sheath of satin.

Basquet knew what was on her mind but, for the life of him, he knew he'd never be up to the job. So he'd taken the second brandy and stayed up a little longer. By the time he got himself upstairs, the satin gown had been replaced by a cotton nightie, Célestine was fast asleep, and he was off the hook. With a pregnant mistress to contend with, the last thing on Basquet's mind was sex with his wife.

Remembering Anais's pregnancy brought Basquet more fully awake. Head hammering, he shifted in the bed, reaching down to disentangle his shorts from his scrotum, trying to ignore the healthy erection this constriction had caused – the damn thing that had got his mistress pregnant in the first place.

Wadding up his pillow, Basquet closed his eyes and gritted his teeth. How in God's name could he have got himself in this mess? The whole thing had seemed so perfect, so easy, so amenable. It wasn't as if he owed Anais anything; it wasn't as if he'd taken years out of her life. He'd always been kind to her, hadn't he? Treated her well, been generous, always little gifts? Yet this was how she repaid him.

The two of them had met nearly a year earlier, at an industry fund-raiser in Avignon where Anais and another girl had been responsible for presenting the lots at the charity auction that followed dinner. Basquet's table was right next to the stage and every time Anais made an appearance, his eyes latched onto her, mesmerised by the blue sequin dress she wore, the split up its side revealing a length of lush brown thigh, its plunging front an enticing expanse of tawny cleavage. And the way she presented each lot – tipping her knees to one side, pushing out her *derrière*, and always bowing low enough to show that there was no room for underwear beneath those sparkling sequins. She was sinfully pretty, in a kittenish sort of way, eyes dark as old timber, lips a glistening, outlined red, teeth white as sugar. He judged her to be in her early thirties, of Caribbean rather than African extraction – which later proved the case – and found himself intoxicated by her presence, prickling with excitement whenever she made an appearance. As a result Basquet bid outrageously on things he really hadn't needed – a dinner for four at the Jardins des Sens in Montpellier, a pair of super-ski downhill Rossignols used by Jean-Claude Killy in the 1967 World Cup and, with Célestine tugging at his sleeve to stop him bidding, a jet ski owned by Elton John, the vehicle pulled on stage with Anais draped seductively across its driving seat dressed in a one-piece, high-cut fluorescent pastel swimsuit. It was the swimsuit that had done it.

Basquet introduced himself an hour later, discreetly, and handed Anais his card. Marvellous performance, he'd told her. If she was ever in Marseilles . . .

Of course she'd called, a week later, and he'd driven up to Avignon to see her, an hour there and an hour back on the autoroute, and three hours in a dingy apartment near the old city walls. Five hours out of his day. But worth every second. Every *sou*. Once a week, for close on a month, Basquet made the same journey. Until Anais let it be known that she would have absolutely no problem relocating, moving down in his direction, and . . . maybe he could help her find someplace?

Two weeks later he found her a small villa in Endoume, twenty minutes from his office in La Joliette, and she moved down from Avignon. She signed the papers, he paid the rent and twice a week – sometimes three times – he'd pay a call.

Until now. Now it was over. Dead in the water.

Easing himself gently from the bed, wincing with the effort, Basquet hobbled to the bathroom, reaching for support from a bedpost, an armchair, and the side of a chest of drawers. It was a pitiful display, one that he was grateful Célestine had not been present to witness. He was getting too old for all this, he thought glumly – late nights, drinking too much. Maybe Célestine was right. Maybe it was time to slow down, get Laurent in to help, all the day-to-day stuff. Of course he'd still keep his hand in, keep an eye on things. But generous with the leash. Not like Célestine's father. The old man never let up, never got off his back. He'd do well to remember that, Basquet reflected, as he closed the bathroom door with a gentle click.

Ten minutes later, after gulping down a couple of ibuprofen with a glass of Resolve and clinging to the taps under an alternating shower of hot and cold water, Basquet decided that he felt marginally better, though the process of cleaning his teeth, stooped over the sink, made his stomach heave and his head pound. Back in the bedroom he dressed slowly – a crisp cotton shirt, a knitted tie, a lightweight linen suit – and as he buttoned and knotted and zipped himself up, selecting a pair of slip-ons that he didn't need to bend down to put on, Basquet acknowledged gratefully that his hangover did appear to be receding.

Downstairs, the breakfast table had been cleared, so he went through to the kitchen where, shakily, he poured himself coffee and chewed on a croissant. Across the counter, Adèle was preparing a meal for Célestine's pack of house cats, one of which mewed and coiled irritatingly around his legs. If he'd had the strength, and the necessary coordination, he'd have kicked the fucking thing through the window.

At that precise moment Célestine came bustling in from the garden, carrying a trug-load of flowers. She gave him an accusing but forgiving glare for his failings the night before and, after an affectionate peck on the cheek, she started up a breeze of happy chatter as she searched for scissors and began snipping away at the flowers' stems.

And then Basquet was in his car, speeding south, only moving into the slow lane when he saw a blue light flashing in his rear-view mirror. An ambulance, thank God, racing past, siren wailing. Which reminded Basquet of the cop from the *Judiciaire* who'd turned up the previous day asking questions about a building they'd developed, an apartment belonging to a murder victim. As he'd told the fellow, it was nothing to do with him what the occupants of his apartment blocks did with themselves. But afterwards he'd remembered that Raissac owned one of the apartments and the butterflies had begun to flutter. Could the murder have taken place in Raissac's apartment? And if it had, could it have anything to do with Raissac? Or was Raissac, as leaseholder, as blameless as Basquet the freeholder?

Somehow, Basquet suspected not.

He reached across for his mobile and brought up Raissac's number. The least he could do was warn him about the apartment, the visit from the *Judiciaire*, let him know that he could probably expect a similar call.

Or not. Maybe that dullard cop would call it a day, not bother to follow it through.

Basquet listened to the ring tone and was about to disconnect when he heard Raissac's voice on the other end of the line.

50

F ive blocks beyond the marble-slabbed slopes of the Gabriel
Cemetery on the northern side of the A7 flyover, Jacquot spotted
the sign for Piscine Picquart. A gaudily painted board set at roof level
ran the length of a square, single-storey building, one in a line of
similar commercial enterprises – timber yards, kitchen-supply outlets,
garden centres and furniture warehouses – each with a parking lot out
front, each strung with bunting and every one of them flagged with
offers of 'once-only' promotions, boldly advertised in extravagant
poster colours to pull in what there was of passing trade.

At some time in the past the premises presently occupied by
Piscine Picquart had been a garage and car showroom, closed down
and sold on when the autoroute opened. Under a spread of sun-
warped roofing, the raised island where the petrol pumps had once
stood was now laid in AstroTurf and furnished with a Californian hot
tub, the showroom was filled with an assortment of poolside furnishings and accessories, and the old used-car lot outside was crowded
with Jacuzzis, more hot tubs and a range of blue, ear-shaped moulds
for suburban swimming pools, lined up according to size and pitched
against a wall of peeling whitewash. The only place that appeared to
retain its original role was a large workshop at the back of the lot, its
shadowy workbench interior slashed by a wedge of sunlight and filled
with the tinny sound of a transistor radio.

Pulling into the forecourt, Jacquot parked beside the Californian
hot tub and got out of the car. Fifty feet above him, traffic roared

past, out of sight on the flyover. He was grateful for the shade and a tug of breeze that pulled the shirt off his skin. It had taken him nearly forty minutes to reach Piscine Picquart from Roucas Blanc and the drive had left him feeling cramped and grubby. As he walked across the forecourt to reception, Jacquot stretched, worked his shoulders and wondered how long before the ache behind his eyes eased off. If he'd known the day was going to start with an early wake-up call and another body, he'd have been more circumspect the night before.

Inside the showroom, behind the reception counter, a young woman two-fingered her way across a computer keyboard, black roots showing in her centre parting, a wad of gum rolling round her mouth. Jacquot was leaning across the counter to ask for the manager when a brown-skinned lizard of a man scuttled out from behind a frosted-glass door.

'Picquart,' he said, snatching at Jacquot's hand and shaking it furiously. His ears were the size of side plates, brown and freckled, and he wore a jaunty little sailor's cap braided with coils of gold. Salette would have taken one look at him . . .

'So, what can I do for you, Monsieur?' he breezed. 'Jacuzzi? Hot tub? Or maybe you're looking for something bigger?'

Jacquot reached into his jacket pocket and pulled out his badge.

The man's face lost its showroom glitter and set itself in stone. 'Let's go through to the office,' he said, indicating that Jacquot should follow.

'So,' he continued, dropping into a chair behind his desk, gesturing for Jacquot to make himself comfortable. 'What can I do for you?'

'The de Cotigny residence. Roucas Blanc. I believe they have a service contract with you?'

'They certainly do,' said Picquart, nodding behind him to an open cupboard, hung with keys on hooks. 'And there's many more besides them, I can tell you. Contract work for more than fifty owners. Pool cleaning, filtration units, pump servicing – we do the lot.' Even with a policeman in his office, it was clear that Picquart couldn't resist the spiel. 'And very competitive prices, too, I don't mind telling you. You'll not find cheaper. Or maybe you will but there's no one in this town that'll look after you quite so well for the price.' Picquart caught the look on Jacquot's face. 'So. Anyway. You were saying. The de Cotignys?'

'You keep a key of theirs here. For a garden gate on Allée Jobar.'

'That's correct.' Picquart extended a finger under his cap and scratched his scalp with a raspy fingernail. Jacquot guessed that a toupé lurked beneath the braid.

'Would you mind seeing if the key is there?'

Picquart tipped back in his chair and peered into the cupboard.

'Up there, second row, fourth from the left.'

Jacquot looked. The only single key on the row. The rest in pairs or threes. Simple enough to replace with one from another bunch.

'And that's where the key has been for the last twenty-four hours?'

Picquart nodded. 'Lock the cupboard myself. Every evening. I'd see if one was missing. Stand out like a sore thumb, it would, one of those keys goes missing.'

'And when was the last time you visited the de Cotigny property?'

Picquart pulled open a drawer in his desk and his fingers danced across a rack of files until he found what he was looking for. He flicked through some pages, ran his finger down the last and said: 'Monday. Test for chlorination and a check on the overflows.'

He pushed the file over in case Jacquot wanted to take a look.

He didn't. 'And since then?'

Picquart shook his head, closed the file and slid it back into the drawer.

'You do the job yourself?'

Picquart waved to the wall behind him. 'Leave all that to the grease monkey out back. Sardé's his name. Not the most reliable when it comes to starting a day's work, you get my drift. But good with his hands. Real mechanical-minded. Cleaning, servicing. That sort of stuff.'

Jacquot took this in.

'You have anyone else working for you? Apart from Sardé and your receptionist?'

Picquart shook his head.

'And how long have they been with you?'

'Maxine, six months give or take. Always need a pretty face out front, even if she's not so hot with the typing and the filing.'

'And Sardé?'

Picquart gave it some thought. 'Two years. Could be longer. Like I say, he does have his off days but he's real good with machines. Got the touch.'

'He married? Single?'

'Not married, no.'

'Girlfriend?'

Picquart shrugged, spread his hands, didn't think so.

'And yesterday? What time did you close up?'

'Around five. The usual, give or take. Sometimes we got a customer comes in last thing we don't send him packing, you understand my meaning.'

'And you were here all day?'

Picquart thought about that. 'Well, not yesterday. Not the whole time. I had some things to collect for the boat. My cruiser, down on the Vieux Port. Thirty feet of fun. Marvellous. Nothing like it. Do you sail, Chief Inspector?' He tapped the peak of his captain's hat.

Jacquot gave him a look, got to his feet and started moving round the office. Filing cabinets, a cork board pinned with business cards, notes and flyers, a couple of pictures of Picquart aboard his boat, and a Sunseeker calendar hung on the back of a second door. Picquart's eyes never left him.

'Well, like I was saying, I needed some supplies. Brush, gas, some tarp, so round three I went up to Marina Supply – 'bout half a mile back.'

'Leaving Maxine here, and Sardé?'

Picquart nodded. 'Just the two of them.'

'And you locked the key cupboard? Your office? While you were away.'

Picquart shrugged. 'No reason to. Like I say, it wasn't more than fifteen minutes I was out.'

'Could you ask Maxine to step in here a moment?'

Picquart shouted out her name and a moment later Maxine shuffled into the office, straightening her sleeves and brushing the lap of her skirt. The waist was too tight and a salami-sized roll of fat bulged under her button-fronted jumper. Also, without the gum to disguise it, her bottom lip was too full and gave her face a sullen slant.

'When Monsieur Picquart left the showroom yesterday, did he have any visitors while he was out?' Jacquot asked. 'Anyone go into his office?'

Maxine looked at Picquart, as though it was her boss who'd asked the question. 'No one, Monsieur. Nobody was in here.'

'Thank you, Maxine,' said Jacquot.

She bobbed and left.

'You want me to call in Sardé?' asked Picquart.

'And he would be where . . . ?' asked Jacquot.

'Workshop, most likely,' replied Picquart. 'Out back.'

Jacquot pointed to the calendar and the second door. 'Can I get there through here?'

'Sure, go ahead.' Picquart started to get to his feet. 'I'll show you over there.'

'No, no, it's fine,' said Jacquot, opening the door. A gust of warm breeze pushed its way in and riffled through the pinnings on the cork board. 'Just a word and then I'm on my way.'

'You mind my asking what it's all about? The de Cotignys?'

Jacquot paused in the doorway, as though considering Picquart's request.

'Yes. I do,' he replied with a smile and stepped out into the sunshine. The man would find out soon enough.

It was only a few steps from Picquart's office to the workshop. A Citroën van with *Piscine Picquart* painted on the side had been backed up into the entrance since his arrival. Jacquot noted that the offside flank had been crumpled and when he saw Sardé gathering up a coil of hoses from the workbench – the white shorts and T-shirt, the limbs brown and muscled, the bleached hair – he knew he'd seen the man before. In a side street off rue St-Ferréol on Monday night, the Citroën wedged up against a bollard and Sardé getting out to inspect the damage, lifting a finger to the beeping drivers held up behind him and unable to squeeze past. When he was good and ready and not before. Like he couldn't give a damn. Like he'd like to see anyone step out of their car and discuss it with him.

'You want the boss, he's in the office,' said Sardé, lugging the coil of hoses to the van, hefting them into the back.

'And you are?'

'What's it to you?' asked Sardé, returning to the workbench for another load.

'Whatever I want to make of it,' replied Jacquot, flashing his badge. 'So why don't you put down the hoses and pay attention?'

Sardé tossed the second load of hoses into the van, then took a stance, stuck his hands in his pockets and gazed over Jacquot's shoulder to the flyover.

Jacquot suspected this wasn't the first time that Sardé had dealt with the police. The other thing Jacquot could see, behind the bored look on Sardé's face, was a sudden discomfort. This was a man with something to hide.

'Last evening,' began Jacquot. 'Between five-thirty and eight, you were where?'

Sardé shrugged, stalling while he thought up a convincing answer. So that was what this was about. Roucas Blanc. There'd been a complaint.

'I dunno. Having a beer someplace?'

'Where, exactly?'

Another shrug, digging the toe of his trainer into the dirt. He nodded along the strip. 'Henri's. Up Plombières way.'

'And how long were you there?'

'Hour. Maybe two. Played some pool.' As soon as he gave the additional information, Sardé knew he'd gone too far – volunteered too much.

Jacquot knew it too.

'And you were playing pool with?'

'Couple of the lads.'

'Friends?'

Jacquot could see Sardé trying to work out whether it was better to say friends, or some guys he didn't know.

'Sure,' he said, sounding even more uncertain.

'Names? Addresses?'

'Look . . .'

'You said they were friends. So they'll confirm you were there. Right?'

'Sure. Sure.' Sardé could see that he'd dug himself a hole and was standing on the edge. 'So what's all this about, then?'

Jacquot didn't mind the dodge, the sidetrack. He knew the man was lying. No point pursuing it.

'You worked here long?'

'Two years.'

'You like it?'

Jacquot could see that Sardé had no idea where this was going.

'It's okay.'

'You get out a lot? Deliveries? Better than an office.'

Sardé nodded, eyes flickering.

'When was the last time you visited the de Cotigny property? Roucas Blanc?'

Sardé made the mistake of trying to repeat the name, as though he couldn't quite place it. The two words came larded with a throaty guilt.

'De Cotigny?' He pulled a hand from his pocket and scratched the side of his nose. 'Couldn't say. A month, maybe. You'd have to ask the boss.'

'He says Monday.'

'Yeah, well. Maybe. We got a lot of contract work, you know. Difficult to remember every place. One pool's much like any other.'

'You know Madame de Cotigny?'

'Sure. Seen her around, you know.'

Jacquot nodded. 'Attractive woman.'

'You say so.'

'You got a coat, *mon ami*?'

'No, I . . .'

'So what are we waiting for? Let's go.'

It took just seven words, in the car back to town, to get the truth out of Sardé.

'Madame de Cotigny was murdered last night,' said Jacquot lightly as he turned into Boulevard des Plombières.

'Jesus!' said Sardé with some feeling. But nothing more.

Halfway along Plombières, Jacquot slowed the car and pulled up outside the bar where Sardé had claimed he'd been playing pool the night before.

'Isn't this Henri's?' asked Jacquot, turning to look at his passenger. He didn't switch off the engine; he knew they wouldn't be getting out of the car.

'Look . . .' began Sardé.

And Jacquot had him.

'Okay. I was there, right, out at Roucas Blanc,' said Sardé.

'Doing what?' asked Jacquot, as he pulled away from Henri's and headed on towards town.

'Waiting.'

'Waiting for what?'

'For . . . you know . . . Getting it together. There's a lot of ladies like her in my line of work. Bored, you know. Want some fun.'

'Madame de Cotigny?'

'Sure. Look,' Sardé said, a little desperate now, realising what a fix he was in. 'You didn't know her. She was up for it, right? Asking for it. Giving me all sorts of come-ons. I was just goin' round to collect.'

'So she called you, set up the meet?'

'No, I just . . .'

'Just thought you'd call by?'

Sardé gave a kind of non-committal shrug.

'So you get the key from the boss's office while he's out?'

'Right . . .'

'Replace it with another?'

'Right . . .'

'So how did you know last night would be a good time to call?'

'I didn't. I mean, I knew it was the staff's day off, but that's all.'

'So you were going to take a look, see if the coast was clear?'

'Right. Right.'

'And what happened?'

'When I got there she wasn't alone. She had some friend with her. A woman.'

'You see who it was?'

They were stopped at lights on rue Malève. When they changed to green, Jacquot glanced in his rear-view mirror and pulled out for the A7 feeder ramp.

'Some girl . . .'

'And?'

'Young. Twenties. Shortish hair.'

'So what did you do?'

'Stayed out of sight.'

'In the trees. You hid in the trees?'

Sardé nodded.

So Chevin had been right.

'And?'

'And then the girl leaves. I hear a car start up, drive away. When Madame comes back to the terrace she's alone.'

'She come through the house?' asked Jacquot, reaching the auto-route and joining the stream of traffic.

'No, round the side.'

'Which was when you made your move?'

'No, no. I stayed where I was. Watched a while, you know. Make sure it's all clear.'

'And?'

'And then someone sees me, in the trees, calls out, you know. "Hey, you!" kind of thing. Scared the shit out of me.'

'And?'

'Well, I legged it, didn't I?'

'You see anyone?'

'Hey, I wasn't hanging around, you know.'

'Man or woman?'

'I told you I didn't see no one.'

'The voice, man or a woman's?' asked Jacquot patiently.

'I don't know. A man? Hard to say.'

'Did Madame de Cotigny hear the voice?'

'I dunno. I was out of there, wasn't I? Didn't stay to look.'

'So the last time you saw Madame de Cotigny she was alive and well?'

'Absolutely. Large as life. You gotta believe it.'

Back at police headquarters, Jacquot took Sardé up to the squad room and handed him over to Serre.

'Our friend here was out at the de Cotigny place last night. And he'd like to cooperate in any way he can. Isn't that so, Monsieur?'

Sardé nodded, started to look hopeful.

'Seems to think I believe his story,' continued Jacquot, who had no doubt at all that Sardé was telling the truth. 'Maybe he'll be able to persuade *you*.'

51

The boys were young, sixteen and eighteen according to Carnot, with the bodies of angels, skin coloured an ashy brown, hair black and curly, limbs loose and long. Coupchoux had brought them over to Raissac's house in Cassis the evening before. Now the two boys were preparing breakfast in Raissac's kitchen, sashaying out with cutlery and china to lay the table on the terrace where Raissac sat, his hand reaching out to caress their bodies whenever they came within reach. Which was as often as they could manage.

Raissac couldn't remember their names. Or rather, which was which. Was Hamid the older of the two, the one with the ring through his ear? Or was it Abdul, with the long eyelashes and sleepy brown eyes? It should have been a simple matter to tell the difference between a sixteen-year-old boy and an eighteen-year-old man, but it wasn't. Dressed in sarongs, knotted low around slim hips, their bodies were similar in every way – height, colour, muscle tone. They were like twins, heavenly twins, and really, thought Raissac, watching them, who gave a damn how old they were, or even what their names were? In an hour Coupchoux would be there to drive them back to town and Raissac would never see them again. Unless he chose to. For now, sitting at his breakfast table, the sun prickling its morning warmth across his pitted shoulders, it was enough just to watch them, a pair of young, supple bodies brushing together, the two of them squabbling like children over how to use the juicer, the correct way to prepare scrambled eggs, and how long to bake the freezer baguettes.

Pushing back his chair, its legs grating against the flagstones, Raissac pulled off his own sarong and stepped down into the pool, wading forward until the water was up to his armpits before striking out for the deep end. While he swam – the only exercise apart from sex that he ever took – Raissac listened to the giggles and chatter drifting pleasantly across the water. What a marvellous way to start the day, he thought, and was pleased that he'd decided to have the boys brought to Cassis, rather than be entertained in the city. So much nicer to be at home.

A month back it had been three girls here in Cassis, again supplied by Carnot, and the pleasure he'd had from them was on a par with the pleasure he'd found in the attentions of Abdul and Hamid. Distinct and different, of course, but no less gratifying, Raissac decided, sliding his way through the water. How fortunate he was to enjoy the two, men and women both. He tried to decide which he liked the most. Boys or girls. But it was impossible to say . . . Maybe if he'd slept with more of one than the other, that might somehow show a preference, but he'd long ago lost count of the men and women who'd shared his bed. What Raissac *did* know was that he invariably alternated between the sexes. After sleeping with a woman, he usually felt a deep compulsion to sleep with a man, both encounters providing the diversion he sought, the pleasure he needed, but neither doing more than leave him with a dull dissatisfaction, as though he'd asked for directions but still couldn't find his way.

After a dozen languorous lengths, Raissac stepped dripping from the pool to be dried and pampered by Abdul and Hamid, led to the table and fed his breakfast, the two of them bickering over who buttered the croissants, who poured the coffee, and who served the scrambled eggs. Raissac reached out a hand and stroked his fingers over the closest thigh. Skin smooth as glass. Not a blemish. Raissac often wondered what it would be like to have smooth skin.

It was over the eggs, a little dry for his taste, that Raissac began to feel the first faint stirrings of impatience with his youthful companions. And when he heard the soft bleating of his mobile, he was pleased for the interruption. The boys were starting to tire him with their petty tantrums, endless chatter and pathetically eager advances. They had done what had been required of them and now it was time for them to go. Reaching for his mobile, he told them to clear away breakfast and get their things together; his driver would be arriving soon to drive them back to town.

Leaving the boys to get on with it, Raissac strolled out onto the lawn to take the call.

It was Basquet.

'I thought you should know,' said Basquet. 'I had a visit from the police. Some Inspector. Apparently a tenant at Cours Lieutaud was murdered. Drowned.'

'You don't say,' said Raissac.

'He wanted to know who held leases. Rentals.'

'And you told him?'

'I said I didn't know. I told him to contact Thierry at Basquet Immo. Said he'd have the relevant information. It only struck me after the cop had gone that you had an apartment there.'

'So you think he might pay a call?'

'If it's the same apartment, it's possible. He didn't seem the most energetic detective. Just thought I should let you know.'

'That's kind of you. I doubt he'll follow up, but I'll be on the lookout.'

The conversation over, Raissac headed back to the table and flicked through the papers. There was no sign of Abdul or Hamid, which was a relief. Five minutes later they came downstairs from his bedroom, dressed identically in T-shirts, jeans and flip-flops, just as Coupchoux drew up at the front of the house. Without needing to be told, Coupchoux herded them up and took them to the car where they started to argue over who should sit in the front.

While they squabbled over the seating arrangements and then which tape to play for the drive back to Marseilles, Coupchoux came back to the terrace where Raissac handed him an envelope: money for the boys when he got them home to Marseilles.

Coupchoux slid it inside his jacket and turned to go, but Raissac caught him by the arm.

There was one more thing.

'Is it done? Doisneau?'

'Tonight, boss.'

'Make sure of it.'

52

I t didn't take long for the squad to make progress.

Gastal was first to report in, calling from the gym.

'Latest victim was a club member. Registered as Suzie Cotagnac. Gotta be the same. They're getting me a list of people using the gym the same time as her. Last two weeks. Staff and members.'

'Great,' said Jacquot. And meant it. The only problem, as Madame Bonnefoy would icily point out, was that it had taken four Waterman kills, and likely as not a fifth – to be confirmed in the next few hours – to get as close as he now felt they were. But somewhere along the line, as he'd told her, there'd be a break, a weakness, a flaw and Jacquot's squad would maximise it. Maybe this was it.

'There's something else,' said Gastal. They were Jacquot's favourite words.

'Yes?'

'The victim's address. According to the gym, it's some place in town. Up on Paradis. Not, repeat, not Roucas Blanc.'

'Sounds interesting. Why don't you check it out? You're in the area.'

'I'm on my way there now. I'll get back to you.'

Serre was next, popping his head round Jacquot's door, the usual cigarette burning between his fingers.

'That guy Sardé's clean, you ask me. Been through the same story three times since he came in. Whatever he was doing there – taking a peek, making a play – he wasn't alone. You ask me, the Waterman stole his pitch.'

'Does he remember anything more about whoever it was caught him?'

Serre shook his head. 'Didn't see a thing. Someone in the trees, is all. Couldn't say whether it was a man or a woman, old or young.'

'Let him stew a couple hours more,' said Jacquot. 'Then give it one more go. If his story holds together, have him show you where he lives. Take a look. Anything belonging to any of the victims, anything that might tie him in. I'm not banking on it, but we better make sure, cover the bases.'

Serre gave a thumbs-up and disappeared.

Next into Jacquot's office were Muzon and Dutoit who'd paid a call on Carnot at his apartment.

'Some kid called Alice making him breakfast,' said Bernie with a grin. 'Seems they met up around seven last evening. The girl confirmed it.'

'And the English lads?'

'Same with them,' replied Dutoit. 'Both accounted for.'

And then a call came through from Al Grenier, one of the longest-serving officers on the squad. Jacquot had asked him to chase up Hervé Thierry at Basquet Immo when he got back from La Joliette the day before, but it had slipped his mind. It came sharply into focus when he heard what Grenier had to say.

'Monel's flat is owned by a leasing company. Raissac et Frères.'

Jacquot sat up at that. 'You got an address?'

'Head office Rabat. Morocco.'

'Anything closer?'

'Not a thing. That's it. Since it's not a publicly-quoted company there's no records available.'

'What about the other girls who lived there? Before Monel. Did Thierry have any information about them? Forwarding addresses?'

'Nothing,' replied Grenier. 'Said they left rental to the leaseholder. Not their business. Maybe this Raissac operation will be able to help.'

When Grenier signed off, Jacquot put a call through to Toulon; an old pal on the local force, Massot.

After the usual pleasantries, Jacquot got straight to the point.

'Raissac. Ever hear of him?'

'We know the name but that's it,' said Massot. 'Has interests all over. Building supplies mainly, but there's hotels, gambling. But nothing on him, though we'd love to find something. Three, four years ago we were certain he was behind some pretty big drug movements. Had the docks round his little finger. We pretty much cracked the scam, took out a lot of big names, but we never could prove a thing far as this guy Raissac went.'

'You got an address?'

'Is this official?'

'Just interested, is all. Anything comes up you'll be the first to hear.'

'He has a place near Cassis,' said Massot. 'Off the road into town. Very private. Perimeter walls. Security cameras. The business. All you can see from the road is sky.'

'Easy to find?'

53

Shortly before lunch, the body of Suzanne Delahaye de Cotigny arrived at the Marseilles City Morgue on Passage de Lorette and was prepped for autopsy by the state pathologist's three assistants. The victim was weighed, sheeted, and laid out face down on a stainless steel 'deck'. Instruments were set out on clean cotton squares, weighing scales were rolled over to the head of the deck and tested, and a new tape was inserted into the recorder. A blood sample was taken and sent for analysis with an instruction to check for pronoprazone and get back soonest with the result.

When everything was ready, Doctor Laurent Valéry was summoned from his office.

Normally any body arriving at Passage de Lorette joined the queue. There were rarely fewer than half a dozen corpses in the cool room awaiting examination and a strict rota was observed. First in, first out – the way Valéry liked it. But a call from Clisson had persuaded him to put aside other work and concentrate on Madame de Cotigny, which was probably why Valéry was in such a waspish mood that morning. He didn't like his schedule being messed with, even if there was a killer on the loose. Pathology was all about method, he liked to tell his students, and method was the mistress of patience and discipline. When his three assistants heard his white boots squeaking down the tiled corridor towards the autopsy room, they straightened their backs and fell silent.

Bustling through the swing doors and dressed in green hospital scrubs, the state pathologist resembled nothing so much as a sprightly goblin intent on mischief. Sixty years old, a fraction over five feet tall, with a horseshoe of grey hair teased into extravagantly curled side-burns, Valéry was a stooped but energetic man who'd been cutting up bodies for the last forty years. In the next two and a half hours, Suzanne Delahaye de Cotigny would surrender all her secrets to the silvery blade of his scalpel and his probing, rubber-clad fingers.

The first thing Valéry did when he reached the table was to whip off the sheet that covered the body, letting it drift to the floor for an assistant to retrieve. As usual, the examination began with a visual, his assistants stepping back while Valéry moved freely around the 'deck', peering down at the body through wire-framed, half-lens bifocals. At the end of the circuit, Valéry had his assistants turn the body face up and he repeated his drill.

'White female,' were his first words. 'Mid-thirties . . .' A flick of his fingers, and rubber gloves were snapped on him by an assistant. With the same fingers, he parted the victim's hair an inch behind her ear, looked over the top of his glasses, then stood back. 'Natural brunette. Weight . . .'

'Sixty-five point three kilos,' said one of the assistants.

'Sixty-five kilos.'

With a thumb and forefinger Valéry lifted an eyelid and top lip in one movement. 'Eyes brown. Teeth her own . . .'

And so it had gone, the state pathologist noting all external characteristics, from the colour of the victim's nail varnish to the bruising on her arms and the lump on the side of her head. Across the room, the sound-level needles of the tape recorder jumped at his high, nasal commentary. When he completed his autopsy, the tape would be typed up and a summary sent to Jacquot, along with Valéry's usual handwritten observations.

Before taking up the scalpel, however, there was one further procedure that he wished to carry out. With a nod to his assistants, the victim's legs were lifted into stirrups, spread apart and the bolts on the table's lower quarter were released, making room for Valéry to sweep forward on a roller chair, pulling a magnifying lamp with him and reaching for a speculum.

For what seemed an age, there was silence in the autopsy room, just the squeak of springs from Valéry's chair as he leant forward between Madame de Cotigny's thighs. Then, bringing the magnifying lamp into play, he gently exhaled as though he'd been holding his breath.

'Well, well, well,' said Valéry, as though he'd just bumped into an old friend. Discarding the speculum and selecting a pair of tweezers from the instrument tray, he settled back behind the magnifying lamp.

Standing around him, the three assistants watched as he eased apart the victim's labia with two gloved fingers and leant forward with the tweezers.

'And what have we here?'

54

Jacquot took the old D559 east out of Marseilles, winding up into the hills of Ginestre before spooling down to the valley beyond. On his left the craggy limestone ridges of the Carpiagne chain rose up against a sky as blue as gentian, the sea away to his right glittered distantly in the morning sun, and the warm air rushing past his open window was rich with the heady scents of pine, salt and wild fennel. Jacquot took a deep breath. The best perfume in the world, he decided, as he reached the sign for Cassis and turned back to the coast.

The trip to Cassis had taken Jacquot a little more than forty minutes, not only a glorious, invigorating drive from the city on such a beautiful morning but an opportunity to review the facts that had occasioned the journey. Facts, Jacquot well knew, that added up to nothing more than a sliver of coincidence and a whisper of intuition. Facts he could as easily have reviewed over a lukewarm cup of coffee in the office.

One of the Waterman's victims lived in an apartment block owned by Valadeau et Cie, and a second victim had been found in the open-sea pool built by a subsidiary of that company. Both companies were run by Paul Basquet, the tiresome little *couillon* whom Jacquot had visited in his office on La Joliette, and instantly disliked. Which was maybe why he'd slipped so easily into his slow, stupid cop routine.

And now the latest twist. According to Grenier, the lease on Vicki

Monel's apartment had been bought from Basquet's property company by Raissac et Frères. The first time out with Gastal, his new partner had had him check on a man called Raissac. Then, the very same evening, Jacquot bumps into an old, old friend from way back, who tells him that this Raissac has something to do with a big drugs deal going down in the very near future. Which explained why Lamonzie had given him such a mouthful for putting his stake-out at risk.

Which was why Jacquot had decided to make the trip to Cassis, on the off chance that he might be able to get a look at this Raissac character. Just like he'd done with Basquet. Maybe it was something. Maybe it wasn't. Maybe it was just . . . well, a coincidence. Nothing more.

As he followed the twists and turns of the road leading down to Cassis, lazily playing the steering wheel to left and right, Jacquot wondered if Raissac and Basquet knew each other. Had to; even with lawyers doing all the work on the apartment purchase, the two principals must have met up at some time or other. If Raissac was at home he'd be sure to ask him, Jacquot decided, as he pulled off the road and drew up at a pair of high wooden gates two hundred metres past a roadside stall selling melons and peaches, just as Massot had described it. He wondered idly if Lamonzie's men were about, keeping a watch on comings and goings, but didn't give a hoot if they were.

Jacquot got out of the car and went over to the entryphone grille, stretching as he did so, feeling the heat beat down on him, the swell of insect noise drowning out the Peugeot's idling engine.

A minute after pressing the button, the entryphone speaker clicked into life.

'Yes?' A man's voice. Immediately familiar. The entryphone on rue des Allottes. Raissac himself.

Jacquot leant forward. 'Chief Inspector Jacquot, *Police Judiciaire*, Marseilles. Be grateful for a word with Monsieur Raissac.'

In answer the connection went dead and the gates began to ease open, one ahead of the other.

Jacquot got back into his car, waited for enough space between the opening gates and then pulled into Raissac's drive.

Raissac had a knack for faces and he knew this one immediately. As he came down the steps of his house to greet his visitor, he noted the shoulders, the broken nose, the ponytail. Rugby. Jacquot. One of the great tries. France versus England. In London, fifteen . . . maybe sixteen years back? Raissac knew his rugby. He probably had a video somewhere.

'Chief Inspector, *bonjour*,' said Raissac.

'Monsieur Raissac,' Jacquot replied, coming round the side of his car. 'Thank you for seeing me at such short notice,' he continued, reaching into his jacket pocket for his ID. But he didn't get a proper grip on the card and it flipped out of his fingers onto the ground at Raissac's feet.

Raissac bent down, picked it up and handed it back, not bothering to check it.

'My pleasure,' he replied, sensing the policeman's surprise at the way he looked – trying as hard as he could to keep his eyes off the ravaged cheeks, the splash of colour. 'Anything I can do to be of assistance, Monsieur. Here, let's go out to the terrace,' he said, leading the way round the side of the house, the path bordered by banks of lavender.

Following behind, Jacquot took in the lines of the house and grounds – a two-floor cube of glass and concrete terraced into a tutored bank of lawn, the mountains of the Baume Massif rising up above the pine and cypress that bordered the property, a feathering of clouds on their peaks. It wasn't quite Jacquot's style – too lean, too modern – but there was no denying that it was a very impressive property.

'Jacquot. Jacquot,' Raissac was saying, as if the name seemed familiar. 'Tell me, Chief Inspector, you're not by any chance *the* Jacquot, are you? Flanker? Number Six shirt?' They'd reached the terrace and Raissac led the way to an umbrellaed table and cushioned chairs. 'Can't remember the Christian name, I'm afraid, but your face is very familiar. And, if you'll excuse my saying, you do rather look like you play rugby.'

'You have a good memory, Monsieur,' Jacquot conceded, taking the seat that Raissac indicated. 'Daniel. Daniel Jacquot. Debut match. And you never saw me again.'

'But that try . . .'

'The right place at the right time, Monsieur. A loose ball and fresh legs. I came on as a substitute, remember?'

'But still . . .'

There was a moment's pause as they made themselves comfortable, and Raissac took a look at his companion, trying to get the measure of him – a useful strategy when the police came calling. The flattery, the recognition, was water off a duck's back with this one, he noted. His visitor from the *Judiciaire* wasn't interested in reliving past glory. That was done and gone. And no bad thing, thought Raissac. Living in the past was the fast lane to nowhere.

A man in an embroidered cream burnous came out of the house and walked over to them. He looked to be in his sixties, thin, a little hunched, and carried a tray under his arm.

'I'm sorry, sir. I didn't know you had a visitor.'

'Ah yes, Salim, thank you. Chief Inspector, what will you have?'

Beers were requested and Salim retreated.

'So, what can I do for you?' continued Raissac, getting down to business.

Jacquot didn't waste any time: 'I believe you own the lease on an apartment on Cours Lieutaud, Marseilles?'

Raissac pretended to give it some thought. 'I believe so, yes.'

'You seem uncertain?'

Raissac waved his hand at the house and grounds. 'I'm afraid I need more than one city leasehold to keep me in my old age, Chief Inspector. As far as I remember, my company, Raissac et Frères Maroc, has a number of residential and commercial properties in the city. Two of the properties are used for business – colleagues from out of town, meetings, that sort of thing. I don't actually have an office in France since most of the day-to-day business is carried out in Rabat. The remaining properties will have been purchased for rental income and market speculation.' He waved his hand dismissively. 'Just a sideline, really.'

Another silence settled between them as Jacquot took this in.

Raissac smiled helpfully. He had no reason to hold anything back. And knew better than to do so. The policeman sitting in front of him might have the looks and build of a bruiser, but there was a fineness to the features, an intelligent set to the eyes. Unlike Basquet's take on the man, Raissac recognised an operator when he saw one, and this fellow was not to be underestimated. He was also, Raissac decided, a very attractive man. Fleetingly, he wondered what this Jacquot would look like with his hair untied, loose, hanging around that wide breadth of shoulders . . . and those strong legs, the slim hips.

Salim returned with their beers on a tray, set them on the table and retired.

'So property is your main business, then, Monsieur?' continued Jacquot, raising his glass to Raissac and taking a sip.

Raissac shook his head. 'Not at all, Chief Inspector. Not at all.'

Give him everything, he thought. There was nothing to hide.

'Property, of course, is always a sensible investment,' he continued, 'and it's how we started. But our company has many other interests.'

'You said "our company". You have partners, then?'

'Just the one,' replied Raissac. 'My brother, Henri. When our father died, we took over the family business. Building supplies, that kind of thing. Based in North Africa. Morocco. My brother, who is ten years older, went in first; and I followed later. We did well in the Sixties when tourism opened up. New hotels meant building on a large scale. Supplies, materials, workforce. And local know-how for foreign companies coming in. We made sure we were the best operation in town. Since then,' Raissac spread his hands, 'we have, of course, tried to expand. Import, export, a little shipping, maritime trade . . . We try to cover the board.'

'And your brother lives here in France?' asked Jacquot, his eye caught by the swallows diving at the swimming pool to scoop up beakfuls of water, leaving a pattern of circular ripples across its surface.

Raissac shook his head. 'Venezuela. Caracas. We have other operations there – mining, drilling, natural resources. Another string, you understand . . . Nowadays, "diversification is the key to economic health", as they say.'

'Coming back to your properties . . .' asked Jacquot. 'Do you know any of your tenants personally?'

Raissac shrugged. 'With so many properties, Chief Inspector, it would be extraordinary if I knew every tenant's name,' he said, regretting the words as soon as they were out of his mouth. Not for any information he'd disclosed, but for the way he'd said it. Rather pompous, on reflection. The kind of thing Basquet would say. 'What I mean is, Chief Inspector . . .'

But Jacquot was holding up his hands, deflecting Raissac's attempt to right the situation. 'No, no, of course, I quite understand.' He took another sip of his beer. 'So, then, it's unlikely you'll have heard that one of your tenants, in a block of apartments on Cours Lieutaud, has been found murdered?'

'*Mais non*, I hadn't heard that.' Raissac put on what he hoped was a suitably concerned expression. 'But then . . .'

'But then it would be dealt with by someone else. In Rabat?'

'Through our legal department there.' Raissac nodded. 'Or the various agents we use. For all purchases, sales and rentals we use local *immobiliers*. On the spot. They know the markets and we leave things to them. Something like this . . . a murder . . . If they don't already know about it, they soon will, I'm sure. But it's not something I would get to hear of.'

'And you haven't read about the murder? In the papers? Or seen anything on TV?'

Raissac shook his head. 'Just the business pages,' he replied with an easy smile. 'And sport, of course. Nothing else, I'm afraid. As for TV . . . well, it's for morons, *n'est-ce pas*? All those game shows . . .'

Raissac caught himself. Again, he'd said too much. The wrong tone. For all he knew this Jacquot watched TV the whole time and just loved game shows. He might not look like it, but you never could tell.

Much to his relief, his guest nodded in agreement and smiled. It didn't look to Raissac like his visitor had taken offence.

'I wonder,' Jacquot began again, 'do the names Grez, Ballarde, Monel or Holford mean anything to you?'

Raissac gave the names some thought. There was only the one he recognised. Monel. Vicki Monel. He shook his head. 'I'm sorry. No, not a single one. Is one of them the girl who was murdered?'

'Actually, they are all murder victims.'

Raissac put on a suitably concerned expression. 'I'm sorry to hear that. Terrible. Terrible.'

Jacquot drained his beer and got to his feet. 'Well, Monsieur, thank you for giving me your time,' he said.

'My pleasure, Chief Inspector,' said Raissac, also standing, a little surprised that this Jacquot should have driven all the way to Cassis for such a short meeting. 'As I said, anything I can do to help.'

They shook hands and Raissac led him back the way they had come.

At his car, opening the door and sliding into the driver's seat, Jacquot paused, as though he'd just remembered something.

'One last question, Monsieur . . .'

Raissac held out his hands – anything.

'Do you happen to know a Monsieur Paul Basquet? Of Valadeau et Cie?'

'Of course I know him, Chief Inspector. Not well, of course. Not socially, you understand. But we do have certain business interests in common. The apartment, building supplies, that kind of thing.'

Jacquot nodded, pursed his lips. 'I see. Well, Monsieur. Thank you again, for your time and for the beer.'

Raissac shrugged off the thanks with a wave of his hand and stood back as the car moved off.

But as it disappeared into the trees Raissac felt a gentle unease settle on him. An increasing sense of discomfort. Something was niggling and he couldn't quite put his finger on it. Something had slipped out, something he hadn't meant to say, or shouldn't have done, maybe. Something small and elusive. He tried to think what it was but couldn't place it.

As he joined the Marseilles road, Jacquot played the meeting with Raissac back in his head. Like Massot had said, the house was something else. Very, very impressive – a couple of hectares by the look of it, with a driveway long enough for a car to reach third gear in. No more than a mile or two from the beach at Cassis, and not another house in sight. The place must have cost a fortune.

Then there was the man himself. Raissac. Even if Jacquot hadn't known about Massot's suspicions, or Lamonzie's interest in him, or Doisneau's tip that Raissac had some big drugs thing coming up, he'd still have known that the man was more than he seemed. No amount of amiable hospitality and easy charm could cover the fact that this man smelled bad. He might affect the corporate style, but it didn't work for Jacquot. The flickering eyes, the thin mouth. And that skin, that stain, that wash of pink scarring with its puckered edges. The man looked like bruised fruit.

But that wasn't all. There was something else, something of much greater interest. Something that made the journey to Cassis worth the time and the fuel.

'Is one of them the girl who was murdered?' Raissac had asked. This from the man who'd made a point about how he only read the business and sports pages and rarely watched TV.

Yet Jacquot had never once specified gender. 'Tenant' and 'victim' were the words he'd used.

Of course, it wasn't the kind of evidence that Solange Bonnefoy was looking for; a slip of the tongue, an innocent assumption, both possibilities easily explained it away. But right now that slip of the tongue, that assumption – whatever you chose to call it – was good enough for Jacquot.

That, and what might soon prove to be a lie.

For even though Raissac claimed that he knew none of his tenants, Jacquot was convinced he was lying. He was certain Raissac would have known one of the names. Monel. Vicki Monel. And if he knew Vicki, then he probably knew Carnot. Taking another step in the dark, Jacquot decided that friend Raissac might even know about the bathroom cupboard on Cours Lieutaud. And with his fingerprints all over Jacquot's identification card, it wouldn't take long to find out.

As the road climbed up through the Ginestre hills, Jacquot slid in the Coltrane tape that César had given him that morning, let his arm hang out of the window and waited for the music.

55

De Cotigny stood at his front door and watched his mother's car pass through the gates and turn out of sight. The ambulance and police cars were long gone and the two men from the Forensics team who had stayed on to examine Suzie's room had packed their bags and departed at about the same time as his daughter. Apart from Hortense, Hubert de Cotigny was now alone in the house in Roucas Blanc.

The day had begun with a shout that he had registered as part of a dream, but Hortense's lilting scream had brought him fully awake. He'd leapt from his bed, pulled on his dressing gown and was halfway down the stairs when Hortense came running in from the terrace, shoes clacking across the tiles, hands waving. All he could make out was 'Madame . . . Madame . . . Madame'. And then, when Hortense saw him on the stairs: 'Monsieur. Monsieur. Come quick. Madame.'

Outside, wielding the pool-cleaning net, Gilles was trying to coax an inflatable chair to the side of the pool. The first thing Hubert saw was his wife's hand trailing backwards through the water.

It was de Cotigny who made the call to the emergency services, the acid remains of his mother's dinner rising into his mouth.

'An ambulance. My wife . . .' he'd said, and given the address, as though he believed she was still alive, as though there was some slim possibility that she could be revived, when he knew with an absolute certainty that she was past help from anyone. That slim pale hand, fingers dipping in the water; the head lolling; the fall of black hair across her shoulder. That was all it had taken for him to know that his wife was dead.

The first police car arrived with the ambulance. The rest followed soon after. The paramedics hurried through the house, hefting their bags and a tank of oxygen. It took them only a few moments with the body before one of them looked up at him, shaking his head, confirming what de Cotigny already knew.

The two policemen, gently solicitous, encouraged him back inside the house, offered to get him some coffee. A drink? One of them stayed with him, asking, de Cotigny supposed, the kinds of questions policemen ask. Who? Where? When? How? This policeman, rather squat and overweight, spoke quietly, took no notes. Just nodded at each answer, pursed his lips. Looking for some nugget of information, de Cotigny realised, at a time of greatest vulnerability. Wasn't that the way they did it?

Then another policeman, a big brute of a man, came in, offered condolences and, in a warm and comforting tone, had asked more questions, seeking clarification, then asked to see the guest room where Suzie had said she'd spend the night. He'd taken them upstairs, pointed them down the hall and gone into his bedroom.

Alone, he called his mother and his daughter. They arrived within minutes of each other.

It was the two of them who took over from there, his daughter dealing with everything downstairs, his mother sitting on the bed beside him, stroking his hand. And he'd gone to sleep. Just like that. His mother stroking his hand.

The house was quiet when de Cotigny woke. His daughter had gone, but his mother remained.

'I'm so sorry, my darling,' she said, though de Cotigny suspected that she wasn't that sorry. His mother was back in his life again, the way she liked it. And the American, as she sometimes referred to Suzie, was gone for good.

Which was why de Cotigny dressed in his office clothes. To get away from his mother.

'But it's past three. Isn't it too late?' she'd remonstrated. And then, thinking of her plans: 'Are you sure you're up to it?' she'd asked, affecting concern.

'There are things I need to do, Maman,' he told her, making her nod understandingly, approvingly. 'I'll call round later. Say seven?'

Which had sealed it.

'Well, if you're sure, dear . . .' And, pleased that he appeared to be taking it so well, she'd acquiesced, got her coat, left him there.

For an hour or more after she'd gone, de Cotigny wandered through the house, pausing here and there, touching his wife's belongings, picking up photos of her in their heavy silver frames, trying to get some tangible sense of her as though that would somehow replace what was missing.

It was unbearable. Suzie was gone. And his life seemed suddenly empty, without purpose, stretching ahead. Finally, he went through to the study, poured himself a brandy, drew a cigar from the humidor and sat at his desk. Turning to the bookshelves, he selected a disc from his collection, slid it into the CD player and reached for pen and paper.

In the kitchen, sitting at the table with a third glass of cognac and a cigarette, Hortense decided she was just a little tiddly. Pleasantly so. Philosophically so.

The whole thing was shocking, of course . . . and she was so sorry for dear Monsieur de Cotigny . . . But still . . . Life goes on, *n'est-ce pas*? You always have to look at the positive side of things. The bright side. And for Hortense, that meant never having to put up with that lazy, good-for-nothing, spoiled young *torchon* a moment longer.

First of all, it seemed to Hortense, these Americans had no idea how to treat staff. Never a 'please' or a 'thank you', never a moment to yourself without a call from Madame – do this, fetch that. It was good to get the in-house accommodation but there'd been a price to pay. On call twenty-four hours a day, she was, her ladyship no respecter of after-hours and the like. By the time Thursday came round Hortense was always at her wits' end, desperate to get away. Wouldn't dare stay, in case she got hauled in to cook something, clean something, whatever it was Madame fancied.

Hortense was tapping her cigarette against the lip of an ashtray when, somewhere above her, a door slammed shut, which made her jump in her chair, spilling a goodly portion of cognac onto her wrist and the sleeve of her uniform.

Damn police, she thought, wandering around like they owned the place, leaving all the doors wide open.

56

'I didn't think it would take you long to get back to me,' said Clisson grimly, looking up from a pile of paperwork when Jacquot appeared in his office, 'but I didn't anticipate a personal visit.'

'You've lost me,' said Jacquot, taking one of the two chairs set in front of the long oak table that served as Clisson's desk. Making himself comfortable, the first thing he noticed was how cool the room was. On the second floor of a building across the road from police headquarters, Clisson's office might have been on the wrong side of the street to benefit from any direct sunshine, but at least, one block back from the Metro works, the deafening rattle of jackhammers and the steady thump of piledrivers were muted here, the clouds of dust from the earth movers dispersed. Which meant that he was able to keep his windows open, shutters latched at an angle to catch the breeze.

'I left you a message,' continued Clisson, running his fingers through his wiry, ginger thatch. 'Something I thought you'd like to know. Something from Valéry.'

'Pronoprazone?'

Clisson nodded. 'And something else.'

Jacquot's favourite words again. Twice in one day. 'Yes . . .?'

'A splinter.'

'A splinter?'

'Valéry found a splinter. A wood splinter. In Madame de Cotigny's . . .'

Clisson cast around for the right word. For a man who'd seen more than his fair share of broken and abused bodies and recorded the full horror of human violence, Clisson was often surprisingly fastidious when it came to talking about certain things.

'In Madame de Cotigny's . . .?' prompted Jacquot.

'In her . . . vagina,' sighed Clisson.

'Jesus.' Jacquot's head reeled. He'd been thinking a splinter in her finger, her foot – something small but possibly significant, one of Valéry's little observations. Like the salt crystals in Jilly Holford's hair. But this was altogether different.

'It would appear that Madame de Cotigny was not raped. Not in the usual sense. She was . . .' Clisson paused, trying to decide how best to describe, exactly, precisely, the nature of the assault. 'She was . . . bludgeoned. According to Valéry, it looks like penetration was effected with . . . some kind of blunt wooden instrument.'

'Some kind of blunt wooden instrument?' repeated Jacquot.

Clisson spread his hands. 'It's impossible to say exactly what . . . a wooden handle of some description, a truncheon, a kitchen pestle . . .'

'And the other victims?'

Clisson nodded. 'Of course it's too late to re-examine the first two victims – we'd need an exhumation order – and Monel was in the water far too long for any positive confirmation. But it's Valéry's considered opinion that the, uh . . . this method of penetration, the nature of the assault, is certainly consistent with the, uh . . . injuries sustained by the Holford girl. And, so far as he can recall, with the other victims as well.'

'Which explains . . .'

'The lack of semen. Spermicide. Lubricant. Quite so.'

This was clearly progress but Jacquot was uncertain how far it would take them. All it did was confirm that the Waterman was a few *sous* short of a franc. But then, they knew that already.

'What I don't understand—' began Jacquot.

'I know, I know. How come it took a splinter before he realised—'

'Well, you see my point. A blunt wooden instrument . . .'

'All he's prepared to say is that the condition of the victims' vaginas initially suggested intercourse, penetration, albeit of a, uh . . . of an aggressive nature. "A violent, abusive penetration" was the way he described it to me. Let's say, possibly, a man of some, uh . . . proportion. It's perfectly feasible, I'm sure you'd agree. However, it

257

wasn't until Valéry found the splinter that he, uh . . . was able to revise that initial assumption.'

Jacquot got up from his chair.

'Thanks, Clisson. I don't know where this takes us, but it's certainly something.'

'My pleasure. Any time. We're here to help.'

'And on this one we're going to need all the help we can get,' continued Jacquot, reaching into his pocket and pulling out his ID card. 'Which reminds me . . .'

'Yes?' said Clisson, looking at Jacquot suspiciously.

'The reason I came by,' said Jacquot, holding the card between his fingers as he laid it on Clisson's desk. 'A favour.'

Clisson peered at the card.

'I'm looking for a match. Vicki Monel's apartment.'

'But it's Friday afternoon,' replied Clisson.

'I appreciate it,' said Jacquot.

57

If Jacquot was quietly pleased with developments – Raissac's slip of the tongue, getting his fingerprints on the ID card, the confirmation of pronoprazone in the latest victim's blood and Valéry's discovery of a splinter, for whatever that was worth – there was even better news waiting for him when he got back to police HQ from Clisson's office.

The atmosphere in the squad room was electric, a bustle of restrained excitement behind the frosted-glass partitions. He could feel it the moment he stepped through the door.

'We got a match from the flat on Cours Lieutaud,' said Peluze, getting up from his desk and following Jacquot into his office.

'Whose?' asked Jacquot, pulling off his jacket and slumping behind his desk.

Peluze gave him a grin. 'Our friend Carnot. Everywhere – handles, shelves, sink, loo flusher – you name it.'

'Anything else?'

'Charlie called to say he's checked out Sardé's place. Walk-up in Baille. A pit, by the sound of it. But sure looks like he's a peeker. Got an expensive photo habit – Nikon camera, telephoto lens, darkroom. And lots of pictures, mostly naked women at home. Swimming pools, bedroom windows. Long-lens stuff. But he hasn't changed his story. He was staking her out and got disturbed. And Charlie believes him.'

'So do I,' said Jacquot.

'What do you want to do with him?'

'He can go.'

'And Carnot?'

'Find him. Bring him in,' replied Jacquot.

Peluze nodded and turned back to the squad room. As he closed the door behind him, Jacquot's phone rang. It was Gastal.

'I'm in the apartment. Real little love nest.'

'Tell me.'

'Top floor on Paradis. The usual layout. Just a small place with the one bedroom. Under the roof. But nicely done. Music, a few books, magazines. But no address book, diary, correspondence. Some clothes, bedlinen, towels and that's it.'

'Neighbours?'

'There's three other flats in the building and a *pharmacie* on the ground floor. Old woman on the second floor, right below, says she sees her now and again, but said she doesn't live there full-time. Didn't know her name.'

'Callers?'

'She says she sometimes hears voices from the apartment, steps on the stairs, that kind of thing. But she's never seen anyone. Not her business, she says.'

'She say how long Madame de Cotigny's been there?'

'Couple of years. Said she couldn't remember for certain.'

'Any news on the gym? The Renault?'

'I've got some names. Thought I'd sit here and chase them up.'

'Call me when you've got something.'

Jacquot put down the phone. Then picked it up again, and tapped out the harbour master's number.

There was something on his mind, something he wanted to follow up – maybe another piece in the jigsaw, maybe not – and Salette was the man to help him. After the usual pleasantries, he got to the point.

58

S alette had always kept an eye out for Daniel Jacquot, always ready to help. But last thing Friday afternoon and on his way out of the office? That was asking too much, surely? Yet the old harbour master did what Jacquot asked, settling back at his computer keyboard, accessing the information that his godson had requested.

Jean-Marie Salette had known the Jacquot family way back, long before it was a family. Long before Daniel arrived on the scene, or his mother for that matter.

Vincent had been first. Daniel's father. Built like a real *gorille* but with a heart made of butter and a voice like an angel. A real crooner. Should have gone professional was Salette's opinion; he could have made it. Really. Trenet, Rossi, Gabin, he could sing them off the stage any day. In his striped sailor shirt and white ducks, moving round the tables at the old Bateau Bleu off Canebière, you'd see the girls twitch when he reached deep for 'Chagrin d'Amour', or knelt at their tables for 'Romance de Paris' or 'O Corse, Ile d'Amour'. But you suggested it, and he just smiled that smile of his and shrugged. 'For what?' he'd say. 'I got everything I need right here.'

And it was true. For six years, from the day he arrived on the mainland, Vincent played the Vieux Port for all it was worth. The girls who fought over him, you just wouldn't believe. A real one for the ladies. That dark Corsican complexion, the fall of hair, the green eyes and that big, beautiful smile of his. Scores wept themselves to sleep when Vincent Jacquot moved on to pastures new.

Then, out of the blue, this girl turns up. Out of nowhere, living some place over in L'Estaque. Wants to be a painter, Vincent says. Marie-Anne Something, from out of town. A lady – you only had to look at her. Expensive schools. Good family. And that's Vincent – *fini*. Four months later they're married and Daniel's on the way.

Salette had his own boat back then and Vincent, fresh off the island, had signed up as crew, and stayed that way till the end. A good worker and knew the water like he knew the streets of Le Panier, where he and Daniel's mother shacked up together. Top floor, Moulins, next house along from Foraque, the cobbler, where Dan lived right now, above the old shop. Done it up, of course. Different. But the Widow Foraque was still there. Keeping an eye on him, too.

Just like they'd always done, she and Salette and a few others, since the time it all went wrong.

First there's Vincent out on the boat and some freak summer storm catches them, the only day Salette ever missed. Never came home. Then it's the bomb. Blows the mother to Kingdom Come. Both parents gone in as many months, with the boy Daniel just in his teens, starting to run a bit wild but a good lad. Sharp like his father, tough and determined, but gentle too, like his mother. And suddenly left on his own, bundled off to the orphanage at Borel as quick as that. Gone, never a word. According to the authorities, the boy's grandfather turned up and took him on. Out Avignon way. Aix-en-Provence, wasn't it? A new life. A better life. But Marseilles was in the boy's blood, sure enough, and it wasn't long before he was back where he belonged.

Just look at him now, thought Salette, printing out the information he'd been asked for, then closing down the computer with a sigh of pleasure. A cop. Who'd have thought it? But, of course, being a Jacquot he'd turned out the best *flic* on the beat.

As promised, Salette reached for the phone and put a call through to police headquarters. While the number connected, he pulled off his glasses and sorted through the printout, humming those old songs.

When Jacquot answered he didn't waste any time.

59

'Putting an old man to work like that. And at six o'clock on a Friday evening, too.'

Jacquot listened to the patter. It was Salette reporting back.

'So you want to hear it?' came the harbour master's voice, gruff and put-upon.

'That would be a help,' replied Jacquot. 'If you've still got the energy.' On the other end of the line, he heard the rustling of paper and the old man clearing his throat.

'Basquet Maritime's fleet consists of six ships,' began Salette. 'Mostly transatlantic, West Africa coast, all good routes and profitable if the passage is fast . . . Current status. One in port for refit. Three en route for Venezuela and two coming home.'

'And they are?' asked Jacquot. 'The ones coming home?'

'*Balon*, just left Cape Town, should be back by the end of the month,' replied Salette.

'And the other?'

'Vessel called *Aurore*. Out of Venezuela. Bound for Accra and home. Expected this weekend.'

'What's she carrying?'

Jacquot could hear Salette leafing through his notes. At last the place was found, the voice came through. 'Mixed cargo of rubber, kaolin and sugar cane from its three South American ports of call. Offloaded the sugar in Accra and took on timber, cocoa and ground-nuts.'

'Whose cargo?' asked Jacquot.

'Half a dozen importers,' replied Salette. 'Basquet Maritime's just the shipper.'

'Names?'

Salette read through the list.

'Thanks,' said Jacquot, and before Salette had a chance to make further complaints at such inhuman treatment on a Friday evening, he'd hung up. Which was when Chevin swung into the room.

'You'll never b-b-believe it.'

'What?' said Jacquot.

'Luc just called in. De Cotigny. He's shot himself.'

'You're kidding me.'

'Not me, boss. And he left a n-n-note.'

It was a replay of the morning save for the position of the bodies. Madame de Cotigny propped up in an inflatable chair in the swimming pool. Her husband flung back by the force of a single bullet, awkwardly folded between his upturned chair and the bookshelves behind his desk, his eyes wide, as though surprised at seeing his knees so close. The gun he'd used lay beside him on the floor, the burn-ringed hole the bullet had made an inch below his hairline no bigger than an old, dark *sou*.

Luc Dutoit had been waiting for Jacquot on the steps of the house and led him through to the study. Dutoit lived out past Prado and was on his way home, he told Jacquot, when he heard the emergency call go through Dispatch. He'd recognised the address and got there within minutes.

'The maid, Hortense Lagarde, said she heard the shot, thought it was a door slamming, so came upstairs,' reported Dutoit, nodding towards the sound of her wailing in the kitchen.

'Was this how she found him?' asked Jacquot, squatting down beside the body.

'Exactly. Nothing's been moved,' replied Dutoit, perching on the edge of the desk.

'And the note?' asked Jacquot, getting to his feet.

'There, boss. On the desk.'

Jacquot turned and reached for it, a single sheet of thick cream vellum lying between an empty brandy glass and a half-smoked Cohiba resting in a crystal ashtray. Two lines. Signed and dated. A spatter of blood was traced across it like a flick of red ink but the words were easily legible.

In case you were wondering, the note read, *I did not kill my wife*.

Jacquot replaced the note and looked round. On a shelf behind the desk, the lights of a CD player glittered a luminous green. Jacquot leaned across the body and pushed the *play* button. Seconds later a Baroque adagio rose mournfully from a pair of speakers set among the books on a higher shelf.

Jacquot and Dutoit looked at each other. The cognac, the cigar, the music – it wasn't difficult to imagine the scene that had played out here an hour earlier.

'It looks like he didn't want her to see,' said Dutoit, drawing Jacquot's attention to half a dozen silver-framed photos around the room – on the desk, on the bookshelves, on a small occasional table behind the door – all of them laid face down.

Jacquot picked up the nearest, a black and white snap of de Cotigny's wife leaning on ski poles, a line of peaks behind her, then put it back as he had found it.

'Thanks, Luc. I'd say we're done here.'

'You want me to hang around? Till the medics get here?'

Jacquot cocked an ear, shook his head. 'Sounds like they've just arrived.'

On his way back to town, Jacquot phoned Peluze to see how they were getting on with Carnot, whether they'd brought him in, whether he should call by?

'Nothing yet,' reported Peluze. 'He's not at his apartment so we're checking known haunts. I'll call as soon as we've got him.'

Jacquot hung up but seconds later his mobile bleeped again.

It was Jouannay, working late.

'The print you gave Clisson? On your ID card?' Clisson's assistant began.

'Yes. And? Any matches with the apartment on Cours Lieutaud?'

'Not a thing,' replied Jouannay. 'Matched against thirty-seven retrieves but not a glimmer. Either the guy wore gloves or he was never there.'

'Thanks,' said Jacquot, running a light and turning for home.

It was time for something to eat and an early night.

60

Despite his jet lag – and his general weariness after three months' courtroom duty in Palm Beach – Max Benedict had not been idle. In the last two days at La Ferme Magny he'd unpacked more than a dozen cases – paintings, rugs, linen, his books – filled the kitchen cupboards with china and the fridge with supplies from the shops in nearby Rocsabin and St Bédard-le-Chapitre, stocked the wine racks in the cellar beneath his terrace and, that very afternoon, bought himself a flat-screen TV and Sony hi-fi at a warehouse on the outskirts of Cavaillon. It was only when he returned home that he discovered, with a jolt of irritation, that neither the TV nor the hi-fi came with plugs. Which had meant another trip to Rocsabin. Finally he managed to get them connected. But since he had no idea which packing case contained his collection of CDs, he tuned the radio for a classics station, poured himself a glass of champagne and settled himself on the terrace to watch the sun slide behind the distant slopes.

Twenty minutes later, at the end of one of his favourite arias, eyes closed, Benedict's peace was interrupted by the babble of a news bulletin. The usual things – war, famine, corporate greed, political wrangling. Benedict let it all wash over him, unwilling to get up from his lounger and find another station, knowing that the music would start again soon enough.

But then the newscaster's voice dipped in a way that caught Benedict's attention. Some final piece of significant news had yet to be

266

imparted. Something domestic. Something that mattered. A double tragedy was the handle here, a murder and suicide in Marseilles.

And then, something that made Benedict frown – a name he recognised. But before he could properly access the information, the bulletin was over and the music began again.

Benedict hauled himself from the lounger, walked through to the salon and switched on the TV. Longer than the radio bulletin, the TV news was still going over the latest peace accords in the Middle East. Benedict went through to the kitchen, refilled his glass, then returned to the salon.

When the story came, it occupied Benedict's full attention, the pictures flitting across the screen. When it finished, tiredness and the last of his jet lag suddenly kicked in and he felt drained. He turned off the TV and radio, closed the terrace doors and went up to bed, the sheets crisp, cool and welcoming.

At three o'clock the next morning, nine in the evening New York time, Benedict sat up in his bed, reached for the phone and punched in a number.

When the connection was made, he got straight to the point.

'Tina? It's Max. Listen . . .'

61

Tense. Relax.
Tense. Relax.
Two thousand nine hundred and ninety-seven . . .
. . . ninety-eight . . .
. . . ninety-nine . . .
Three thousand.

Coupchoux let his fingers ease off the steering wheel, felt the muscles in his arms sing. A gentle, pleasurable ache. A curious weightlessness to his arms as he let go the wheel and wiped the palms of his hands on his jeans. He clenched his hands into fists, felt the whitened fingers creak, the blood flow. He straightened his back and flexed his shoulders, stretching the tightness away.

Three thousand. Not bad. He wondered what he should do next: calves, diaphragm or lower back? He had a dozen or more exercises he could do behind the wheel of a car to keep himself occupied – and fit. But Coupchoux also knew that he had to be careful. One time, he'd done too many reps on his upper thighs and when he got out of the car he'd nearly crumpled to the sidewalk. It must have looked funny to anyone passing by, his stumbling around like that, but it made him cross. He'd left it too late to loosen up, and he'd nearly got the hit wrong. It was like he was using someone else's body, his reactions a couple of beats behind his brain. It had been a close call and no mistake.

Lifting his watch to the light, Coupchoux checked the time.

Eleven-twenty. He'd been sitting there an hour now, in a line of parked cars along Tamasin. He'd wait another hour if he had to. And an hour after that. However long it took. Raissac had made it clear that the job had to be done tonight, and Coupchoux knew well enough not to disappoint his boss.

Fifty metres ahead, on the other side of the road, was the back entrance to Restaurant Molineux, an arched opening between a travel agent and a *patisserie*, a block of shadow between the lit shop windows. Raissac's fixer, Carnot, had shown him the place Wednesday evening. They'd sat there a half-hour, watched three of the staff come out onto the street, when Carnot nudged him and nodded forward.

A fourth figure, the hit. Pausing cautiously in the shadows like an animal sniffing for predators, he'd looked one way and then the other before stepping out into the light. According to Carnot he lived six blocks along in a basement room off République. He didn't have a car or a bike, and he never took the bus. They'd watched him pass, head down, hands in pockets, keeping close to the shop windows across the street. Fast, steady, anonymous. Coupchoux had turned the wing mirror, adjusted the rear-view mirror. Take your eyes off him a second and he'd be gone.

Coupchoux was the same. Coupchoux could lose you. It was one of his many talents. Sliding through the city, day or night, unseen, silent as a cat. Do the job and disappear, like he'd never been there. He practised, of course. Like the flexing. All the time. You had to keep the edge sharp. Like this afternoon, after dropping those kids back in town, he'd parked the car and paid a call on Galerie Samaritaine. Just coasting – fingers tingling – and saw his chance. A lighter on a velvet presentation square, while the customer pointed out another model and the assistant reached down for it. They'd never even known he was standing there, waiting his turn. They could have been working it together, the customer and him, it was so seamless. Perfect timing. A team hit.

But Coupchoux never worked doubles. Coupchoux only worked by himself. It was a lesson he'd learnt early on.

Then, in the very same shop, not thirty seconds later, with the lighter feeling heavy in his pocket, an open bag, up ahead, swinging on an arm. A tricky steal but too tempting to resist. The gentle acceleration, brushing alongside in the crowd of shoppers at the door, fingers like darts, a single, fleeting dip. And into his own pocket a long, leather purse stuffed with the woman's cards and cash. Later he'd slid out the notes and dumped the purse. Which was a pity. He'd like to have kept it, for the leather had her scent on it, warm, lingering, intimate. But the cash made up for it, a little under three thousand francs. For five seconds' initiative. Now that's what he called work.

Coupchoux could have stolen the guitar strings too, neatly coiled in their see-through packet on a rack in Sacha's Music Store. But he didn't. He paid cash, waited for the assistant to bag it, give him his change, and then left. Never once looked up, never gave the assistant a glance at his face. Practice, that's what it was. Every day, in every way, you got better and better.

Of course, he couldn't help but feel guilty. He always did. Thieving like that, and the killing. But Coupchoux knew how to ease the pain, and five minutes after leaving Sacha's he slid through the felt-backed doors of the Basilica Grandes Carmes. Not as clean and lean as the church in Cassis, and not as dark as the Réformés at the top of Canebière, but it was still a peaceful, comforting space. Dipping his fingers into the holy water, he made his way down the aisle and took a seat. It was too early for confession, so he knelt forward in the pew and began his litany of prayers, pleadings and promises.

Afterwards he'd gone home to prepare, and at a little after ten he'd found this parking space on Tamasin, one of the guitar strings he'd bought at Sacha's lying on the passenger seat beside him.

It had taken him an hour to get it right, winding the tape around the ends of the nickel-wrapped E-string, doubling them over, thickening them up, then reversing the tape for a grip. Satisfied with his handiwork, he'd gone through the motions in front of the mirror, stripped to his shorts, watching his pectorals flicker beneath the skin as he raised the wire, crossed his hands, right over left, and looped. Slow at first, then speeding up as he got the rhythm. Fifty, sixty times, working the stiffness out of the springy coil, conditioning his limbs to the movement.

For the job he had in mind, the crossover was essential. If you looped the wire, you could pull straight out, left and right, keep the victim on his feet. If you didn't do the loop, you had to pull back and down, which meant you could lose your balance, your hit could twist free, turn, come at you. But looped, there was nothing they could do. Fifteen seconds and they go limp. Thirty and it's over. But only if you used the E-string, Coupchoux had learnt, the thick one. The other strings were just too fine, with a tendency to cut, and that could be messy.

The lights in the shop window beside him blinked out, but Coupchoux didn't take his eyes off the entrance to Molineux's backyard. Five of the crew had already come out, but they'd all turned left. Doisneau would go right, up rue Tamasin, heading back home. Like he always did.

He should have known better, thought Coupchoux. Break the pattern. Pattern was never good.

And then, there he was, stepping out from the archway and turning, head down, hands in pockets. Almost a lope. Passing Coupchoux and making for the steps down to République, where lights were few and doorways deep and shadowy.

Reaching for the wire, Coupchoux wrapped it around his fist and slid out of the car, his eyes never once leaving his quarry.

62

Saturday

Jacquot had slept in the same sheets all week. Boni might have taken everything that belonged to her, but she'd left her scent, intoxicatingly close on the pillow. It was the first thing that Jacquot recognised when he woke on Saturday morning, staying still a while, breathing her in. Like he'd done at exactly the same time the week before, her head right there beside him. The spread of hair, the sprinkle of freckles between her shoulder blades, the sheet draped over a hip. The soft rise of her breath.

That was the moment when Jacquot decided he'd try his best to make it up. He didn't think it was for him to do, but that wasn't the point. She was unhappy about something and he needed to know what. Getting dressed, quietly so as not to disturb her, he'd made up his mind to give it one more go, tomorrow, when he got back from his trip to Salon-le-Vitry. They'd talk it through. Sort things out. It would be all right, she'd see.

Now, all that was left was the smell of her, and a dull, deep pain that had squeezed at his heart all week. Always right there if he let his defences drop for a moment. Like Nocibé's shop window on St-Ferréol. Something stupid like that was all it took.

Jacquot rolled over and tried to get comfortable again, away from the scent of her. But it drifted back. Sinuous, sweet, breathing life into memory, begging for attention.

272

There was only one thing for it. Naked, Jacquot slid from the bed and pulled the pillows from their slips, hauled off the sheets until the mattress was bared, its buttoned depressions wadded with lint. Then he scooped up the pile and took it through to the kitchen, dropping it in a heap in front of an already loaded washing machine. He was contemplating the dubious pleasures of emptying it, hanging up the clothes to dry somewhere, to make room for the bedlinen, when the phone rang.

It was Isabelle Cassier.

'We've got another floater,' she told him. 'Man. Out at Radoub Basin.'

63

M ax Benedict snapped shut his mobile phone and slid it into his breast pocket.

Since leaving La Ferme Magny, negotiating the turns down to Chant-le-Neuf with only one hand on the wheel, he'd made three calls. One to a sleepy security manager at JFK in New York, one to the reservations manager at the Crillon in Paris, and the third to his contact at the Nice-Passédat, Marseilles's most illustrious hotel – and certainly the most expensive – set on its own headland off the city's coastal Corniche.

Yes, he was told by his sources, the Delahayes' Gulfstream had departed JFK; yes, they had spent last night at their favourite hotel in Paris; yes, they were expected at the Nice-Passédat that very morning; and yes, of course . . . Monsieur Benedict's usual room? No problem.

It hadn't taken Benedict long to realise that the Marseilles double header – a murder and a suicide in the same family in a single day – was his beat. He'd realised that before the TV newscast was over. But he'd kept his cool, surrendered to the last traces of jet lag seeping into his bones and had gone upstairs to sleep on it.

Sometime in the early hours, Benedict had woken from a deep sleep, called his editor in New York, and run her through the story. Murder and suicide, he told her. An illustrious French family, socially connected, political. And a wealthy American family, big-time New Yorkers, with much the same credentials.

'Absolutely your territory, Max,' she'd said, and the deal was done. Five thousand words, 'Postcard from the Riviera' kind of thing. She'd hold three pages for the next issue if he could make a Friday deadline. He told her he could and signed off with a punch in the air. A whole week. It was a shoo-in. He'd have it wrapped by Monday and the five thousand words e-mailed to New York just in time for the Friday deadline.

Sure he was tired, sure he wanted a rest after Palm Beach. But this story was irresistible. Equally irresistible was the notion of charging his flights, his jeep rental, his fuel, his accommodation at the Nice-Passédat and a *bouillabaisse gourmande* at Molineux's to the magazine. As to the fee, that would neatly cover the expenses he'd incurred by having the builder, Armande Vaison, look after the property during his latest, extended absence.

As he skirted Cavaillon and followed signs for the autoroute, Benedict went over the facts that he'd picked up from the TV broadcast the night before. Madame Suzanne Delahaye de Cotigny, only daughter of Leonard and Daphne Delahaye of Park Avenue, Manhattan, and Bedford Hills, Connecticut, had been found dead by her gardener. She had drowned. She had also been murdered – how else could she have been found propped up in an inflatable pool chair? A grisly detail that Benedict just knew he would use to intro the story, already forming in his head. And then, not twelve hours after her body was discovered, the husband, Hubert, son of the late Auguste de Cotigny and his wife Murielle, went to his study, put a gun to his head and pulled the trigger.

The question that needed answering was this: did de Cotigny kill his wife, or did someone else? And why?

For Max Benedict, it would be fun finding out.

As it happened, Benedict knew both families professionally. The de Cotignys were old-school aristocrats, Hubert's late father a war hero, senator and presidential confidant who'd come to prominence in the summer of 1968 when, from his seat in the Senate, he had railed against the student uprisings in Paris and given the French police every encouragement to be brutal. Water cannon, baton charges, give no quarter had been his remit. Which had proved the spark for even greater enthusiasm at the barricades. But his closeness to de Gaulle (the general and he had fought side by side during the Saar Offensive and at Sedan) had protected him in the political fall-out that followed, the satirical newspaper *Le Canard Enchainé* bold enough to suggest on its front page that the president wouldn't get out of bed unless his old friend was standing there with his slippers and dressing gown.

Which was how Benedict had first come to hear of old man de Cotigny, when he was sent to France on his first foreign assignment to cover de Gaulle's state funeral for the *New York Times*. Through their Paris correspondent, he'd secured an interview with de Cotigny, the only non-family member at the great man's deathbed. Benedict had found him an insufferable bore and snob, while the grieving senator, done out in starched collar and black tailcoat, had noted Benedict's long hair, jeans and open shirt with a cool, disapproving look. The interview had not gone well.

As for the Delahayes, they were closer to home. Benedict had written about Mister Delahaye during his spat with Winston Lowell over a disputed plot of land on the Hamptons; and again when Delahaye was finally voted chief executive of Wall Street's Gravyll-Windham; and, of course, when his daughter, Suzanne, was arrested for possession of cocaine after the home of a transvestite drug dealer was raided by police.

In the Hamptons debacle it wasn't difficult taking the Delahaye side, when you knew what a twister Winston Lowell could be; and tipping his editorial in Delahaye's favour during the battle for Gravyll-Windham had been more about supporting the underdog than approving his corporate ethics – if GW's directors hadn't behaved so disgracefully in trying to keep Delahaye off the board, it would have been a more difficult tale to tell. As for the daughter's drugs bust, it was the story of stories, and there had been no other way he could spin it. Anyway, it was widely acknowledged that the girl had had it coming.

Suzanne Delahaye, younger of two children, had led a charmed life. Her mother was independently wealthy, her father a self-made man, and her brother Gus married by the time she hit her teens and head of his own brokerage firm by the time she was twenty. Spoilt and wilful, quietly sacked from The Mercy School in Manhattan and sent down from Vassar at the end of her first semester, she'd provided grateful gossip columnists with yards of salacious copy, not an inch of which came anywhere close to the spirit of the truth.

More than the drugs, the drink and the shoplifting, more than the tantrums in restaurants and nightclubs and a wildly acrimonious divorce from her first husband, it was Suzie's questionable sexual orientation and dubious low-life liaisons that raised eyebrows among those in the know. People like Benedict, whose diary column in one of New York's hottest society magazines often required the closest legal scrutiny prior to publication.

It was in that same column that Benedict broke the news of Suzie Delahaye's engagement to Hubert de Cotigny, following a chance summer meeting in Martha's Vineyard. But despite all the predictions of doom, the marriage seemed to have worked. For the last five years, living in France with her new but not so young husband, not a word had been heard of the wayward young lady. Until now.

Up ahead, Benedict saw the toll-booth outside Salon swing into view across the autoroute. He slowed the jeep, took a ticket and, when the barrier was raised, sped on towards Marseilles, a little less than an hour south.

And beckoning.

64

The Radoub Basin, in the shadow of the autoroute, was one of the smaller docking bays beyond the Quai d'Arenc, with enough berths and turning space for six large motor cruisers awaiting service or refit in the Radoub works. That Saturday morning the cranes threw long, fretted shadows across the cobbled quays while a stiff breeze off the sea feathered silent spray over the breakwaters and kept the roar of the autoroute to a background hum.

Isabelle Cassier was waiting for Jacquot just inside the main gate. She was wearing a black leather jacket over belted jeans and a blue T-shirt which rippled with the breeze, her bob of black hair flicking around her cheeks. Tucking the ends behind her ears, she briefed him on the circumstances surrounding the discovery: the crane operator who'd spotted the body floating in an empty berth and raised the alarm; the two mechanics who'd hoisted the body out of the water; and the crane operator's boss who'd phoned the police. As for Isabelle, she just happened to be in the squad room before anyone else and took the call.

The body had been laid out on the cobbles and covered by a tarp. Neither Clisson nor Jouannay had yet made an appearance and it was a small and sombre group that stood around the crumpled, feature-less shape, not quite knowing what to do with themselves, huddled, smoking, whispering to each other.

'It's not like the others,' Isabelle told him, as the four men around the body stepped aside to make room for them.

'You mean it's a man?' asked Jacquot.

'Fully dressed, not naked. And garrotted. Very professional job, by the look of it.'

Jacquot knelt, and reached for the tarpaulin.

The face hit him like a thunderbolt. The punctured cheeks, the hook nose and tented eyebrows, a jagged line of browning teeth revealed by the snarling lips, eyes already glazed from exposure to the water.

It was the fifth body that Jacquot had seen in the last eight days. Apart from Hubert de Cotigny it was the only face he recognised.

Doisneau.

Tipping up the chin, Jacquot saw the red wire-burn across the throat, a scarlet necklace trimmed with an edging of black that disappeared into Doisneau's collar. Isabelle had been right. A very professional job. A crossover loop, had to be. The skin only broken below the Adam's apple, more like a graze than a cut. On the right-hand side of the throat, close to the ear, the red line was interrupted by a large yellowing bruise.

Isabelle, kneeling beside Jacquot, lifted Doisneau's right hand and opened the palm. Traced along the tops of his fingers was the same red line that stretched across his throat.

'It looks like he managed to get his fingers up before the wire went tight,' said Isabelle. 'But that's all.'

Jacquot looked at the fingers Isabelle held in her hand and, from somewhere far back in the past, he remembered those same long fingers, the dirty nails, expertly working a palmful of tobacco with a crumbling nub of Moroccan hash that the *Chats* had got hold of, rolling the mix in a cigarette paper, licking it down and lighting up. 'Here, Danny, try this . . .' he'd said.

Jacquot dropped the tarp over the corpse's face and stood up, took a short, sharp breath of salt air and looked around. An empty, desolate, weekend landscape. The cranes, the workshops, the empty offices of La Joliette, oily black cobbles scabbed with tarmac, the pillared flyover beyond the gates and, far above them, a scatter of clouds so high they looked like they could pass behind the sun.

He turned to Isabelle.

'His name is Paul Doisneau. You'll find all you need in Records.'

And with that, Jacquot turned on his heel and walked back to his car, stepping on his shadow as it flickered ahead of him across the cobbles, feeling a strange mixture of anger, guilt . . . and not a little excitement.

65

They were waiting for him when he got back to his apartment building. Two of them, getting out of a grey Peugeot as he paid off his cab, the big one with a buzz-cut and rough-looking five o'clock shadow, his companion smaller, older, rolling his shoulders as though to loosen a stiffness, tugging his cuffs, the pair of them buttoning their jackets, coming towards him. The car was unmarked, the two men wore no uniform, but Carnot knew who they were.

With twenty metres between them, and closing, Carnot felt a sudden, burning instinct to turn and run. So he did.

Before the cops had registered Carnot's reaction, a handful of coins were spinning on the sidewalk, the cabbie had started swearing and the twenty metres between them had become thirty and rising. Pumping his arms, his lips tight, head back, Carnot sprinted for the corner, looking ahead for a break in the morning traffic. When it came – or as near to a break as you'd get on a Saturday morning in Belsunce – he leapt into the road and wove between the cars, pirouetting like a bullfighter around boots, bumpers and bonnets, oblivious to the hoots of car horns and the squeals of brakes.

He didn't look back so he didn't see the two men split up. It wouldn't have mattered if he had. Carnot knew where he was going, knew that he could shake them off. They might be cops but he knew the streets and alleyways around this city as well as he knew the face he looked at every morning in the mirror.

The day before the cops had caught him napping – no chance of escape. But his alibi was preparing breakfast and he'd sent them packing. Now they were back and that wasn't good news. Not today. Not this weekend. This weekend was booked and there was no way he could afford to spend a few idle hours in an interview room on rue de l'Evêché.

As Carnot ran, his mind raced with his feet. He was certain he knew what they wanted. Vicki again. They were closing in on him, he was sure of it. And all because of that loudmouth Vrech. He'd known straight away that it was the tattooist who'd given the cops their lead. The bones in the Dutchman's fingers would heal in due course, but he'd have to find someplace else to put his name, the two-by-four-inch rectangle of tattooed skin neatly razored from his scalp and bandaged round his broken fingers. All of which would teach the man a useful lesson.

But then, as he ran, Carnot considered another possibility. It might be a long shot, but maybe it had something to do with the woman in the pool. De Cotigny's wife. It had been all over TV the evening before. Maybe de Cotigny suspected that his wife's death was tied in with the blackmail, a little persuasion to keep his mind on the job of passing the development permissions? And maybe he'd said something to the police? Given them a description before he'd gone and shot himself.

Carnot gritted his teeth, sucked in a lungful of air and ran on. De Cotigny dead. Who'd have believed it? Now they'd have to find someone else to put the screws on, someone else to set up. Because Carnot knew that another pair of buttocks in the planning chief's chair wouldn't deter Raissac when he had his mind set on something.

At Canebière, Carnot dared a glance behind him, saw nothing, then caught a friendly light and sprinted across the road. Thirty metres further on, he took a right into rue des Feuillants, and right again into the Capucins market where, for the first time, he allowed his pace to slacken. Jostling his way through the early-morning market crowds, using his shoulder and elbow to clear a path, he glanced back again but could see no disturbance in the flow of shoppers behind him. He had to be fifty metres clear, maybe more, he estimated. Enough to make his move and lose them.

And Capucins, he knew, was the place to do it. Although the throng of shoppers and market stalls slowed him down, this narrow passageway provided a means of escape he'd used more times than he could remember. Halfway down, he ducked to the left between a fish stall and a display of wrinkled dates and pink pomegranates and into a covered alleyway that doubled back onto rue du Musée. The opening was so narrow that his pursuers would pass right by without seeing it. Another five minutes and he'd be clear.

His only problem now, he realised, turning out of Musée and heading up to the Boulevard Garibaldi, was that with the cops after him, he'd have to stay clear of the apartment. And then he remembered Sylviane. Only four blocks away. He could hole up there. Perfect.

Loping down Garibaldi, Carnot took another look behind him. Nothing. He'd shaken them. He slowed his pace and stopped at a newsagent's kiosk on the corner of Mocquet, checking through the racks of magazines, glancing up and down the street while he caught his breath and wiped the sweat from his forehead.

He was about to stroll off when he felt the barrel of a gun press against the ledge of bone behind his ear, and heard a gravelly voice whisper in his ear:

'I know these streets too, Monsieur.'

66

It was Gus Delahaye, Suzie's brother, that Benedict saw first, coming down to specify room numbers for the luggage, a stack of matching Vuitton cases and trunks which, for the last few minutes, had been piling up in the foyer of the Nice-Passédat. A nod of understanding from the concierge and a clipped wad of bills appeared from Delahaye's trouser pocket, the notes peeled off and pressed into the man's hand with fluid ease.

Gus Delahaye did a lot of that, reflected Benedict as he sipped his drink and watched the performance. Never the parents, he'd been told. Always the brother. The Wall Street broker, the son and heir. Usually to buy silence, kill a story; there were men, Benedict knew, who were paid not to write about the Delahayes. Now there was a profession worth having.

Having dealt with the luggage and the concierge, Gus Delahaye came through into the bar, ordered himself a drink and stepped out onto the terrace where Benedict was sitting, shading his eyes from the sun-glare off the sea. He was short and heavy-shouldered, with trimmed black hair and a pasty complexion. Almost as soon as he'd settled himself at a table, the barman was at his side, dispensing his order: a tumbler of caramel-coloured bourbon laid out on a paper coaster, a silver jug of iced water and a plate of tapenade toasts, the same type of toasts that Benedict had received with his own drink and promptly dispatched.

The two men were no more than thirty feet apart, their rooms even closer. According to his man behind the front desk, Benedict had established that the Delahayes had arrived that morning, only minutes before him, the parents billeted on the second floor at the front, looking out towards the Frioul Islands, their son on the third floor, at the side, next to his room, facing the Corniche J.F. Kennedy.

Benedict wondered if Gus Delahaye would recognise him, here on the terrace, or in the lift, or passing one another in reception or in the corridor outside their rooms. They'd never met but the stories Benedict wrote were always accompanied by a byline photo. It wouldn't have been the first time that someone had recognised Benedict's trade-mark half-tortoiseshells, and shaved, sun-freckled head.

Across the terrace Gus Delahaye caught Benedict's eye and nodded, cordially, one guest to another. Benedict was tempted to say something, but held back. Better by far to observe and record the small diminishings of grief – the stoop of a shoulder, the wipe of an eye, the whole sad, stately procession of it – than risk all access by dropping his cover with an ill-judged remark. And anyway, he'd already decided that this was not a dialogue story. There was nothing the Delahayes would know or could say that he wouldn't be able to find out for himself. Enough for them to be there, silent, unsuspecting players in his stagecraft.

It would be the same with Madame de Cotigny, the grand, grieving matriarch. Benedict's man at the front desk had told him where the old lady lived and he would station himself there, in a bar or a café, to observe and record. All the bustling comings and goings, the black tulle, the flowers, the fluttering veils that would feature through the next few days.

But in all of this there was one person that Benedict did want to see, someone he did want to talk to. The man he'd read about in the newspapers. The man in charge of the investigation. Chief Inspector Daniel Jacquot.

Jacquot. Number Six shirt. The man who'd scored that winning try against the English. Benedict had done his homework. The man was a legend. And a policeman. The copy near wrote itself.

Benedict finished his drink, licked the tip of his finger to pick up the last crumbs of tapenade toast and called for the check. He signed with a flourish, nodded to Delahaye and headed for his room.

He'd made contact, a first sighting. The game had begun.

67

Raissac watched the TV coverage in his dressing gown. From his bed, from his breakfast table, and from the ottoman in his sitting room. Flicking on the TV in every room he entered. Missing nothing. National and local. Aerial shots from a helicopter hovering over de Cotigny's tutored lawns, terraces and pool; footage of the ambulance turning out of de Cotigny's gates; reporters speaking to camera with de Cotigny's home visible through the trees behind them.

With a grim expression, Raissac watched it all.

Everywhere dismay and disbelief – stunned responses from friends and neighbours, official statements from the steps of the Préfecture and, every few minutes, the victims' photos flashed onto the screen. Hubert and Suzanne de Cotigny. Suicide and murder. De Cotigny with his brisk, old-fashioned haircut and just-off-centre parting, dressed in tailcoat and sash at the opening of Aqua-Cité; his wife Suzanne, elegantly coiffed, in elbow-length gloves and haute couture at the opera.

What an extraordinary couple, thought Raissac; so utterly unalike. And it wasn't just their different styles – the outfits, the hair – or even the difference in age, he decided. The husband, a chill, humourless figure who looked like his childhood hadn't been much fun, something concealed and repressed about him – tight and coiled, with a smile he must have had to search for. And then the wife, firm and fresh, skin the colour of young cognac, up for anything and looking for trouble, with a smile to launch a fleet of ships. How on earth had they ever got that one together? If he hadn't known better, Raissac would have said Money. Or Position. Some kind of Advantage. One of those things that come with a capital letter. Like Sex. Which was why Raissac did know better, and had the film to prove it.

Except the film wouldn't do him any good now. Difficult to blackmail the dead.

So now he'd have to start all over again; have Carnot sniff out someone new. Raissac went through the likely names for de Cotigny's job – all of them loaded with the usual petty indiscretions, but none of them with anything big. Nothing like a video. Nothing like de Cotigny.

How long, he wondered, would it take to get the ball rolling? Two months? Three? It had taken Carnot and Vicki weeks to set things up with the de Cotignys, throw them the lure, draw them in. And now Raissac was back where he'd started.

As far as he could see, there was only one advantage to be gained from the previous day's body count. With a murder and a suicide to investigate, it didn't look like the *Judiciaire* would be much of a nuisance over the next few days. And with a first consignment of two hundred kilos of cocaine about to land on French soil, that could well prove a blessing.

The last time Raissac had checked with Carnot, Basquet Maritime's *Aurore* was only a day's sail from port. And everything in position – skipper and Customs all squared away. As good as it got. If it all went according to plan, he'd have a new route and a new carrier by the following week.

As for the *calanques* deal, well, Basquet would just have to wait for his *permis*. No other option – take it or leave it. At least they'd have the money. And, if the gods were with them, all it would take to get that *permis* from whoever replaced de Cotigny on the planning committee was a large bundle of that money *sous table*. It would never have worked with de Cotigny, of course, but it sure as hell might with someone else.

Filling his cup with the last of the coffee, Raissac reached for his mobile and put a call through to Carnot. Check up on progress. See how everything was going.

The answering service came on instead, but Raissac didn't leave a message.

It was the same when he tried later.

And later still.

68

Patience had never been one of Carnot's strengths. And today of all days. So much to do, so much to arrange. When the *Aurore* dropped anchor, everything had to be in place. Or Raissac would be all over him. Which was why he'd run.

He'd been at police headquarters over three hours now, sitting in the same chair, pacing the same interview room with its barred and frosted window overlooking rue de l'Evêché. And no one seemed to know what to do with him. Except bring him coffee. Strong and black. So far he'd tossed three empty styrofoam cups into the bin and his foot was beginning to tap.

Of course he knew their game. Make him sweat. Stretch him a little. Once again, he tried to guess what they'd brought him in for. Monel or the de Cotigny woman? It had to be one or the other. The lid was too damned tight for anything else.

Carnot was speculating how much longer they might hold him, whether or not he should start making a fuss, demand a lawyer, when the door opened and a cop came in. Plain clothes like the others, a file in his hand, long hair tied in a ponytail. A big guy. A real *gorille*, and clearly someone you didn't play around with. The same guy, Carnot realised, who'd tapped him on the shoulder outside Club Maras a few days earlier.

Monel. It was Monel he was here for. That's what all this was about. But him making a run for it wouldn't have helped.

The cop pulled out a chair and sat down, put the file on the table and flicked it open.

Carnot didn't move, sprawled back in his seat as though he had all the time in the world, watching the man leaf through the pages, trying to remember what he'd told them before. All he had to do was keep the story level, just keep it straight. That was all he had to do. But he knew he'd have to watch his step.

The cop took a pack of cigarettes from his pocket, offered him one.

Carnot shook his head. Not a word more than was necessary.

The cigarettes and a lighter were left on the table and from his other pocket the cop took a cassette tape, unwrapped it and slid it into the player. He pressed a button and a red light came on.

'My name is Jacquot. Chief Inspector Jacquot. It's a Saturday. May seventeenth. 2:40 p.m.' He turned towards Carnot. 'And you are . . .?'

Carnot said nothing.

The cop looked to his file. 'Jean Alphonse Carnot. Born Tunis. Resident Marseilles for . . .' The cop looked up, gave a little smile. 'Twenty years? Off and on?'

The man held his eye, waiting for an answer.

'If you say so,' replied Carnot. Then, tipping forward, laying his arms on the table, he said: 'Maybe you can tell me what I'm supposed to be doing here?'

Jacquot spread his hands. 'Helping with police inquiries, Monsieur. Of course, if you'd like to have a lawyer present . . .?'

'I don't think there's any need for that, do you?' replied Carnot carelessly.

The policeman shrugged. The kind of shrug that suggested the facts to hand certainly pointed in that direction. But he wasn't going to push the matter, not if Carnot was happy to continue.

'Entirely your decision, Monsieur. But I have to warn you that I am recording this interview and that anything you say . . .'

Carnot held up a hand. 'Please. Let's get to the point. Whatever it is I'm here for.'

The cop gave him a long look.

'Vicki Monel,' he said. 'You knew her. Remember?'

'You know that already.'

'You said, let's see . . .' The cop looked back to his notes, turned a page. 'You said you haven't seen her for more than a year. Maybe two.

That you thought she lived somewhere up round Gare St-Charles. That correct?'

Carnot nodded.

The cop raised his eyebrows, indicated the tape recorder. He needed words.

'Yes. That's right.'

'You said she came from Toulon, Hyères, someplace down the coast?'

'That's right.'

'She live with you when she arrived in town?'

'To start with,' replied Carnot, pushing back cuticles with a finger-nail.

'Where and when did you meet?'

Carnot let out a *pouff* of breath, stopped his manicure. 'Like I said, a couple years back. Some bar.'

'You told us "a party" last time.'

'Party. Bar. It's two years ago, man. Maybe more. I don't remember.'

The cop nodded, shook out a cigarette and lit it. Smoke spiralled upwards into the still air.

'And the nature of your relationship?'

'The usual. Girlfriend.'

The cop nodded.

Carnot became aware that his foot was dancing, fast, to some unheard beat. He tried to stop it. Damn coffee.

'She work for you?'

'Work?'

The cop gave him a patient look. Carnot remembered the pictures on the Internet.

'This and that. Few odd jobs here and there,' replied Carnot with a smirk. Which he knew immediately was a mistake. The smirk.

'You put her on the game? When you finished with her?'

Carnot decided to go along with it. The smirk. He didn't have much of a choice.

He nodded. Then, for the tape: 'Yes.'

'How long?'

'Four, five months.'

'Tell me about her.'

Carnot shrugged. Where to start? 'She was a looker,' he said. 'Stop you in your tracks, man. But she was wild, you know. Unreliable. Say she'd be there and then not show. Hopeless. It wasn't going to work out. Took drugs, you ask me.'

'You supply her?'

Carnot shook his head. 'No, I didn't.'

'So you lost touch?'

'Like I said, she took off.'

'And then you heard she had some place up by Gare St-Charles?'

'That's right.'

'But you never saw her?'

'There was no point.'

'Never saw her around?'

Carnot shook his head. 'No.'

'Well, that's where we have a little problem, Monsieur.'

Carnot rearranged his shoulders, not quite a shrug, but a movement, he hoped, that suggested indifference to the policeman's 'problem'. Which was certainly not the case. He didn't like that word, 'problem', nor the way it was delivered.

'Problem?'

The cop stubbed out the cigarette and stretched back in his chair, hands clasped behind his head.

'You said St-Charles. Where she lived?'

'That's right.'

Carnot spotted what was happening. The cop was backtracking and the trap was closing. He could smell it. And now he knew what it was.

'But you never went there?'

'No. I said.'

'So what about Cours Lieutaud, Monsieur? Which is where she must have moved to after she left St-Charles. Or maybe she never lived in St-Charles?'

Carnot let his face go along with it, but his mind raced. Prints. They had his prints.

'Lieutaud. Of course,' said Carnot. 'Up Noaille way. Yeah. That's right. She moved. I heard.'

'According to the concierge she moved in just about the time you said you split up.'

'Yeah, well . . .' Carnot let it trail away.

'But you didn't go there? Drop by? Say "hi"?'

Carnot went back to his fingernails.

292

'Yeah. Maybe. I don't recall,' he said at last, not looking up.

'Yes or no.'

'Yeah. I remember now.'

'This was what – calling by? Another party?'

'Must have been a party.'

'When?'

'Christmas. Round then.'

'She invite you?'

'No, course not. Just went along with friends. Some party was all they said. Didn't know who was throwing it. Didn't realise it was her place. Just a party, you know?'

'So you were surprised to see her?'

'Yeah. You could say.'

'And how did she react?'

'She was cool.'

'And did she tell you it was her party? Her apartment?'

Carnot nodded, going along with it. He was feeling safe. The prints. The party. He'd got it covered.

The cop gave him a look.

'Yeah. She did.'

'And did you ever go back? Call in after the party? Old times?'

'No. I never did.'

'So Christmas was the only time you were there? The last time you saw her?'

'Or New Year, maybe.'

'But around then?'

Carnot nodded. 'Yeah. Around then.'

There was a knock at the door and a fat guy came in, suit jacket tight under the arms, fingers thick and red as *merguez* sausages. Sweaty skin and short black hair coming to a point on his forehead. He leant over and whispered in the cop's ear. Carnot recognised him, the one leaning against his car the night they questioned him. You could feel the weight of him. Near lifted the car.

The one with the ponytail listened, then nodded.

'Nice one,' he said. 'Leave it to you?'

The fat cop nodded. 'On the case,' he replied and left the room without a look in Carnot's direction. Like he wasn't even there.

'So. Where were we?' asked Jacquot.

Carnot knew he didn't expect an answer.

'Right. Cours Lieutaud. What was it? First. No, second floor.'

'Fourth. Top.'

The cop swung a look at him.

Carnot tried not to flush. He'd blown it, knew it. Trying to be too smart. Just keep it short and sweet.

'Hey! You remember? One visit. Remarkable.' The cop pushed back his chair and stood up, stretched and walked to the window. 'Tell me,' he began, leaning against the window ledge and looking back at Carnot. 'She must have been making some money, that place?'

'Could be. Neat address.'

'You know how? You know how she was making that kind of money?'

'Like I said, it was a party. We didn't talk incomes.' He didn't bother to look at Jacquot, just kept his gaze idling on the empty chair. He felt more comfortable with the cop at the side of him like that.

'So she didn't show you the cupboard?'

Carnot was surprised. They'd found the cupboard. The first time he'd taken Vicki to the apartment, she'd searched the place high and low. Even took her in the bathroom, told her it was there, and she still couldn't see it. The cops must have gone over the place with a fine-tooth comb.

Carnot sniffed, breathed out slowly, knew he was being boxed in. If they had his prints in the apartment, and they'd found the cupboard, then they'd have his prints there too. But if he'd told this cop he'd only gone to the apartment once, for a party, how come he knew about the cupboard? He gave it some thought.

'Cupboard?' he asked, to give himself some space. 'You got me.'

'In the bathroom. Behind the mirrored tiles.'

Carnot shook his head slowly. And then: 'Oh yeah. Yeah. You had to look, right.'

'So she showed you?'

'Nope. Found it myself. I was taking a leak. I was looking for a towel.'

Carnot smiled. Looking for a towel . . . That was a good one. He licked his lips, starting to enjoy himself. They didn't have a thing on him. He was out of there.

Jacquot nodded. 'So what happened to the camera?'

'Camera?'

'The one in the cupboard, Tarantino. The one you and Vicki used for your little films.'

'Like I say, you got me there.'

'You're right. We have.'

The cop smiled and something turned in Carnot's belly. Shit.

'Right now three of my men are picking up a search warrant with your address on it,' Jacquot began. 'And it's my bet they'll find a camera. Maybe not the films, but enough to tie you in to Vicki's death.'

'That's crazy, and you know it,' said Carnot, turning in his seat to give Jacquot an insolent look. 'It's got nothing to do with me. It's like they say in the papers. The Waterman. The one they're all talking about. I read it.'

Jacquot smiled, came back to the table. 'If it was just Vicki,' he said, 'we wouldn't have much to go on. But there's more.'

'What "more"?'

'A shop-assistant. Worked at Galerie Prime. We found her body in the Longchamp fountain. Name of Grez. Joline Grez. Remember her?'

The name meant nothing.

Carnot frowned, shook his head. What was all this?

And then . . .

'She had a picture of you,' the cop continued. 'In her bedroom. The two of you out together – a club, a bar. Real blonde hair. Cut short. Remember?'

After they took Carnot down to a holding cell, Jacquot was in the washroom when the Duty Sergeant, Calliou, came in and took a stall. He was off duty, his jacket undone. Jacquot glanced at his watch. A little after five.

'You get the message from Gastal?' asked Calliou.

Jacquot looked over. 'About the girl? Yeah.' More good news. Gastal had traced the driver of the Renault. A beautician in a local salon. He was going to check her out.

Calliou shook himself off, zipped up and turned from the bowl. 'Funny how it happens like that.'

'How do you mean?'

'The mobile. Your suspect's mobile.'

'Carnot's?' Jacquot shook his head. 'You've lost me.'

Calliou rinsed his hands and wiped the palms down the sides of his tunic. 'The suspect's phone,' he repeated. 'Soon as we get his stuff bagged up, the thing goes off. Three, four times.'

'You answer it?'

Calliou shook his head. 'Not at first. But it never stops, see. So in the end I switch it off. But I get the wrong button and this name pops up. The one who's calling.'

'And?'

'So I tell the Inspector. He said he'd pass it on. Thought it might be useful.'

'Remind me.'

'Some guy called Raissac.'

'Right,' said Jacquot. 'Yeah. Could be.'

69

'You'll love him. Believe me,' said Delphie to her younger sister, as their cab turned off Canebière and started winding through the back end of Belsunce.

'A policeman, for God's sake? A cop?' Claudine exclaimed. 'That's all I need. Nasty habits, suspect friends, unsociable hours; probably has a drink or a drug problem, maybe likes beating up wives or girlfriends . . .'

'Shush,' said her sister. 'You've been reading too many books. This one's nothing like that. A real hunk. I mean, if Sydné likes him he's gotta be special, don't you agree? And I'll tell you something else . . . If I wasn't so happily married I'd . . .'

Delphie paused. She realised the moment she said the words 'happily' and 'married' that she was moving into dangerous territory. Six months earlier Claudine had come home unexpectedly to find her husband in bed with her best friend. In just six months her sister had gone downhill fast. Furious with her husband and furious with herself. It was probably the anger that kept her sane. How she'd managed to complete the work for her exhibition, Delphie had no idea.

Beside her, Claudine continued in a softer voice: 'I just wish you hadn't. Right now, you know . . . It just doesn't feel right.'

Delphie felt for her sister's hand in the darkness of the cab's back seat and squeezed it. Heartache and hard work, she decided, might have blunted Claudine's usual enthusiasm for life but they didn't seem to have hurt her looks. Typical, thought Delphie, who'd long ago accepted that her younger sister had gotten the lion's share of the Eddé family's best features: their father's high and haughty cheekbones, their mother's lustrous auburn curls and *calisson*-shaped eyes, and a smile – when she managed one – as warm and wonderful as it had always been, tempered now with a wan sadness. All she had to do, decided Delphie, was put on a little more weight. She'd lost too much in the past few months and it didn't suit her. She needed fattening up. Some good, wholesome home cooking. That, and a new man in her life.

Up ahead the Gallery Ton-Ton came into view, its picture window a square of white, welcoming light on an otherwise dull street. Their cab slowed and pulled into the kerb.

'Well, you never can tell,' said Delphie brightly, letting go her sister's hand, reaching for the door handle and bustling her out. 'He might even buy a picture.'

But he didn't buy a picture. Because he didn't show.

Which made Delphie, keeping an eye on the door of the gallery, just a little cross. Three days earlier, at Sydné's party, he'd promised her he'd make it for the first-night show. Had sounded really interested. And according to Sydné, whom Delphie called the very next morning to check him out, he was on his own. The ring on his finger, Sydné had told her, didn't mean a thing. Some girlfriend had given it to him and then, clearly not in her right mind, she'd walked out on him. And good riddance, Sydné had remarked tartly.

As for Claudine, her sister's no-show was just that. A relief, if she'd thought about it. Which Claudine hadn't, beyond considering the possible nuisance factor of this unknown man being steered in her direction on the first night of her first-ever exhibition. Right then, there was too much on her mind, too much at stake to waste her energies on some man her sister was trying to set her up with. That first night, it was the gallery, her work, and nothing else.

It began the moment Claudine stepped through the door: the way her paintings looked against the whitewashed brick walls, the order in which they'd been hung, the play of the down-lighting, the title cards, catalogues, the trays of canapés, the wine. So much to feel anxious about, so much to test her nerve. But too late to do anything about it.

And then, suddenly, the way the room started filling, the crush, the noise. All directed at her – friends to greet, a word with her agent, introductions, watching people break off from the hubbub to approach her work, take it in, Claudine straining for their unguarded comments amongst all the hellos, how-are-yous and friendly but clearly fraudulent congratulations. If she was as good as they said she was, she'd be living in St-Rémy-de-Provence by now and not on the outskirts of Cavaillon.

But three hours later, when they closed the gallery and walked down to the Vieux Port for a late supper, Claudine felt reprieved. She'd done it. She'd come through. Her first night had been a success and so elated was she – some really genuinely flattering 'overheards' – that all she wanted to do was talk to her sister about the show, hear all the things she'd missed and badger her agent about the critic from *Côte Sud* who'd just turned up out of nowhere, asked her some questions, scribbled notes on his catalogue. What did he think? What would he say? When would it appear? Questions, questions.

Better still, she'd even sold some paintings. A half-dozen red dots on the title cards. A little over thirty thousand francs. Enough to cover her week's rental of the Ton-Ton, and pretty much her total framing costs.

That night, against all her expectations, Claudine was bursting with delight.

After the last six months, life was just . . . beginning.

70

Ever since the post that morning, the Widow Foraque had been waiting for him.

Now it was past ten and Jacquot still wasn't back. And a Saturday. A soul could work too hard, and that was the truth. Even if there was this Waterman stalking the streets. Disgusting, she called it. Her day, things were different. All this TV and stuff. Wasn't good for you.

Which hadn't stopped her switching on *Celebrity Lives of the Rich and Famous* after she'd had her supper, fed the canaries and poured herself a small *digestif*. Then, halfway through the show, she heard the outside door squeak open and close, the same squeak they'd had when the same front door opened onto her husband's shop.

Madame Foraque reached for the TV remote, turned down the volume and listened out. She heard the familiar footsteps cross the tiled hall, a pause at the old sideboard and the shuffle of mail. She'd put the postcard at the bottom of the pile. The one from Washington. An aerial shot of the White House.

Madame Foraque had spotted it right away, among the bills and circulars in the postman's hand. The vibrant colours beside the cream and the buff. The stiffness of it. The glossy, exotic shine to it. And the foreign stamp. She knew immediately who'd sent it, and was desperate to be rid of the talkative postman so that she could take a proper look. Finally he bid her *adieu* and, closing her front door, she flicked the card over and read the message.

Her first impulse had been to throw it away. It had never arrived;

he'd never know. But just as quickly she changed her mind. He needed to know, had to know that it was over and she was gone. The words on the postcard were clear enough on that score. The man was paining for her and it wasn't right, shouldn't be, oughtta stop. Before it got a hold on him.

All week the Widow Foraque had seen it: the frown, the tight lips, the tired eyes and weary wave of his hand as he made his way upstairs. And an equally weary look, behind the put-on smile, when he went off to work each morning.

Outside her door, the footsteps moved off. Lighter this time, it seemed to Madame Foraque. No heavy tread, but a brisk, jogging ascent. And was that a whistle she heard, a few faint notes, or was it one of the canaries? Settling herself back in her chair, Madame Foraque turned her attention to the TV screen, satisfied with the way things had turned out.

But it didn't take long for the Widow Foraque's mood to change dramatically. Something was wrong. Something was badly wrong. She sat bolt upright in her chair. She knew at once what it was. The TV presenter. She couldn't hear a word he was saying. Not a single thing. She'd lost her hearing. She'd gone deaf. Just like that. In an instant.

Then, with a flood of relief, Madame Foraque found the TV remote in her lap and realised that she hadn't turned the volume back up.

71

Sunday

S itting out in early-morning sunshine on the gravelled terrace of the family *bastide* a few kilometres west of Aix-en-Provence, Paul Basquet shuffled through the Sunday papers one last time, dropping them one by one onto the table. There was nothing else he'd been able to find on the deaths in Roucas Blanc that he hadn't already read – the front-page news reports, the inside editorials, the leader comments and, of course, the obituaries. Or seen on TV – all the breathless newscasts and updates that had followed the discoveries of the bodies.

It was all so . . . astonishing. So close. The man who on three separate occasions had turned down his proposals for development in the *calanques* and who, according to Raissac, would be passing said proposals at the next meeting of the planning committee. Dead by his own hand, and just a few hours after the murder of his wife. According to the papers and TV, Suzanne de Cotigny was the fifth victim of a serial killer the newspapers had dubbed the Waterman, all his victims murdered by drowning.

Extraordinary. Quite extraordinary.

Basquet, in the course of his various development businesses, had met with Hubert de Cotigny on a number of occasions – at formal presentations, on the cocktail circuit, even dinner on one occasion, the last time at the opening of the Aqua-Cité open-sea extension –

302

but he had no reason to like the man. In Basquet's book, de Cotigny was a snob, pure and simple. Old school. *Le gratin.* Well up there with the great and the good of Marseilles. The kind of people his wife, Céléstine, had grown up with. But he still felt sorry for the man. A shocking tragedy. Losing his wife to such a random, senseless killing – as the papers would have it – and then, within hours, reaching such depths of misery and despair at the loss of his young wife that he saw no alternative to taking his own life.

Basquet wouldn't have wished that on anyone – not even de Cotigny.

He was wondering again what impact this would have on his *permis*, how long they would be delayed, when Céléstine joined him at the breakfast table, back from her morning jog. She picked up a table mat and, with a whoosh of breath, fanned it against her face. Basquet gave her the once-over. Too like her father to be beautiful: the same drooping heaviness in the face; the same strong nose and thinning hair; and three children over a dozen years had done her figure no favours. Standing there in her sweats, a mist of perspiration on her top lip and flushed cheeks, she looked dumpy and shapeless. For the life of him, he couldn't understand what she thought she was up to and was grateful there were no near neighbours to witness her absurd efforts. One time, driving home from the office, he'd seen her out there in the lane, her arms high to the shoulder, elbows pumping, the lower half of her legs splaying out to the left and right with every step, the way women run, like the way they throw a ball. Completely uncoordinated. He'd slowed to offer her a lift but she'd waved him on – 'No, no, I must finish.' She was so breathless that she could hardly speak. In the rear-view mirror he'd seen her push back her shoulders and pick up her pace. She knew he'd be watching.

Basquet also knew, as Céléstine put down the place mat and wiped the wristband across her forehead, that she had something to ask him. She had that look about her. Hesitant but determined, waiting for the right moment.

He wasn't mistaken. 'We've had an invitation from the Fazilleaux. Dinner and piquet. This evening. Chantal says the Durets will be there too.'

This last detail she'd found out from Chantal the previous afternoon, a fact that she was certain would sway her husband. Xavier Duret was the man who'd designed and financed the Concept Tuillot in Nice, who'd built the Grimaud yacht basin and pioneered the use of firewall construction that halved structural weights, diminished project costs and increased safety at a single stroke. But she could see at once, as she finished speaking, that even the prospect of meeting Monsieur Duret wouldn't budge her husband.

Basquet sighed, gave her a sad smile, reached for her hand even.

'I'd love to, really. But I'm up to here. It's been a dreadful week and I'm way behind. Maybe I could call in later, when I'm finished?'

Céléstine nodded. 'I'll let Chantal know.'

Then she stood, took up one of the papers, and walked back to the house.

72

Rully and Jacquot knew each other too well to be bothered by silence. Which was what was happening right then – a deep, contemplative silence settling between them. Rully, eyes fixed on the steel cord that held his plastered leg, Jacquot with his arms folded on the back of his chair, chin resting on his hands, staring at a square of sunshine splashed across the bottom of Rully's bed, ribbed with the shade of the blinds.

Beyond Rully's room, there was silence too. No rattling of trolleys this Sunday morning, no urgent ringing of phones, no distant voices or squeaking plimsolls on the shiny lino. The whole hospital could have been empty, just this one room occupied.

Jacquot had brought lunch. Two steak-and-salad pittas in a foil wrap from Gassi at La Carnerie, some wine, cheese and bread. A glass of red down and halfway through the pittas, Rully had started the ball rolling, prompting Jacquot to take him through the leads and the breaks of the previous week: the gym, the splinter, Carnot's fingerprints all over Monel's place and, finally, Saturday afternoon, tying in Carnot with the second victim.

It had been one of the squad, Bernie Muzon, who'd put it together – seeing Carnot at the front desk as Calliou itemised and bagged his possessions, and recalling the picture in Grez's apartment. But he didn't make the connection straight away. It just set him thinking. What Jacquot always loved about police work. A familiar face – you've seen it before somewhere. But where, exactly?

It took Muzon a while to place it. As Carnot waited in an interview room, Muzon went through the files, going back over the evidence, the reports, the statements, until he found what he was looking for. The photograph they'd taken from Joline Grez's bedside table. The photograph of a man with his arm draped around her shoulders. Black curly hair, dark eyes, a bored, arrogant slouch. After they'd found Grez's body in the Longchamp pool, they'd done the rounds with that photo – showing it to the staff at Galerie Prime, Grez's family, her friends – but nothing had come of it.

Until now. The man downstairs. The man he'd passed at the Duty Sergeant's desk. And when Muzon heard Jacquot was about to question the same man about another victim, Vicki Monel, he knew they were on to something.

He'd caught Jacquot on his way down to the interview room and filled him in.

'One of those lucky breaks,' said Rully, reaching up for the metal-frame bedhead and stretching his upper torso.

'And that's the truth,' said Jacquot. 'Sometimes it just piles up on your doorstep.'

'So you *really* think it's this Carnot character?' continued Rully.

Jacquot sighed. 'It would be nice just to have one more piece, you know? Just one more link. Ballarde, or the English girl, Holford, or de Cotigny.' He spread his hands. 'Take your pick. Right now, two out of five, it could just be coincidence. It could go either way. And there was nothing incriminating at his apartment. The boys searched top to bottom. Not a thing to tie him in.'

'But you're holding him?'

'Oh yes. Friend Carnot's going nowhere for the moment.'

'But you're not happy?'

Jacquot gave his partner a rueful smile. 'It's just a feeling. Nothing. Something. Who knows? Sure, we can place him with two of the victims. And yeah, sure, he could do it, kill – he's nasty enough. And maybe we can even come up with a motive – Vicki taking on the side, Grez not playing ball.' Jacquot paused, shook his head. 'It's just . . . what the Waterman does to the bodies. The sex. It doesn't . . . it doesn't fit. Carnot's not the kind of guy who'd go round using some wooden . . . some implement, when he's got the real thing.'

It was then that the two of them fell silent, Rully thinking through what Jacquot had told him, Jacquot trying to make sense of everything else that had cropped up in the last few days, all of it centred around Raissac, something flitting around at the back of his mind, still shadowy, insubstantial, not quite fitting in: Gastal's interest in the man at the start of the week; Vicki Monel's apartment owned by one of Raissac's companies; Raissac's slip of the tongue out at Cassis; Doisneau's warning about Raissac and the subsequent discovery of Doisneau's body floating in the Radoub Basin; and, thanks to Salette's efforts, the information that a Raissac subsidiary appeared on a cargo manifest as an importer on a vessel due in port that very day, a vessel owned by Basquet Maritime.

Then, last thing the evening before, yet another connection – a call coming through from Raissac to Carnot; something that Gastal had failed to mention when he dropped by the interview room to let Jacquot know he'd tracked down the Renault driver. Maybe Gastal would say something about it tomorrow. Or maybe he'd just forgotten, didn't think it was important.

But how could that be, given his interest in the man? Was he keeping it to himself – something to take to Lamonzie? For the moment, Jacquot decided to let it wait. It could all yet come together. Right now it was enough to know.

It was Rully who finally broke the silence.

'So what does your new partner think?' he asked, picking crumbs from his chest hair.

'Gastal? Difficult to say. Start of the week he was a real pain. Told me he wasn't interested in homicide, nothing in it, couldn't wait to join up with Lamonzie. As good as told me he was just marking time. Then, towards the end of the week, he starts getting into his stride. Now, of course, he thinks it's in the bag. Plain sailing. We got our man.'

'So you're not going to say anything to him? Your doubts about Carnot?'

'Not much point. Just wait it out, I guess. See where the ball goes.'

'Just don't go breaking any legs,' said Rully, packing the remains of his lunch in the foil wrap, balling it up and tossing it at Jacquot.

After leaving La Conception, Jacquot made a detour into Belsunce.

He'd remembered something the night before, as he went off to sleep, thinking about Boni. And he'd felt bad about it.

That Sunday, he had one more call to make.

73

C laudine Eddé had her eyes on him from the moment he came into the gallery. She sat at the small desk with its computer, telephone and pile of catalogues and busied herself with the keyboard. Apart from her nod of welcome and his return smile, there had been no further communication. Each behaved as if there was no one else in the room. Or rather, as if someone was.

But now it was time to do something about it.

He'd been there long enough now, shown sufficient interest, for her to start the ball rolling. When customers realised they were talking to the artist, it was often all that was needed to tip the balance and secure a sale. Her agent had told her that when he advised her to rent the Ton-Ton and work the gallery for a week; he'd look after all the rest.

Which she was doing. The Sunday after the night before.

Claudine had calmed down since her first-night show and celebratory supper, waking in an empty bed to all the usual doubts and uncertainties. It had been a haul getting herself up and coming in to work, sitting alone in the same gallery that had hummed the night before, manning the desk in case someone stopped by and felt like buying.

Like the man who'd just come in. Only the second that afternoon. The morning had been fine, a load of people passing by and coming in, but after lunch she might as well have closed up. In fact, she'd been thinking of doing exactly that when the buzzer sounded and the door opened. And in he came.

Claudine had just about plucked up enough courage to leave her desk and introduce herself, when he turned to her and said:

'She's very good, isn't she?'

Which stopped Claudine in her tracks. How to respond? She could either say it just so happened she was the artist and thank you so much. Or pretend she wasn't; play along as the gallery assistant he clearly imagined she was.

'She'd be very pleased to hear you say that,' she replied, feeling her neck redden, cross with herself that she hadn't had the nerve to tell the truth. 'Any artist would.'

'She's really got a touch.' He was standing in front of the canvas entitled *Ripe 2*, two glass preserving jars filled with figs, the fruit strangely disfigured by the varying thickness of the glass. 'She's got the colour, the shade. Real texture. And seeing the figs pushed up against the sides of the jars gives them a real sense of . . . I don't know . . .' He looked to the floor as if he'd find the word there. 'Form, I guess. Life.'

For a moment Claudine wondered if this was the start to a pick-up line. The kind of thing he tried on shop girls – which he now assumed she was – to start up a conversation. A gentle flirting.

But Claudine wasn't convinced. He'd really been looking at the piece, and everything he said about it – the way the jar changed the shape of the figs, either through the thickness or touch of the glass – was exactly the effect she had sought to achieve.

Then he looked at the title card to see the price and nodded, as though he'd expected as much.

He moved on. 'I was supposed to be at the opening last night but I got held up. Did you go? Was it fun?'

Which knocked the breath out of her. It couldn't be, surely not? Not her sister's no-show? The man Delphie had tried to set her up with? No, it couldn't possibly . . .

'Yes, I did. It was great. Do you know the artist?'

The stranger shook his head. 'I met her sister at a party. She invited me. I'm sorry I missed it.'

So it really was him. Claudine couldn't believe it. Her stomach started doing cartwheels. Somehow she managed to speak. 'Well, you're seeing it now. That's the main thing.'

'Looks like she sold some, too,' said the man, indicating the red dots.

'They went mad.'

'You don't have to be mad to know talent like this,' he replied.

He came to the desk, turned and looked around, as though he were about to share a secret – or ask her out. It was neither.

'Is there anything, you know . . . ?' He cast around for the right words.

Claudine looked up at him, prepared herself.

'. . . Just a little less . . . expensive?'

Not what Claudine had been expecting. She could hardly speak. 'There's a small one. By the window. The lemons on a plate.'

He went over and looked at the painting, stood back from it, then leant forward to see the price. Which she liked, his looking at the picture first, before checking how much it cost.

'It's four thousand,' she said, the only words she could manage. As if he couldn't read.

'It's really nice.' And then: 'I'll take it.'

He came back to the desk and took a chequebook from an inside pocket. When he opened it she could read, upside down, the name – D. Jacquot. Was that what Delphie's no-show was called? She couldn't remember if her sister had mentioned a name. But she could remember how her sister had described him. And he certainly didn't look like a policeman. A cool-looking linen jacket, shiny black hair tied in a ponytail, lovely fingernails, and barefoot, just a pair of espadrilles with the jeans. He reminded her of the footballer, Ginola, the one in the coffee ad. But not so pretty. A little bit of Depardieu roughening up the mix. But very, very attractive all the same. And a lovely voice, soft and hard at the same time. And those eyes. She'd have trouble mixing a green like that, soft and shifting, translucent, like the undersides of certain leaves.

'To whom should I make it payable?' he asked, glancing up at her.

'To the artist, Claudine Eddé,' she replied.

He filled in the cheque, tore it out and handed it to her.

'Thank you, Monsieur. I'm sure you'll enjoy the painting.'

'I'm sure I will.' And then: 'Tell me, how long before I can pick it up?'

'If you leave your address we can send it to you. Or otherwise you could collect it when the exhibition closes.'

'Which is?'

'Friday,' she replied, knowing that she was saying all the wrong things, but unable now to do anything about it. 'We close at six.'

He nodded, gave her a smile. 'I'll come back,' he said. 'Maybe get to meet the artist, and say thanks personally.' And with that he pocketed his chequebook, nodded goodbye and left the gallery.

Leaving Claudine Eddé not a little cross with herself – that she'd played the shop-assistant and not told him who she was; and how embarrassed she'd be when he found out the truth. Which he was sure to do, when he came back to collect his painting on Friday evening.

And he hadn't even made a pass.

She wasn't sure which was worse.

For the next two hours, and despite herself, Claudine tried to recall whether or not he'd been wearing a wedding ring.

74

A mistake. The Waterman had made a mistake. An error of judgement, a momentary whim that came from nowhere, and the joint was hopping.

The cool, clean dispatch of Berthe Mourdet and the discovery of her body at Plage de Corbières in L'Estaque would have raised few eyebrows: just another name added to the list of Waterman kills. A beautician from Saint-Pierre. So what? There'd be a few TV news reports, some hand-wringing prose in the local papers and, from the police, the usual empty promises of renewed efforts to track down her killer. But that would be all. In other words, not much. That was how it had been in La Rochelle, in Dieppe . . . That was how it should have been here, in Marseilles.

But Berthe Mourdet had not been dispatched. Coolly, cleanly or otherwise. On a powerful, unexpected whim, she was allowed to get in her car and drive away. Just like that. Five weeks following her, getting to know her – coming up right behind her in the line for coffees and croissants at that café of hers on rue des Trois Rois, close enough to smell the soap on her skin. But in a single instant, the plan changed and she escaped. Lucky girl. All that work for nothing.

Except, of course, that all that preparation had led to the house in Roucas Blanc and that bewitching woman. *Dieu*, she made Berthe look like a sack of beets.

So the Waterman stayed, saw off the opposition – some pimply kid in shorts holed up in the trees to take a peep – and spent some quality time with Berthe's delightful companion. Out there on the lawn, their bodies rolling on the grass as one, and then to the pool, wading into the deep, dark water, everything they did together accompanied by the gorgeous, heart-warming bubbling of her laughter.

Great, great fun. But a very, very major mistake. Which was why the Waterman was so cross.

Unlike Berthe, the companion wasn't a beautician in Saint-Pierre and her death did not go unnoticed. According to the press, the TV and radio broadcasts, Madame de Cotigny was a very important lady – the daughter of a wealthy American family who'd flown to France in their very own private jet when they heard the news, and the wife of a leading local politician, who'd been so mortified by her death that he had taken his own life. It was a story that had been playing for two days now and it showed no signs of slowing down. This one would run and run.

It had taken the police a while to make the right connections. At first the response followed the usual pattern: a scatter of TV broadcasts, a spate of breathless editorials, and that front-page photo of a fat policeman driving out of Aqua-Cité, talking it up to the press. Not that any of this bothered the Waterman. Indeed, there was a certain satisfaction to be had in following your own investigation, watching the authorities run rings around themselves. So confident, so cocky, they were. But that as far as they ever got. Running around in circles.

Yet suddenly here was this man, Jacquot, heading up the investigation – not the fat one any more. There'd been a photo of him in Saturday's paper and he'd appeared on a TV news bulletin, making a statement outside police headquarters. Well-set in the shoulders, with hair drawn back off his brow and tied in a ponytail, his eyes held the camera with a level, steady gaze that put a chill clean through you. He looked the kind of man who didn't like things upsetting his day. With someone like him in charge, the Waterman decided, life was definitely going to get more difficult.

Indeed, it had already started – at the Café-Bar Guillaume across from the gym. A few days earlier there'd been this girl who'd come in. She wasn't a regular, you could tell. The way she couldn't make up her mind where to sit – by the window, by the bar, in an alcove by the *toilettes*? Half a dozen times now she'd been there, chatting up Patrice and Nadine when they brought her another coffee, looking up from her newspaper every five seconds as though deep in thought.

Going through the classifieds? Looking for a job? Who did she think she was kidding? She already had a job. With the cops. Stood out a mile. Which was funny for a while, having her sit there, only a scatter of tables between them. But the message was clear. The police were getting close. They'd found the gym, and had clearly decided that the Café-Bar Guillaume was just the kind of place the Waterman might use as a lookout spot.

Smart. Very smart. Which meant that the time had probably come to move on, find somewhere else, just when all the fun was starting. And Marseilles was such a great place to be.

Pulling on a coat that Sunday evening, the Waterman knew what had to be done. A pleasant drive out to Callelongue and a stroll along the *quai*, looking out for a quiet spot to say goodbye, committing to the ocean the memory of friends: their watches, rings and bracelets, their gold chains, crosses and silver clips, even that weighty solitaire eased off the unresisting wedding finger of Madame Suzanne Delahaye de Cotigny.

And maybe on the way home from Callelongue – if something presented itself – just one last, little adventure. Something to keep that cop Jacquot on his toes.

75

Anais pulled at her watch, held up her wrist and checked the time. Just past midnight. She sat up in bed and listened. Had she heard the door buzzer or not? She couldn't be certain. Had she dreamt it? Or was there really someone there? She waited in the darkness, listening for a second ring. Then she would know. Around her the silence was deep and pure. Not a sound, save for the sigh of her mattress springs, the warm whisper of her sheets and, stirring the air, the soft pulse of the ceiling fan.

Then it came again. Out of the darkness, a low insistent buzzing from her front door, jolting her fully awake. But who on earth could it be? At this time of night?

Paul. It could only be Paul, thought Anais as she slipped from her bed. He must have left something – his phone, his briefcase, his glasses. The man was hopeless, always forgetting something. But that was ridiculous, she decided. He'd left two hours earlier. Why would he bother? He'd be home by now. In bed, asleep, like her, glad that everything had been sorted, arrangements made. And no explosive tantrum this time, just an acknowledgement that what she was asking for wasn't that unreasonable, that she'd keep her word, that he'd never hear from her again.

As she tugged on a gown and tied the belt, Anais remembered what she'd been dreaming in the instant before coming awake. The small house in Martinique that she'd bought, in the hills above La Lamentin, where it was cool, close to her parents, with her child playing in the yard, with not a care in the world.

But she wasn't in Martinique now. She was in Endoume. At night. Alone.

Hugging the gown around her, Anais moved to the bedroom window and parted the blinds. The driveway was empty: no Porsche, no light, no movement. Closing the blinds, she went to the hall and, trailing her fingers along the wall, tiptoed to the front door and listened.

Nothing.

And then the bell rang a third time, making her jump from her skin, longer this time, more urgent, the sound so close, the finger pressing it only the other side of the door, inches from her.

'Who is it?' she called out and then regretted she'd said a word.

'It's me,' came a whispered reply.

'Paul,' she said with a burst of relief and slid the chain from its runner, turning the lock and opening the door. 'What on earth . . .'

Part Four

76

Vallon des Auffes, Marseilles, Monday

It was the seagull that saw it first, a fledgling, pink webbed feet splayed for a grip on the prow of a fishing skiff. His feathers were still grey, flecked with white, ruffling in the breeze, wide yellow eyes hard and sharp, and his call, screeching plaintively around the cove, still high-pitched, uncertain. And unanswered. The seagull was alone. Somehow he'd missed the others leaving, out of sight now, circling in the wake of a fishing boat edging past the Malmousque Heads and bound for the Vieux Port.

And so he stood there, waiting, looking. Hungry.

Which was when his attention was caught by a wink of something in the water. A flash of light catching the morning sun. A fin? A darting scatter of silvery scales? The young seagull blinked his honey-coloured eyes, straightened his neck and peered into the water not ten metres from his perch.

Whatever it was, it was not familiar. So not a fin, then, not scales. But something. Moving gently with the pull of the tide, breaking the surface. Something dark and shadowy. Caught, by the looks of it, in a shred of netting.

The seagull might have been young, but he knew netting. And he didn't like it. His sister had died dragging a webbed train of it from her ankle. Two weeks it had taken before they found her, washed up *on the slipway, her thin pink leg still tangled in the net. That was enough for him.*

But still . . . he was hungry. And the glint. That promising glint. There it was again. Buried, so far as he could see, not in a web of netting but in a coil of shifting black seaweed, winking out now and then with the movement of the sea. It was big, too, whatever it was that produced the flash of light, rounded, and . . . somehow tentacled, limbs angled down, lost against the glare of the water.

Big enough to land on, the seagull speculated. Worth a look. So he pushed off from the prow of the pointu, *a few half-hearted beats of his wings through to reach the bundle. Legs down, feet spread for landing, neck and head rearing back, wing-tips meeting, he felt himself make contact.*

But not solid contact. The bundle was smaller and lighter than he'd estimated. Not bulky enough to bear his weight. For it dipped beneath the surface and sent him skittering up into the air, flapping for purchase, before dropping down again for a second try. Only this time the thing seemed to roll like a log, bringing those tentacles sparkling into the sunlight, fingers curled at the sky, slicking black coils of hair over an ashen face.

Twenty metres away, on the steps of Chez Fonfon, coming down from the restaurant to the quay, a woman looked hard at the water, pointed, and put a hand to her mouth.

77

Senior Customs Officer Emile Jalons, of the State Customs and Immigration Department, arrived early, and nervously, at his office on Quai d'Arenc, parking his car in a spill of shadow. It was a little after eight o'clock in the morning and the sun was already starting to bite. In the warm, ticking silence, he sat at the wheel and fought down an impulse to turn the car round, head home and call in sick. But Jalons knew that he couldn't do that. It was bad enough as it was, but if he chickened out now, at the last minute, he knew there'd be a far higher price to pay than the one already on offer. Let them down, refuse to do what they wanted, and Jalons had not the slightest doubt that they'd come looking for him. Tomorrow. The day after. A year, even. But come they would.

Of course he should have known right from the start that it was a set-up. The club, the boy, the apartment, the ease of the whole thing. Forty minutes after that first drink – so sweet, a fruit cola – the lad was sliding a key in the lock and showing him into a not-bad one-bed apartment overlooking the steps of the Gare St-Charles. Five hundred francs for the best personal attention he could remember receiving. Just the five! The boy must be new in town, Jalons decided, as he made his way home to his wife and children.

Three days later, the videotape of their activities that night in St-Charles had been left in a padded brown envelope on the front seat of his car. The accompanying note, sellotaped to the cassette, carried nothing more than a local phone number. After Jalons watched the tape that evening, he picked up the phone and tapped out the number with a shaky hand.

The voice that answered was cool and soothing. Knew who was calling without needing to ask. There was a little job they needed doing, the voice on the phone told him, and if he did exactly as he was told the original tape that recorded his indiscretions would be destroyed. Otherwise . . .

There'd been no need for Jalons to be told what the consequences would be. Better the offending video destroyed than on his boss's desk. Or, God help him, in the mail to his wife.

Up in the office, its ceiling fans turning slowly, its dusty, metal-framed windows giving onto a stretch of hawsered quay and the peeling hulk of a Japanese tanker, Jalons checked through the movements board behind Sergeant Dupuys's desk. He found what he was looking for and flicked through the three single pages on the merchant ship *Aurore*, just as he'd done every morning since receiving the tape.

Launched 1976. Registered Senegal. Eighteen thousand tonnes.

Current owners: Basquet (Maritime) et Cie.

Ship's Master: François Mallet. Three other officers all French. Mixed Asian crew.

Two for'ard holds. Three stern holds.

Incoming from Venezuela, Surinam and Cayenne in French Guyana, to Accra and Marseilles.

Mixed cargo of rubber, kaolin, timber, cocoa and groundnuts. And whatever else it was that Jalons was being asked to overlook. With South America as the ship's point of departure, it wasn't difficult to work out what that cargo might be.

Jalons had also noted that the *Aurore* was scheduled for a refit after her arrival and wondered whether the contraband – which she was surely carrying – was hidden amongst the cargo or somewhere in the superstructure. Concealing contraband in a ship's superstructure for pick-up during refit was harder to police than contraband hidden in the cargo. But given that the voice on the phone had instructed him to supervise unloading and arrange Customs clearance himself, Jalons could only assume that the drugs – for that was surely what this was all about – were part of the cargo about to be unloaded on his quay. Once cleared by Customs, the shipping line was then free to release that cargo direct to its owners.

This morning, Jalons noted, there was only one further notation on the *Aurore's* file – made earlier that morning by Sergeant Dupuys in blue marker pen. '*Arrivée.*' Which meant, Jalons knew, that right now Dupuys would be down at the *Aurore's* berth, inspecting her crew documentation and confirming her registration papers and cargo manifest.

Jalons replaced the clipboard on its hook and, taking up a pair of binoculars, he walked onto the deck outside the office. A week earlier, with a berth still to be assigned to the MS *Aurore*, he'd decided on Bay Seven, at the end of Quai d'Arenc. As far away as possible. He trained the glasses on the spot, adjusted the focus, and there she was, all but hidden at the end of a long line of bulkier merchantmen, a low-slung rust bucket with white upperworks and mud-red flanks. The paintwork was patchy and she looked like she'd done some sailing. Jalons settled his binoculars on the flying bridge where two officers leant over the rails, one of them shouting at his crew through cupped hands.

Since there were no quay-crane facilities at Bay Seven – the steel track fell short by a hundred metres – the shore crews had already started unloading cargo using the ship's own gantries, each netted load to be transferred by pallet and fork-lift to Bond Hall Seven, the most distant of the dockside warehouses. Dropping the glasses from the *Aurore's* bridge to the bustling quayside, Jalons picked out Dupuys making his way through the shore crews and pallets to his car. He watched him open the door, lean in and pick up his radio.

Behind him, in his office, Jalons heard his own radio crackle into life. He left the terrace, went to his desk and acknowledged Dupuys's call confirming that the *Aurore's* hatches were open and derricks operating. Signing off, Jalons slumped behind his desk and ran a dry tongue across parched lips.

Now it was his turn.

An hour later Jalons pulled on his cap and headed down to his car in front of the Customs building. Procedure required that a senior Customs officer should be in attendance on at least two occasions during cargo discharge. At which time said senior officer was entitled, if he saw fit, to authorise searches using whatever means he judged appropriate – dogs, electronic sweepers, X-rays, even random sampling.

But, of course, Lieutenant Emile Jalons had no intention of doing any such thing. He knew that it would be enough for him to follow the code of practice as set down for investigating officers, put in his regulation appearances and then wave the cargo through.

That was all they'd asked him to do. Go easy. Look the other way. As if he'd never turned a blind eye to illicit cargo before.

It was going to be, he reassured himself, a piece of cake.

78

Adèle hadn't seen Monsieur Basquet in such high spirits for a long time.

'Morning, Adèle,' he bellowed, patting her arm as he took his seat at the breakfast table, thanking her as she poured his orange juice, which she couldn't remember him ever doing before.

Then thanking her for the yogurt and honey she brought him.

And the croissants.

And the *omelette fromage* that he'd requested.

In fact, everything Adèle put in front of him, served with a tiny bob, Basquet thanked her for it, tucking in as if he hadn't eaten for a week. Which, she reflected, preparing another pot of coffee in the kitchen, had been pretty much the pattern for the last few days.

Back in the breakfast room, Basquet finished his omelette, leant back from the table and felt a great wave of contentment sluice over him. Anais finally out of his hair. The problem solved. And unexpectedly easy to negotiate. He'd been quite surprised how little trouble she'd caused him, how little fight she'd put up.

At that moment Célestine appeared, thankfully not in her jogging gear, Basquet observed, but more suitably dressed in her preferred slacks and cardigan. She came over and kissed the top of his head, scolded him for his snoring and for driving her off to Laurent's room once again, and told him he'd missed quite an evening.

'What party?' he asked, not aware that he'd been snoring.

'The Fazilleaux,' replied Céléstine, taking her seat at the table. 'Remember?'

'You meet that Druet chap?'

'Duret,' his wife corrected him. 'Xavier Duret. Charming man. You'd have loved it.'

'The two of you get on?'

'Like a house on fire.'

'So call him,' said Basquet expansively. 'Get them round for dinner.'

Céléstine looked at her husband in amazement.

'You mean *dinner*? Here?' she asked, as though she must surely have misunderstood. It had been months since they'd last had guests at the house. Lately, her husband liked to do his entertaining in restaurants, usually without her.

'Why not? Live a little.'

Either her husband had lost his senses, Céléstine decided, or he wanted to meet this Duret more than she realised.

Adèle came into the room with a fresh pot of coffee.

'Good morning, Madame,' she said with another little bob, and filled their cups.

'Thanks, Adèle,' said Basquet, and Céléstine blinked.

79

Crossing République, Coupchoux never saw the autobus that hit them.

He'd just finished breakfast at Café Samaritaine and was on his way to the car when his attention was caught by two nuns headed in the same direction as him but on the other side of the road. Their hands were tucked into their sleeves, their robes billowed in the sunshine and the knotted cords of their belts slapped against the folds of their skirts. He watched them as they walked, the white wings of their starched wimples glaring bright in the morning light like the sails of a ship. He wondered where they were going. It had to be St Cannat, he decided; the cloister there was a favourite of his. Perhaps there was a Mass. A saint's day, maybe.

Coupchoux checked the time. He was supposed to be in Cassis at eleven, picking up Raissac, but he reckoned there might be time for a detour. After all, he was in need of some spiritual cleansing. Thanks to a change in plans, he'd been up half the night. All of it for Raissac. Hard, bloody, dirty work it had been, too. And Carnot off gallivanting somewhere. Raissac would have his balls for that and no mistake – maybe even get Coupchoux to do the honours. Which would be fun. Coupchoux didn't like Carnot one little bit. Playboy type, a nasty piece of work who thought he was the dog's bollocks. And Arab, too. Pretended he wasn't, but you could see it a mile off. It was the pretending that Coupchoux particularly disliked.

Across République the two nuns stepped into a side street off the boulevard and in an instant they were gone. But Coupchoux had been expecting it. If they were headed for St Cannat, that sharp turn and shadowy street was the only way they could get there.

Fifty metres ahead of him the lights changed to red and the westbound traffic slowed to a stop. By the time Coupchoux got there, he knew they'd be back to green and he'd have to wait. He decided to cross République where he was, slipping between the traffic, and save himself the delay.

Which was just what the man in front of him decided to do, tugging his poodle's lead to indicate the change of direction. The poodle yelped and hunkered back but its owner lifted the lead to shoulder height and dragged the dog to heel, the two of them squeezing between the line of waiting cars.

Coupchoux didn't see the dog again until he reached the middle of the road, where the poodle and its owner were waiting for a break in the eastbound flow. It was difficult to say exactly what made the poodle snap and dart at Coupchoux's ankles – maybe nervousness at the closeness and noise of the traffic – but the kick that Coupchoux aimed back at it certainly inspired the dog to fresh acts of bravado. In an instant of snarling, yapping aggression, it had snatched up the slack in the lead from its owner's hand and gone for Coupchoux, making him dodge to one side, then forwards, in a kind of tiptoe dance with the poodle jumping at the back of his knees, the two of them stepping into the path of an eastbound autobus, accelerating through the lights and making for the Prado *Rondpoint*.

There was no time for the bus driver to avoid them. First a thump on the bonnet right below the driver's cab, and then a fearsome jolt that lifted the driver out of his seat as the front nearside wheel ploughed over the obstruction.

At almost the same moment, in the nave of St Cannat, two nuns took their places in the choir stall and Mass began.

80

There was some commotion on République which meant that Max Benedict had no trouble finding a table at Café Samaritaine. He chose one by the window, in the shade, and as he ordered a *café-calva* an ambulance squealed round the Canebière corner, sirens wailing, blue lights flashing. Cars pulled over and the white van hurtled past.

Marseilles, thought Benedict. Another gunfight at the OK Corral. France's Wild West. It beat Paris hands down. The contemplative, style-conscious, soft-bellied northerner, and this impulsive, hot-blooded southerner. He knew which he liked the most.

Benedict also knew the nightmare of driving in this city. So rather than face the horror of trying to find parking spaces for his jeep, he had taken a cab to the Vieux Port after an early breakfast on his balcony at the Nice-Passédat. Watching the sun come up over the crumpled, shadowy ridges behind Montredon. He'd been quietly pleased to see the shutters closed the next balcony along, Gus Delahaye's room. His compatriot was way behind him in the jet-lag stakes, and it would be hours before he, or his parents, made an appearance.

This was exactly what Benedict had hoped for, dining alone at Molineux's the evening before and planning his strategy. With the Delahayes shuttered away, now was the time to track down this Jacquot character. In half an hour he'd present himself at the Préfecture and secure his press accreditation, which would give him access to press briefings on the de Cotigny murder and suicide but not much else. What it wouldn't do was get him into police headquarters, which was where he was going after the Préfecture. He had thought about calling ahead to say he had information, arrange a meeting, but over a wicked Molineux soufflé he'd finally decided the best course of action was simply to arrive unannounced, try to make it as far as Jacquot and take it from there. If they hustled him out, if Jacquot proved difficult – it didn't matter what – Benedict would have enough for his piece however they wanted to play it. Maybe, along the way, he'd strike some kind of gold and the story would be made. Sometimes it happened as easily as that.

Benedict stood, pulled on his jacket and hefted his shoulder bag. As he slipped some money under his empty glass of *calva*, he saw the ambulance come back down République.

Its lights were off, its siren was silent and it seemed in no hurry to get anywhere fast.

Benedict knew what that meant.

81

M aître Denis wasn't telling Jean Carnot anything that his client didn't already know.

'They have nothing on you. It's all circumstantial.'

They were sitting in an interview room, waiting for the officer in charge of the investigation – the one who'd interviewed Carnot on Saturday afternoon – to make an appearance. They'd been told by the Duty Sergeant that he was on his way.

'. . . But I must impress on you,' the lawyer continued, 'the need to be, ah . . . cooperative. To be of assistance. Otherwise our friends here could be very . . .'

The door opened and Chief Inspector Jacquot came in.

'. . . Unhelpful,' finished *Maître* Denis in a whisper.

Jacquot took a seat and smiled at them both, pleased to note that Carnot was not looking his best – tired, anxious and unshaven after two nights in police custody.

'So, Messieurs.'

'Chief Inspector,' began Carnot's lawyer, gathering himself. He was plump and well nourished and looked too large for the chair that he sat in. 'I really must insist that my client be released without delay. You have kept him here far longer than is strictly, even legally permissible; you have yet to make any formal charge; and, despite a few thin coincidences . . .' *Maître* Denis waved his hand dismissively, '. . . I would suggest you have no good reason to hold him a moment longer.'

'Quite so,' said Jacquot. 'As you say, nothing more than a few thin coincidences. If I were a betting man I'd say it's unlikely that your client is the person we're looking for.'

The two men across the desk glanced at each other, then got to their feet, Carnot first, almost springing up, *Maître* Denis much more slowly, heaving himself from his chair.

Jacquot remained seated. 'However, there is one more question I would like to ask.'

'My client is under no obligation—' began *Maître* Denis.

'And I am under no obligation to be so understanding,' interrupted Jacquot coldly. 'If Monsieur Carnot decides not to cooperate, you can be assured that some kind of charge will be made.' He looked at the two men. 'Believe me.'

The lawyer turned to his client, narrowed his eyes and gave him a 'Remember-what-I-just-said' look.

Carnot nodded. 'One question.'

Jacquot nodded back. It was all he needed.

'Tell me about Alexandre Raissac,' he said.

82

Raissac was not amused.

First Carnot had gone missing – Saturday, of all days – and Raissac's calls had gone unanswered. It hadn't taken Raissac long to realise that there was only one possible explanation – Carnot had been picked up by the cops. He was a naughty boy, after all. What else had he been up to that Raissac didn't know about? Putting a call through to his contact on rue de l'Evêché, Raissac confirmed it: Carnot was indeed in custody at police headquarters, and looked like he'd be there some considerable time, helping the Waterman investigators with their inquiries. According to his source, Carnot was now a prime suspect.

Vicki, thought Raissac. That fucking girl again. When he and Carnot had work to do.

That Saturday, with his fixer out of action and the *Aurore* just hours away, Raissac realised that he'd have to move fast. Since his man on the inside had still not been able to establish whether an action was scheduled, Raissac decided that he couldn't risk waiting for the *Aurore*'s cargo to be unloaded, as originally planned. Far too risky – the place could be crawling with cops. It had to be sooner. He'd have to reschedule for Sunday night. Direct. Ship to ship. Out in the Rades. Tricky but possible. Which was what Raissac arranged. Coupchoux and the boys had shifted the lot. Not a hitch. Every single kilo.

But now, Monday morning, it was Coupchoux that he couldn't reach. Not a word since breakfast when his driver had called to say he was on his way. Which meant that he should have arrived by now. It didn't take two hours to drive from Marseilles to Cassis. And why wasn't Coupchoux answering his mobile? For a moment Raissac was tempted to call his mole again and find out if Coupchoux, too, had been picked up by the cops. But there was no way they could have made any link between Carnot and Coupchoux. And through Coupchoux to him. Unless Carnot had talked . . . But that was ridiculous. Carnot knew better than that. At least, Raissac hoped he did.

At close to midday and still no sign of Coupchoux, Raissac realised there was no option but to drive himself. It was an important meeting, the last piece of the jigsaw, and he didn't want to keep his man waiting.

In Coupchoux's absence, Raissac decided on the Bentley – the only car he ever drove himself – and in a leathery cocoon of chill air-conditioning, he swept out of the Cassis compound and headed for the autoroute. He was having lunch in Bandol with Monsieur Condé, an associate from Toulon days. Arrangements had to be made. Time, place, people. Raissac didn't want two hundred kilos of uncut cocaine sitting in one of his rented lock-ups in Marseilles any longer than was necessary.

An hour later the two men met at L'Auberge du Port, on the first-floor terrace overlooking the harbour. Condé, as ever, was keen to get moving, agreed to the price and conditions that Raissac suggested and the deal was finalised over a dish of grilled red mullet washed down with a Pibarnon rosé. All most agreeable. As soon as Raissac had confirmation that the money was in place, he'd have his man deliver the merchandise.

At three Raissac was on his way back home, easing off the autoroute and heading down the slope towards Cassis. In a funny sort of way he was glad that Coupchoux had failed to make an appearance. He'd enjoyed the ride – the leather closeness of his Bentley, the wheel sliding through his hands, its seamless, silent power. Ten minutes later the gates to his property swung open and then, one after another, closed behind him.

As he steered the Bentley up the drive, Raissac let his gaze wander across the gardens, admiring the sweep of lawn, the clicking rainbow spray of sprinklers and, rising above the stand of cypresses that lined the northern boundary of his property, the craggy ridges of the Baume Massif.

What Raissac didn't see, as the garage doors slid down behind him, was a man dressed in black biking leathers waiting in the shadows.

Raissac had switched off the ignition and was reaching for the door handle when the rounded tip of a silencer tapped against his side window, a black hole rimmed with a halo of grey steel. There was no time to do anything. The last thing that Raissac saw was a gloved finger squeezing the trigger.

In the space of four seconds Raissac took six nine-millimetre bullets at close range. The first, a bull's-eye in the centre of his birthmark, punched him over onto the passenger seat. The remaining five followed a rough line from his upper chest to his kidneys, the sound of the gunfire reduced by the silencer to a hollow popping.

When the last note died, leaving only the subsiding tick of the Bentley's engine and the tinkle of glass falling from the shattered window, the killer slipped the gun into his jacket and left the estate the way he had come in. Starting up his bike a few hundred metres down the road, he decided his dad would've approved of the way that things had worked out.

Two hours later Paul Doisneau's son joined the Autoroute Languedocienne at junction twenty-six outside Nîmes and turned south-west, heading for the Spanish border.

·

83

Jacquot's thumb played with the ring on his finger.

Standing at the table, Carnot gave Raissac's name some thought, then shook his head.

'Alexandre Majoub Raissac,' Jacquot repeated, watching Carnot's eyes shift around the room. 'Not at all familiar?'

'Not at all,' said Carnot, turning to *Maître* Denis as if to let him know that he'd done what he'd been asked – a single question – and now it was time for his attorney to get him out of there.

'One question, remember, Chief Inspector . . .' began *Maître* Denis gently, light-heartedly admonishing Jacquot in a finger-wagging tone.

Jacquot's reply was anything but gentle or light-hearted. 'Well, that's unfortunate, *Maître*, because I have to say I'm not at all happy with your client's reply. So. If you wouldn't mind, Messieurs . . .' Jacquot gestured to their chairs and the two men sat down again.

Jacquot watched them settle themselves. For the first time since they'd picked him up, Carnot looked worried. Raissac's name had rattled him. As for *Maître* Denis, Carnot's lawyer looked perplexed, clearly unprepared for this new line of questioning. This had not been a part of his brief – no mention of Monsieur Alexandre Raissac, a man he had never met but whose name rang many bells. *Maître* Denis, decided Jacquot, was starting to look as ill at ease as his client.

'I don't want to waste any time here,' continued Jacquot, pulling a tape from his pocket, sliding it into the cassette machine and pressing the *record* button. 'So let me begin by telling you what we know.

Since you were taken into custody, Monsieur Carnot, a number of calls have been received on your mobile phone. All of them from a certain Alexandre Raissac. So I'm sure you'll agree that it's pointless your trying to persuade me that you don't know him.'

Maître Denis was about to say something.

'Wrong number?' Jacquot asked. 'I don't think so. According to phone records, *Maître* Denis, your client and Monsieur Raissac have spoken together on numerous occasions in the last three months.'

Which wasn't exactly accurate. Muzon was still chasing down the phone company for information, but Jacquot was certain he wouldn't be too far off the mark.

Carnot swallowed.

'So. Let's begin again, shall we? Alexandre Raissac.'

'Okay. I know him. I do the odd job for the guy.'

'What kinds of jobs?'

'Personal security. That kind of thing.'

'So why didn't you say so?'

'It's just . . . well, in the protection business you need to be discreet.'

'So you protect him?' Jacquot leant back in his chair, stretched out his legs and crossed his ankles.

'That's right.'

'From what, may I ask?'

'He's rich. Needs to look after himself. Needs someone like me around. Just in case.'

'Just in case?'

'You know how it is with these guys. Marseilles's no playground.'

'So how long ago was this? How long have you been working for Monsieur Raissac?'

'Must be . . . six, eight months.'

'Not longer?'

Carnot shook his head.

'And it's just protection?'

'That's right.'

'So what about girls? Does he get you to provide those kinds of services? Or is it boys?' Jacquot remembered his visit to Cassis and the way Raissac had eyed him up over their beers. He'd recognised the look for what it was.

Carnot sighed. 'Sometimes Monsieur Raissac has business colleagues need setting up, entertaining, you know? With girls.'

'Girls like Vicki?'

Carnot nodded. 'Yes. She was one.'

'And Grez?'

'No. That was just . . . you know, personal, a fling. Couple of times was all. I can't hardly remember. It was just . . . nothing. Nothing to do with business.'

'And Ballarde? Was she one of your girls?'

Carnot frowned. The name clearly meant nothing to him. He shook his head.

'And Raissac? Did Raissac know these girls? Maybe use them himself?'

'Sure.'

Jacquot took this in. 'Monel? Did Raissac know Monel?'

'I suppose . . .'

'Yes or no?'

'Yeah, I guess.'

'How?'

'I took her round to his place a couple of times.'

'Here, or in Cassis?'

'Usually here.'

' "Usually"? So sometimes to Cassis as well?'

'That's right. A few times.'

'So he knew her? Knew her name?'

'Yeah. Course.'

Which was not what Raissac had said. Inconsistencies – Jacquot loved them. For a moment he wondered whether Raissac was the Waterman? It was an intriguing possibility, but Jacquot wasn't convinced. Not yet.

But then there was his old friend Doisneau. What about him? Did Raissac kill Doisneau? Or have Carnot kill him? To keep him quiet. Maybe Raissac found out that Doisneau was talking to the cops. Or maybe Doisneau tried a little blackmail on Raissac. A foolish thing to try, by all accounts.

'And Grez? Did he know Grez?'

Carnot shook his head. 'No, he didn't. Like I told you . . .'

'You're sure about that?'

'Yeah, I'm sure. She was just a girlfriend of mine. A couple of times and that was it. I told you.'

'And what about Cours Lieutaud? Vicki Monel's apartment. Did Raissac ever visit there?'

'No.'

Jacquot nodded. 'But you knew he owned the apartment?'

Carnot looked surprised. 'Yes,' he replied.

'He told you that?'

Carnot looked uncomfortable. How much to say? How to say it? After a pause, not seeing how he was giving anything away, Carnot nodded. 'Yeah. He told me. Said if I knew anyone who wanted to earn a bit of money . . .'

'They could stay in the apartment in exchange for . . .?'

'That they could maybe do some work for him.'

'And what work was that, Monsieur?'

'Like I said, entertaining. Clients and things. Business people.'

'And he cut you in?'

'No. That was between me and the girl. He didn't charge no rent, just expected us to do what he asked. Arrange things. Be available.'

'So it wasn't just personal security. He set you up with the apartment. And you supplied the talent. Girls like Vicki. And Alina, Nathalie, Rose.'

The names that Madame Piganiol had given him. Somehow Jacquot had remembered them.

Carnot's eyes widened. He couldn't help himself.

Jacquot slipped his hands behind his head; he was starting to enjoy himself. He'd found the end of a piece of string and was pulling it in for all he was worth, confirming everything he'd suspected – and a few things he hadn't.

'Well?'

Across the table Carnot nodded. 'That's right.'

'So it's a little more than six months you've known Monsieur Raissac? Would that be correct?'

'I suppose . . .'

'So let's talk about these "business colleagues". The ones Monsieur Raissac sent to the apartment. You know any of them?'

Carnot shook his head. 'No. I didn't.'

'You're certain?'

'I told you – no.'

'And how many of these "colleagues" do you suppose you filmed?'

Carnot sighed. The cop seemed to know everything. 'Five. Maybe

341

six,' he replied, picking at his fingernails.

'So what happened to the films?' continued Jacquot.

'Just gave 'em to Raissac.'

'That's all?'

'That's it. That's the truth.'

'You know what he did with those films, our Monsieur Raissac?'

Carnot held out his hands. 'Look, in my line of work you don't ask too many questions.'

'Well, I'll tell you. He used those films, those indiscretions you recorded, to put pressure on people. Not "colleagues", as I'm sure you already know, but people he wanted to control. Important people, people in positions of authority. To get them to do whatever it was that he wanted doing. A little bit of leverage.'

Carnot gave a shrug.

'Which, Monsieur Carnot, is very much against the law. Is that not so?'

'If you say so,' replied Carnot, trying to be flippant, trying to distance himself.

'And you helped him. Helped him break the law. The word we're looking at here is "accomplice". In case you didn't know . . .'

'It was just a job. I didn't know why he wanted the films. I didn't ask. Not my business.'

Jacquot nodded. 'You ever hear the name Basquet? Paul Basquet?'

Carnot gave the name some thought, shook his head. Another name, another line. This was getting complicated. 'No. Never heard of him.' Then he turned to *Maître* Denis with a threatening look – get me out of this, now.

Which Jacquot had been expecting.

The lawyer took the cue.

'Chief Inspector, I really must—'

Jacquot pulled in his legs and leant forward. 'At this moment, *Maître* Denis, your client is helping us with our inquiries. Depending on the level of that assistance, then certain arrangements might be put in place to help Monsieur Carnot here out of a very nasty situation. Conspiracy, aiding and abetting, blackmail . . .'

'Look, this is a load of bull,' said Carnot, finally losing patience. 'So I lay on some girls for him. So what? And maybe I take a few films. So what? That's it. It's nothing. This is just a crock.'

'You know someone called Paul Doisneau?'

'No. I don't,' replied Carnot, far too quickly.

And Jacquot knew he was lying. Just like he'd lied when Jacquot had asked about Raissac. The same shift in the eyes.

'You mind telling me what you were doing Friday night?'

'Out clubbing,' replied Carnot. 'Maras, Dugong, Chai. Gotta dozen people saw me.'

'So why did you run?'

'You mean, your guys coming to my place? They could have been anyone, man. I didn't know.'

'But you can give us names? The people who saw you at these clubs?'

'Sure.'

'Well that's fine. Give us a list and we'll check them out. Until then, however, I very much regret we'll have to keep you here . . .'

'Now just a fucking minute . . .' said Carnot, hands reaching for the table, glaring at Jacquot.

'Please, Chief Inspector,' interrupted *Maître* Denis, pulling Carnot back. 'Really, my client has been most helpful.'

'Not nearly helpful enough,' replied Jacquot. 'I think a little more time to think things over is needed. Then we can talk again.'

And with that Jacquot pulled the tape from the machine and left the room.

84

Max Benedict jogged up the steps of the headquarters of the *Police Judiciaire* on rue de l'Evêché and presented himself at the front desk.

Sergeant Calliou was on duty. He gave Benedict a questioning look: 'Monsieur?'

'I would like to see Chief Inspector Jacquot.'

The sergeant shook his head. 'I'm afraid the Chief Inspector is busy,' he said. 'And you are . . . ?'

'It's about the Waterman,' said Benedict.

Calliou shot him a look. 'He's still busy. I'll call one of his team.'

'It has to be Jacquot,' said Benedict.

Calliou gave it some thought.

'Then you will have to wait, Monsieur. There is seating over there. In the meantime I will let him know that you are here.'

Benedict took a seat and checked the time. He was in no hurry. He could wait all day if he had to. And whether he actually got to see Jacquot or not, he'd decided, was unimportant. Already he was getting the kind of material he was looking for. Atmosphere. A real sense of place, activity. The uniforms and the babble of French, the posters on the walls, the comings and goings, the strong, stale smell of tobacco in a room that, in three separate places as far as Benedict could see, had signs prohibiting smoking. All so different from the bland, soulless station house in Palm Beach where he'd spent so much time in the last few months.

As things turned out, he didn't have long to wait. Twenty minutes after arriving at police headquarters, a few brief observations scribbled into his notebook, Benedict spotted a policeman heading across the hall in his direction. He was in plain clothes but you could tell him a mile off.

'You wanted to see Chief Inspector Jacquot?' said the man, taking up a position in front of him. He spoke English with a heavy accent, but the words were correct and courteous.

So his French wasn't as good as he thought it was, Benedict realised. He was out of practice after only a few months away and the Duty Sergeant had spotted it. 'Yes, yes, that's right,' he replied, then continued in French: 'If it's not too much trouble.'

'And you are?' Infuriatingly the policeman kept to English, as though he couldn't be bothered wasting time with halting schoolboy French when his own English was so much better.

'Max Benedict,' he replied, a little chastened.

'And may I ask what this is about?'

'The Waterman case.'

The policeman nodded, gave it some thought. Then he came and sat beside Benedict, leaning forward, elbows on knees, eyes looking straight ahead as he spoke, his hair, tied in a ponytail, coiling over his collar.

'If you have any information, Monsieur. Any one of the team . . .'

'It has to be Jacquot.'

The policeman sat back, gave him a look. 'I'm Jacquot.'

Benedict was delighted. He couldn't have crafted it better. What an introduction.

'I thought I might be able to help,' began Benedict. 'You see, I knew Suzie de Cotigny. That's to say . . .'

'How? Where?'

'In New York. She . . .'

At which moment the policeman's mobile rang. He flipped it open, holding up a hand to silence Benedict.

'I'll be there,' he said and snapped it shut. Then, turning to Benedict: 'You ever see a dead body?'

'Many times.'

Jacquot gave him a penetrating look as he took this in.

'Then we'll talk in the car.'

85

With most of her cargo unloaded, save for the timber in her forward holds, the merchant ship *Aurore* sat higher in the water than she had done earlier that day, her mud-coloured flanks now greened with a glistening coat of seaweed. Pushing back his *képi*, Emile Jalons watched a net bellied with sacks settle onto the quayside and sighed with relief. This was his second, and final, visit to Bay Seven and the unloading could now continue without further interference from him. He'd put in his two official visits – just like the book said. If the Drug Squad were going to make an appearance or bullets were going to fly, they were cutting it fine. Once the cargo was signed off and the bond hall doors secured, he was out of the firing line, safely back in his office at the other end of the quay, his interest in whatever the *Aurore* was carrying, and the interest of the Customs service, at an end. In a couple of hours his shift would be over and hang the lot of them.

Thirty metres away, a gang of dock workers unhooked the load's netting and transferred the last of the kaolin onto pallets. Belching clouds of black exhaust, the fork-lifts moved into action, picking up the loads and bearing them off to the bond hall. As they disappeared into its shadowy interior, Jalons rested his clipboard on the bonnet of his car and signed off each sheet of the manifest with a flourish. Slipping the originals into his briefcase, he handed Dupuys the copies.

As his sergeant loped off to the *Aurore*'s gangplank and made his way up the steep incline, Jalons shaded his eyes and looked up at the flying bridge. Was that Mallet, the skipper, the one with the beard and no cap? The one looking down at him. Was he in on the act, Jalons wondered? Did they have a tape of him? It wouldn't have surprised him. Jalons waved, snapped off a quick salute. As he lowered his hand, he cut it across his throat.

Up on the *Aurore*'s flying bridge, François Mallet glanced down at the senior Customs officer. The man had been a gem. No asking to have cases unpacked, no demand for sacks to be opened. Just a routine inspection, by the book. For a moment Mallet wondered whether the man was in on it. A little backhander, something to keep the wolves from the door. Mallet suspected so. Unloading a freighter was rarely this straightforward.

Not that he had anything to worry about, of course. Not now.

Stifling a yawn, he watched Dupuys claw his way up the gangway with the clearance papers. Once he had them, Mallet could call the shipping-line manager and confirm Customs clearance for owners and distributors, sign off the crew for shore leave, secure the ship and head into town.

Down on the quay, the senior Customs man gave him a wave, saluted, then ran the side of his hand across his throat. Job done. See you next time.

Which was when Mallet's attention was drawn to three unmarked Peugeots drawing up alongside the Customs officer's car. Before they'd come to a stop, a dozen armed men had bundled out onto the quay. They clearly knew what they were doing and in a matter of seconds the docking bay was secured: two men disappearing into the warehouse, three herding together the dock workers, another pair standing guard at the warehouse doors and four of them hammering up his gangway. The last member of the team was talking to the senior Customs officer, showing his ID and clearly intent on taking over.

Mallet's heart sank. The way things were shaping up he'd be lucky to make town any time soon.

At least the ship and its cargo were clean.

86

It took Jacquot twenty minutes to reach the fishing port of Vallon des Auffes on the road out to Fausse Monnaie. It took nearly the whole of that time before he realised that his passenger, with the freckled scalp and tortoiseshell glasses, had nothing to tell him that he didn't already know or suspect. All Benedict had done was provide some interesting New York background, verify their speculation about Suzanne de Cotigny's sexual preferences, and confirm that she enjoyed recreational drugs – which squared with the presence of cocaine in the guest bedroom at Roucas Blanc.

But that was all.

'How long did you know her?' asked Jacquot, after a short silence.

'We never actually met.'

'You never met?'

'Not directly, no. It was my job. It brought me into contact with them.'

'And what job would that be, Monsieur?' asked Jacquot.

'I'm a journalist,' said Benedict quietly. 'I work for—'

Jacquot didn't hesitate. He pressed his foot to the brake, changed into neutral and pulled into the kerb. There was a beep of protest from a car close behind that had been taken by surprise by this manoeuvre but Jacquot paid no attention. He reached across and opened his passenger's door.

'Thank you for your help, Monsieur. It has been invaluable.'

'You're letting me out here?'

'The walk back to town will do you good. Clear your head.'

After a moment's stunned silence, his passenger hefted his knapsack and got out of the car.

Merde, said Jacquot to himself as he drove off, leaving Benedict on the sidewalk. A journalist, for God's sake. How on earth could he have walked into that one? Glancing in his rear-view mirror, Jacquot could see the man a hundred metres back, standing at the kerb. Serve him right, decided Jacquot, as he turned off the Corniche road and followed the steep hillside lane into Vallon des Auffes.

Down on the quay a gendarme lifted a *Do Not Cross* perimeter tape and Jacquot pulled up behind Grenier's unmarked Peugeot.

Vallon des Auffes, thought Jacquot, getting out of the car and looking around. The place where his father had lived when he first arrived in Marseilles, a pocket-sized fishing port enclosed by a slope of fishermen's cottages and the towering arches of a Corniche flyover. It was different back then, in his father's day – a real working harbour: chandlers, metalworks and, as the name suggested, rope-makers. Now, most of the port-side premises had been turned into expensive seafood joints, of which Chez Fonfon was the oldest and most celebrated. A bouillabaisse here was even pricier than at Molineux's but, in Jacquot's opinion, not half so good. Here, in Vallon des Auffes, you paid for the view as much as the food. At Molineux's the only thing worth looking at was your plate.

Ten metres from the steps leading up to Chez Fonfon, in a space between two fishing skiffs, stood Grenier and Peluze. The body, covered in a dirty blue tarp, lay at their feet. Above them, inquisitive faces peered from the restaurant's picture windows.

'It's not the Waterman,' said Grenier, the only man on the squad who didn't call Jacquot boss.

Jacquot squatted down and lifted the covering, peered inside. The body was naked, small, almost childlike, but the breasts and the tuft of pubic hair were unmistakable. A very petite, dark-skinned lady. Somewhere in her thirties, Jacquot estimated. Toe- and fingernails painted red, and professionally cared for by the look of them.

'You ask me, it's a copycat,' continued Grenier.

'What makes you think that?' asked Jacquot, trying to see what Grenier had spotted that he had missed. The victim was a woman. She was naked. She looked to be close in age to the other victims. She had bruises on her cheek and neck and since she'd been pulled from the sea the chances were that she'd drowned. Or been drowned. He couldn't see what Grenier was getting at. He lifted the tarp a little higher and noted an injury to the victim's foot. Her ankle lay at an odd angle and the skin was badly abraded.

Jacquot lowered the tarp and looked up at the flyover. And the line of pilings beneath. His money said the body had been tumbled off the Corniche from the boot of a car, but not far enough along the bridge to miss the rocks below, where the victim had sustained her broken ankle. She'd then slowly drifted ashore, much like the body of Jilly Holford at Aqua-Cité.

'Turn her head, boss,' said Peluze. 'In the neck. You'll see what Al means. And there's jewellery, too.'

Jacquot did as instructed and there, wrapped with strands of hair, was the gold hilt of a dagger, wedged at an angle between shoulder and neck. If this was a Waterman victim, it was the first time the killer had used a weapon. And the first time he'd left jewellery on a victim, a thick gold bracelet on one wrist and a pair of gold ear-studs.

'Lucky strike, that,' said Grenier. 'All the bone there. You ask me, the killer's right-handed, taller than the victim and came at her from behind, a little to the side.'

'Anything else, professor?' chuckled Peluze.

Pushing aside the tarp Jacquot leant closer and studied the entry wound, the blade buried deep, a circle of bruised scarlet clearly showing against the caramel-coloured skin. Grenier was right, he thought, a lucky strike. First hit. And delivered with considerable force. It was a wonder the blade hadn't snapped. Pulling a handkerchief from his pocket, Jacquot reached for the handle, got a grip on it with both hands and began to rock it back and forth, the victim's head moving with the action. Deep down, he could feel the blade grate and scrape against bone, then start to loosen, until finally it slid free. Jacquot got to his feet and turned the weapon between his fingers, the sunlight glinting off it. It was long and slim, more like a letter-opener than a dagger, but surprisingly hefty in the hand. It was also exotically styled, the thin silver blade sliding between the lips of a golden serpent whose scaled body formed the handle, its tail coiled around a large blue stone.

Where the blade appeared from the serpent's mouth two words had been engraved into the silver.

Avec tendresse.

'I think you'll find it's a Zoffany,' came a voice from behind them. 'Got one just like it back home.'

Jacquot turned to see Benedict's blue eyes peering through his tortoiseshell spectacles, his freckled face wreathed in a helpful smile.

'They have a branch here in town,' he continued. 'Rue St-Ferréol, I think.'

87

E mile Jalons wanted very badly to go to the lavatory but the possibilities for a discreet pee on Bay Seven were limited. The side of his car, the wall of the warehouse, or over the edge of the quay – all of them out in the open and none of them dignified. Which was why he had left it so long. Trying to make up his mind. And now he was getting desperate.

He looked across at the Narcotics man, Lamonzie was his name, wondering if he could make his excuses and leave, but knowing that as senior Customs officer he'd probably have to stay till the bitter end. And right now, it was clear that this Lamonzie was in no mood to let anyone go anywhere. They'd searched through the goods in the bond hall without finding a thing and were now preparing to board and search the *Aurore*, Lamonzie and three of his men leaning over the bonnet of their car, poring over plans of the ship.

Which was good news for Jalons. It wouldn't have looked very good if they'd found something amongst the cargo that he'd signed off only minutes before their arrival. If the drugs were on board, at least that gave him a margin of professional security. His only concern was that if things did go wrong and they did find something on board, then a copy of the tape might still find its way to his wife or his boss.

But right then that prospect wasn't half so bad or pressing as his need for a pee.

Lamonzie was in a foul mood. After three hours in the warehouse searching through the *Aurore*'s cargo they'd found nothing amongst the hefty black blocks of rubber, dusty sacks of kaolin, and woven bags of cocoa and groundnuts, all of them itemised on the ship's manifest. Nothing extra. Nothing unaccounted for.

Which, as far as Lamonzie was concerned, meant one thing. The cargo they were looking for was still on board, either concealed amongst the timber in the forward holds or scheduled for a later pick-up during the refit that Jalons had told him about. But searching a ship the size of *Aurore* was no easy matter.

Snatching up the plans, he passed out instructions to his men: clear and secure the vessel; release the shore gangs; and bring in lights, dogs, sensors – the works.

Lamonzie glanced at his watch. It was going to be a long night. And he had no doubt whose fault it was. Trying to order his thoughts – what to do next, how to proceed, please God let us find something – he caught sight of the senior Customs officer, Jalons, flies open, pissing against a stack of pallets. Already a long stream had wound a coiling path between his boots and out onto the quay where it had started to puddle.

'Hey, you, Jalons,' shouted Lamonzie. 'When you've got a moment . . .'

88

Sometimes an investigation went so fast that it left the head spinning. Which was how things proceeded that Monday afternoon.

As Grenier said, the Vallon des Auffes body looked like a copycat killing. Sliding the letter-opener into a plastic evidence bag, Jacquot was certain they'd find no trace of pronoprazone, nor any evidence of a sexual assault comparable with the other victims. And the chances were that the victim hadn't even drowned, dead before she hit the water. No, Grenier was right. The jewellery, the weapon. This was no Waterman kill. If it had been, Jacquot reflected, walking to his car, it would have been the Waterman's last.

Which was when Clisson and Jouannay swung down into the port, parking their car beside his. Jacquot had hoped to make good his escape before the scene-of-crime boys arrived and for a moment he was tempted to say nothing about the knife in his pocket. Grenier or Peluze could tell them what he'd done. But as Clisson got out of the car, gave him a nod, Jacquot decided to play it straight. He pulled out the knife, told Clisson he'd removed it from the body and said he wanted to borrow it.

Clisson gave Jacquot a sharp, angry little look. But since the knife had already been removed from the body, there wasn't much he could do except make the point that it was Forensic's duty to secure a scene of crime and his job to collect and record evidence. Behind his boss, Jouannay raised his eyebrows and shook his head wearily.

Jacquot said he understood, apologised, but five minutes later he was reversing his car back past the police tape, the knife still in his possession and Benedict, knapsack on his knees, in the seat beside him.

'Where are you going to drop me this time, Chief Inspector?' the journalist asked, as they pulled away from the port and wound their way up to the main road.

'Back in town, Monsieur. Or at your hotel. Whichever you wish. It's the least I can do. But first . . .'

Up on the Corniche, Jacquot parked his car, told Benedict to stay where he was and, fingers idling along the stonework, he set off along the seaward edge of the flyover above Vallon des Auffes.

He found what he was looking for quickly enough: a smear of dust on the parapet as if something had been dragged across it, and a dry, dark bloom of scarlet. He looked over the edge. Far below the sea lapped at the pilings. At night, you'd never see them.

As Jacquot headed back to the car, his mobile bleeped. It was Gastal reporting in. The driver of the Renault, he said, was called Berthe Mourdet. Apparently she and the victim had met at the gym just a few days back and, under pressure, she'd admitted why she'd gone to the house in Roucas Blanc. According to Mourdet, Suzie de Cotigny had been alive and well when she left the de Cotigny house round 6:30 p.m. and she'd gone straight home. Her flatmates had backed up her story. They'd ordered in pizzas and watched a video. "She said she heard about the murder on the radio at work the following morning. Some beauty salon up on rue Sibié. At first she didn't realise that it was the woman she'd met at the gym and spent the afternoon with because the victim had given her another name. It wasn't until she saw the evening TV news and the pictures of Suzie and the house that she realised it was the same woman. After that she decided to keep quiet, keep out of it."

'You give her a hard time?' asked Jacquot.

'Oh yes,' replied Gastal.

'Good,' said Jacquot, and told him to meet up with him at the jeweller Zoffany on rue St-Ferréol.

Twenty minutes later, after dropping Benedict at the top of the lane leading to the Nice-Passédat, Jacquot left his car in the underground car park beneath Place de Gaulle and started along rue St-Ferréol. He didn't have far to walk. As Benedict had said, there was indeed a branch of Zoffany here, the kind of shop where you rang a bell for the door to be opened by a uniformed commissionaire. Waiting outside was Gastal.

The saleslady who greeted them was of a certain age, exquisitely polite and elegantly turned out, a silk cravat tucked into the collar of a blue Chanel suit. When Jacquot showed her the knife, a trace of blood from its blade smearing the inside of the sealed plastic bag, she blanched a little as though she'd been shown something that Gastal might have picked up on the sole of his shoe. But she confirmed that it was indeed a Zoffany piece, a silver-gilt letter-opener.

'It's the latest design,' she told them. 'It's called "Serpent". We've only stocked it for the last few months.'

'Have you sold many?' asked Gastal.

'Lots,' she replied. 'They've been enormously popular.'

'Could this be one of them, Madame?'

The sales lady spread her hands, shrugged. 'It's possible . . . But we have many branches, Messieurs. It could have been bought in any of them. In Paris, in Nice . . .'

'There is an engraving, Madame,' said Jacquot. ' *"Avec tendresse".*'

She smiled, shook her head. 'I'm sorry, Monsieur, I don't remember it. But I have only been here since March. It could have been done before I arrived.'

'So you do carry out that kind of work? Engraving? If a customer wants something . . .' asked Jacquot.

'*Bien sûr.* We have a workshop in the basement. If you like, I can check for you. It shouldn't take too long.'

Five minutes later she was back, bearing the workshop's order book. According to their records, she told them, resting the book on the counter and flicking through the pages, the engraving had indeed been carried out on the premises. In February. She found the page she was looking for and gave them the precise date. And the address where the letter-opener had been delivered after the work was completed. And the name of the recipient.

'Ba-da-boum,' said Gastal, with a leery wink.

'And the purchase, Madame?' asked Jacquot. 'Would you have records of the purchase?'

'*Mais certainement*, Monsieur. It's here in the book.'

Jacquot's heart lifted.

'Cheque? Credit card?'

The saleslady consulted the ledger once more, running a long, lacquered fingernail along the line.

'Purchase price. Engraving costs. Delivery. *Tout compris.* Cash,' she replied, and smiled helpfully.

89

B asquet left work early. Negotiating his Porsche up the ramp from the underground car park, he joined the flow of traffic along Quai du Lazaret in the shadow of the autoroute and set off along the Littoral for home. There was still an hour or more before rush hour clogged the road, so he found the outside lane quickly – it was pleasingly empty – and put his foot down.

It had been a good day and he was in a buoyant mood. Valadeau-Basquet's tendered offer on a planned hospital extension in Aix had been accepted, a shopping-mall development in Capelette was ahead of schedule and below budget for the month, and Valadeau et Cie's share price was up after a report in the financial press had listed them among the South of France's most energetic and forward-looking companies. All of it most gratifying.

And there was more. According to Raissac, whom he'd spoken to that morning, the *Aurore* had docked and was unloading cargo. But there was no need to worry, his friend had assured him. Their merchandise was already safe, spirited away. In a matter of hours it would be off their hands, and the money in their pockets.

With Anais finally out of his hair, Basquet reflected, the only rumple in the fabric of his happiness was the *calanques* deal, the still-to-secure *permis*. The re-presentation of his plans before the planning committee had been scheduled for a week on Wednesday, but with de Cotigny's suicide there'd clearly be delays until Raissac could work his magic. At least the money would be in place. No going

358

cap in hand to the Valadeau trustees. His first, very own, personal project. Not a *sou* to borrow, to beg for. A Paul Basquet project.

Céléstine was resting when he arrived home. Upstairs in his dressing room, tiptoeing round so as not to wake her, Basquet changed into tennis shorts and polo shirt and went down to the terrace where he had Adèle fetch him a drink. Carrying a chair onto the lawn and positioning it in the last rays of the setting sun, he made himself comfortable and gazed contentedly over his land: the barns and outbuildings coated in thick, rustling ivy, the pool and tennis court, the slopes of striped lawn, the braided sweep of the family vineyards – the vines greening and thickening, a soft emerald haze – and not another house in sight.

And beyond it all, rising up against the evening sky, the crumpled flanks of the Montagne Sainte Victoire. It was an awesome sight, Basquet decided, its steep, stony slopes brushed by the setting sun, a different colour every time you looked. Now the pale blush of peaches, now a soft, rosy blue, now a shifting violet, now mauve. Simply magical. Maybe when he retired, he'd follow Céléstine's example and learn to paint. Another Cézanne in the family.

Basquet was on his second Scotch and soda when he spotted Adèle coming out onto the terrace followed by two men. She pointed in his direction, bobbed a curtsy and disappeared inside. The two men crossed the terrace towards him. One of them seemed familiar. As they drew closer, Basquet remembered where he'd seen him before.

90

Anais Cuvry's front door had been easily forced, Gastal's shoulder enough to splinter the frame, free the lock and effect entry.

The first thing that struck them was the lingering scent of a woman's perfume, a warm, musky, intimate fragrance. Jacquot breathed it in; Gastal sniffed appreciatively. And then the colours: soft pastels, creamy shades, nothing bold or bright. This was a woman's home. A single woman's home. No children here.

And no men apart from those just passing through, guessed Jacquot, sizing the place up. At lunchtime. During the afternoon. Early evening on the way home. But never overnight.

Which was how it was starting to look to Jacquot. The petite, dark-skinned body, the perfectly manicured nails, the discreet little villa, expensive gifts from expensive stores. If Mademoiselle Cuvry wasn't on the game, she was clearly a well-maintained mistress.

The two men walked down the hallway and into the salon. It was a night-time room – the blinds closed, the ceiling light still on – and clearly the scene of a struggle: a rug in the centre of the room was rucked; a chair lay on its back; and a blue silk gown, tossed onto the sofa, was darkly stained around its lacy cream neckline.

Gastal went to the gown and picked it up. The silk and lace were stiffly creased. He pulled at the material and the stained patch parted with dry, resisting ticks. The two men looked at each other. They had the right place.

While Gastal stepped through into the kitchen, Jacquot went to the bedroom. The same scent, but stronger here. The curtains half drawn, stirred by a ceiling fan, a soft evening light showing through open shutters. But no lights on in here, unlike the salon. Nothing out of place. Jacquot walked over to the bed, which was garlanded with pink silk drapes hanging from the ceiling. Only one of the pillows was crumpled, one side of the bed slept in, the top sheet pushed aside, just as anyone would push aside a sheet when they got out of bed. Whoever had slept here the night before had slept alone.

Jacquot crossed the room to a small dressing table set into a wall of panelled cupboards. Amongst the paraphernalia of make-up was a single silver-framed photo. He picked it up. A posed studio shot. Head and shoulders tilted to the lens, something a model might keep in her portfolio. A younger, prettier Anais Cuvry; the features were unmistakable. The face he'd seen at Vallon des Auffes.

Back in the salon, Jacquot tried to work it out. From the beginning.

First, and most important, no damage to the front door. Which meant one of two things: either Mademoiselle Cuvry opened it herself, or the killer had a key. One of her clients? A lover calling by late? Since the bed had been slept in, it seemed unlikely that the visit had been expected. As far as Jacquot could see, the victim had been woken by someone coming into the house or ringing the doorbell late at night.

But certainly the caller was someone she knew. Either because he had a key, or because she had let him in. Since there was no spyhole in the front door, and she wouldn't have been able to see who was there, a visitor without a key must have said something, made himself known. Or Mademoiselle Cuvry would surely have put the chain on its runner before opening up.

Gastal came out of the kitchen. 'Nothing in there, or the bathroom,' he said. 'You check the bedroom?'

Jacquot nodded, but Gastal went to take a look all the same.

So. Someone the victim knows arrives at the house. They come in here, into the salon. But they don't go through to the bedroom. Significant? Possibly.

And here in the salon, judging by the chair and the rug and the bloodstained gown, some kind of confrontation had taken place, a struggle, which ended with the murder of Mademoiselle Cuvry.

One thing Jacquot knew for sure, the late-night caller hadn't come to kill. If he had, he'd have come prepared, brought his own weapon. This killing had been spontaneous, the heat of the moment. Snatching up the closest thing to hand, the Zoffany letter-opener, the killer had buried the blade in the victim's neck when her back was turned.

Afterwards, Jacquot guessed, the body had been stripped and carried out to a car, to be rolled off the Vallons des Auffes flyover, no more than a couple of miles from where he stood. Right now, in the evening rush hour, it would be nose-to-tail down there. But late at night, last night judging by the dried blood, a Sunday, it would have been a far quieter stretch of road – easy enough to pull over, dump the body and drive on without anyone seeing a thing.

Just like Grez's body at Longchamp. Make it look like another Waterman killing. Something to cover the killer's tracks.

Then, standing there in the middle of the room, something caught Jacquot's eye.

On the table by the sofa.

Just lying there.

A round yellow tin.

Lajaunie's *cachou* pastilles.

'So?' said Gastal, coming out of the bedroom, fingering a slip of silk he'd found, lifting it to his nose. 'What next?'

'La Joliette,' Jacquot replied quietly. 'A company called Valadeau on Quai du Lazaret. There's a man there we need to see.'

91

It was rare that Célestine took a nap in the afternoon and she felt strangely out of sorts as she pushed aside the sheet and swung her feet to the floor. She'd slept longer than she'd intended, the room cooler now than when she'd come up here, and the sun so low that shadows tented its corners. It was almost dark enough to switch on a light, but Célestine left it as it was. She showered, and felt revived, selected a pair of slacks and a blouse and dressed quickly. It was nearly seven when she arrived downstairs, a cardigan draped over her shoulders, her hair brushed but still damp, the taste of spearmint on her tongue, a lick of lipstick, and a spray of Heliotrope on throat and wrists.

In the salon she mixed herself a small vodka tonic and was twisting a slice of lime into it when Adèle appeared to say that Monsieur Basquet was in the study, with two gentlemen.

Detectives, she added, from Marseilles.

Jacquot and Gastal missed Basquet at his La Joliette office by minutes. According to Geneviève Chantreau, his personal assistant, Monsieur Basquet had just left for home. Was there anything she could help them with in his absence, she enquired?

Rather than ask for Basquet's home address, and risk Chantreau calling ahead to let her boss know that two policemen were looking for him, Jacquot told her that it was nothing urgent and that maybe she could fix a meeting for later in the week? This she had duly done, an appointment, Jacquot was sure, that would not be kept.

Back in the car, a call to Headquarters had secured Basquet's home address and an hour later Jacquot and Gastal were sitting side by side in leather club chairs in front of Paul Basquet's desk.

As soon as they'd introduced themselves on the terrace, explained the reason for their visit – investigating a murder, a body found at Vallon des Auffes – Basquet had struggled to his feet and suggested that the library might be a more appropriate place for their questions, leading them from the garden back into the house. On the way he'd offered them drinks, which they'd politely refused. Tea or coffee? Again refused. Now, looking ridiculously out of place in shorts that were too tight for him and too high in the leg, Paul Basquet stood by the windows behind his desk, looking inquiringly at his guests.

'Does this have anything to do with . . . with the other murders you were investigating, Chief Inspector? The last time we met?' He said this with the trace of a smile, as though he didn't expect Jacquot to be any more challenging than he'd been at their previous meeting.

'It's not clear at the moment, Monsieur, but there could be a connection. Once again, it's just a question of following up.'

'Following up. Of course. So how can I be of help this time?' There was a tired, tolerant tone to his voice.

'We believe you may know the victim,' Jacquot began.

It took a moment for Basquet to register what Jacquot had said.

'Really?' he replied. 'Are you sure? I do hope not.'

'Anais Cuvry,' said Jacquot.

If Jacquot had been expecting a reaction, he was disappointed. The name should have hit Basquet like a tyre iron, but the only response was a deep drawing-in of breath, a thoughtful frown and the closing of his eyes, as though he was giving the name his full consideration.

'No, Chief Inspector,' he said at last. 'I'm sorry. The name doesn't ring a bell.' Then, digging his fists into his pockets, Basquet turned abruptly and looked out of the library windows, towards the distant slopes of the Montagne Sainte Victoire.

It was a masterful performance, delivered with cool, controlled assurance. But turning his back to look through the windows was the give-away – a cover, a chance to gather himself. Jacquot had seen the same move many times. The man was lying. There was now not the slightest doubt in Jacquot's mind that the *cachou* pastilles in Anais

Cuvry's home belonged to the man behind the desk. That round yellow tin, he was certain, would be plastered with Basquet's fingerprints.

But what of the Zoffany letter-opener? Had Basquet bought it for his mistress? Had he had it engraved? *'Avec tendresse.'* It seemed a reasonable bet; the kind of gift a wealthy man like Basquet would give a mistress. Expensive, but suitably anonymous. No name or initials for the engraving and paid for in cash.

Which would mean, Jacquot had concluded on the drive up to Aix, that Basquet could not be the killer. If he was going to murder Anais Cuvry he'd hardly use a letter-opener that he'd bought for her, thoughtfully leaving it lodged in her spine for the police to find and trace.

But then, maybe Anais Cuvry had other lovers? Lovers that Basquet didn't know about. Any one of whom could have given her the letter-opener, ordered the engraving.

Which would certainly put Basquet back in the frame. If they were looking for motive, jealousy was always a good place to start – Basquet finding out that Anais was two-timing him with other men and having it out with her. And in his rage, killing her.

Jacquot decided it was time to change gear, toughen it up. He couldn't be bothered to wait for fingerprints to confirm what he already knew. That Basquet was lying. That Basquet was Cuvry's lover – and possibly her killer.

Across the desk, Basquet turned from the windows and gave the two policemen a questioning look, as though surprised that they should still be there. 'Was there anything else, Messieurs?'

'She lived in Endoume,' said Jacquot, crossing his legs, making himself comfortable. And making it clear he was in no rush to leave. '34 Avenue Corbusier. Maybe you know the address?'

Again Basquet shook his head. 'Of course, I know the area, but not . . .'

'So you're saying that you do not know the victim and that you never visited her home? Is that correct?'

'It most certainly is,' replied Basquet indignantly. 'I already told you . . .'

At which point there was a soft knock on the door and Céléstine Basquet appeared, drink in hand. 'Gentlemen?'

Jacquot and Gastal got to their feet, and Basquet came bustling round the side of his desk, his trainers squeaking on the polished wood floor.

'I won't bother to introduce you, my dear,' he said, kissing her on the cheek. 'These two gentlemen were just leaving.'

'On the contrary, Madame,' said Jacquot with a light smile. 'Actually we do have some more questions we would like to ask your husband.'

'Questions?' asked Céléstine.

'These gentlemen are investigating a murder, my dear, someone . . .' Basquet groped for words, an explanation.

'Someone we believe your husband may have known,' said Jacquot. 'A friend of his.'

Basquet threw Jacquot a menacing look.

'How dreadful,' said Céléstine, patting her husband's hand as though to comfort him. Then, going to a sofa and arranging herself there, a look of concern settled across her features. 'But which friend? Who? Tell me.'

At this point, Jacquot reasoned, Basquet had two possible options. He could either maintain his indignation and deny everything – particularly with his wife present. Or he could make an effort to cooperate, covertly, without arousing her suspicions. If he opted for the latter route, Jacquot knew that they'd find his prints on the tin of pastilles, confirming that Anais Cuvry had been his mistress.

'It appears that someone from Valadeau, one of the staff, has been killed,' said Basquet to his wife, returning to his desk, pulling out the chair and sitting down.

As they took their own seats, repositioning their chairs to include Madame Basquet in the conversation, Gastal caught Jacquot's eye and mouthed what looked like 'Badaboum'.

They had him.

Now all they needed to do was find out if Paul Basquet was the killer.

'So,' continued Jacquot. 'You were saying, Monsieur. Mademoiselle Cuvry worked at Valadeau?'

'I think so. I think so,' replied Basquet, tapping a finger against his temple as though to jog his memory, but using the cover of his hand to shoot Jacquot a meaningful look without his wife seeing. 'Human Resources? I can't quite recall. Something like that.'

'Is it the Waterman? The one in the paper?' asked Céléstine, sipping her drink, eyes bright with curiosity.

Jacquot turned to her. 'We don't think so, Madame. There are certain similarities, but also certain differences . . .'

Céléstine nodded but said nothing more. For a moment there was silence in the room.

'So, Messieurs,' said Basquet, trying to regain his composure, clearly anxious to bring the meeting to an end. 'Is there anything else I can help you with? Perhaps you should come to the office tomorrow. Maybe we can check our records . . .'

Jacquot knew what Basquet was after. Now that he'd as good as admitted that he and Anais Cuvry were lovers, he was rather hoping they'd be kind enough to get the hell out of his house before they got him into any trouble with his wife. They were men, after all. They would understand the position he was in. Surely.

But Jacquot had no intention of going quite yet. Or of letting Basquet off the hook, interested to note that it had still not occurred to him that he might be a suspect.

It was time to apply more pressure. Play the advantage.

'Did you ever visit Anais Cuvry at home?' he asked, starting to enjoy the man's discomfort.

'At home?' repeated Basquet, giving Jacquot another hooded look. 'Not that I recall. It doesn't seem likely.'

'Valadeau employs well over a thousand people, Chief Inspector,' said Céléstine, from the sofa. 'You can't surely expect my husband to know everyone? Or where they live?' She gave them a patient smile, then reached for a silver box on the coffee table, took out a cigarette and lit it.

Jacquot nodded. Of course, it was ridiculous. Nevertheless . . .

'So that would be a "no", Monsieur?' he continued.

Basquet frowned fiercely, pretending for his wife's benefit to give the question some thought, but actually levelling another look in Jacquot's direction. He began to shake his head. 'Not so far as I can recall. Endoume, you said?'

'Tell me, Chief Inspector.' It was Céléstine, from the sofa. 'How exactly did this Mademoiselle Cuvry die?'

'The victim was stabbed, Madame. In the neck, with a letter-opener.'

Out of the corner of his eye, Jacquot registered a look of surprise on Basquet's face.

'So far as we can establish,' he continued, 'it appears that the letter-opener was bought from a jeweller called Zoffany. Here in town. Rue St-Ferréol. Four months ago.' Jacquot turned back to Basquet. 'Are you familiar with the store, Monsieur?'

'Zoffany, you say? It certainly sounds familiar.'

'It certainly should,' said Jacquot. 'According to their records, your credit card was used to buy that letter-opener. Your signature is on the payment slip.'

Across the room, on the sofa, Jacquot noticed Basquet's wife stiffen, pale.

Basquet saw it too.

'My credit card?' he blustered, suddenly uncertain, trying to remember if he'd paid with cash or by card. Surely, he'd have paid cash? He'd never have used a credit card, would he?

The uncertainty threw him off balance, just as Jacquot had intended. But he still clung on, desperate to keep control of the conversation, desperate to keep his wife from finding out about his mistress.

He began nodding, as though he'd just remembered something. 'Cuvry, you said? Cuvry. Yes, yes . . . I do certainly recall the name . . . But, but . . . You know something? I'm wrong. I've got it wrong. Not Human Resources. Not at all. Come to think of it, I believe she might have helped us with some contract work. Some consultancy, perhaps. This gift, this . . . letter-opener must have been a kind of thank-you. That sort of thing, for helping us out . . . I can't actually remember buying it, but if you have my credit-card payment slip, Chief Inspector . . .'

So Basquet *had* bought the letter-opener. Or, at least, he hadn't denied buying it. Which meant . . .

Jacquot let the moment hang, then moved on: 'Might I ask where you were last night, Monsieur?'

'Last night? Sunday, you mean?' asked Basquet.

'That's correct. Say, from nine in the evening onwards?'

'Why, here, of course.' He looked at his wife, who nodded helpfully. 'Célestine was at a dinner party,' he continued, clearing his throat. 'Friends. The Fazilleaux. In Aix. I'm afraid I didn't fancy it, so I cried off . . . stayed home. Did some work here in the library and then went to bed.'

The clearing of the throat, like his turning to look through the window when Jacquot told him the name of the murder victim, was enough for Jacquot to know at once that Basquet was lying. Or rather, not telling the whole truth. His wife might have gone out to dinner, and he might have cried off, but Jacquot doubted that Basquet had spent the evening working here at his desk. He'd gone out as well. To Endoume? To call on Anais Cuvry?

There was something else, too. For the first time since they'd told him about the murder, Jacquot could see that Basquet now realised it was no longer just a matter of keeping his wife from finding out about his mistress. It was the sudden, chilling realisation that he was a murder suspect.

'So you were in bed when your wife returned home?' continued Jacquot, keeping up the pressure.

'That's right. That's right,' stammered Basquet, reaching across to snap on a desk lamp in the gathering gloom. The pool of light that splashed across the desk made the rest of the room grow suddenly darker. Jacquot couldn't have wished for better stage management.

'Asleep?'

'Dead to the world,' Basquet's wife answered for him, leaning forward to put out her cigarette. 'And snoring like a lion. I had to sleep in our son's room.'

'And that would have been at what time, Madame?' asked Jacquot, turning in his chair to face Basquet's wife.

'I'd say, oh, around eleven.'

'And you, Madame,' continued Jacquot lightly. 'Did you go straight to bed? After you returned from your dinner party?'

'I had a glass of warm milk in the kitchen, then went upstairs to bed.'

'To your son's room, you said?'

'To ours first. But it wasn't easy getting to sleep . . .' She gave a little laugh, smiled forgivingly at her husband, then twirled the ice in her glass.

But Basquet, Jacquot noted, did not return the smile. He was looking at his wife intently, a puzzled frown forming, as if he was trying to remember something, as if something didn't quite add up, the lines on his face thrown into stronger relief by the play of the light.

'So from eleven onwards,' continued Jacquot, registering Basquet's frown, his silence, 'you were both here, asleep? In different rooms?'

Madame Basquet nodded. 'That's correct, Chief Inspector.'

'Tell me, Madame,' said Jacquot. 'And please forgive the forthright nature of this question . . .' He paused, drew a breath, let the moment stretch into expectant silence. 'Tell me,' he continued at last. 'Did you know that Anais Cuvry was your husband's mistress?'

'Good God, man . . .' exclaimed Basquet, leaping to his feet, eyes wide with indignation.

'If you wouldn't mind, Monsieur,' said Jacquot, holding up a hand, but never taking his eyes off Madame Basquet for a second.

'But I do mind. I mind a lot,' spluttered Basquet, rapping his fists against the blotter on his desk. 'Coming here . . . coming to my home with these . . . with these outrageous allegations . . .'

'Yes, I did know,' came Madame Basquet's voice, quiet, resigned.

Her words stopped Basquet in his tracks. He turned and looked at his wife. Then, stunned, he reached back for his chair and lowered himself into it.

Jacquot knew how he must have felt. All that effort to keep it from her – here, this evening, and for however long the affair had been going on – and she'd known the whole time!

Jacquot pressed on. 'And how long have you known?'

'From the beginning, Chief Inspector.' She leant forward to put her drink on the coffee table, then sat back and composed herself. Calmly she returned Jacquot's gaze. 'What do they call it? *Cinq à sept?*' She gave another of her little laughs, a touch more brittle this time. 'I believe it's quite common. Men of a certain age.'

'And how did you feel about your husband's . . . activities?'

'So long as it didn't upset the status quo . . . So long as the children didn't find out . . .' Céléstine shrugged, spread her hands. 'And she was nothing special.'

'So you knew Mademoiselle Cuvry? You met her?'

'No. I mean . . . I know my husband. It is probably not the first time he has . . . strayed. And it probably wouldn't have been the last. It was just . . . not important. I'm sure you understand, Chief Inspector.' She waved her hand, as if at a fly. Inconsequential.

But Jacquot was not convinced by Madame Basquet's quietly dignified admission, nor by her calm acceptance. There was something up ahead. He could smell it. Almost taste it. He pressed on.

'Tell me, Madame. Do you drive?'

Basquet's wife nodded, then looked perplexed – as though she couldn't quite see where this was headed, what Jacquot was getting at. She didn't have to wait long.

'Might I ask what kind of car, Madame?'

'A Citroën, a Xsara,' she replied.

Jacquot nodded.

'It might interest you to learn, Madame, that a Citroën Xsara was seen on Avenue Corbusier. In Endoume, where the victim lived. Late last night. A man walking his dog reported seeing it.'

Of course it was a lie, but Jacquot had played the same game with her husband – the signature on the credit-card slip – and that had worked, so he saw no reason not to try it with Basquet's wife. Just a bluff, to unsettle her. That was all it was.

'And later a Citroën was seen on the Corniche road,' he continued. 'Parked on the flyover above Vallon des Auffes. Where Mademoiselle Cuvry's body was dumped.'

For a moment there was silence in the room as the implication took shape in their minds.

Céléstine Basquet shivered, pulled the sleeves of her cardigan around her.

'I can't imagine what you mean,' she began, but her voice faltered. 'If you're suggesting, Chief Inspector . . .'

'I think, Madame, you know exactly what I'm suggesting.'

'This is getting ridiculous,' began Basquet, but Jacquot could see that his interruption was half-hearted; the man didn't know what else to say, how else to proceed. Basquet knew something they didn't. Something about his wife. Something to do with their sleeping arrangements.

And that was enough for Jacquot.

He slid his hand into an inside pocket and drew out the plastic bag, reached across and laid it on Basquet's desk. There was a dull clunk as the weighty silver-gilt letter-opener wrapped inside the bag came into contact with the wooden surface.

The effect was exactly as Jacquot had wished. Both Basquet and his wife stared at the object with horrified fascination, the gold handle and silver blade glinting in the light, a smear of blood still visible on the inside of the plastic.

'The murder weapon,' said Jacquot. 'You, of course, will have seen it before, Monsieur.'

But Basquet didn't speak.

Which Jacquot had expected.

'And so will you, Madame,' continued Jacquot, turning towards Madame Basquet, leaning his elbows on his knees. 'Last night. In Anais Cuvry's home. When you went round to confront her. After dinner. When your husband was asleep. To scare her off? To save your marriage? The letter-opener you snatched up when she refused to play ball. The same letter-opener that your husband bought for Mademoiselle Cuvry, a gift you couldn't have known about.'

Madame Basquet straightened her back, raised her chin, clasped her hands in her lap. But said nothing.

Jacquot turned to Basquet. 'I think, Monsieur, that you should call your lawyer.'

Basquet dragged his eyes from his wife, and looked blankly at Jacquot.

'My lawyer?'

'Or maybe your wife has her own?'

Beside him, Gastal sniffed, sat back in his chair and pinched the creases in his trousers.

92

Tuesday

The Widow Foraque fed her two canaries, Mittie and Chirrie. Pouring seed into their bowls, changing the water in their cups, twittering at them as she did so, she waited for footsteps on the stairs.

He'd come home late the night before, long past midnight. She'd heard the key in the latch, the screech of the door, the scuff of his shoes across the tiled hall. She listened from her bed, lifting her head from the pillow so that she could bring both ears into play. And there it was, she was pleased to note, a lightness to the step. As she settled back, Madame Foraque decided her tenant was finally on the mend.

She was carrying the birdcages to the front door that Tuesday morning, for an hour or two of fresh air and sunshine, when Jacquot appeared at the foot of the stairs. She put down Mittie and Chirrie and placed her hands on her hips, four-square and confrontational.

'So?'

'Happy birthday,' he said, and bent down to give her a kiss, not easy to do when she made no effort to offer her cheek.

'Who told you it was my birthday?' she asked, taking the small parcel he offered.

'You did. Last week. And the week before. And the week before that. Just like you do every year, *Grand'maman.*'

Madame Foraque shrugged off his reply, scrabbled to untie the ribbon, then wound it round her fingers; opened the wrapping, then folded the paper neatly, putting both in her apron pocket. Only then did she inspect the gift. Five cheroots from Tabac Delorme, also bound in ribbon.

'Have you got that Waterman yet?' she asked, lifting the cheroots to her nose and sniffing suspiciously. 'You look as if you have.'

Jacquot shook his head. 'Not yet, we haven't,' he told her. 'But you don't have to worry yourself. I have a feeling that our friend has moved on.'

'You have a feeling? Just a feeling?' Madame Foraque clucked disapprovingly. 'And that's supposed to make me feel better? A woman on her own? With a madman on the loose? *Pppfff.*'

'You'll see,' replied Jacquot, heading for the door. 'Mark my words. *C'est fini.*'

And as he made his way down the sloping steps of rue Salvarelli, a sweet salt tang in the air, Jacquot knew he was right; knew in his bones, that bright Marseilles morning, that their man was packing his bags, or already gone.

First off, Jacquot decided, turning along rue des Honneurs, all the brouhaha over the de Cotigny killing would have unnerved him. All that press and TV coverage over the weekend. Suzie de Cotigny was too big, too important a name, to be ignored. Her murder would become a high-priority, high-profile case and the killer would know that Marseilles was no longer the safe billet he'd enjoyed so far. The heat would be turned up, all police resources directed at this one case, and he'd have to watch his step. Easier, if he was the transient Jacquot suspected, just to move on.

Secondly, if the Waterman was still hanging around, too cocky or confident to worry about increased police activity, then the Cuvry murder would certainly see him off. When they got their confession from Madame Basquet, currently residing down the street at police headquarters, and the press splashed the story saying how she'd tried to disguise it as just another Waterman kill, that would be an end to it. Killers like the Waterman hated copycats. Hated them. He'd move on for sure. Somewhere new – another city by the sea, on a river, beside a lake.

Not that they'd stop looking for him, of course. As far as the *Judiciaire* was concerned, a file remained open until the killer was apprehended. But that wouldn't happen in Marseilles, Jacquot knew. Not now.

One day soon, though, a call would come through from some other force – more murders, more drowned bodies. It was the way it went. As Jacquot had said to Solange Bonnefoy, sooner or later, wherever he happened to be, the Waterman would make a mistake.

And then they would have him.

Toulon. Nice. Biarritz.

Wherever he pitched up next.

93

The body of Suzanne Delahaye de Cotigny, in a shiny mahogany casket furnished with sturdy brass handles, was released to the Delahaye family at mid-morning and taken from the city morgue to the airport at Marignane by a firm of undertakers. Suzanne's brother, Gus, supervised proceedings, watched by Max Benedict who'd followed in a taxi from the Nice-Passédat.

So far as Benedict could see, Delahaye handed out tips to nearly everyone he came into contact with that morning – the concierge at the front desk, the busboy who brought round his rented Mercedes, the two medical orderlies who wheeled the trolley from the back entrance of the morgue to the undertakers' limousine, and undoubtedly, though Benedict was unable to confirm this, to the undertakers at the airport after the body had been loaded onto the family jet, possibly even to the Immigration officials who dealt with the paperwork and cleared the casket for the journey home.

From Marignane, Benedict followed Delahaye's Mercedes back to town and the Nice-Passédat where the tip-happy Wall Street broker joined his parents for lunch on the terrace.

It was the first time that Benedict had seen the older Delahayes since their arrival three days earlier. Either they'd stayed put in their room or they'd managed to evade him. Like his son, Leonard Delahaye wore a black suit and tie, while his wife wore a narrow black dress and jacket, black shoes and pillbox hat. Benedict sat three tables away, close enough to see the dishes they were served – a slice of foie gras and toasts for Gus Delahaye, a simple green salad with quails' eggs for his mother and a small steak *frites* for his father – but not close enough to overhear their conversation, an occasional, whispered affair. The brother drank his customary bourbon and branch but his parents made do with mineral water. They rarely looked up from the table, either at each other or at the waiters who attended them. Benedict sensed an air of unsurprised despair in the way they held their forks – in the American manner – and in the way they sipped their drinks, as though they had somehow always known that it would come to this. How Suzanne had disappointed them once again, albeit for the last time.

An hour after their lunch a chauffeur-driven limousine, as black as their suits, drew up at the front of the Nice-Passédat and the Delahayes were taken to the Cathédrale de la Major for the funeral service of Hubert de Cotigny. Max Benedict watched them pull out of the hotel forecourt, then waved up a cab and followed at a discreet distance.

The roads around the cathedral were packed, the city's finest turning out to bid farewell to their friend and their colleague, a sway of black umbrellas to protect against a blazing sun. Benedict watched it all from the back seat of his cab – a milling swarm of the great and the good in tails and frock coats, top hats and dress uniforms, sashes, gloves and veils making their way through the cathedral doors. He waited there in the dusty heat until the service was over and he watched as the two grieving families reappeared – Delahaye Senior with a stooped Madame de Cotigny on his arm, Mrs Delahaye with her son, de Cotigny's daughter with her husband – followed by the pall-bearers, de Cotigny's casket hoisted onto their shoulders and draped in a rippling *tricolore*.

Across town, at the Saint Pierre cemetery, ahead of the cortège, Benedict paid off his cab and took up position on a rise of headstones some fifty metres past the intersection of Allée du Japon and the Grande Allée, the main cemetery concourse where his man at the Nice-Passédat had told him the de Cotignys kept their family mausoleum. Pulling a pair of Leica binoculars from his pocket Benedict scanned the miniature *faux* Greek temples and Palladian palaces, the Gothic towers and arabesque tents that faced the Allée.

It was not difficult to identify the de Cotigny mausoleum, nothing less than a miniature chateau with witch-hat turrets and marble battlements, its wrought-iron doors wide open, its grassy bank strewn with wreaths. Above the doors, between lowered and furled banners, was the family name, the letters boldly carved in capitals but spread with yellow lichen.

Ten minutes later, Benedict watched the hearse turn through the gates, enter the walled cemetery and lead a column of black sedans between the shadowing lime trees to the family plot. It was immediately clear that there were fewer people here than at the church and, as the guests stepped from their plush back seats, Benedict raised his binoculars and scanned the faces. There the Delahayes, there a weeping Madame de Cotigny now supported by her granddaughter, and gathering around them a smaller circle of family and friends.

Slowly, the casket was drawn from the back of the hearse and four frock-coated undertakers took a handle each. Carrying it slung between them, they slow-stepped to the mausoleum where a Monsignor in papal red gave the final blessing and the casket passed into the darkened crypt. A minute or two later the pall-bearers trooped dolefully back into the sunlight, one of them securing the mausoleum doors, another presenting the *tricolore* that had adorned de Cotigny's coffin to his mother.

It was over. As simply and as finally as that. Car doors slammed, engines started and ten minutes later the only thing that moved on Saint Pierre's Grande Allée were the leaves of the lime trees, rustling their own indistinct adieus.

Stepping out onto Grande Allée, Benedict made his way back to the cemetery gates, pausing only briefly to note the flattened grass outside Hubert de Cotigny's final resting place, the mourners' wreaths and the messages of farewell.

Outside the cemetery he cast around for a cab and knew it didn't look good. Most of the traffic was heading north into the suburbs. In order to find a ride back to town he would have to cross the road for the southbound flow. He was trying to decide how best to do this when a grey city cab slid out of the line of traffic and pulled up at the kerb. In the back seat he could see a woman lean forward with money for the fare.

As she opened the passenger door, Benedict stepped forward, drew it wide and offered a hand to help her out. Her eyes were concealed behind sunglasses, and only a border of dark curls showed beneath a tightly wrapped headscarf. She wore a blue mackintosh draped over a light cream trouser suit and she carried a single rose. Without looking at him, she murmured what he presumed were thanks and hurried through the cemetery gates.

Sliding into the back seat, warm from the sun and scented from the previous passenger (Eau de Flore, he was certain), Benedict gave instructions for the Nice-Passédat and the cabbie, with the heel of his hand on the horn, nudged his way through the flow of northbound traffic.

As they made the turn, mounting the far kerb and bumping off it, Benedict glanced back down the long, lime-treed length of the Grande Allée and noticed that the lady in the coat and pants suit appeared to be standing in front of the de Cotigny mausoleum.

As the cab straightened and accelerated away, Benedict wondered who she could be? A mistress, maybe? Coming to her lover's grave after the family had departed? So discreet. So stylish and so French, he thought, sitting back in his seat, not a little surprised that a man like de Cotigny, if indeed it was his mausoleum the woman had stopped at, should have had a mistress.

As the cab headed back into town, Benedict wondered if he should follow it up, ask around, another angle for the story. But then he dismissed the thought. The piece was just about wrapped. It was time to check out of the Nice-Passédat, and go home to La Ferme Magny. Tonight he would do a final edit and send his story off to New York. If it worked, maybe he'd just add a final sentence about the lady in the trouser suit. The single rose. Something unresolved. Enigmatic.

Benedict liked the feel of it.

A sweet little touch.

94

It was the news, delivered by Jacquot, that Anais Cuvry had been three months pregnant which finally broke Madame Céléstine Basquet. Whether it was knowing that her husband Paul had likely fathered the child, or the fact that she, Céléstine, had unwittingly ended two lives instead of one, it was impossible to say.

Up until that moment Madame Basquet had stuck steadfastly to her story. Dinner with friends, cards, returning home at about eleven. She'd made herself a warm drink and gone upstairs to bed. But her husband had been snoring so loudly that she moved to her son Laurent's room where she spent the rest of the night.

And that was all she would admit to.

No, she did not know Anais Cuvry personally, though she did know that her husband had a mistress.

No, she did not know where Mademoiselle Cuvry lived.

No, she had not driven to her home late Sunday night when her husband was fast asleep.

And no, she had not killed this . . . woman. Quite preposterous. Why should she? What was it to her? He would tire of her soon enough.

And that was how, the previous night, they had left it, her lawyer *Maître* Arrondeau and her husband Paul Basquet retreating into the night, leaving Madame Basquet to ponder her situation in a holding cell in the basement of the Hôtel de Police.

But with no forensic evidence to tie her to the scene of crime, her obstinate denials regarding the murder, and some heavy guns brought to bear by her attorney Arrondeau the following morning, it was looking increasingly likely that Madame Basquet would be released.

Until Valéry's preliminary report was delivered to police head-quarters shortly after lunch.

As they'd suspected, no trace of pronoprazone had been found. And the victim had not drowned. She had died from a single stab wound to the neck, the blade lodging fatally between the second and third thoracic vertebrae, severing the spinal column. In addition, Valéry noted, the victim had sustained a compound fracture to the left ankle, the wound containing fragments of stone and grit which, Jacquot had no doubt, would match any sample taken from the Vallon des Auffes pilings.

Valéry also noted that the victim was a little over three months pregnant at the time of death.

That was all it took.

Later that afternoon, Madame Céléstine Basquet was formally charged with the murder of Anais Cuvry and arrangements were made for the accused's immediate transfer to the women's wing of Les Baumettes until a formal application for bail could be made by *Maître* Arrondeau.

Jogging up the stairs to his office, Jacquot felt justifiably pleased with the day's work. A murder solved in less than twenty-four hours. It didn't get much better than that. He was on the last landing when Peluze leant over the banister one floor above.

'Call from the Chief,' he said. 'You're wanted. You and Gastal.'

95

I n his top-floor office, Yves Guimpier looked tense and irritable, his fingers playing with a plastic ruler.

'I've had Lamonzie in here. And he's looking for blood. Your blood.'

Jacquot nodded. Gastal cleared his throat.

Both men were standing in front of Guimpier's desk, their boss swinging to and fro in his chair. Neither had been invited to sit. Over Guimpier's shoulder, through his closed window, seagulls wheeled around the spire of the Cathédrale de la Major, the rattle of drills on the Metro extension just a dull, distant jangling.

'What's he say?' asked Gastal, sounding concerned.

Guimpier stopped swinging and gave him a glowering look over the bending ruler. Jacquot could see that Guimpier didn't much like Gastal.

'Says you've been hampering his investigation . . .'

'Not so . . . no, no . . .' spluttered Gastal.

'. . . Treading on his toes,' continued Guimpier. 'Despite being told to keep off. Said you alerted the suspect, this Raissac fellow, and blew the bust.'

'No way,' said Gastal. 'He's got it all wrong.'

'You're telling me that a senior officer is lying, Gastal? The head of Narcotics? You're saying that—'

'There was no choice,' interrupted Jacquot, coming to Gastal's aid. He knew what this was all about. Lamonzie playing prima donna, looking for fall guys. News of his quayside bust gone wrong had been doing the rounds all morning, much to everyone's amusement. 'Raissac was linked to the Waterman inquiry,' Jacquot continued. 'What else could we do? Turn a blind eye because Lamonzie's cooked up some plan and not bothered to tell anyone?'

Guimpier turned from Gastal and fixed Jacquot with an icy look. 'Linked? Linked to the Waterman investigation? How? Because an apartment he owned was rented to one of the victims?' Guimpier started shaking his head. 'You'll have to do better than that, I'm afraid. I shouldn't be telling you this, but right now friend Lamonzie is looking for an official inquiry. And I can't say I blame him.'

'Look,' began Jacquot, 'there was more to it than just—'

But Guimpier didn't want to hear it. 'According to Lamonzie – and I have no reason to disbelieve him – he told you, personally, last week, steer clear or else.'

'Which, so far as possible, we did,' replied Jacquot, keeping his temper in check but feeling a knot of impatience tighten in his chest, not at Guimpier but at Lamonzie. Lodging an official complaint? Just who the hell did he think he was?

'So visiting Monsieur Raissac at home last Friday was just a social call?' Guimpier put down the ruler and set his hands on the arms of his chair. 'You were seen. In and out.'

'He was part of our investigation,' Jacquot repeated, slow and quiet. 'It would have been out of order not to follow it up. We had bodies piling up and we didn't want another . . .'

'You didn't think to talk to Lamonzie?'

'Talk to Lamonzie? Why? He doesn't talk to us. And what would he have said, anyway? "Back off, this is my investigation." ' Jacquot shook his head. 'There was no point, nothing to be gained.'

'So what exactly's happened?' interrupted Gastal.

Jacquot glanced at his partner, not altogether sure whether Gastal was trying to cool the situation or was simply motivated by self-interest – how this might affect his forthcoming transfer to Lamonzie's unit.

'According to Lamonzie, a new route was opening up,' replied Guimpier. 'Old players. New source. Seems they'd decided to bypass the Spanish ports and go the extra mile. Here. To Marseilles. Like the old days. Lamonzie's been on the case nearly a year, working with the boys in Toulon. Some grass told them Raissac was behind it, moving his operations along the coast. Bigger loads, greater frequency;

apparently he'd also set up a new carrier. And yesterday, according to Lamonzie's sources, the first consignment was due to land. Several hundred kilos of cocaine. So when the ship ties up and starts unloading, Lamonzie's team arrives and sets to. Only there's nothing to find. Either it was never there, or someone got hold of it. And now, to cap it all, this fellow Raissac's dead . . .'

'Dead?' Jacquot was stunned by the news. He had a sudden image of the man, bending down to pick up his ID card and handing it back with a smile, a smile set in a pool of pitted scarlet.

'He's dead?' repeated Gastal. 'How?'

'One of his staff found him last night. In his garage. He'd been shot. Looks like a professional hit, according to Lamonzie.'

'Jesus,' said Gastal.

'So, not only does Lamonzie not get hold of the consignment,' continued Guimpier, 'he also loses Raissac and a whole line-up of supporting characters – after working on the case close to a year. A year's work down the drain. Because you two set off alarm bells.'

'Well, I guess you can see his point,' said Gastal, shaking his head.

It took a moment for Jacquot to register what Gastal had said. 'You can see his what?' he said, turning to his partner. 'You can see his point? Just exactly whose side are you on, Gastal? You're working Homicide, remember? And it was you . . .'

'Listen here,' replied Gastal, squaring up. 'I said we should leave it. I told you it was Lamonzie's call.'

Jacquot couldn't believe his ears. 'You said what?'

'Hey, hold on, Danny. Don't try and tell me—'

'Hey, hey, give it a break, you two,' said Guimpier, reaching for his ruler and slapping it on the desk. 'Gastal,' he said, pointing the ruler at him. 'You got something to say, say it. Jacquot . . .' The chief held up a shaking finger. 'Not a word.'

'It starts last Monday,' Gastal began, stretching his neck out of his collar. 'We meet up after lunch and my friend here says we've gotta check a name. Turns out it's Raissac's place in town. We wait around all afternoon, wasting time, and end up with zero. Which is when Lamonzie lets Danny know in no uncertain terms to keep out of the way. The man's under surveillance. Which seems fair enough to me. I mean, you got an ongoing, you don't want someone messing the ground.'

Jacquot looked at Gastal in astonishment. He could hardly believe what he was hearing. This was all wrong. This was not what had happened. It was Gastal who'd suggested calling on Raissac. Not him. He'd had Monel's tattoo to check out. Instead, he'd spent a couple of hours drumming his fingers on the roof of his car, hanging around for Gastal. Checking out someone he'd never even heard of till that afternoon.

And then, standing there in Guimpier's office, Jacquot suddenly recalled what Doisneau had told him in the café on Tamasin. Doisneau's warning that Raissac had a man on the inside. At the time, Jacquot had assumed it was someone in Toulon, or someone on Lamonzie's team.

Or maybe someone about to join Lamonzie's team?

Gastal.

Who'd come to Marseilles from Toulon.

Gastal. It had to be. It fitted. No wonder Gastal hadn't said a word to him about Raissac calling Carnot's mobile on Saturday. Trying to keep his paymaster out of the frame.

And then, like he was reading a passage of play, Jacquot knew what was coming, could suddenly see what all this was about, where the ball was headed.

It was a set-up. And he, Jacquot, was the fall guy, the one who'd gone for the dummy and would likely end up paying the price for a bust gone wrong. A bust gone wrong because his own partner was on the take – sending him to ring on Raissac's doorbell instead of doing it himself, the only way Gastal could find out if the place was under surveillance without putting himself on the spot. Because Gastal knew that if Raissac's place *was* being watched, then Lamonzie would be down on them like a sack of shit – for jeopardising their stake-out, possibly alerting the suspect. And that was exactly what had happened, providing Gastal with the information he needed, information that he could pass on to Raissac without arousing anyone's suspicion.

Jacquot's fault, not Gastal's.

And here was Gastal busily covering his tracks, playing the innocent.

Jacquot felt a rising swell of anger.

'I told Danny we should leave it be,' Gastal was saying, 'but he wouldn't listen. Couldn't get this guy Raissac out of his head. Like he's obsessed. He can't get a handle on this Waterman so he starts off on this other line of inquiry – hanging round Raissac just because, like you say, boss, the guy owns this apartment. I mean . . .'

Gastal paused, took a breath, but started off again before Jacquot could order his thoughts and get a word in. 'Then, Friday, knowing how I feel about it – me transferring to Lamonzie and all – he deliberately sends me off on some wild-goose chase to some sleazy little gym downtown while he jumps in his car and heads off to Cassis. To Raissac's place down there. You ask me—'

But Gastal got no further.

Jacquot's knuckles brushed past the point of Gastal's jaw but connected an inch below the cheekbone, lifting Gastal back onto his heels. He staggered a few steps, hands reaching for the point of impact, then stumbled over a chair.

'Badaboum,' said Jacquot under his breath and launched himself at Gastal.

In the struggle that ensued Gastal's nose was broken and Guimpier, trying to separate the two men, had an eye blackened by Jacquot's elbow.

96

Friday

'So. Policeman. How come?'

'The uniform,' Jacquot replied lightly.

She looked at the linen jacket, the T-shirt, and smiled.

They were sitting at a corner table in Molineux's, the progress of their meal observed by a pair of lobsters in the fish tank beside them. It was after ten. They'd finished their main course, but the plates had still to be cleared away. She'd ordered the grilled oysters, served under a duvet of bubbling cheese, and a fillet of bream, its silvery skin crisply browned and curled. Jacquot had gone for the whitebait and Molineux's bouillabaisse.

'How long?'

'Quite some time,' he said. 'It's all I've ever done.'

'Don't you find it . . .?' She couldn't seem to light on the right word.

'Depressing?' he suggested. 'Dangerous?'

'Yes. Both those, I guess.'

'Of course. But there's a lot else besides. Good things. Like being part of a team. Not letting the good guys down or the bad guys get away. Settling accounts. It's like . . . playing a game. A game you have to win. A challenge every time.'

'Just like any business, I'd have thought. Not just the police.'

'Sure, I suppose.'

'Wasn't there something else you could have done?'

Jacquot shook his head. 'Maybe. But you know how it is. Things happen. You get drawn in. Life.'

For a moment there was silence between them as she took this in. And then:

'You married?' she asked.

Jacquot shook his head. Smiled. 'Not so far.'

She noticed the wince that accompanied the smile, a small vertical cut on his top lip that had tightened the skin as it healed. He looked, she thought, more tanned than the last time she'd seen him, more relaxed. And more attractive too, his hair loose, black wavy curls reaching to his shoulders.

Which, given the last three days, was no surprise.

Suspended from duty with immediate effect pending an internal inquiry after breaking his partner's nose and blacking his boss's eye – apart from any action that Lamonzie might be planning – Jacquot had presented himself first thing Wednesday morning at Salette's office and the two of them skipped school and played truant. A case of beers and some Armagnac stowed in the bow, they'd taken Salette's boat and set off for a couple of days' sailing and fishing, anchoring overnight in the *calanques*, cooking their catch over driftwood fires, sleeping on deck under the stars. On the second night, when Jacquot told him about the bust-up with Gastal, the reason for his suspension, old Salette had laughed, punched him on the shoulder and told him that he was just like his father, all that stormy Corsican blood on the boil. Which had made Jacquot laugh too, suddenly warmed by the thought of his father's proximity.

Now Jacquot was back, sitting there in Molineux's, the bubble-wrapped painting of the lemons which he'd bought the previous Sunday and picked up earlier from Gallery Ton-Ton resting against his chair leg.

It had been a fun evening. Starting at the Ton-Ton where they'd met, moving on to O'Sullivan's where she'd matched him Guinness for Guinness and, finally, arms linked, swinging along the quays of the Vieux Port to Molineux's.

He looked at her now. The dark hair, the brown eyes, an eyebrow arched.

'So how come the ring?' she asked, nodding at his left hand, like she needed an explanation.

388

He looked at the band of silver, twisted it on his finger. 'It was just . . . a joke, I suppose. Someone I knew.'

'But it was serious?' she asked.

'It wasn't long enough to be serious,' he replied.

'But you kept it? The ring? Kept wearing it?'

Which surprised Jacquot. He hadn't thought about it like that.

'It doesn't mean a thing any more,' he replied. And he realised he meant it. It didn't. Not a thing.

She gave him a look.

He looked right back, liking what he saw, knew what was going to happen and was glad for it.

But first he needed to do something. For her. And for him. So he did.

Slipping the ring from his finger, he showed it to her, looked at it one last time, then dropped it with a clink into the remains of his bouillabaisse. A small bubble marked the spot where it had broken the surface of the soup. Then the bubble burst and there was no sign.

A moment later a waiter came to their table, cleared the plates, and asked if they needed anything more. Perhaps they would like to see a menu?

'You should try the soufflé, it's very good,' said Jacquot. 'Lemon, with a shot of vodka.'

'If you say so,' said Isabelle Cassier and gave him a long, cool smile.

97

Saturday

Sylviane had just about reached the end of her tether. Another day of this and she'd go mad, she was sure of it. There was just so much a girl could take. Gritting her teeth, she stepped into the bath she'd drawn for herself and slid down into its foaming, scented warmth. How much longer, she wondered; how much longer would she have to put up with her unwanted, unexpected guest and his endless, unwelcome demands? Food, clothes, newspapers, whisky, cigarettes and, when he felt like it, her. She'd been run off her feet all week.

He'd been waiting for her in the shadows when she returned home on Tuesday evening. She'd been out of town for five days, invited by a girlfriend for a weekend party in Cannes, some American film producer over for the festival and looking for fun and company. The girlfriend, Sylviane and two other girls had been holed up in a spectacular villa in the hills, fabulous grounds, a pool the size of her apartment, with enough coke to keep them buzzing merrily along. All day, lying by the pool, working on their tans, and maybe just a couple of hours keeping the client happy – putting on a show for him last thing at night when he got home from the festival, or first thing in the morning before he headed off for his meetings along the Croisette.

Five days of fun in the sun, well-paid fun at that, and then, the moment she gets home, it looks like she's going to get mugged. She'd just turned the key in the lock when she heard someone scuffle up the steps behind her and barge her through the opening door, propelling her forward, an arm closing round her waist, her hip grazing against the door handle, the side of her suitcase banging angrily against her shins. She was about to struggle, pull herself free, fight back, when a mouth pressed against her ear.

'Quick, quick. Get in and close it.'

And there, in the hallway, with the door kicked shut behind them, the arm releasing her, she turned to find herself face to face with Jean Carnot. He hadn't shaved, his clothes were filthy, and he smelt bad.

Four days later he was still there, sharing her home and her bed. He needed to lie low, he'd told her. Just a few days. And there was nothing she could do about it. Not if she wanted to get her hands on that place on Cours Lieutaud, the apartment he'd promised her, even shown her round the previous week. It was sorted, Carnot had told her. Any day now. It was the only reason she'd put up with him all this time.

Then, this afternoon, sprawled on her bed, swinging a set of keys on his finger, he'd told her there was this little job he needed her to do. A favour. And then the place on Lieutaud was as good as hers.

Sylviane was just about to haul herself from the bath when the door opened and Carnot strolled in. He was wearing a black T-shirt and nothing else. Without saying a word, he went to the toilet, planted his feet either side of it and, not bothering to lift the seat, started peeing, the water in the bowl bubbling at the force of the stream, spraying out in extravagant arcs onto the seat and floor tiles. Sylviane could even see the soft tissue of lavatory paper puckering with damp spots. She clenched her teeth. Jesus Christ, what an animal.

When he'd finished, he turned to her, still shaking the last drops off him.

'When you're ready,' he told her and walked back into the bedroom, not bothering to pull the flush.

Jean Carnot parked a block past the lock-up and handed Sylviane the key. They'd driven past the row of garages five minutes earlier and he'd pointed out the one he wanted her to check, the one with the looping scrawl of purple graffiti.

It was the third lock-up they'd checked that evening. Three more to go.

Carnot lit a cigarette and watched Sylviane walk back past the row of garages, pause at the graffiti and fit the key to the lock. In the setting sun her shadow was long and thin.

Maybe this one, he thought to himself. Maybe this time. And if the place was being watched, if the cops were waiting, all he had to do was put the car in gear and drive away. They wouldn't see him for dust.

Up ahead he watched the door to the lock-up spring open and Sylviane step out of sight.

It had been one hell of a week, Carnot reflected while he waited. So much had happened since that bastard had pressed a gun against the back of his head and taken him into custody. But judging by the way things had gone down, it was maybe just as well he'd missed the party.

Raissac dead.

Coupchoux dead.

He'd seen the newspaper report of Raissac's murder half an hour after the cops released him Tuesday morning, pending inquiries. Then, searching the pages for more information about the hit in Cassis, he'd chanced upon the single paragraph devoted to Coupchoux's unfortunate accident on République.

But nothing, nothing at all, about any drugs haul. Not a single word. As Carnot saw it, either the two hundred kilos of cocaine scheduled for landing the previous day were sitting in a bonded warehouse down at the docks, waiting for a pick-up that would never happen. Or, in his absence, they'd been spirited away by Raissac and Coupchoux before the ship docked. It wouldn't have been the first time someone had done a transfer at night, ship to ship, and with Carnot sitting in a cell on rue de l'Evêché it was just the kind of move Raissac would have made. Plan A compromised. Go to Plan B. It's what Carnot would have done in Raissac's shoes.

And if they'd done that, Carnot reasoned, then the chances were high that the load had been secured in one of the half-dozen lock-ups that Raissac kept in town. Stored safely until the deal went down.

And he, Carnot, had the keys to every single one of them.

But there were still risks. If Narcotics had made a connection between him and Raissac they'd be watching him like a hawk, looking to trace the coke. And collar him in the process. So he'd gone back to his apartment and stayed only long enough to pick up the keys and get out of there. What he needed was somewhere to hole up, some place they didn't know about.

It hadn't taken him long to work out where. Sylviane's apartment. There was no chance she'd turn him away, not with the Cours Lieutaud place on offer. Even if she'd read about Raissac, he'd easily persuade her it was still a runner, that he could fix it. No problem. So that's where he'd gone, waiting for this moment, waiting for the dust to settle.

Two hundred kilos of pure, uncut cocaine. And all his, no one left to chase him down. No Raissac. No Coupchoux. No one. If it worked out right, he was made for life. And Sylviane wouldn't be a problem. He'd sort her.

Five minutes later she was back in the car, the key dangling on the end of her finger.

'Sacks, you said?'

Carnot nodded, taking the key.

'Well, they're there okay. Eight of them.'

Carnot pursed his lips, gave a short, non-committal grunt, and started up the car.

But inside he whooped with an exultant, crazy, disbelieving delight and his heart soared. Oh *yeah*!

98

Cavaillon, Friday, October 21st

J acquot felt the chill as he stepped into Place Lombard and he turned up his collar against it. It was warm enough during the hours of daylight, but once the sun slid away over the rooftops it wasn't long before the shadowy lanes and empty squares of Cavaillon grew grim and cheerless. Which just about summed up how Jacquot felt in this small provincial market town where he'd been transferred following his spat with Gastal.

It was Guimpier, still nursing a black eye, who had made the call. Gastal was pressing charges, Guimpier told him, which meant there'd have to be a disciplinary hearing. And then there was Lamonzie. The old man was sorry but there was nothing he could do. Three weeks later Jacquot had been given two choices: Cavaillon, and a spell with their undermanned regional crime squad. Or early retirement. Take it or leave it. As for the ongoing Waterman investigation, Guimpier was handing it over to Bernie Muzon.

So Jacquot packed up the apartment at Madame Foraque's, paid her three months' rent in advance and told her to let the place out as soon as she could. He'd be back, he told her, but he didn't know when. There were tears in the old girl's eyes as he jammed his bags in the back of the Peugeot and drove north to Cavaillon.

Of course, Isabelle Cassier had made everything easier. She came up to Cavaillon the first weekend and helped him find a place to live, helped him furnish it and kept him company whenever she could get away, keeping him up to date on all the gossip: how Gastal had been bypassed by Lamonzie and then, out of the blue, promoted to an ill-deserved posting in Lyons; how the Waterman seemed to be lying low; how Guimpier was already hustling for Jacquot's reinstatement; and that Lamonzie was blocking the move at every turn.

Then, the beginning of October, Isabelle phoned him one evening, an evening she was supposed to be visiting, and announced that she wouldn't be coming after all. Gently, without any anger or resentment, she explained that she knew his heart wasn't in it, and that she understood. Sure, it had been fun, but it wasn't doing her any good, she told him, and maybe the time had come to call it a day. Best to stay friends, she'd said. And Jacquot hadn't pressed her, just thanked her for all she'd done and wished her good luck. Told her to take care.

Two weeks on, unlocking the street door, checking his empty mail slot in the hallway and then scuffling up the four flights of stairs to his apartment, Jacquot knew she'd been right to end it. His heart hadn't been in it. But that didn't mean he didn't miss her. The weekend off and no one to share it with, two whole days stretching out ahead of him with no prospect of company.

Letting himself into his apartment, a cramped one-bedroom space under the eaves overlooking Cours Bournissac, Jacquot hung his coat on the peg behind the door and pulled off the rubber band from his ponytail. Fifteen minutes later, showered and shampooed, wrapped in a dressing gown, he went back to the front door, dug around in his coat pockets and pulled out a small brown paper bag. Inside was a nuggety black truffle presented to him that afternoon as a thank-you from a farmer he had helped out a week or two earlier. 'Makes a woman soft and a man hard,' the old fellow had said as he pressed the bag into Jacquot's hand. Already the apartment reeked of its scent, as did his office.

Taking it through to the kitchen, Jacquot rolled the gnarled tuber between his fingers, savouring the woody, earthy aroma, and tried to decide what to do with it. There was a good stock he'd made the previous day – though nowhere near as good as the Widow Foraque's – and he decided a plain risotto would do the truffle justice. Until he discovered he was out of rice. There was only one thing for it. Cracking some eggs in a bowl, Jacquot whisked up an omelette, shaved a good half of the truffle into its heart and folded it over. Atrocious waste, he thought to himself, taking his plate through to his sitting room, switching on the TV and settling himself in the sofa. Shameful. Wicked. He sliced off a corner of the omelette with his fork, popped it into his mouth and smiled luxuriously. He was still smiling half an hour later when the phone rang.

It was Bernie Muzon in Marseilles.

Although the two men hadn't spoken since his suspension in May, when Muzon had interrupted Jacquot's desk-clearing to wish him luck and help him lug his belongings down to the underground car park, Jacquot recognised the voice immediately.

'So,' prompted Jacquot, after the preliminaries were dispensed with – the how-are-yous, the catching up, a grumble about Guimpier, and the news that Isabelle had transferred to Paris.

At the end of the line, Muzon cleared his throat.

'Thought you'd like to know. He's started again.'

Jacquot didn't need to be told who Muzon was talking about.

'Marseilles?'

'Not Marseilles. You were right, there. Not a thing since you left. This time it's Aix.'

'Aix-en-Provence?'

'No, Aix-les-Bains.'

'How did you find out?'

'An old friend from Academy days. Lescure. Ferdie Lescure. He heads Serious Crime in the Savoy. Based in Grenoble. Two bodies so far. Out of the lake. Lac du Bourget. At first they thought it was just drownings. Or rather, that's how the local boys filed it. Until Lescure discovered the bodies had washed up naked. He knew about Marseilles and ordered tests . . .'

'Pronoprazone.'

'Dioxy . . .' There was a pause on the end of the line, Muzon trying to get his tongue round the word. 'Dioxymi . . . Di-oxy-mi-ro-pla-zo-hyp-nol.' The name came out in laboured syllables. 'Jesus,' said Muzon. 'Why don't they ever use words you can pronounce?'

'And?'

'Same basic effect as pronoprazone, but even faster acting. There's a derivative, much weaker, called Rohypnol. Remember? The date-rape drug? But this one, this dioxy-whatsit, it's a whole heap stronger. Just a scratch with a needle and you're out.'

'Easy to get hold of?'

'Very difficult,' replied Muzon. 'Only a dozen or so hospitals in the country. Geriatric centres for the most part. In dilution, it's used as a pre-med in geriatric surgery. According to Clisson, who got it from Valéry, it lowers the risk of blood clots forming during anaesthesia.'

'And these hospitals are where, exactly?'

'Well, there's two in Aix for starters. Which got Lescure geared up. He checked their dispensary records against stock and found a discrepancy at one of them. Very small, but a discrepancy all the same. Something like two phials unaccounted for. Just fifty milligrams total, but enough to put a whole street to sleep.'

He's made a mistake, thought Jacquot. The Waterman's made a mistake. Changing the drug: his only access a very limited, secure source. Which he probably didn't know about.

'He's in the business,' said Jacquot. 'Has to be. A doctor or a nurse.'

'Looks that way,' said Muzon. 'And there's something else.'

Jacquot's favourite words.

'Yes?'

'They've had a complaint. Came in while Lescure was visiting. Seems there's a girl reckons she's being followed, stalked.'

'Any description?'

'Nothing. She said she'd never seen anything. Anyone. Said it was just a feeling. Nothing she could put a finger on. But she was certain someone was tailing her. And she was scared. Really spooked. If Lescure hadn't been there, the local boys would probably have filed a domestic and done nothing about it.'

'So what got Lescure interested?'

'This girl, she works on the lake. Ferry terminal.'

'He's a smart one, your friend. So why's he calling you? Sounds like he's got it stitched up.'

'He wanted to speak to you. Didn't know you'd . . . moved on. I told him about Gastal. What happened.' Muzon paused. 'They're setting up something. He thought you'd like to be in on it. Maybe do the honours.'

Three days later, after calling Lescure, Jacquot arranged a leave of absence from Cavaillon and took the autoroute north, branching east at Valence for the final lap to Aix-les-Bains.

397

99

Aix-les-Bains, Friday, October 28th

It was time to move on, the Waterman decided. Time to move again.

In Aix-les-Bains the tourist season was over. From now till the spring the old and infirm, the lame and the halt would reclaim this ancient place. Grey-haired *curistes* with their sticks and their stabilisers, their hobbling and shaking, their crumpled, anxious faces.

The Waterman strolled along a gravel path that followed the shoreline, watching the ferry from Chanaz scratch a rippling, feathery path across the dark waters of Lac du Bourget. Already, the Waterman noticed, its decks were more thinly packed than the previous week. There were clouds, too, gathering behind the peaks of the Dent du Chat and a chill breeze was sweeping the leaves along. Winter knocking at the door.

At a drinking fountain beside the path the Waterman leant down to take a drink, a loop of cool water, eyes searching out the ferry office a hundred metres away, at the entrance to the landing quay.

There was a girl there . . .

Two Sundays back the Waterman had bought a ticket from her, a half-day cruise across the lake to the Abbaye de Hautecombe. Their fingers had touched as money changed hands and the ticket was issued. As close as that. Young, blonde bobbed hair with a clip either side, dressed in a black polo neck and short check skirt. And so much

398

prettier than the others. Not a trace of make-up. Freckles and blue eyes. She'd even smiled.

The Waterman had been watching her for more than a month now, drawing the moment out. Here at the quay, idling past to take a look, to see if she was there; and sometimes calling in at the Casino where she worked nights behind the grille of the *Caisse*.

It just seemed the right thing to do, getting to know her like this. It suggested respect, a sense of closeness. The Waterman knew where she lived, knew where she shopped and, even, what she liked to eat. Once, in the *supermarché* on the corner of Boulevard Wilson, there'd been a small steak in her basket and a bag of *frisée* salad. The Waterman bought the same, cooked the meat that evening, prepared the salad and laid two places; it was like having dinner together.

The Waterman even knew her name.

Ginette. Ginette Brunet.

Just one more time. That was what the Waterman had decided. Just one more time. Before moving on again.

Fresh water, too. The Waterman's favourite. So pure and clean. And here in Aix-les-Bains, so much of it, springing up from the earth, lapping at the shore, gushing here, there and everywhere. Urgent. Persuasive. The pulse of it. Irresistible.

The Waterman found a park bench and sat down, watching the ferry manoeuvre into the dock. The last of the day. When the final passenger disembarked, they'd secure the terminal for the night, close the ticket office, and Ginette Brunet would make her way home, along this very path.

Like so many times in the last few weeks, the Waterman would follow. Past the Marina, the short cut through the woods, across that little stream with its deep swirling pools. Only this time the Waterman would catch her up, take her . . .

'*Excusez-moi, Madame?*'

The man had come from nowhere, startled her. There was an unlit cigarette in his hand.

Did she have a lighter, the stranger asked? Some matches?

She knew she didn't, but felt in the pockets of her mackintosh all the same, patted the pockets of her nurse's pants suit, really just to be polite. She looked up to shake her head and paused. A familiar face. Somewhere, she knew, she'd seen that face before. The size of him. The bulk. The gently broken nose, those sleepy green eyes and the way his hair was tied back in a ponytail.

The stranger smiled, flicked away the cigarette and sat down beside her, gathering his overcoat into his lap. He took a deep breath, savouring the evening air, and looked out across the lake.

The Waterman looked too. But it wasn't the view that drew her attention, the darkening sheet of water, the sheer sides of the Dent du Chat rising above them a mile across the lake. It was the girl she saw, Ginette, her dear Ginette, standing outside the ticket booth, arms folded across her chest as though she were keeping off the cold, hunched, shivering. Two men stood beside her, either side, as though shielding her. One looked to be speaking into his lapel. A radio.

The Waterman glanced back along the path, towards the town. A police car had drawn up in the small car park and three men leant against it, looking in her direction.

She turned and glanced behind her, into the trees. Uniforms. Capes. *Képis.* Five, maybe more, closing in.

And somewhere far off the wail of a siren.

The man beside her stretched out his legs, crossed his ankles, and sighed.

'It's been a long time, Madame,' he said.

100

'*C'est une femme?*'

Solange Bonnefoy didn't need to introduce herself. The voice was enough for Jacquot to know exactly who was phoning him that blustery Friday morning.

'*Une femme,*' he replied, settling behind his desk. Rain rattled against his window, still dripped from the coat that hung behind his door.

'Not what we expected, Chief Inspector?'

'Not at all, Madame.'

'But she is the one?'

'Without question.'

There was a pained sigh at the end of the line. 'You forget, Daniel. I'm an examining magistrate, remember? I don't do "without question".'

'From the beginning, then?'

'If you please.'

Jacquot reached for his cigarettes, lit up and pulled the ashtray closer. He swung his chair round, put his feet on the corner of his desk, crossed his ankles and made himself comfortable.

'The man in charge of the investigation, Ferdie Lescure, hears about two bodies washed up near Aix-les-Bains. Both female. Both in their twenties. Both naked. The bodies were found about three miles

from each other, seven weeks apart. Both women were tourists. One was staying in Aix, the other further up the lake at a campsite near Brison-les-Oliviers. According to the pathologist both women had been drinking heavily just before they died, which was why the local boys put them down as accidental drownings. The girls get drunk, decide to go skinny-dipping; it's night-time, they get into trouble . . . it happens.'

'Stop making excuses,' scolded Madame Bonnefoy.

'Anyway,' continued Jacquot. 'It's too late to check the first body because she's been flown home to Stockholm and cremated. But the second's still in the Aix morgue. So Lescure orders a test for pronoprazone . . .'

'And it's positive.'

'Negative. No pronoprazone. Not a trace. But the pathologist finds something else, something even more effective. Another drug – don't ask me to give you the name – but from a very limited source. Maybe a dozen hospitals in the country. And in Aix, just two private clinics, something like forty beds between them. The other nearest outlet is Lyons. So Lescure checks their dispensary supplies, finds a minute discrepancy at one of them and takes a look at personnel . . .'

'We didn't think of doing this in Marseilles?' There was a vexed edge to Madame Bonnefoy's voice.

'We thought of it, of course, and we had people working on it. I told you that, remember? But Marseilles's a whole lot bigger than Aix, Madame. By a long way. Which means more hospital beds, more staff, and less efficient paperwork. Just think . . . State and private, specialist and general – convalescent homes, geriatric centres, hospices, asylums . . . you name it. All with access to pronoprazone. Maybe we would have got there in the end, but . . .'

'Yes, yes, yes . . . I remember. Resources. So what does our enterprising Lescure discover?'

Jacquot smiled. He could tell from the way she said it that Madame Bonnefoy had savoured the 'enterprising'.

'Nothing,' he replied. 'Every single member of staff at the clinic, from doctors down to orderlies, lives in Aix. At least three years. As far as their records show, everyone's local. So then, as a last resort, Lescure checks leaves of absence, holiday rosters and discovers that over the last eight years one member of staff, a Julianne Perot, comes and goes on a fairly regular, and significant, basis. A month away.

Four months. It varies. But she always comes back to Aix. According to the clinic, she was employed part-time, got called in when they were busy, or to cover for staff holidays or illness. A first-class orthopaedic nurse, apparently; they'd tried to contract her full-time but she said she couldn't do it. Something about having to care for an elderly relation.'

'You said "significant".'

Jacquot leant forward and stubbed out his cigarette. 'The dates of her various absences. Although the clinic had no idea where she went, Lescure discovered that her trips away, ostensibly to care for this elderly relation, appeared to coincide with known Waterman activity.

'There was something else, too. While Lescure was in Aix, he happened to hear about a local girl who'd put in a complaint that she was being followed. No description of the stalker, but when he heard that she worked at the ferry terminal he set up surveillance on our friendly nurse. Sure enough, she seemed to spend a lot of time lakeside, walking the shoreline, taking the ferry, that kind of thing.'

'So what do we know about this Julianne Perot? Her background?'

'Well, she's not Aixoise. And nor is she Marseillaise. We were right there. According to her employment records she comes from – you'll love this – Villars-les-Dombes.'

'The Dombes? Lakeland?'

'The same. Just along the road from Aix.'

'What else?'

'Forty-three years old. Unmarried. Only child. Both parents dead. Taken into care when she was thirteen. Finished school in Villars and trained as a nurse in Lyons, going on to specialise in orthopaedics. Co-workers at the clinic said she was friendly and conscientious but she kept to herself. After her arrest, the local police searched her home – a small, one-bedroom apartment a few streets from the clinic – but found nothing of any significance. Except for a stack of tourist brochures, maps and guides to—'

'Don't tell me,' interrupted Madame Bonnefoy. 'Marseilles, La Rochelle . . .'

'. . . Cherbourg, Dieppe, Annecy. In Marseilles, Lescure discovered that she worked at La Conception. Four months.' Jacquot thought it prudent not to add that it was the same hospital where his partner, Rully, had been laid up. The possibility that Jacquot might have passed the Waterman in a corridor, shared a lift with her, or that Rully might have had his pillows plumped by her had not escaped him.

There was a long pause at the end of the line. And then:

'What else? There's something you're not telling me, Daniel. I know it.'

Jacquot smiled, recrossed his ankles. He was enjoying this.

'Her parents.'

'Yes?'

'They both drowned.'

'*Drowned?* You *are* joking?'

'Absolutely not, Madame.'

'So? Tell me.'

'After Perot's arrest, Lescure had a couple of his boys go to Villars, ask around. According to police files, her father died first. Nearly forty years ago. The family had a smallholding, a few hectares outside Bouligneux. Maize in the summer, fish, a few ducks. He was clearing a channel between two ponds when a sluice gate gave way. The weight of water crushed him against the second sluice gate and that was that. Accidental death.'

'And the other?'

'Perot's mother died ten years later. Cause of death, a heart attack, in the bath.'

'Incredible.'

'But that's not all,' continued Jacquot, saving the best for last. 'She'd been raped first.'

After a second's delay, Madame Bonnefoy came back on the line: 'Did they find who did it?'

'They drew a blank. No suspects. No arrest.'

'What about the daughter? She was what, fifteen, fourteen? Didn't she see anything, hear anything?'

'Asleep in bed, according to the reports. Didn't see or hear a thing. And there's something else. While Lescure's boys were in Villars they traced a journalist who'd covered the case for the local paper. Old fellow, retired now, called Davide. According to him, it wasn't the happiest of families. Father was a drunk, mother a loud-mouth and bully. People he spoke to after her death seemed to think "good riddance". She wasn't popular. There were even whispers that she might have been responsible for her husband's death. Apparently his

skull had been fractured, but this was put down to the force of water
hurling him against the sluice gate. Whatever, no one had a good
word for her, but they all said how sorry they felt for the daughter,
growing up in a home like that.'

'Abusive?'

'Who can say, Madame? It was a long time ago.'

'So where is she now, the daughter?'

'Police custody in Grenoble. But not for much longer. Lescure says
he'll have to release her for clinical evaluation. If she won't talk, won't
cooperate, he has no option.'

'Maybe the doctors will get somewhere with her.'

'I'm not holding my breath.'

'You don't think so?'

Jacquot shook his head as though Solange Bonnefoy was across the
desk from him. 'She was blank, Madame. Just closed down.'

'You were there?'

'At the lake. Sitting beside her, Madame.'

'In Aix? That's Savoyard jurisdiction.'

Jacquot smiled. Just the kind of thing Marseilles's examining
magistrate would latch onto. 'Chief Inspector Lescure was kind
enough to include me in his team,' he replied.

'Impressions?'

'Lescure or the Waterman?'

There was silence down the line, then another sigh.

'Resigned,' said Jacquot. 'Not particularly happy at being picked
up, but not sorry either.'

'I heard she tried to make a run for it.'

'Hardly a run, Madame. When I introduced myself, she gave me a
long, hard look, as though she recognised me from somewhere, then
got up and started walking away – like I'd said something offensive,
propositioned her, you know? It was Lescure who did the honours,
falling in beside her. Took her arm in his and just steered her along
the path to a car.'

'A good result, then.'

'A good result, Madame.'

There was another silence from Solange Bonnefoy. And then: 'So
when are you coming home to Marseilles, Daniel? We miss you.'

'Who can say, Madame?' replied Jacquot, swinging round in his
chair, watching the rain spatter across his window. 'Who can say?'

Dorothy Linda O'Brien
April 17th 1921 – September 4th 2000